Darkened Eyes

Michael Schroeder

Mobile, Alabama

Axiom Press
P.O. Box 191540 • Mobile, AL 36619

Acknowledgments

This book has been a long time in the making and so many people have helped to forge this work with their ideas and inspiration that I couldn't possibly name them all, but I did want to highlight a few.

First, I'd like to thank my sister, Elise Schroeder, who has been a sounding board for me throughout the whole process. She was the first to read it chapter by chapter as I finished each one, and her input and feedback shaped the book as I wrote it. I couldn't have done it without you, Elise…thank you!

My mom, Elaine Schroeder, is my best ally, consultant, and critic. Not just with this book but with my whole life. Thanks for being there for me no matter what, Mom.

Denise Cuthbertson, the first person to do an in-depth edit and catch all the initial grammatical mistakes. Thank you, Denise.

I never could have gotten all my skateboarding terminology right without the help of my skateboarding expert, Matt Zamba.

Others who edited and gave me feedback include Amy Bohannan, Rebecca Felber, Richard Garza, Anthony Barr, Stephanie Hills, and Lauren Copu. Your insights have been invaluable to me. I appreciate you all so much.

And, of course, special thanks to my literary agent Keith Carroll and the team at Axiom Press. You put in a lot of hard work to get this book out.

I am so grateful for all of you who have had such an impact and influence in my life. I am a composite of so many people and am humbled that God has surrounded me with such great relationships. I pray that this book blesses you and finds its way into the hands of people that it can truly help.

PROLOGUE

With a crack, the window shattered and shards of glass flew across the floor. The warehouse was suddenly lit up by the flashing red and blue lights outside. Immediately, a blinding light shone through the window and a voice blared, "We have the building surrounded. Don't make any sudden moves."

Cursing, Al rolled over and grabbed a bag. Fear and anger struggled for superiority. That stupid runner had betrayed them—he knew it! Zane jumped up, and Al caught his wild eyes in the flash of the blue and red lights. The other guys were grabbing stuff, starting to panic. He saw Junior grab his gun. Al needed to calm everybody down, but he had to calm himself down first.

"Stay down!" Al whispered sharply to Zane, but as soon as he said it, he heard a loud crack at the door. The gang members were shouting. A bullet whizzed by, smacking into the window. Instantly, policemen began shouting outside, and the bright light disappeared from the window. The guys were grabbing boxes and snatching bags that were lying around.

"I knew this was a bad idea!" Zane cried hoarsely.

Al was on his feet now, grabbing two guys who were about to run. "Nobody panic," he ordered in his gravelly whisper as he tried to keep a grip on himself. "Just follow the plan."

He whirled to two guys moving the boxes away from the doorway and pushed them aside. He had to remain calm! Moving quickly, he knelt down and uncovered the trap door.

Daemiem appeared by his side. "Al, we gotta get everybody out!"

Al nodded tersely. "And we gotta get the goods out."

The shouts from both the policeman and the gang were growing more intense. The police would break through any minute.

"Gimme the gun," whispered Daemiem.

Al shot a glance at him, then the door. "A'right, here. Cover us!"

Daemiem leaped to his feet. He nodded to Junior, who began motioning everyone toward the back of the warehouse. The guys grabbed all the boxes and bags that they could and scrambled for the trap door, which Al had now unbolted. Some of them quickly pushed past Al. Those who hesitated, Al moved along with a string of obscenities and rough shoving.

Daemiem and Junior stood at separate windows, firing shots. But they wouldn't be able to hold back the police for long. Al glanced over at Michael and Zane who were the last ones. *What's going on over there?* Al silently cussed them out. They were both on the floor, gathering up some small bags. Zane must have spilled his box, the clumsy oaf. Al hunkered down and crawled over, keeping his head well below the two windows. "Michael, get outta here," Al ordered. "I'll take care o' this."

Michael nodded, scrambling towards the trap door and down into the tunnel.

"You idiot!" Al shouted, shaking his head at Zane, adding a few more flavorful words as he began scooping up the bags.

Zane froze. "I can't get caught by the police! I can't! You know—"

He wasn't able to finish his sentence before tear gas began pouring into the room. Junior and Daemiem both dropped to the floor, coughing and gasping. Junior crawled over to the trap door and disappeared down the tunnel. Al held his breath and mentally cursed. His eyes were watering and his chest was burning.

Zane leaped to his feet and began staggering blindly in the wrong direction. Al grabbed his ankle to pull him down to the floor, but the stupid idiot shook him off. *Zane ain't thinkin' straight! He needs to grab ahold o' hisself,* Al thought. His eyes burned, and he was having trouble seeing where Zane was. His chest had never been so tight. Daemiem apparently saw what was happening, even with blurry eyes, because he grabbed for Zane's legs.

At that moment, the door cracked open and a bullet flew into the room. Zane toppled to the ground. Al grabbed Zane's shirt, only to find it sticky with blood. He looked at Zane's eyes, which were now rolled back into his head. The bullet had gone right through his chest.

Al's stomach rose up into his throat, and he was glad the tear gas gave him an excuse for the tears streaming from his eyes. Daemiem violently motioned for him to take the bags he had in the box down into the tunnel. Al paused but there was no time to wait. Daemiem kicked at him, and Al grabbed the box and fell down into the tunnel.

Michael and Junior caught Al as he fell down. Before he could see what was happening, the trap door closed, and some boxes were shoved up against it. "What's Daemiem doin'?" Al mumbled as he rose and shoved Michael and Junior away from him. Panicked, he rubbed his eyes and looked through the crack of the trap door into the room. He saw Daemiem fire a gun, then a policeman tackle him from behind. It was over.

Al motioned wildly for Junior and Michael to move out. Full of rage, he grabbed his own box and began running down the tunnel. There was no time to dwell on his anger—they had to get as far away from here as they could and find Adikema. He would have a plan.

○———○

Far away . . . a streak of light, unobserved by human eyes, shot through the night sky. Heading for its mission, it flew over corn fields, cities, streets, and highways. Shadowy figures saw and shielded their eyes, spitting as the streak passed by. Other beings waved in salutation.

The light being zoomed closer and closer towards its destination, arriving at a small town in Colorado. He slowed his speed and scanned the terrain underneath him, searching for his next assignment. Passing over some railroad tracks, he entered the town. Over a trailer park and a few subdivisions he flew. A bank, a couple of restaurants, what must be the main street, a fast-food joint, a little grocery store, a video rental store . . . *Aha!* Gaddiel declared as he neared his destination—a sports park with a small deserted swing set, and some picnic tables and pavilions off to the side. And there it was—a small skate park sat to the left of the playground.

Bright street lights shone down on the skate park, illuminating the ramps for the nocturnal skaters. Two skaters were there now, laughing and making lewd remarks. Standing regally atop a ramp, another angelic being already stood watch, his wingspan spread out in protection, a flaming sword ready in his hand. He was adorned with shining white clothes, and light emanated out of every part of his body. But despite this impressive show, nobody noticed, except Gaddiel, who now veered toward the skate park and glided downward.

Zimri looked up and smiled in greeting. "Worthy is the Lamb who was slain to receive glory," he said, nodding at Gaddiel.

"Glory to Him who sits on the throne and to the Lamb forever and ever," Gaddiel responded with a smile. He landed gracefully next to Zimri. "So, who's my assignment?"

Zimri nodded and pointed to one of the boys skating. He looked to be about fourteen years old. The boy had long, curly brown hair and wore tight black pants, a loose T-shirt, beat-up skater shoes, and a backwards ball cap. "Right there," the angel said softly.

Gaddiel looked at the one Zimri had pointed to and grimaced as the boy shot out a cuss word. "Mmm. Not a Christian?" he asked.

Zimri nodded. "That's right. His mother has been praying."

Gaddiel eyed a demon across the street and warily laid a hand on his sword. "I see."

"You have a tough job ahead of you," Zimri said with a soft smile.

Gaddiel gave him a wry grin. "It wouldn't be the first time. So what is this one's name?"

The two of them felt the gentle Spirit of the Lord empowering them as they watched the two skaters. God's great love for this teenager was evident, and Gaddiel tightened his grasp on his sword.

Zimri laid a powerful hand on Gaddiel's shoulder. "His name is Greg."

The war for another soul had begun.

1

One last time up the ramp, he thought. He glided along the pavement on the skateboard then sailed up the ramp. The bright white lights shone like a search beam against the black night sky, giving the surface of the ramps at the small skate park a glossy look—just the way he liked it. Grabbing his board, he jumped and did a kick flip before landing on it again and riding back down the ramp. *What a rush!* He jumped off the skateboard and snatched it up off the ground, leaving its wheels spinning.

Taking off his cap, he ran a hand through his thick brown hair. Renae clapped her hands, and his chest swelled with pride. "What do you think of that, huh, Doug?" he yelled to his friend, grinning at him.

"My grandmother could've done that!" Doug said, grinning back. "You're a pansy!"

"Oh yeah?" Greg set his cap back on his head and rushed at him. Doug was too fast, though, and grabbed his wrists, shoving him to the ground. Doug laughed. "You're going to have to do better than that . . . pansy!"

Greg laughed too and cussed at him. *My mother would freak out if she heard me talking like that,* he thought with a grimace. *She probably asked for prayer for me at her women's prayer meeting tonight. I wouldn't be surprised if those hypocrites prayed that God would strike me down for being rebellious. God is just and won't put up with my sin—blah, blah, blah.* He sat up, shaking his head to clear it of the thought. *Don't need to think about that right now.* Hey, this was his moment of freedom, and this was the one place he could be himself and be rid of all of that Christian garbage. But thinking of his mother had reminded him of the time. He looked at his cell phone and groaned. She would be home by now. He had stayed out too late—again.

Renae walked up to him and slid her arm around his waist. Her dark hair hung around her ears. She was wearing pink shorts and a white sweater whose folds flapped on her slim legs in the slight breeze that whipped through the skate park. "Your mom is home, huh?" she murmured. Embarrassed, Greg shrugged.

Renae was more than a girlfriend . . . she was a true friend. Greg couldn't talk to anyone else like he could Renae. Whenever he was upset with his mom or irritated with Doug, he could tell her all about it and she would sweetly listen. Greg couldn't talk to Doug like that, even though he was his best friend. Doug was too self-absorbed. And he certainly couldn't talk to his mom like that!

Doug picked up his skateboard and gestured toward the ramps. "Let me show you how it's done," he said, calling Greg a crude name.

Greg started to grab his skateboard when Renae grabbed his hand. "Greg, you probably shouldn't make your mom mad tonight," she said.

He turned to free his hand, but she looked at him so sweetly with her big brown eyes, he couldn't. He hesitated. "You don't want to do anything to mess up the contest tomorrow," she reminded him.

Greg groaned. She was right. He didn't want to mess up the contest. This was the chance of a lifetime.

"Come on!" Doug called impatiently. "Hey, groupie, let him skate!"

Renae tossed her brown hair and pouted her lips at Doug. "Don't be jealous."

"Jealous of you?" Doug asked. "You're dreaming! You wish you had me! You'll be begging to take back your words after you see this trick! Greg, wait till you see this!"

"Can't." Greg spat on the ground, letting another bad word slip. "Have to get home. My mom's back by now."

"So what? Stay out." Doug shrugged, throwing his skateboard back down and resting his foot on it.

Greg grunted. "Yeah, I would, except last time she grounded me from the skate park, remember? I don't want to miss out on the contest tomorrow."

"Oh, right." Doug frowned. "Man . . . you let groupies hang around, and soon all your friends go soft."

Renae rolled her eyes. "I've gotta go too. See you tomorrow, Greg!" She reached up and kissed him on the cheek, sending an electric feeling buzzing through his body.

"Gross!" Doug yelled. Renae ignored him and took off towards her house, texting as she walked.

"Well, I better go," Greg said, scuffing the ground with his foot.

Doug shrugged and skated to the other side of the skate park. "Yeah, whatever. Later, dude. Go dream of me winning tomorrow."

"Yeah, later," Greg said softly, ignoring Doug's dig as he began to make his way toward his house. Why did his mom have to be so uptight? *It's because she's religious,* he thought, leaving the bright lights of the skate park to trudge through the wet grass in the dark. Several years ago, his mom had started going to the Pentecostal church down the road. It was a weird place where people shouted, danced, screamed, shook, jumped, and did what his mom called "speaking in tongues." Whatever that meant. He was freaked out the first time he went there. Then his mom started having Bible studies, and soon she was a regular member.

And to make matters worse, they had these bizarre customs. They required ladies to wear dresses and let their hair grow long and made guys cut their hair. And that was just the beginning of all the rules. No drinking. No smoking. No jewelry. No popular clothing. No tattoos. No makeup. No drugs. No cussing. Lots and lots of noes.

No way was he was going to compromise his freedom to follow that list of crazy rules. What had God done for him? Nothing. God had never sought him out. The church people always said, "God loves you!" *Oh yeah?* Greg thought bitterly. *Then why did He let my dad leave? Why did He let me move to this stupid little town in Colorado? Why did He let my little sister die?* He bit the inside of his cheek. The last one was too hard to think about.

No. God had never helped him, and he had no reason to follow the long list of rules God laid out for him. He could still hear an old lady at the church, glasses perched on the end of her nose, her gray hair tied up in a bun, as she screeched, "Turn to God, or you'll go to hell, boy!" Greg rolled his eyes. *Sheesh, I don't care. Just lay off, okay?*

As he reached the doorway of his house, he squeezed his eyes shut, pausing with his hand on the knob, dreading the tirade that was likely to come. Maybe she'd already be asleep and he could act like he got in earlier. He slowly turned the knob, willing the door not to creak. Stepping quietly into the house, Greg turned back to carefully slide his skateboard in, trying not to let it bump against the door.

"Gregory?"

Augh. She was awake.

"Why were you out so late?"

Slowly, he turned to face her. She was already in a pink night gown. Wisps of her long dark hair hung around her face, and her questioning, worried eyes looked over him as if to check for any injuries.

"I'm okay, Mom," he said in annoyance, closing the door behind him.

"Where were you? Why didn't you call?"

Greg walked over and leaned his skateboard against the couch, then brushed past her as he went into the kitchen to grab an apple. "I just lost track of time. I was at the skate park. It's no big deal." He bit into the apple.

Her frown told him she thought otherwise. "Yes, it is a big deal. You were supposed to be home by ten o'clock. It's eleven thirty!"

Greg could feel his face getting hot. Doug would never put up with such an unreasonably early time. If he knew that's what she expected . . . "That's so early! None of the other kids have a curfew!"

"They should," she said firmly. "Teenagers get into too much trouble if they stay out late. Besides, if all the other kids jumped off a cliff, would you?"

Oh brother, way to use another cliché, Mom. How many times in my life have I heard that one? Greg shook his head a little, letting his brown locks fall down further over his eyes. He didn't want to talk tonight. He knew his mom had been obsessing about how late he stayed out ever since she had let him off restriction. Greg was almost positive the real reason he had been grounded last time wasn't because he had been late, but because she had smelled marijuana on his clothes and was scared he was at a party. But Greg hadn't even smoked it! He had just been around the other skaters who had. And the worst they did was pot.

Greg had blamed his dad's leaving on the drugs that his dad did and had promised himself that he'd never do the thing that had turned his dad into such a mean, uncaring idiot. The night Greg walked in on him when he was rolling white powder and his dad charged at him, swinging a tire iron, Greg made a decision. He vowed never to touch the stuff. And he hadn't! His mom thought he was such a bad person, but he knew tons of kids at the skate park that were worse than him. They had done drugs, slept with girls. The worst he had done with a girl was make out—and that was with Renae. Either way, he couldn't win. He wasn't good enough for his mom, and he wasn't bad enough for the guys at the skate park. Nobody cared about him no matter what he did.

Greg tossed the partly-eaten apple into the trash and started walking toward his room, trying to brush past his mother. She grabbed his shoulder.

"Wait, we're not finished talking yet."

Greg tossed his head, flipping his hair to the side, and looked at her with blazing eyes. "Well, I'm finished! I'm not in the mood for a lecture, okay? Just . . . leave . . . me . . . alone!" He shoved past and stormed into his bedroom.

"Wait! Gregory! Come back here this instant. Gregory James—"

Greg slammed his door and locked it. His mother was so frustrating! He yanked off his cap and threw it against the wall, then flopped backwards onto his bed. Quickly, he pulled out his phone and shot off a text to Renae: My mom is so stupid!

The simplest little remarks by his mother set him off these

days. Everything she said irritated him. Blame it on those Holy Rollers! If she had never started going to that church . . .

Renae texted back. Why?

She's just being a religious idiot, he sent back. I'll tell you about it tomorrow. No use in thinking about it now. His mom went to church, that was that. He would be better off concentrating his thoughts on the contest tomorrow.

The contest. Ah, that's better. He had looked forward to this Saturday for weeks. The skateboarding contest being held at the local skate park was sponsored by some company in Chicago. The best skateboarder would get to go to Chicago and compete there. The fact that the contest was taking place in their small town was kind of strange, but none of the local kids questioned it. This was the opportunity of a lifetime! Chicago— home of hot dogs, skyscrapers, smog, Lake Michigan, and deep dish pizza! And whoever had the longest grinds, biggest airs, and best flip tricks would get to go.

Greg smiled thinking about it. This would be his chance to show his stuff, maybe impress some chicks, and prove himself to the guys. I might even get the chance to get away from Mom's nagging about church and go to a big city for a few days! That alone was worth it. He couldn't wait. With that thought, he drifted off into a dream about seeing Chicago from the top of a skyscraper.

Shobab cackled with glee. With wicked intent, his small, ugly black form sat hunched over on the windowsill. Suddenly, the small devil felt the hair at the back of his neck rise. He knew this feeling. He spun around but too late. A blinding flash of light caused him to shriek as he covered his eyes.

A tall, muscular form stood before him, displaying an enormous silver sword that shone in the moonlight. Shobab spat and flapped backwards a few feet. "Who are you?" he demanded angrily.

The angelic being didn't flinch a bit when Shobab advanced and bared his claws. "My name is Gaddiel," the angel said in a calm, strong voice. "I have been sent to protect this child."

"What game are you playing?" said Shobab, his eyes narrowing. "He's under my influence right now. He isn't a child of your King!"

Gaddiel hadn't moved since he made his appearance. "Nevertheless, the Lord has great plans for him."

Shobab's scaly talons raised in defiance. "You may have plans, but so do we!" he said, hopping up and down on one foot. "You can't take him! We're going to use him for—" Suddenly, the small devil thought the better of revealing their plans to the enemy, and he shut his mouth. "Just wait, angel," he finally said. "He's not going without a fight. We have big plans for this one." He grinned wickedly. "Big plans."

o———o

The water in the sink somehow seemed ridiculously cold this early in the morning. Greg cupped the water in his hands and splashed it on his face, then shook like a dog, his shaggy hair spraying water droplets on the mirror. He looked closer in the mirror. *Ugh, a zit. On today of all days. Blech. Whatever.* Nothing was going to spoil this day for him. A whole Saturday of skateboarding. He grinned at himself in the mirror. *That's what I call living!*

A sudden knock at the bathroom door interrupted his thoughts. "Greg? Honey, what are you doing up?"

"Today's the contest," he yelled through the door.

"I know," his mom said as she tried to stifle a yawn. "But that doesn't start until ten, right?"

"I wanted to get in some early practicing."

"Gregory, it's still dark outside."

"If I wait, people will be there setting up and stuff. I want to have the whole skate park to myself. And Mom? Don't call me Gregory, okay?"

"Honey, you need to get some sleep."

Greg sighed. He couldn't explain it to his mom. She didn't understand how he felt when the wind was blowing through his hair as the skateboard sped along the concrete. She didn't know how it felt to finally master a trick nor did she understand the free-floating feeling he got when the skateboard left the ramp and he was flying through the air. When he was skateboarding, he was free. That's why he wanted to be out right now, in the predawn hours. Just him and his skateboard, with nobody else around. He had hoped to slip out of the house while his mom was still sleeping. No such luck.

He opened the door to face his mom. "I'm all ready. Can't I just go?"

His mom put her hand on her hip. "What if something happens to you?"

Greg groaned. "Mom, I'll be okay. Nothing could happen to me at the skate park! The worst thing people do in this town is jaywalk. Come on!"

She looked at him for a moment then sighed. "All right. I guess it's okay. Are you going to be back for breakfast, before the contest?"

He shrugged, in a hurry to be off. "Don't know. Guess so." He started edging toward the door. Suddenly, his mom gasped. "Gregory! Look at how long your hair is!" Greg closed his eyes and gritted his teeth. *Oh, no. Not this argument again. Not now.* She reached up and pulled a strand of hair down as far as it would go on his face. "It's past your eyes! When's the last time you had a haircut? Thank God you've got naturally curly hair! At least that keeps it up a little."

Greg let out an exasperated sigh. "Why do you care if I have long hair or short hair? Can't I just do my own thing?"

"'Doth not even nature itself teach you that if a man have long hair it is a shame unto him?'" his mother quoted the now familiar Bible verse. "You know that, Gregory. The Bible says it; I didn't make it up."

"Well, I think you and your little Pentecostal friends take it too far," Greg said under his breath. "And besides, I'm not a Christian. I'm not trying to follow all that!"

He saw his mother wince and knew that had stung a little. "We're only doing what the Bible says," she said, trying to keep her voice even. "And I am responsible for training you and raising you before God to . . . to . . ."

"Yeah, well, maybe I don't want you training me," Greg shot back. "All your rules are so retarded! You're so rigid and legalistic and . . . and . . ." He struggled to find another insult. "And the whole church is just full of hypocrites!"

His mom grabbed the doorframe as if for support and pressed her fingertips to her forehead. "Gregory, how can you judge the people in the church as hypocrites when you don't know them, and you hardly ever go?" She was getting agitated, and her voice raised a few decibels. "Greg, the reason I make rules is because I care about you—"

Greg threw up his hands in disbelief and interrupted his mom. "You're telling me the reason I have to have short hair is because you care about me? You're just a control freak! Let's face it, Mom! Ever since Dad left, the only one you care about around here is yourself! That's why you're doing this whole church thing. It isn't 'cause you care about me!"

Mrs. Martin's voice quavered. "You listen to me, Gregory Martin. The reason I'm working at a dead-end job is for you. I have sacrificed and—"

"Well, nobody asked you to!"

His mom took a deep breath then said, "I'm just trying to do what God says. He made it up, not me."

Greg looked around for his skateboard. He couldn't stand being around his mom when she got like this. "Well, maybe I don't care what God wants." Just then, he caught sight of his skateboard by the couch where he'd set it last night. He walked towards it, but suddenly his mom stepped in front of it, blocking his path. Greg felt his anger rising.

"Well, maybe you should care," she said. He tried reaching for his skateboard, but she moved in front of it again, demanding his attention. "Greg, can't you see that God loves you? That He wants to save you?"

"Let me have my skateboard." Greg wanted nothing more than to leave the house.

"Gregory, listen to me! Why can't you see it? God loves you. I—"

"Give me my skateboard!" Greg shouted.

"Do not raise your voice to me, Gregory. Just tell me why you won't go to church!"

Greg clenched his fist and gritted his teeth. *Why is my mom such an idiot?* He tried to shove past her, but she grabbed his shoulders and tried to make him look at her. "Look at me, Gregory!"

That was it. Greg's exasperation got the better of him and half screaming, he spat out a string of cuss words.

His mom gasped and jerked back like she'd been slapped.

Greg jumped at the opportunity to snatch up his skateboard, but just as quickly she grabbed the other end and yanked it back. "Gregory Martin! I never, ever, ever, ever want to hear you talk like that again!"

"I don't care what you want! Just give me my stupid skateboard!"

His mom's eyes spilled over with the tears that had already been threatening to come, but she held onto the skateboard. "All I want you to see is that God loves you!"

Greg threw his hands up in the air. That was the clincher—because it wasn't true. "God doesn't love me!" he shouted. "If such a person as God even exists, there's no way He loves me! God doesn't care about us humans! If He exists, He's evil and cruel and—"

"Stop that right now! I will not have you talking like that!" His mom sank down on the couch, as if unable to stand any longer.

"You say God is such a loving, merciful God. Then why do bad things happen all the time? Huh? Isn't God big enough to stop it?"

"God doesn't cause the evil in the world. He . . . He allows it because—"

"Is that supposed to make it okay? It's okay because God 'allows' it? In my mind He's still responsible. If He doesn't stop it, that's just as bad!"

"Watch your attitude, young man! I will not have you disrespecting God under this roof!"

"Fine! Then I'll leave!"

Greg snatched his skateboard out of his mom's hands and stormed to the door, flinging it open. His mom jumped up to her feet and reached out her hand, stifling back a sob. "Gregory, stop! We are going to talk through this . . ."

Greg ran out the door and bounded off the porch into the damp grass. "Gregory!" he heard his mom call after him as she ran to the doorway.

"Don't call me Gregory!" he yelled over his shoulder and kept running.

"Greg! Gregory!"

A neighbor's porch light turned on, and his mom bit her lip and slumped against the door. She stared as her son vanished into the darkness. Light streamed out from their open door, forming a pool of light on the grass. Crickets chirped. His mom leaned against the door frame. "Oh, Gregory . . ."

Greg kept running blindly, his head down, his face flushed with anger. A dog barked at him as he ran past the fence. Fuming, he turned toward the dog. "Shut up, you—" he cussed the dog out. A light came on in the house, and Greg could see a man in boxer shorts through the glass sliding door. He turned and kept running.

The sky was turning that gray color it turns right before the sun comes out. The lights at the skate park had clicked off sometime during the night. Greg could see the black silhouettes of the ramps.

Angrily, he slapped his skateboard against the concrete and jumped on, pushing it with his foot as fast as it could go. He zoomed closer and closer to the ramp. Suddenly, the skateboard hit a loose pebble, which sent him flying. He landed hard on his shoulder.

For a long time he lay there, sprawled out on the ramp, as the sky grew lighter with the approach of dawn. His chest heaved up and down. Why was everything so hard? An ache hit his heart. He felt so alone, so lost. Staring up at the sky, an overwhelming sense of insignificance engulfed him.

Greg sat up, hugged his knees to his body, and rested his

forehead against his arm. He thought of texting Renae, but she probably wasn't awake yet. She almost always slept in late. His mind drifted back against his will to the conversation with his mom. If God really cared, why did it seem like He had forsaken Greg's family? His sister was dead. His dad was gone. His mom was miserable. *I'm miserable!* Right now he almost wished that God did care and that He could help him. But he knew God wouldn't. God probably didn't even exist. Doug said God was a crutch for people who couldn't make it through life on their own. Maybe Doug was right. Greg just didn't know.

Finally, Greg staggered to his feet. He wasn't out here to lie on a skateboard ramp. He picked up his skateboard and rubbed his fingers along a scratch. If anything could make him forget his problems, skateboarding certainly could. Greg put one foot on his skateboard and pushed off with the other one. He slowly took a lap around the park then began to gain speed. With the speed and style of a pro, Greg ollied onto a rail and grinded across it. This was familiar territory. Soon Greg was lost in his skateboarding, practicing his flip and grind tricks. He never noticed a shadowy figure standing behind a tree, watching him.

o——o

Stefan stayed out of sight, lurking in the shadows, as he watched the kid skate. His cell phone was pressed against his ear and his sunglasses were pulled down just enough so his sharp eye could study the kid. He didn't know much about skateboarding, but he could tell this kid wasn't bad . . . maybe even good. Not that it mattered. He wasn't here to critique skateboarding techniques.

His loose black suit coat was buttoned against the slight chill, the collar turned up against his neck. He pushed up his sunglasses further on his nose. It didn't matter that the sun had barely begun peeking up over the horizon. Stefan always wore sunglasses.

Slowly, he ran a smooth hand over his slick black hair. "Yes," he said in a low voice into the phone. "I think this kid will work out after all."

2

Cambiano eyed the machine with a critical eye. Sighing, he put his gun on the counter and rolled up the sleeves of his uniform. Suddenly, the door burst open and Officer Purdo stormed in. "Cambiano, we have a problem!"

Cambiano didn't turn around. "We sure do," he said, in a monotone voice.

"The . . . gang . . . got . . . away!" Purdo said. "The entire gang slipped right past us, with most of the drugs!"

"Not the entire gang," Cambiano corrected, pressing another button on the machine.

"Yeah, we took one guy into custody! One!"

"And one corpse to the morgue," Cambiano said coolly.

Purdo ignored him and continued ranting. "Every single punk in that gang should be behind bars right now! Al and his gang have wreaked havoc on this city for too long. We were so close!" he yelled, slamming his hand down on the table. "After months and months of investigating and tracking and searching, we had our chance, and now we are—" Purdo suddenly stopped. "What are you doing?"

Cambiano grunted. "Trying to get this espresso machine to work." He hit the top of the machine and sighed. "I can't figure out what's wrong with it."

Purdo's mouth dropped open. "We're in the middle of an investigation! A dangerous gang is running loose around our streets, supplying numerous gangs with illegal narcotics. These are the guys who are responsible for all the drug traffic in this section of the city, you know. They've run off all the other gangs, and have kept this area of our beat under their control for too long. If we can cut them out of the picture, we can stop the traffic of so much illegal contraband. We have to get them before the trail grows cold—and you're in the break room making coffee!"

Cambiano didn't turn around. "Look, Purdo, this isn't the first drug ring we've busted, and it won't be the last. As soon as we incarcerate the members of one gang, another gang springs up to take their place. Believe me, the five minutes I spend getting coffee isn't going to do much to affect the entire underground drug network here in Chicago. In fact, if I don't get my coffee . . ." The older officer banged the machine again.

Purdo threw up his hands. "Look, Cambiano. We have a chance here before the trail gets cold to bust these guys! We know the general area they're located. I want you to make my beat in that part of the city."

Finally, Cambiano stopped fiddling with the machine and faced Purdo. "If I put you on that beat, you'll have to be by yourself. I can't spare two officers to constantly patrol the small beat you have in mind."

Purdo's eyes gleamed with triumph. "As long as I'm there and can have backup within a moment's notice, I'll get 'em."

Cambiano eyed him for another moment. "Fine. Get out there."

The breaking dawn turned the eastern sky pink. The sun

was just peeking over the horizon, emitting its blinding light into the world.

Brushing some hair out of his face, Greg dropped the skateboard on the pavement with purpose and began skating towards the grinding rail. He geared himself up, popped up the end of the board and ollied over the rail, barely clearing it. He made a mental note to ollie higher at the contest. If he were going to win, he had to be in top form. Weaving between two ramps, he decided he was about ready to head home and grab some breakfast. This practice time hadn't turned out like he thought it would. The whole time he kept thinking of his mom and God and . . . He shook his head. Maybe he could shake his mind clear of the thoughts that refused to leave him alone.

Let's see if I can get that ollie a little better before I go. Greg skated toward the rail. He had almost reached it when a voice startled him.

"You may need to pick up a little more speed if you're going to clear that."

Greg spun around and lost his footing. His skateboard sailed out from under him and clanged against the rail. Greg tumbled backward and landed hard on the concrete.

A man stood at the edge of the skate park, leaning against one of the lampposts, arms folded, a sly grin toying at the corners of his mouth. He wore sunglasses and all black, with no collar on the black shirt under his suit coat. A low chuckle escaped the stranger's lips as Greg scrambled to his feet. Heat spread up Greg's neck and he mentally cussed, grabbing his skateboard with one hand and slipping the other hand into his pocket so the stranger wouldn't notice it shaking. *What was this creep doing here?*

"Oh, I'm sorry, did I scare you?" the stranger asked dryly, not the least trace of apology in his tone.

Greg stood there, warily watching the stranger. *Who was this guy, anyway?* "Well, normal people don't usually sneak up behind kids at the skate park early in the morning for fun."

The man laughed again—that low, humorless chuckle that grated on Greg's nerves. "And normal people are at the skate park skating before it's even light out?"

"When did I say I was normal?" Greg shot back, turning slightly away.

"When did I say I was?" the stranger countered.

Greg turned back and stared at the man for a moment. He was starting to get annoyed. *What did this guy want?*

The man strode over to Greg and held out his hand. "Allow me to introduce myself," he offered. "I'm Stefan Adikema. And you are . . .?"

Greg ignored the man's hand. "Why should I tell you who I am?"

"Why wouldn't you?" There was that annoying smile again. "Listen, kid, I've been watching you. And I think I could help you—if you helped me in return."

"You could help me?" Greg took a few steps backward. "Listen, dude, I don't even know you. How could you possibly help me?"

The man used the hand he had been holding out to Greg to gesture to the skate park. "You're obviously planning on entering the competition today, correct? Why else would you be out here skateboarding?"

Greg shifted uncomfortably and looked around at the park. "What if I am?"

The man smiled. "I could arrange for you to win."

"You got some tips for me or something?" Greg ran his fingers through his hair.

The man didn't change his stance. "I know people higher up. I could arrange for you to win."

Greg shook his head disbelievingly. "I don't need your help."

"Oh? Well, it's been my experience that skateboarding competitions usually require the contestants to be able to stay on their skateboards."

Greg clenched his pocketed fist and tightened his grip on his skateboard. Before he could say anything, the man held up his hands. "Listen, I'm not trying to pick a fight. I wouldn't ask you to do this for free." Stefan reached into his suit coat pocket and withdrew a wad of bills. "Besides, there is no guarantee that you will win . . . unless I intervene."

Greg eyed him for a long moment. *What in the world? He wants to pay me to take his help to win the contest? There's gotta be a catch. Maybe he wants me to promote a brand in Chicago . . . that might actually be kind of cool.* "What's in it for you?"

"Your assistance. When we get to Chicago, I need somebody to run a few errands for me and keep quiet about it. That's all. Nothing else."

So he doesn't want me to promote a brand. Greg shifted from one foot to the other, still eyeing the guy suspiciously, but his curiosity was piqued. "Why pick me?"

"I like you, kid. You've got spunk. I think you could prove to be valuable."

Greg flipped his hair out of his eyes. Something about this was actually appealing. "No, I mean why not pick some kid in Chicago? Why come all the way to Small Town, America?"

"Why do you think? I need somebody the locals won't recognize. You'll fly in for the contest, run the errands for me, then be out of there. Nobody in Chicago will be able to trace you back to me."

Greg's heart was pounding. He knew he had just stumbled onto something big, something illegal. Stefan made no effort to hide the fact that he was doing something very wrong. That was obvious from the way he was offering to cheat all the kids at the contest. The question was, why? He studied the man. Stefan appeared cool and collected. He was simply standing there, patiently waiting for Greg's response.

The rebellion in Greg's heart stirred. *Why should I care if it were illegal?* Because you could get arrested, a small voice inside him argued. *No I couldn't. It's not like I know what's going on!* Greg tried to convince himself. The other voice argued back, You know enough to know this isn't something you should be messing with. Your mom would be really disappointed. That last thought roused up all the anger and bitterness he had been feeling for the last hour. *Yeah, she would,* he thought, smoldering. *Her and her God.* Greg became angrier and angrier as he thought about it. It was all God's fault! All the bad things in his life God could have stopped from happening but He didn't! Maybe . . . just maybe, this was Greg's chance to get back at Him.

Stefan was still standing there. "Well?"

Slowly Greg held out his hand. A big smile spread across Stefan's face. He gripped Greg's hand and shook it. "Excellent. A very wise choice. When else will you have an opportunity like this one?" Suddenly he grew serious, and he stared at Greg through the sunglasses. "Now, this is what I want you to do," he instructed. "Behave just as you normally would. Do your best at the contest. We don't want it to be obvious that the contest is rigged. I will take care of everything."

Greg nodded. Stefan's scheme was obviously well-planned. This might even be kind of fun. It would definitely a good story he'd be able to tell later.

"I will contact you after the contest. For now, go home and above all else, act completely normal."

Greg nodded again and turned to go.

Just before he walked off, Stefan caught his shoulder with a firm hand. "One more thing." Greg turned his head. "Don't breathe a word of this to anyone. If you do . . ."

Greg cursed and glared at him. "Do you think I'm stupid? I can handle myself!"

Stefan smiled and released Greg's shoulder. "I like you, kid. You can be a great help to me. But make sure you remain on my good side." Greg raised an eyebrow, but Stefan didn't elaborate. Greg turned and walked off.

As he left the skate park, Greg glanced over his shoulder. Stefan was still standing there, watching Greg leave, the same smile plastered across his face. But in that smile was something else—something malicious, cold, and cunning.

What have I gotten myself into? Greg shivered and hurried home.

o———o

Officer Cambiano walked slowly into the small interrogation room and shut the door behind him. The prisoner was already sitting there, hunched over, with his hands folded in front of him.

Cambiano eyed the young man for a minute as he began sorting through his folders. The bright interrogation lamp reflected light off the bare table onto the prisoner's bulging biceps. Rather than brightening the room, the lamp seemed to suck all the light out of the rest of the room and concentrate it into one place, leaving the prisoner mostly in darkness. Still, he could see that the young man was probably six feet tall when standing up, well over 200 pounds, African American, mid-twenties. The senior officer shuffled through the papers, then tapped the stack in his hands on the table to make it straight and orderly. Finally, he sat down with a grunt and reached over to click on the voice recorder. The young man on the other end of the table sat as still as a statue—he hadn't moved a muscle since the officer had made his appearance.

"All right, well, let's get through this, shall we? It doesn't have to be too difficult, if you'll cooperate." The prisoner didn't answer. "What's your name?" Cambiano asked, opening up a pad of paper.

Silence. He glanced up from his pad. The prisoner hadn't even acknowledged him. Cambiano glanced over at the records. "Says here your name is Daemiem. Is that true?"

Daemiem finally grunted. "You got my records. You know who I am." The gang member still didn't look up.

Cambiano sighed and leaned back in his chair. "All right, Daemiem, well, why don't you level with me? I'm here to help you, if you'll just let me. I need information about your sup-plier—where you were getting the drugs, where you were hiding them. That sort of thing."

The gang member gave a derisive grunt but didn't say any-more. Cambiano waited, tapping his pen. "The more you tell me, the better it will go for you," he finally offered.

At last, Daemiem looked up. "You ain't gettin' nothin' from me. You may as well save your breath."

Cambiano leaned forward and interlocked his fingers in front of him. "We're going to find them anyway. The only thing you're doing is hurting yourself."

"I got a right to remain silent. You can't make me say a thing. I ain't gonna betray nobody."

Frustrated, Cambiano looked him in the eye. "How about you just tell me about where you initially got the drugs? I'm not even asking for information about your gang. I just want to know about the suppliers."

Daemiem looked down with a shake of his head and spat

out a noise that sounded like a cross between a snort and a laugh. "You ain't gonna catch them." He paused then looked back up, making eye contact with Cambiano. "Dis bigger than you realize, copper. Dey got plans and more power dan you know. It in your own best interest to stay away. Dey ain't messin' around."

Cambiano locked eyes with him. "Neither are we."

Pink? Or purple? Renae held the two tops up, trying to decide. She looked at herself in the mirror and squinted. She wasn't really a girly-girl, obsessed with fashion and how she looked. At least not like Tonya. But she did put thought into each outfit, usually based on who she was going to be with and what she thought they liked. She tried to imagine which color Greg would like best, then half-smiled. Greg probably wouldn't notice one way or the other, especially since he was going to be skateboarding. When he was skateboarding, it was as if he saw and heard nothing else. Every fiber of his being was devoted to his passion.

Deciding on pink, she grabbed a pair of jeans to go with it. Glancing at the clock, she quickly put on the clothes. The contest would be starting soon and she wanted to be there for Greg. She couldn't waste too much time getting ready. But what should she do with her hair? Again, she evaluated herself in the mirror. A couple blemishes on her skin made her wince. She needed to do something quick. She liked her hair length. It was long enough to do a few pretty things with but short enough that it wasn't a hassle. A ponytail would be good enough for today. As she grabbed a hair tie and began pulling her hair through it, she hesitated, looking a little longer at her top.

Greg's mom probably wouldn't think it was modest. She felt a pang of uneasiness and quickly looked behind her shoulder as if someone were watching her.

Her discomfort didn't come from what Greg's mom would think of her but from what Greg would think of the fact that she had gone to a few of his mom's church's Bible studies. Despite what Greg thought of his mom, she really liked Mrs. Martin, and she had been intrigued by what she had told Renae about God one day while she was waiting for Greg. Mrs. Martin had invited Renae to a Bible study, and Renae had agreed but told her it would be best not to mention it to Greg. At the time, it had seemed like no big deal, even though she knew Greg would be crazy mad. But Greg didn't rule her life and she could go wherever she wanted. But it hadn't just been that once. She had gone back several times.

Renae's family wasn't religious, but Renae had always had questions about God and what happened when a person died. It was interesting to hear answers. She hadn't realized how opposed Greg was to religion until he had vented to her a few days before about how much he hated his mom's faith. It had surprised her so much, and she was glad she hadn't said anything about the couple times she had gone to the Bible study. To be honest, it seemed like Greg was overreacting. Sure, they had some strange beliefs that seemed a little too conservative maybe, but it really wasn't as bad as he made it out to be.

She looked down at their last couple texts.

My mom is so stupid!

Why?

She's just being a religious idiot.

I'll tell you about it tomorrow.

Renae sighed. She wished Greg and his mom got along better. Maybe if he knew she went to the same Bible study, he would ease up on Mrs. Martin a little bit. She bit her lip. Suddenly, the time on her phone screen caught her eye. She was going to be late for the contest! She shoved her phone in her back pocket and hurried to the door.

o——o

Greg scanned the skate park. When he had arrived that morning, a white tent had been erected on one side of the skate park with some chairs and a table set up for the judges. A man with a megaphone scurried around bellowing orders. Judges made last-minute preparations. Skaters milled about, practicing on the street or socializing. Another table had been set up on the other side of the park for the kids to sign in. A line of skaters were already waiting by the table. More kids were there than he expected.

Doug waved at him from over by some yellow tape, blocking off the skate park. "Hey, dude, over here!" Greg walked over to him but continued watching for Stefan. He didn't see Renae anywhere either.

Breakfast had been uneventful. Tension was still in the air at home, but he and his mom hadn't said a word to each other. She had left out the materials to make breakfast and then left for work before Greg was done eating. Greg was glad he hadn't had to talk with her, especially with the skating contest and the mysterious offer from Stefan on his mind.

"Checking out chicks?" Doug teased as he noticed Greg's eyes wandering, shoving Greg's shoulder and shaking him out of his reverie. "Better not tell Renae. Not that I blame you. There are some hot girls here!"

Greg nodded distractedly.

"Dude, you should see Stephanie. She's—"

Greg whirled around. "What? Did you say Stefan? Where?"

Doug backed up with his hands in the air. "Whoa, cool it! I said, 'Stephanie.' What are you talking about?"

Greg's face flushed. "Oh, sorry . . . I . . . uh, I just heard wrong." Mentally he cussed at himself. *Get a hold of yourself, man! You're supposed to be acting normal.*

Doug looked at him suspiciously until his eyes turned away and he groaned in mock disappointment. "Oh great! Renae is here!" he said loudly enough for her to hear. Just then Greg felt someone's arms wrap around his waist. He lurched forward then turned around to Renae, whose eyes were twinkling mischievously.

"Did I scare you?" she asked, winking. He hugged her, glad for the distraction.

"You didn't scare me," he said. "I just had to turn around quickly to protect myself from whatever you were planning."

"Just seeing you scared me," Doug cut in.

Renae smiled sweetly. "Good to see you too, Doug. Did you both already get signed in?"

"I did, but Rip Van Winkle here hasn't," Doug said.

"Well, let's walk over there and get in line," Renae suggested.

Greg's eyes darted over to the line of kids at the registration table. He tried to see if Stefan was over there, but he still couldn't tell. Renae nudged him. Greg looked over at her and saw that she had been watching him.

"You okay?" she mouthed.

Greg shrugged the concern off and forced a laugh. "Sure, why wouldn't I be? Come on, let's get in line. At this rate, I'm going to be the last one."

Doug punched his shoulder. "Dude, you might as well not even waste your time. I'll be skating circles around you!"

Greg shoved him, but before they could get into a playful fight, the man with the megaphone clicked it on and cleared his throat. "Testing . . . can everyone hear me?" The guy turned for a moment as a man yelled something to him, then he turned back to the megaphone.

"Excuse me, skaters. We're about to get started. We may need a couple more minutes," he said, glancing at the man who had yelled at him. "But we're almost there. If you haven't registered, now is the time to do it." The man put down the megaphone and walked over to the other guy, yelling and waving his arms. Several skaters who had been practicing moved towards the registration table.

As they walked to the table, Renae held onto Greg's arm as she surveyed all the kids. "There's a lot more people here than I thought there would be," she said. "Do you still think you have a pretty good chance of winning?"

Better than anyone here after meeting Stefan, Greg thought.

"Are you kidding?" said Doug. "None of these kids has a chance against me!"

Renae rolled her eyes. "I was asking Greg."

Just then, Greg caught sight of Stefan. The man still had his sunglasses on and had approached the man with the megaphone and was conferring quietly with him. The megaphone man was nodding a lot, and Stefan kept gesturing with his hands. Greg saw Stefan point at him, then keep talking.

Doug tapped him on the shoulder. "Hey, dude?" Greg jumped, and his friend smirked. "Man, what's wrong with you? You're all jumpy. Have too many energy drinks or something?"

Greg glared at Doug. "Well, I wouldn't be so jumpy if you weren't always sneaking up behind me."

Renae smiled and glanced over at Doug.

Greg forced himself to take a deep breath. *Act normal. Not jumpy. Normal.* The line had moved up and now it was Greg's turn to sign in. The man who had been holding the megaphone had walked over behind the table. He looked at Greg intently for a moment and then said, "Go ahead and put your full name and phone number down here."

It seems pretty self-explanatory, Greg thought, but he just nodded and signed in.

Greg was one of the last in line, so after two or three of the final skaters signed in, the man with the megaphone jumped atop a ramp and clicked the megaphone on again. "Excuse me, we—" Kids continued to chat. "Uh, excuse me . . . Hey! Listen up!" The skaters began to quiet down. One of them called out a rude suggestion to the man, but he ignored it.

"My name is Rush Stein. I'm the organizer of this contest." The man went through a few preliminaries. One caught Greg's attention. "We'd like to thank the sponsor of this contest, Stefan Adikema." Stefan waved his fingertips at the crowd of kids.

Greg tried to act as bored as everyone else was, but was thinking, *So, Stefan's the sponsor. Why would he rig it so I'd win?* Rush Stein finished the opening remarks and thank-yous and finally moved on to the contest itself. Greg listened intently, as he normally would, so he'd be able to put on a convincing show.

"So that's how this contest will be conducted. Any questions?" Stein glanced at his watch, then without allowing any time for questions looked up and said, "No? Good. Then let's get started. We'll be having you kids compete in the order you signed up, so first up will be . . . Jeremy Duran! Come on up."

The contest lasted almost through lunch. Doug's turn came early on. He fell a few times, after which he was in a foul mood the rest of the day. At last it was Greg's turn.

Rush Stein wrote something on his clipboard and motioned to Greg with his pencil. "Okay, kid. We're gonna start with some ramp stuff—"

"Vert?" Greg asked.

Rush rolled his eyes. "Yeah, whatever you skater kids call it in Colorado. Afterwards, we'll move on to some of the flat ground stuff, all right? So, begin whenever you're ready." Greg looked around for Stefan, hesitating a moment. He didn't see him. Rush waved his arms. "C'mon, we don't have all day! Get goin'!"

It was time to show his stuff. Greg skated over to the half-pipe and swung up the ladder. He dropped in and with all the speed he could muster, sailed up the other side and did a front-side heel flip, landing flawlessly. Greg snuck a glance over to the judges to see if they were impressed. One of them was looking intently at him over his glasses while chewing on a mechanical pencil. The other one was simply watching, his face expression-less.

Greg dropped in again and went up the other side, doing a tail-slide. He decided to take a risk and tried a hurricane grind. *Ooh, bad move.* He stumbled but quickly regained his footing. Pencil-chewing judge shook his head. The stoic one just stared. *Jeez, these guys are hard to impress!* Greg stopped the thought and corrected himself. He was going to win anyway, it didn't matter what the judges thought. The jerks. Greg decided to just lose himself in his skateboarding. *I'm not here for them, I'm here for me.* So that's what Greg did. He skated just as he would if it were just Doug and him. His tricks went smoothly and he didn't have any big errors.

When he glanced over to the judges again, Pencil-chewer was nodding, and Stoic was smiling. At last, Greg finished his run and flipped the hair out of his eyes proudly.

The judge who had been smiling began clapping sponta-neously, until he was met with a glare from Pencil-chewer. His clapping died out. Rush Stein walked out to the middle, making notes on his clipboard. He nodded to Greg. "Thanks, we'll let you know." Then with a wave of his hand, he called another kid up to the skate park.

Greg was smug as he walked away. *Not bad,* he thought. *But really . . . it didn't matter.* Nothing really mattered in this contest. It was all staged. All of the kids here were practicing, sweating, and cursing for nothing. It didn't matter how good any of them were; it didn't matter how bad any of them were. No matter what, Greg would win. A pang of guilt suddenly hit him. He swallowed hard.

Knock it off, he told himself. *It's no big deal. Why should you care if these kids just wasted their time?* But deep down, he did care. Whatever. No going back now.

Renae rushed over and hugged him. "You did so good!" Greg kissed the top of her head, drinking in the praise. It felt good.

Suddenly, he saw his mom standing on the other side of the park, clapping and smiling. He moaned inwardly. When he'd gone home for breakfast, they had avoided each other like the plague. He had eaten then left again to register. *What is she doing here?* She waved at him, and he was tempted to act like he hadn't seen her until Renae pulled his arm. Reluctantly, he shuffled over with Renae to his mom.

"Good job, Gregory! You did well!"

"Don't call me Gregory," Greg said in a low voice. "Mom, what are you doing here?"

"I dropped by on my way home from work for lunch to see if I could catch a glimpse of you skateboarding. Looks like I was right on time! Hi, Renae!"

"Hi," Renae said with a sweet smile.

"Well, thanks. Uh, I gotta go."

"Wait! I thought we could talk."

Greg glanced at Renae. "Not now, Mom," he said, hoping she would take the hint.

"I really would like to talk about what happened last night," she repeated.

Renae let go of Greg's arm. "I'll go get you some water," she told Greg. "You guys can talk." Greg gave her an angry look, but she turned around and walked toward the table with the water cooler.

As soon as Renae was gone, his mom started in. "Greg, I . . . I'm sorry for our argument this morning."

The skater kept his eyes averted, letting his brown locks fall over his eyes. "Mom, I really don't want to talk about this," he repeated.

She forged ahead anyway. "I just want so much for you to see, well, to see how much God loves you." She took a deep breath. "But I shouldn't have gotten as upset as I did."

Greg shrugged. "Yeah, whatever. I'll see you at home, okay?"

His mom stopped him again. "Don't I get to see the awards? When are they going to do them anyway?"

"Mom, there aren't really any awards. The winner gets to go compete in Chicago, and the second place gets a new skateboard. That's all."

"Well, I'd still like to be here when they announce the winner."

"Mom! Do . . . do you have to?" Greg asked.

His mother's face fell, and she took a step back. "Well, no. I guess, I don't have to. Uh, let me know if you win . . . and I'll see you at home."

Greg winced at the pain he saw in his mother's eyes. "Mom, I'm sorry, I—"

"No. No, it's okay." She forced a smile. "I'll see you at home."

She turned and walked slowly back to her car. Greg looked at his mom's receding form for a moment. An inner turmoil reigned for a few seconds. Then he averted his eyes. No. It would be too embarrassing to have his mom at the contest. He walked slowly back towards the water table. Renae was waiting behind two other kids.

"Where's your mom?" she asked in a surprised tone.

"She left," he said shortly. "Where's Doug?"

Renae shrugged. "I think he went home. He knew he wasn't going to get first, so he probably left." Greg nodded. Knowing Doug, that was probably true.

"I wish you wouldn't be so hard on your mom," Renae said.

Greg turned to her in surprise. "Are you kidding? You don't know what it's like, Renae. You're lucky your grandma isn't religious. My mom is always using God as a way to get at me. I hate it! That's all religion is! An attempt to control people!"

The other kids had moved on, and Renae positioned her cup under the water spigot. She bit her lip and said, "Have you ever thought . . ." Greg stared at her. "Thought what?" he asked.

Making sure the water went into the cup seemed to take all of her concentration. "Thought that . . . well, that . . . that maybe she's right?" Renae asked, still not looking at him.

"What?" he asked in a flat tone.

"Greg, there's something I've been wanting to tell you. I haven't before because I knew you'd be mad, but . . ." she took a deep breath like she was about to go underwater. "But I've gone to a couple of your mom's women's Bible studies, and I think you're overreacting." She finally looked up at him, holding out the cup of water like a peace offering. He ignored it.

"You're becoming one of those religious fanatics?" he asked incredulously. "Please tell me you're joking. Of all the people I know, I thought you were the one person I could trust! Confide in! But you're letting yourself become brainwashed?"

She was still holding out the cup of water, but she looked

hurt. Her big brown eyes looked up at him. "Greg, you can trust me. That's why I'm telling you what I really think."

"Why?" Greg felt betrayed. "Why would you take her side? Why would you go . . ."

"Do you really believe there's no God?" she asked. "I don't!"

"If there is a God," Greg said, "then He's a mean, vindictive, bloodthirsty tyrant who just wants to control people!"

"It's not like that at all!" Renae said, raising her voice. "The people at the Bible study talk about God like a father, who loves us and wants to have a relationship with us—"

Greg cursed. He was getting wound up but he couldn't seem to control the anger bubbling up inside him. How could Renae do this to him? "A father like one of our fathers?" Greg was disgusted by the idea.

"Yeah!" Renae said, planting her feet and sloshing some of the water out.

"So, so He gets drunk and curses and hits the people He loves and then abandons them? That sounds about right!"

Renae stamped her foot in frustration. "Ugh, Greg! That's not what I mean and you know it!"

"If He's like my dad . . . or your dad . . . then I don't want anything to do with Him!"

Renae threw down her hands, letting all the water pour out of the Styrofoam cup. "You don't understand!" she said, on the verge of tears. "Why are you being like this? What's wrong with believing in a loving God?"

"Because He's not real!" Greg shouted. A few people turned to look at them, but he didn't care. "And if you're going to take up with those religious zealots, then I don't want anything to do with you!" He turned and stormed off. Renae didn't try to stop him. Instead, she turned and fled in the other direction. That made him even angrier, but he wasn't about to go after her. Not now.

Unsure of where he was going, Greg looked up and saw a gas station across the street and decided to go there. Having refused the water Renae had gotten for him, he was still thirsty.

He strolled across the grass toward the convenience store, carrying his skateboard, trying to cool off. How had this day turned out so badly? He had gotten into fights with two of the most important people in his life. But why couldn't they see that they were restricting him with all this God talk? How could Renae do that to him? He couldn't think about her right now. It was too fresh. Too hurtful. Unbidden, his thoughts turned to his mom. He couldn't help regretting that conversation either. She got on his nerves, sure, but he still loved her and didn't want to hurt her. But having her at the contest would have been awful. It would've embarrassed him and . . . An unexpected thought hit him. It would've made him feel guilty. He was winning the contest illegally, and having his mother there would've just reminded him of the fact. Greg squeezed his eyes shut, trying to block out the feelings that were bombarding him. He felt an unexplainable restlessness, a discontented feeling he'd felt before and hated.

He opened the door of the convenience store and walked in, looking around. A pretty girl with a bored, mundane expression on her face stood behind the cash register. He'd never seen her before. She might prove to be the perfect distraction. He didn't need Renae with her new thoughts about religion and her judgmental attitude! He'd show her!

Greg had caught his reflection in the glass door and decided it might be best to go to the bathroom and maybe splash some water on his face and make sure he was looking good before going to meet the girl. He walked over to the bathroom and swung the door open, stepping inside.

Greg raised his eyebrow at his reflection in the mirror and

tried to put on his best macho look. The zit caught his eye. He looked closer. Was it noticeable? It was on his forehead, maybe he could try to cover it up with his hair. Greg splashed some water on his face and wet his hair a little, arranging it in a way he hoped would cover up the zit.

A dry chuckle from behind him caught him by surprise. "You're really obsessed with yourself, aren't you?" Greg whirled around to face Stefan and banged his knee on something metal. He grabbed his knee and grimaced at the pain.

Stefan's annoying chuckle sounded again. Greg gritted his teeth and fought the urge to punch him. "Maybe I should've picked somebody else," the infuriating man said. "How on earth are you going to compete in Chicago when you're startled so easily?"

Stefan stood by the door to the stall next to the sink, leaning against the wall with his arms folded. Before Greg could give a sarcastic reply, Stefan continued. "Now turn back around and continue what you were doing. I'm going to go in this stall and tell you what to do. Act completely normal if anyone comes in, understood?"

"I've been doing okay so far, haven't I?"

Stefan shook his head. "Actually, no. It was obvious to anyone with eyes that you were nervous about something this morning. You're lucky nobody cared enough to ask."

That last comment stung. Greg felt the urge to slug Stefan again. Who was this guy, coming in and telling Greg nobody cared about him? *What's wrong with me? I don't need anybody to care,* Greg tried to persuade himself bitterly. *I'll look out for Number One, and who cares what anybody else thinks?* But deep inside, it hurt Greg to think that what Stefan said might be true. Maybe nobody did care about him. Renae had betrayed him. Doug was too self-centered to care about anyone else but himself.

Stefan was looking annoyed again. "Now turn back around to the sink. We want to look natural. Nobody should come in, but just in case. Remember, never try to contact me. I'll contact you. You don't know me, got it?" Greg resisted the growing temptation to hurt Stefan and turned back to the sink, running his fingers through his hair. "Now," Stefan said, disappearing into the stall. "Listen carefully. I want you to act completely natural when you receive the award. Though your acting left much to be desired this morning, you were pretty natural when you were skateboarding."

Greg couldn't hide his surprise. "You mean you were there? I never saw you."

"Just because you can't see someone or something doesn't mean he or it is not there." Stefan's tone was amused, but in it Greg also detected something else. A warning?

"I will be the one to give you the award, and I'm going to repeat to you: Give no indication that you know me," Stefan demanded. "This is the last opportunity I'll have to talk to you privately until after the contest. Again, don't try to contact me. Someone will call you probably a day or two after the contest to work out the details surrounding your trip to Chicago. It will just be you going. We will make that clear to your legal guardian. No parents or friends will accompany you. This trip will only be for a couple of days, so your parents won't have a problem with that, will they? We will, of course, allow the necessary phone calls, emails, text messages, whatever's necessary. But you will be going alone. Are you with me so far?"

Greg nodded, even though Stefan couldn't see him. He had a feeling Stefan would continue whether he was "with him" or not.

"The person who calls you will let you know of any other important details. I'll be on the flight with you out to Chicago.

Once we're off the plane, you can get further instructions. I think that's about it. I'm going to leave now. You are to count to ten, then follow. Understood?"

Greg nodded again. Stefan flushed the toilet and emerged, pushing Greg aside and running his hands under the water for a moment. "Wet hands make it look less suspicious," he explained, shutting off the water and flicking water droplets onto the mirror. With that, Stefan pushed the door open and strode out of the restroom.

Greg quickly ran his hand through his hair, checking to make sure it was presentable. He waited a few more moments and then exited the restroom. Stefan was nowhere to be seen. Greg almost left but caught sight of the attractive girl leaning against the counter reading a magazine.

He swaggered up to the counter. The girl sighed as she stood up and set down the magazine. "Yeah?" She was clearly bored.

Greg cleared his throat. "Um, yeah, could I get a water cup?" The girl carelessly handed him a paper cup and gestured to the soda dispenser.

Undeterred, he stayed where he was, leaning against the counter. She sighed. "Can I get something else for you?"

Greg flashed his most winning smile. "How 'bout your number?"

The girl narrowed her eyes at him. "Don't get any ideas, hot shot. Shouldn't you get back to your skateboarding?"

The skater held up his hands and backed off. "Hey, take it easy."

The girl leaned forward on the counter. "Listen, bud, I'm from Chicago. I don't put up with it when some kid's hitting on me."

Greg felt color rise to his cheeks. "Kid?"

The girl didn't let up. "And if you're naïve enough to compete in that skateboarding contest for a trip to Chicago—"

"Naïve?" Greg asked. "What's so naïve about it?"

She smirked. "You're obviously a skater. You think you're gonna fit in Chicago? Unless you trade in your skateboard for a switchblade, you're out of luck."

"What are you talking about?"

The door opened and a couple walked in.

"I've got customers," the girl said. She moved to the other cash register as the man approached. "Hi, can I help you?"

Greg turned to get his water, surprised and irritated. What was she talking about? The cryptic language about switchblades and skateboards didn't make any sense. There was going to be a skateboarding contest in Chicago! Why wouldn't he fit in? He frowned.

No matter what this girl said, he was going to Chicago. And he would have a great time on top of that! Suddenly, he felt water running over his hands. He looked down to see the cup overflowing. He quickly let go of the dispenser button and backed away, taking a long sip so it wouldn't overflow more.

As he turned to leave, he saw the girl smirking at him. *What did she know anyway?* But as the door of the convenience store closed with a jingle behind him, he felt a twinge of doubt. He tried to shrug it off. Chicago would be a blast! He hoped.

3

"Absolutely, ma'am. Rest assured that your son is in good hands. We'll take good care of him, won't we?" Rush Stein leaned over the table and gave Greg's shoulder a squeeze, winking at him. Greg was tempted to roll his eyes, but this was the opportunity to sell his mom, so instead of expressing how he really felt about Rush's empty gesture, he turned to his mom and gave her his most winning smile.

She sat quietly. Greg could tell she was mulling it over. She glanced down again at the paperwork Rush had laid out on the kitchen table. "And he'd be back on Saturday afternoon?"

Rush nodded. "And let me say again that we are willing to accommodate you in whatever way works best with your schedule. We can drop him off, meet you at the airport or whatever we need to do, but know that we will be with him every step of the way."

Mrs. Martin bit her lip and rifled through the papers, not meeting his eyes. Rush took the opportunity her silence provided to direct her attention to a particular piece of paper with Skaterz Inc.'s mission statement on it.

This is taking too long, thought Greg as he rubbed his fingers along the edge of his skateboard while Rush read some cheesy sounding statement about "enabling the youth of America to

46

create their own future" or something. Someone from the contest had already contacted his mom by phone and talked things over with her. But his mother still had reservations, and Rush Stein was doing his best to soothe them.

Greg let his mind drift to Renae. He wondered what she thought about him going to Chicago. He hadn't talked to her much since the contest. She had texted him to congratulate him and they had kinda made up, but Greg still felt uncomfortable with the things she had been saying about God, so he hadn't communicated with her much. It wasn't that he was avoiding her; he just wasn't going out of his way to talk with her. Besides, he had been busy getting ready for the trip to Chicago. If only his mom would stop dragging her heels!

"Our highest priority is your convenience, and doing what's best and easiest for you and our contest winner," Rush was saying.

Mrs. Martin blew out a sigh. She looked up at Rush. "And he will always have a chaperone accompanying him?" This time Greg did roll his eyes. "Chicago is a big, dangerous city," she continued, "and I certainly don't feel comfortable unless there is constant supervision—"

Rush had been bobbing his head in sync with what she was saying, and now he took the liberty to interrupt her by saying, "Yes, ma'am, we understand and share your concerns. This contest would not even be happening unless we were completely assured of all our contestants' safety. Our personnel will always be alert and ready to assist and accompany the competitors. Our staff is very attentive and conscientious. He will be completely safe. You don't need to worry about a thing." He ended his speech by flashing a reassuring smile.

Greg tapped his foot impatiently. His mom picked up another piece of paper. *C'mon, Mom,* he silently pleaded. *Just say yes already.* At last, she heaved another sigh and slowly began nodding. "Well, I guess if you're sure—"

Rush was already standing. "That's great, Mrs. Martin. We appreciate your attentiveness. Remember, we are on your side on this. So you are saying . . . ?"

His mom bit her lip and Greg held his breath in anticipation. *Say yes, Mom, say yes!*

Mrs. Martin blew out a sigh. "I suppose it will be fine."

Greg whooped and leaped up from his chair. In his mind he was already packed!

o———o

To Greg's chagrin, his mom insisted on driving Greg to the airport, following Rush's car; and Rush, unfortunately, was only too happy to comply. Greg almost wished he had accepted Renae's offer to come along, but he was still mad at her and had brushed her off.

The ride to the airport was a painful one consisting mostly of lectures and advice. But at last they stood by the security line. Rush Stein was already waiting by the line, and Greg was anxious to join him. But Mrs. Martin took him by the shoulders and faced him. She stared at him for a moment, making him shift uncomfortably, particularly when he saw tears welling up in her eyes. *Please don't make a scene,* he thought. She hugged him and when they pulled apart, she brushed a lock of hair from his eyes. "Please be careful, Greg," she said in a whisper, remembering to use his preferred nickname.

He nodded hurriedly and glanced over to where Rush was tapping his foot and looking at his watch. "I guess you'd better go," his mom said, wiping her eyes. Greg agreed and picked up his bag, ready to join his chaperone. "Don't forget to call me when you get there!" Mrs. Martin called after him. Greg quickly nodded and joined Rush in the security line.

Rush went out of his way to supervise Greg in the security line. Mrs. Martin continued to watch as they went through the line, and Rush placed a hand on Greg's shoulder as they headed toward the escalator. Right before he went down the moving staircase, Greg glanced up and saw his mom still watching with loving, tear-filled eyes. He allowed himself one more wave before she disappeared from view.

Greg shifted his weight in his seat and glanced around. His pulse quickened and his heart wouldn't stop pounding, though of course he would never admit that to anyone. He peeked around his seat into the aisle, trying to catch a glimpse of Rush or Stefan.

Stefan said he was going to be on this plane too. Greg strained his neck to see if he was. There! Stefan sat a few rows back, casually reading a magazine. As usual, he had black clothes and sunglasses on. Greg didn't see Rush, who had promptly abandoned him to find his own seat the moment they were on the plane.

The skater turned back to face the seat in front of him and took a deep breath, trying to calm himself down. *This is it.* He was going to Chicago!

He glanced over to the people in the seats next to him. A businessman in a suit sat in the middle seat, busily tapping away on his laptop, trying to get some work done before takeoff. A slightly overweight man leaned heavily against the window, beginning to fall asleep. Greg looked out the window, which was partially covered up by the big man's bulky body.

This wasn't the first time Greg had been on an airplane. Only last time . . . Last time, *my sister was with us.* His head felt heavy and his eyes closed. No. He forced his eyes open. *I won't think about it.*

Flight attendants were moving down the aisle, reminding people to turn off their cell phones, to place their carry-ons under the seat in front of them, and to put larger items in the overhead bins. They reached Greg's aisle and the businessman next to Greg hastily saved what he was working on and snapped the laptop shut. The overweight man lifted his head groggily and fastened his seatbelt before falling asleep again.

Greg had already stowed his carry-on bag in the overhead compartment, but he hadn't turned off his cell phone. Stefan had warned him to comply with all the rules to avoid drawing attention to himself. Greg pulled out his cell phone and put it on vibrate. *That's close enough, isn't it?*

As the businessman placed his laptop under the seat in front of him, Greg's attention was drawn to a flustered lady dragging a little kid down the aisle toward the back of the plane. "The plane's going to start flying soon. Why didn't you go when we were in the airport?" she asked with an exasperated sigh. "I didn't have to go then!" the little boy said, struggling to keep up.

Greg smiled. Suddenly he was a little kid again, and his mom and sister were sitting by him on the airplane. "Mommy, when are we gonna start flying?"

"Soon, honey. Samantha, don't play with that."

Greg forced the memory out of his mind and tried to concentrate on something else. Thinking about his sister hurt too much. And it was another area where God had failed him.

“We will be landing shortly. Please note that the fasten seatbelts light is on. It’s been a pleasure having you on board today, and we hope you’ll choose to fly with us again. Welcome to Chicago.”

Greg yawned and stretched. He slowly looked around, blinking a couple times. The businessman was clacking away at his laptop, as he had been for the past hour. After the overweight man woke up, he had tried to start a conversation with the businessman and with Greg but had failed, and now he was reading an old-looking novel, which didn’t seem to be keeping his attention very well because his head was nodding again.

Greg lazily clicked his seatbelt into place. A sudden burst of excitement shot through him, which he did his best to hide. *This is it! I’m actually in Chicago!* He felt the dip as the plane began descending. His stomach jumped in his throat. At last he wouldn’t have to put up with his mom’s Christian rhetoric for a couple days at least. Here, he would be accepted. Here, he would fit in with the other skateboarders! Not to mention the fun he would have at the contest.

He smiled dreamily as he imagined himself doing tricks and flips at an elaborate skate park with huge ramps, sweet grinding rails, and a humongous half-pipe in the center. Greg pictured himself skating toward the half-pipe.

He climbs up to the top, drops in, then . . . lets himself go free! The judges jump to their feet in awe at the skills of this incredible skateboarder prodigy. The other kids stare with their mouths open. Applause echoes through the arena. Then the skater goes for a 720. The audience gasps. Will he land it? In slow motion, he twists around—and lands it! The crowd goes wild. Greg tosses his head and gives a little wave to the crowd, then walks up to receive his award. The judge shakes his hand furiously. "Ladies and gentlemen! Today we have seen the best of a master skateboarder. One that will rival the best skateboarders of all time. Would you all give a great, big hand to . . . Greg Martin!" Greg smiles casually as he waves at the crowd again. Some cute girls swoon. "Would you like to say a few words?" the judge asks.

Greg takes the mic. "Thanks, dude, uuuh . . ."

Ugh. Greg grimaced. That would never work. What would he say if he was asked to give a speech?

Suddenly, he felt the plane skimming across the top of the runway. The wheels bumped onto the surface and the plane began slowing to a stop. People began unbuckling their seatbelts and stretching as a flight attendant asked over the intercom for them to please keep their seatbelts on and remain seated until the plane had come to a complete stop. Finally, it did. People began getting up and getting their bags out of the overhead compartments. Greg was the first one out into the aisle after retrieving his carry-on.

He looked around for Stefan or Rush. With people jostling and moving all around him, it was difficult to see. The businessman began tapping his foot, waiting impatiently for Greg to start moving down the aisle. *Chill out, dude,* Greg thought. *Where is Stefan? Whatever. I guess I'll find him when I get off the plane.* The line slowly moved out the door, past the stewardesses who were profusely thanking everyone for flying with their particular airline.

The first thing to hit Greg was the humidity. It was raining outside but still warm. Greg grimaced. He would have to get used to it.

The Coloradoan skater emerged into the busy O'Hare

International Airport, moved off to the side where he wouldn't be knocked down, and scanned the crowds for Rush or Stefan. After several minutes of looking, Greg became irritated. *Where is that creep? He knows I don't know my way around.* He considered yelling but didn't want to risk drawing attention to himself.

Greg flopped down in a nearby chair and acted as if he were reading the departing and arriving times of various airplanes as he tried to figure out what to do. *I could wait for Stefan, but then again, knowing what a jerk Stefan is, he's probably gone on without me.*

Greg suddenly felt insignificant and foolish. He looked around at all the people swarming around him, all hurrying to do something, to be somewhere. Greg didn't know what to do or where to go. All the people scurrying past him had their own separate lives. They were in control and knew what they were doing at this moment. No familiar faces were waiting to welcome and help him. The only people he knew here were Stefan and Rush, and they could hardly be described as friends. But at this point, Greg would've been glad to see even Stefan, as irritating as he was.

Greg decided he would go to the baggage claim then figure out what to do from there. *Yeah, good plan.* Greg got up and looked around for some sort of directional sign. Restrooms . . . Food . . . *Aha!* Baggage Claim. Greg moved through the sea of endless people toward the baggage claim. He had never been around so many people in his entire life! Chattering in Japanese, a couple absentmindedly pushed Greg aside as they walked by. "Hey, watch where you're going!" Greg called out after them, punctuating his sentence with a cuss word. They didn't even turn around. *Man! Welcome to Chicago!*

Greg adjusted his ball cap, which was of course on backwards, and kept walking. He finally arrived at the baggage claim. Pushing past the people standing around, he moved to the front.

"Hey, watch it, kid!" said a burly man with a beer belly.

"You watch it!" Greg retorted and moved on before the man could respond.

He sidestepped a mother with a stroller trying to keep her hyper kids in line and stood in front of the baggage claim, watching for his bags. The bags on the conveyor belt slowly made their rounds. People shoved their way to the front so they could retrieve their luggage.

After about ten minutes, Greg was getting impatient. Suitcases and garment bags continued getting snatched up, and still Greg hadn't seen his go by. *Am I in the right place?* He looked up at the sign. Yeah, that was his flight number all right. *So where's my bag? It should've been here by now!* Greg looked around in frustration. Now he wasn't sure what to do.

Just then, Greg caught sight of a bald man in sunglasses, casually leaning against a wall holding up a small, white sign. He was a tall African American, and seemed in no particular hurry to go anywhere. At his feet lay a backpack with a skateboard strapped to it that looked a lot like Greg's. It wasn't the man himself that caught Greg's attention. It was the sign he was carrying that read: Gregory Martin.

Hesitantly, Greg took a step toward him. The man caught sight of him and waved his fingertips, his expression never changing. Greg awkwardly made his way over to him, too surprised to be angry about the sign designating him "Gregory."

"You waitin' for me?" Greg asked. The man looked down at him. He dipped his head toward the sign and nodded, instantly making Greg feel foolish for asking the question. The man's facial expression remained the same as he flipped out his wallet, handing Greg a card. Terrance Shekilah. Skaterz Inc. (800-555-

8121) Chicago, Illinois. With that, the man picked up Greg's bag, tossed the sign in a nearby trash can, and jerked his head toward the escalators.

Greg blinked at the card then shoved it in his pocket and followed, hurrying to match the tall man's strides. "You could've told me you were going to meet me," Greg said. "I was waiting at the baggage claim forever." The man didn't respond but just kept walking. "So," Greg said, struggling to keep up. "You must work with Stefan, huh?"

Again, the man nodded. Greg was getting annoyed. *Doesn't this guy speak English?* "Uh, where is Stefan? And Rush?"

Finally the man spoke. He had a crisp, clear voice with just a hint of some sort of an accent. "Stefan and Rush had to hurry off for an appointment. I'll be taking you to your hotel."

"Oh. Which hotel?"

Evidently, Terrance didn't hear him, as he continued his fast-paced exodus toward the escalator. The man didn't say anything the rest of the way out of the airport, and Greg gave up trying to communicate with him. *Whatever. It was just as well. At least this guy didn't ask you a lot of annoying questions about school or what you want to be when you grow up like some adults did. Greg could get used to this kind of silence.*

At last they emerged into the parking garage. Terrance held up a hand to Greg and then stepped out onto the road. Not comprehending his gesture, Greg followed. For the first time since they had been together, Terrance wrinkled his eyebrows and held up his hand again.

"Wait here, please," he demanded in his crisp voice. Greg stepped back onto the sidewalk, and Terrance disappeared into the rows of cars.

Several minutes later, a sleek, black limousine pulled up to the curb. Terrance stepped out and walked around, opening the back door for Greg. Greg's jaw dropped. *No way! A limousine?* Terrance motioned for Greg to get in the back. In awe, Greg climbed in and got comfortable on the leather seat. Terrance slammed the door shut and made his way around to the driver's side. Greg gawked at the size of the limousine. The front seat was separated from the back by a wall. A screen sat in a cove in the wall. Underneath it was a gaming system.

An intercom installed in the wall clicked on and Terrance's voice came over the loudspeaker. "Make yourself comfortable. If there is anything you need, press the button on the wall near the cup holder." With that, he clicked off. Greg eyed the button and then looked around the rest of the limousine. *Yeah, I could definitely get used to this,* he thought with a smirk.

The limousine began rolling smoothly over the pavement, and within minutes Terrance had skillfully navigated his way out of the parking garage into dreary Chicago.

Greg was still confused about where Stefan had gone. *How had he left? And how had he gotten out so fast?* It didn't make sense that he didn't take the limousine with Greg. *Come on, who wouldn't want to ride in a limousine?* But Stefan probably rides in them all the time, Greg mused. In fact, he may even have ridden in a different one on the way to where he was going.

But enough thinking! Greg turned on the screen and began scrolling through the games displayed. Some war games . . . a basketball game . . . ah! A skating game! Greg selected the game on the screen.

Stefan watched the whole proceedings on a small television screen, the only illumination in his dark corner of the parking garage. He smiled to himself and started up the car. *Yes, this*

could work. We'll make sure that Gregory Martin won't betray us anytime soon.

About twenty minutes later, the limousine pulled into the parking lot of a large hotel. Terrance slowed to a stop in front of the sliding doors underneath the awning that always accompanies big hotels and set the parking brake. He exited, swiftly moved around to the big trunk, and removed Greg's bags. Greg shut off the game he had been playing and opened the limousine door.

He looked around. *So this is Chicago.* Gray, gloomy, and overcast. It was drizzling rain, and cars zoomed by on the street, splashing through puddles. Taxis honked at buses that were going too slow for their liking. Umbrella-holders, dog-walkers, and business people strolled by on the sidewalk. Intimidating skyscrapers loomed above him, and Greg could make out the Willis Tower in the distance. *So, this is Chicago. Cool.*

With an almost imperceptible crook of his finger, Terrance motioned for Greg to follow him. Greg ran his fingers through the thick brown hair under his cap, gripped his skateboard, and complied.

Terrance was in the hotel before Greg had a chance to close the door of the limousine. The tight-lipped driver approached the front desk and flashed a credit card, then in a low voice explained the reservation that had been made.

Greg walked through the sliding doors into the hotel. Just inside was an entryway with some luggage carts and a stand that held brochures for various things to do in Chicago. The skater walked around the lobby, observing his surroundings. Several large plants that looked like they belonged more in an African jungle than in a hotel decorated the lobby. A couple of plush, comfortable-looking chairs were placed strategically around a few small coffee tables. A telephone and a computer sat in the corner. Greg's footsteps echoed on the tile floor. At one side of the lobby, the tile gave way to a red carpeted hallway, leading to the first floor rooms. The elevators were situated near this hallway, and Greg made out a sign pointing the way to the pool area, ice machine, and vending machines. Along one wall ran a long brown desk where Terrance was now standing, confirming Greg's room.

After a couple minutes of conferring with the clerk at the front desk, Terrance motioned the skater over. The clerk tossed her brown ponytail as she gave Greg his room key. Terrance pulled Greg over to the side. "You are in Room 317. Stefan will be contacting you soon. I assume you can get your luggage to your room without assistance?"

Something about this guy's attitude was beginning to grate on Greg's nerves. "Yes, I can handle it," he said.

Terrance nodded, twirling his keys. "Well, if you need anything, call me at the number on the card I gave you."

"Sure, sounds—"

Terrance was already going out the automatic sliding doors and heading to the limousine. Greg scowled, then hefted his suitcase and headed toward the elevators.

o——o

Terrance watched as Greg entered the elevator and pushed a button. When the doors closed, Terrance snatched up his cell phone and hit the speed-dial button designated for Stefan.

Stefan picked up on the second ring. "Hello?"

"He's in the hotel," Terrance informed him.

"Fantastic," Stefan replied. "I'll implement the next phase of the plan shortly. I assume there were no difficulties?"

Terrance shook his head, then remembered Stefan couldn't see him. He hated phone conversations. "No."

"So did he ask a lot of questions?"

Terrance shifted in his seat. *No, but you are.* Out loud, he repeated, "No."

"You're sure you didn't alert his suspicions? Did the business card work?"

"Yes, yes, everything went perfectly."

"Good. I'll be along soon. Contact me if anything else happens."

The driver looked at his watch, anxious to end the phone call. "I'll be watching."

"Remember, Terrance, we have to play our cards carefully. We can't afford to let this kid compromise security!"

"I know," Terrance said, nodding his head. He understood the importance of this. Their whole operation was based on secrecy. If that secrecy was betrayed . . . Terrance swallowed his fear and stared out the window, taking a deep breath to calm down. He didn't want to think about it.

4

Greg fumbled with his key, struggling to keep hold of his suitcase and skateboard. After missing a few times, he clumsily slid it into the lock. It beeped red at him. Greg cursed and dropped his bag and skateboard on the ground. He inserted the key in the lock again, and this time it flashed green. He shoved the door open, grabbed his things, and walked into the room.

It was your average hotel room, with two beds, a TV, and a digital clock. Greg strode over to the window, which displayed a view of the side of a building. He looked down into the alley running adjacent to the hotel. Some dumpsters were pressed against the walls, but Greg was surprised to see how clean it seemed. He at least expected some graffiti! *I'll have to get some spray paint and tag a wall before this is over,* Greg mused with a grin.

His phone suddenly vibrated in his pocket. Greg jumped, startled at the sudden movement, then fished his phone out of his pocket and clicked it on. "Hello?"

"Gregory?" the voice on the other end said. *Oh great. It was his mom.*

"Yeah," he said, slumping down into a chair next to the table.

"Have you arrived yet?" his mom asked.

"Yeah." Greg's eyes searched for something to do while he reported to his overprotective mom. "And stop calling me Gregory, okay?"

"You were supposed to call me when you got there!" Mrs. Martin reprimanded him.

Greg rolled his eyes. "Mom, I just got to the hotel."

"Okay, well, that's fine. So how was your flight?"

"Good."

"Oh . . . good. Did you get through the airport all right?"

"Yes." *If only you knew, Mom.*

"Good. I know it's a busy place."

Greg remained silent.

"Have the people from the contest been helpful?"

Not particularly talkative, but the limousine was nice. "Yeah, they've been cool."

"So . . . how is your hotel?"

"It's fine."

"When does the contest start?"

Greg leaned back in his chair, irritated at all the questions. "Tomorrow. At least, that's what the package of information said."

"Oh. So what are you going to do until then?"

"I dunno, probably skateboard, do some sightseeing and stuff . . .with the people from the contest."

An awkward silence hung in the air. "Well, I'm glad you made it safely," his mom finally said. "And . . . hope you do well."

"Thanks," Greg said shortly.

"Uh . . . call me tomorrow after the contest to let me know how you did."

"Sure."

"Um . . . well . . . have a good time. I love you."

"Love you too."

"Bye, Greg." Was it his imagination, or did he detect a hint of sadness in his mom's voice?

"Yeah, talk to you later."

Well, whatever, she's probably fine. Greg ended the call.

Back in Colorado, Greg's mom slowly put the phone down. She sat at the kitchen table and buried her face in her hands. "Oh, Gregory." She hated the wall that had grown between them. This rebellious stage of Greg's exhausted her energy. The people at the church were praying, but it didn't seem as if it were doing any good. Greg was still so distant from her and not just in miles. She had agreed to let him go on this short trip, praying that it would bring them closer together since she had given him something that he wanted. Rush Stein had told her she could have gone along, but Greg was the only one paid for, and she couldn't afford the plane ticket or to take off work. She thought the time away might do him some good. But Greg didn't seem to appreciate the favor.

"Oh, God . . ." she cried, her voice muffled from her hands covering her mouth. "Please, help Gregory. Reach out and touch him, and . . ." her voice wavered. "Do whatever it takes to bring him to You. Please, Father. Bring him to You." With that, she broke down and began weeping for her son.

Greg had changed out of the clothes he wore on the airplane into something a little more eye-catching and checked himself out in the mirror. *There. That looks cool. Now I'm ready for any hot chicks that come along.*

As Greg exited the bathroom, he noticed a slip of paper lying on the floor by the door. It was folded in half and had his name on the front. Greg frowned at it. *That's weird. How did that get in here?* He stooped down to pick it up and read,

Greg, meet me down in the pool area at 7:45.
– Stefan

Greg immediately opened the door of his room and looked around. No one was out there. He ducked back into the hotel room. So, Stefan knew where he was. How did he slip the paper under the door without Greg noticing? Stefan and all his mystery and intrigue still creeped Greg out. *Why couldn't he just be a normal human being, for crying out loud?* Greg glanced at the clock. 7:25. So in twenty minutes . . . Greg stopped his train of thought and slapped the note down on his bedspread. He wasn't going to follow Stefan's rules. He'd show up whenever he wanted.

Twenty-five minutes later, Greg left the hotel room and rode the elevator back down to the first floor. He stepped off and glanced around, rather conspiratorially he thought. Nobody was around. Ponytail clerk must have been in the back. Greg shoved his hands in his pockets and strode down the hallway to the pool. *Casual, casual,* Greg reminded himself, as he brushed a lock of hair out of his eyes. There wasn't anybody around to see him. But just in case . . .

Greg approached the pool door and nonchalantly shoved it open; that is, it would've opened if it weren't locked. Good thing nobody was around. Greg cursed to himself and retrieved his key from his pocket.

As he entered, his footsteps echoed the way everything does in pool areas. The surrounding area was empty. Nobody was in any of the lawn chairs. He could see it raining outside the glass door that led to a small courtyard area. *Was Stefan outside? Or did he get tired of waiting for me and left when I wasn't there in exactly twenty minutes? I bet he's late too.* Greg fumed. *I should've waited ten minutes after the original meeting time.* Since Stefan obviously wasn't there, Greg turned back to the door.

"Leaving so soon?"

Stefan's voice echoed across the pool area and Greg jumped. How did Stefan always do that? Every time he showed up, it was always he who surprised Greg, never the other way around. By the time this trip was over, Greg was going to be jumping every time somebody's cell phone rang.

Greg grunted and turned to Stefan. The still sunglass-clad man made no effort to hide his amusement. Greg made no effort to hide his annoyance. "Would you quit doing that?"

Stefan smiled and motioned for him to come over. "Please, have a seat. By the way, don't think I didn't notice you were late. I'll let it slide this time, but in the future, be on time for our meetings."

Greg sneered at him as he made his way around the glassy pool. "I never thought punctuality would be high on your list of priorities."

Stefan gave him a serious look. "When you're in my business, you learn that every minute counts. You never know what can happen in the few precious seconds we have. Quit mouthing off and wipe that stupid look off your face. Now, I want you to listen carefully.

"Tomorrow we're going to do the first pick-up. I'm going to meet you, I'll let you know where, and give you a package. You are going to take the bus to another part of town where someone will be waiting for you. You'll give them the package, and they'll give you a slip of paper. That's the hardest thing you'll have to do . . . fortunately, considering how you've handled yourself so far." When Stefan said this, a condescending smile appeared on his face.

Greg seethed. *He just had to add that last part, didn't he?* Again, he was struck with the urge to punch that smug face. *Why was Stefan such a jerk?* If it had been one of Greg's friends he could've handled it. But coming from Stefan, this almost complete stranger who managed to make Greg feel worthless so easily, it made him angry. Greg wanted to flash a snappy comeback at him, but he couldn't think of one.

"Why do I have to take the bus?" he finally said. "Why can't Terrance take me?"

Stefan looked at him the way you might look at a dog who hadn't figured out that you hadn't thrown its Frisbee yet. "Why do you think you're here? The whole purpose of using you as an intermediary is so we aren't associated with this business in any way, shape, or form."

"Great, pin the blame on me, right?"

"More or less." Stefan grinned. "The more links we use, the harder it is for the police to trace it back to us. And don't worry, that's why I got you from Colorado. They'll have a tough time trying to follow your trail—not that they'll ever pick it up. After all, the point of you being here is so they don't suspect anything."

Without warning, a prick of uneasiness hit Greg. The nonchalant way Stefan talked about being tracked by the police was unsettling.

"Now about tonight."

"Tonight?"

"Of course. We can't afford to waste time, remember?"

"But you were talking about tomorrow."

"The hardest thing you'll have to do is tomorrow night, but

I still have an errand for you to run tonight. Think you can handle that?"

Greg glared at him. Stefan continued, "I want you to go to a drop-off point in a park near here. You need to arrive at exactly nine o'clock, no later. And don't try your cute rebellion stuff with me. This is important, and we don't have time for you to work out your emotional or psychological problems, got it?"

Greg paused a moment, then muttered, "I can handle it."

"You'll find an envelope underneath a bench on the south side of the park, the bench farthest away from the fountain. All you need to do is get the envelope and bring it back to the hotel. I'll be in touch with you tomorrow to let you know when to get the package and deliver it and all that. Any questions?"

Greg put his annoyance at Stefan aside for the moment. "Is this going to happen before or after the contest?"

Stefan blinked at him. "The contest?"

"Yeah. And where is the contest anyway? Will Terrance be driving me to that?"

Stefan looked at him for a moment, a smirk twitching at the corner of his mouth. He began to chuckle.

"What?" Greg asked.

"Don't tell me you fell for that."

A lump began to form in Greg's stomach. "What do you mean?"

Stefan laughed again. "Oh, Gregory, Gregory." Greg clenched his fists. "There is no contest. The whole thing was a cover-up to get some kid who could run these errands for us here."

Greg fumed. "What!" The sound reverberated across the pool area. "You mean the prize, the contest . . . there's no contest at all?"

"No, of course not. And keep your voice down! Someone

might hear you. I'm sure you could find a skate park somewhere, but officially," he chuckled, "you're on your own."

Greg stared at him with his mouth open. Disbelief numbed his other senses. Stefan snapped his fingers as though just remembering something. "Oh, I almost forgot. I'm going to pay you in advance for this one, just so you know I'm on the up and up." Stefan pulled a wallet out from the inside pocket of his suit coat and withdrew two crisp 100 dollar bills. He slapped them into Greg's hand. "I must be going now. And don't forget nine o'clock!"

Stefan turned and went out the side door of the pool, disappearing into the darkening Chicago night. Greg stood there dumbly, watching him leave. Slowly his rage began to mount, trumping all of his other senses. *How could Stefan cheat me like that? The whole reason I had wanted to come on this trip was to compete in a high-level skateboarding contest. It's not like I care about Stefan's stupid plots and schemes! The only reason I agreed to this was so that I could hitch a free ride to the contest. And now I discover there was never even going to be one?*

Greg angrily shoved the money Stefan had given him into his pocket and marched out the door leading to the hotel, slamming it behind him. He didn't care who saw him now. In fact, it would've given him pleasure to see Stefan squirm about being caught. Unfortunately, no one was around to witness Greg's tirade. Dejected, Greg headed toward the elevator. Once inside, he jabbed the button for the third floor and watched the doors close. When they did, he snatched his hat off his head and threw it to the ground. He slumped against the wall. *Now what am I going to do? And what will I tell Mom when she asks about the contest?* He didn't want to go back home yet. But he wasn't sure what he was going to do here in Chicago either. *Well, I know one thing I can do. The one thing I can do anywhere.*

○——○

The concrete became a blur under his feet as the skateboard whirred down the sidewalk. The rain had stopped and the night sky was relatively clear. Bright street lamps lined the sidewalk. None of the stars was visible due to the intense reflection of the city lights. Greg had no interest in looking at stars anyway.

A man walking his dog jumped out of the way and yelled a warning at Greg as the skater zoomed past. The man's small dog yipped, probably echoing his owner's feelings. Greg ignored them and kept speeding down the sidewalk. He dodged a bench at a bus stop and swerved to miss a girl jogging and wearing earbuds. Greg ollied over a planter and came to a downward slope in the sidewalk. Traffic rushed by at its normal breakneck speed. Nothing had changed for these millions of people. They pressed on, oblivious to Greg's problems.

Anger continued propelling him, as he pushed furiously with one foot. The hill was steep enough now and Greg put both feet on his board, the wind tossing the hair sticking out from beneath his cap. He zipped by what looked like a security guard who was wearing a black suit with brass buttons and a shiny badge. The guard jumped back in surprise, nearly losing his black hat. He shook his nightstick at Greg, yelling something. The skater, already too far down the sidewalk to hear, didn't care.

Greg gave the skateboard another big push with his foot. *It isn't fair! Stefan promised a skateboarding contest! That's what I came here for!*

His mind continued to shout out the arguments it had been replaying over and over ever since he had first heard the news from Stefan, which made him angrier and angrier at the horrible man. These arguments goaded him on in his skateboarding race against himself and did absolutely nothing to change the situation.

He came to a light and without waiting for the walk signal maneuvered across the street. A car swerved to miss him and honked at him. Greg didn't care.

He continued skating down the sidewalk, looking around irritably. *Aren't there any skate parks in this city?* He had been skating for at least fifteen minutes and he hadn't seen any. Stefan said he could probably find one near here. Greg rolled his eyes and pushed harder at the thought of Stefan. *As if I can believe anything that Stefan says!* Well, no matter what Stefan said, there had to be a skate park around here somewhere, and Greg was determined to find it.

The skateboard was moving at a pathetic speed down an alley. Greg was lazily pushing it along with his foot, tired and still angry. It was about nine thirty, and he still hadn't found a skate park. In spite of his anger, earlier at nine, Greg had gone to the park near the hotel and found the envelope under the bench just as Stefan said. He had slit it open to see what was inside, as a kind of act of defiance against Stefan. It was money. Stacks of money and a sealed thick brown envelope lined the inside of the white paper. Greg had thought about taking one but decided against it. Stefan probably knew how much he was supposed to get. Besides, he didn't really need it for anything. Stefan was paying him anyway, the thought of which didn't do much to improve his mood.

The fact that he hadn't found a skate park also really bugged Greg. *This is Chicago, for crying out loud! There are supposed to be skate parks here, aren't there?* Greg had been so determined to find one after retrieving the envelope, he had randomly picked back streets and alleyways, hoping to come across a skate park on one of them, pushing himself extra hard—but the results had been zero.

Now, trudging tiredly through the alley, he was just about ready to give up. The only problem was that he had paid absolutely no attention to where he had been going, and now he wasn't even sure he could get back to the hotel. *Yeah, that figures,* Greg thought, shaking a few curly locks of brown hair out of his eyes. *The perfect end to a perfect day.*

Greg picked up his skateboard and walked out of the alleyway, hoping to get his bearings. He glanced around, looking for some familiar landmark that might tell him where he was. *Ha! A familiar landmark in Chicago?* Greg thought to himself. *I'm so stupid.*

He stood on the edge of some grass and what looked like a parking lot. The grass stretched on the left side to some baseball fields, and immediately to his left . . . *Is that . . . ? No way. It couldn't be!* Greg moved closer, hope thudding in his chest. A chain-link fence surrounded it, with some street lamps set up at intervals, lighting up the inside. A sidewalk with some benches lining it ran around it. And inside the chain-link fence . . . *Yes!* A few skate ramps dotted the inside, grinding rails ran in between, and in the center was a small half-pipe. It was small, but it was a skate park!

Greg just about screamed for joy. He pumped his fist. *Yes!* Finally he had found one! Calming down and trying to appear indifferent, Greg strolled over to the park where several kids were already inside, doing tricks on the rails and ramps. A couple sat on one of the benches on the outskirts of the skate park in the dark, making out.

As Greg got closer, he saw the true condition of the skate park. Graffiti covered everything. Several large holes were in the chain-link fence, and at the top in places it was broken and hanging. Two of the street lamps' glass were shattered, and moths and fireflies were darting around the dim lights. The rails were bent and rusty, the edges of the ramps were chipped, and the paint was faded. Litter, broken bottles, aluminum cans, and trash lined the edge of the fence.

What a big letdown. Greg had come to Chicago expecting it to be the land of skaters, the L.A. of the East, expecting . . . well, expecting the huge skateboarding contest, of course. But Greg now saw that Stefan had completely misled him. The incident with the girl at the convenience store suddenly made sense. The skate parks in Chicago were few and far between, and the ones that were there obviously weren't kept up very well.

But it didn't matter how run-down the skate park was, or how much Stefan had lied to him. He had found a skate park, and here he could lose himself in his skating!

Greg came to the gate in the chain-link fence and lifted up the rusted latch, letting himself inside. He set his skateboard down and put a foot on top. His fatigue faded away as he began to skate. He went up a ramp and did a simple kick-flip, landing it, of course. He grinded across a rail with ease except in one place where it desperately needed wax. Oh, yeah! This is more like it! Greg continued doing grinds and flip tricks, completely absorbed in his skating world.

After a few minutes, though, Greg noticed a couple of the kids had stopped skating and were staring at him. Greg tried to ignore them and grinded another small rail, but their eyes on his back were making him uncomfortable. He turned back and ollied over the same rail and came to a stop.

A kid with spiky blond hair that was partially dyed blue

walked up to him. Greg eyed him warily, not knowing what to expect. "Hey, dude," the kid said as he approached Greg.

"Hey." Greg nodded toward him.

The kid stuck out his hand. "I'm Chris, what's your name?" Greg slid his palm across the kid's and the two pounded fists. Greg felt a wave of relief flood through him. *Good, the kid is friendly.*

"I'm Greg."

"Cool." Chris shifted some gum he was chewing to his other cheek. "Where you from? I haven't seen you around before."

"Colorado," Greg said. "I'm here for a . . . well, for a trip."

"Sweet," Chris said. "You're a pretty good skater." He dipped his head toward Greg's board.

"Thanks." Greg grinned. "I wasn't sure if I could find a skate park here or not."

"Yeah, there aren't a whole lot of kids who are into skateboarding here. I don't know why. But it's cool to find someone like you, who's good at it. Some of the kids were wanting you to show us a few things, but we want to see you do one more kickflip first."

Greg felt his confidence building. This kid was asking for his advice? "Well, sure," Greg said and grabbed his board.

Chris held out his hand to stop Greg and smiled. "No, no...we want you to show us on *this* board." He held out a longboard to Greg with a challenging smile.

Greg locked eyes with him for a minute, and felt unease in the pit of his stomach. *Was this some sort of initiation?* Longboards were for speed not tricks. Doug always said that longboards were for amateurs who didn't know how to use a real skateboard.

The kid was still standing there, challenge in his eyes. Greg instinctively felt that this was a test for acceptance. Fortunately he was prepared.

"All right," Greg agreed, snatching the longboard from Chris. "Watch and learn."

The kid relinquished the board and stepped back, with something like surprise in his eyes. Greg could feel the eyes of the other kids on him, evaluating him, judging what he was about to do.

Brushing a few locks of hair away from his eyes, Greg dropped the board, and placed one foot in the center, and the other on the back of the tail. There was no reason he shouldn't be able to do it—but if he messed up because he was nervous, how humiliating would that be?

Time slowed down for a second, and then, just going for it, Greg performed the trick, skated around and did it twice more just to show off, before snagging the board up again and returning it to Chris with a smug grin.

Respect shown in Chris's eyes. "Dude!" he exclaimed. "I didn't know you could do that on a longboard! What did I tell you guys?" he shouted, turning around to the other kids. "You've gotta show me—but..." he paused. "Won't that ruin the board?"

Greg smiled wryly. "Yeah," he admitted and glanced back down at it. "Sorry about that."

Chris belted out a laugh. "I like you! Could you show me that heel flip you did a minute ago? I've never been able to do that. But on *your* board!"

Greg laughed too. He knew this was Chris's way of accepting him into their group, and he was all too willing to join. "Look, I'll show you," he said. "You put your front foot by your front bolt."

Chris took a skateboard from another kid who only mildly protested before riding off on Chris's longboard. Chris adjusted the board, and mimicked how Greg was standing on it. "Like this?"

"Yeah, now hang your toes over a little . . . good . . . now ollie, and then kick out with your front heel." Greg performed the trick and landed it effortlessly.

Chris nodded seriously, studying the way Greg did it. "Okay, I think I got it."

Chris positioned his feet the way Greg had and attempted the flip trick. The board slipped and clattered to the ground, and Chris fell backwards landing on the concrete.

Greg stifled a laugh, and ran over to him. "You okay, man?"

Chris grinned, as he got up and dusted himself off. "Totally! That was awesome! It's better than I've ever done before!"

"Well, I see what you did wrong. Let's try it again."

The two of them began practicing Chris's heel flip. After they tired of that, Chris introduced him to the other kids and Greg showed off, doing some of the tricks they couldn't do. Greg was beginning to feel like he fit in. For the first time on this trip, Greg was starting to have fun.

Greg was at the top of a ramp getting ready to drop in, when he noticed an adult there that he hadn't seen before. He was talking to one of the other kids over by the gate. "Who's that?" Greg asked Chris, motioning toward the guy.

Chris whirled around. "Who? Oh, you mean Brother Joseph?"

"Brother Joseph?"

"Yeah, well, that's what everybody calls him. He's cool. He comes to the skate park and hangs out with us, and sometimes he'll take us out to eat. And on Fridays, he holds these meetings in the park."

"What kind of meetings?"

"Oh, well, you know, it's him and sometimes a couple other

people from his church will come and help. And we sing, and then he talks to us about stuff out of the Bible."

"The Bible?" Greg groaned. "You mean he's, like, a Christian?"

"Yeah, but he's cool. He's not the shove-Christianity-down-your-throat type. He's . . . I don't know . . . different. Everybody here likes him. C'mon, I'll introduce you."

Greg tried to protest, but Chris was already heading toward Brother Joseph. Greg rolled his eyes and moaned. *I came to Chicago to get away from all this stuff!*

Reluctantly, he shuffled over to where Brother Joseph was just finishing up talking to the other kid. The man turned and gave them both a warm smile when they walked up. "Hey, Chris," he said. "How's it going?"

"Pretty good, how about you?"

"Good, good. Who's this?"

Chris stepped back to make the introduction and dramatically flailed his arm toward the new skater. "This is Greg. He's just here visiting from Colorado, but he's a really good skateboarder. He was showing me some stuff."

Brother Joseph held out his hand and his eyes locked on Greg's. "Nice to meet you, Greg. I'm Brother Joseph."

Greg shook hands with the man and studied him. He had glasses, but his brown eyes sparkled with warmth and seemed to draw you in. Stubble ran along his chin like he hadn't had time to shave for a couple days. He was dressed casually, in jeans and a T-shirt, and stood at ease as if it were completely normal for him to hang out with teenage skaters at eleven o'clock on a Wednesday night. His face was warm and friendly, and his mouth was turned up at the corners as if he were remembering a funny joke but couldn't share it at the moment.

"We're going to go grab some pancakes or something if you two want to come," Brother Joseph invited.

Chris looked at Greg, waiting for his approval. Greg nodded slowly. "Yeah, sure. We'll come."

"All right!" Chris said. "Way to go with the flow!" He clapped Greg on the back.

Greg gave him a quizzical look. "Who says, 'Way to go with the flow'?"

Chris turned back to Brother Joseph. "Did you bring the church van?"

"Of course. Hey, you want to help me gather everyone up?"

Chris nodded enthusiastically. "Are you gonna help, Greg?" He turned to Greg expectantly.

Greg shook his head. "No, I'll wait here for you guys."

Chris nodded and he and Brother Joseph headed toward the other kids.

"So, are you gonna be there Friday?" Brother Joseph asked Chris as they walked away.

Greg slowly did a 360 on his board and watched Brother Joseph and Chris approach the others. Chris seemed to completely open up to this street missionary dude. Then again, Chris was pretty open with everyone. But there was, as Chris had said, something different about Brother Joseph. Greg couldn't put his finger on it, but it was true. Greg wasn't sure what he thought about Brother Joseph yet. He would have to wait and see.

o———o

Shobab crept into the warehouse, peeping and muttering. Fluttering his wings restlessly, he ignored the cackles and jeers of the other demons as he searched for Sharath. He finally spotted him. The leathery, bat-looking demon stood guard outside of Poneros's throne room. Sharath wasn't the largest of demons, but he was taller than Shobab and still intimidated him. Shobab scurried up to him and quickly bowed low. Sharath looked at him for a long moment, his face cold.

"My lord," said Shobab from his place of reverence on the ground, "I have an urgent matter to discuss with Ba-al Poneros that simply cannot wait."

Sharath began picking at his long, pointy teeth one by one with each of his long claws. "What matter?" he asked finally.

"Really, my lord, it must wait for the ears of the Ba-al himself."

Sharath's eyes flashed and he leaned close to Shobab's quivering form with an intense look of anger. "I am appointed to discern what should be told Poneros and what shouldn't be! You can tell me, or you can take your news elsewhere!"

"But, my lord, it is most urgent!"

Sharath shrieked and growled at Shobab, lifting him off the ground with one claw. "TELL ME, OR GET OUT!" he shouted.

Shobab quickly held up his hands and began blubbering, "It is concerning Gregory Martin, my lord."

Sharath sneered. "Yes? What of him?"

"He . . . he . . . uh . . ." Shobab suddenly lost his words and began fumbling, uncertain how to say it.

"What is it?" Sharath demanded, shaking the little devil.

"It . . . it's Brother Joseph!" Shobab blurted. "Whispered murmurings have been heard in the Enemy's ranks that He has ordained for him to make contact with Brother Joseph!"

Immediately Sharath's face went pale, and without another word he dropped Shobab into a heap on the ground and fled into Poneros's presence on his black, leathery wings. Shobab huddled on the ground, nervously waiting for Poneros's response. It didn't take long. A roar of rage echoed through the warehouse, causing some demons to cower and others to sneer. Sharath emerged from the door and motioned quickly with one claw to Shobab before disappearing back into the room. Shobab cautiously took a step forward into the room. Instantly his neck muscles bulged in terror as a hand grabbed him. Poneros snatched him up and flung him across the room.

The other demons in the room looked on in hate. "So Shobab," Poneros said as he stalked over to him. "I understand you have a report for me?"

Shobab huddled on the floor, whimpering as the looming form of Poneros stood over him. The demon's bulky frame towered high above him, and the evil in his red eyes seemed to taunt Shobab.

Poneros' eyes bored into him for a moment, and then with a rumbling growl he swiped his claws across Shobab's face and petulantly flew up a few feet, batting the air with his enormous wings. "You fool!" he snarled. "You have failed in your task!"

"Oh, oh not so, my Ba-al, not so! The Hosts of Heaven are simply too strong. The mother has been praying and—"

"Give me only the facts. Tell me the reason you have not been completing your assignment."

Shobab looked up with a pleading face. "As I said, my lord, the Host of Heaven is strong and it's hard to get through anymore! Especially with the personal detail assigned to my charge."

Poneros's eyes bulged and his face darkened. He whirled around to the room full of demons, eyeing them for a moment. Then he snapped. "Personal detail? There's a personal detail? Why wasn't I informed of this?" The room fell silent. Shobab rejoiced inwardly. He had brought new information to light, and Poneros would surely reward him for this.

Sharath cleared his throat. "There is actually not a 'personal detail' as such, but only one of the Hosts of Heaven."

Poneros howled. "You mean the Lord has sent an angel to protect this skater?"

Sharath held up a non-threatening hand. "This is true, my lord, but only one. We did not see it fit to inform you because we assumed Shobab would be able to handle it."

"As if Shobab can handle anything!" Poneros said in disgust. "Listen to me, Sharath, from now on I want complete reports of the whereabouts of the Host of Heaven at the skate park and everywhere else! Do you think we can afford to let this child be lost to the kingdom of God? Well? Do you?"

"No, my Ba-al!" the demons chorused together. "None can escape our clutches!"

"That's right!" the Ba-al yowled. "We are in this for the dark lord, Satan! And glory be to him!"

The demons broke out into shrieks and cheers, and a presence of evil filled the building. Shobab fled the building to attend to the skater.

5

The light seeping through the dirty glass in the street lamp barely lit the street enough to reveal the forms of Al and two of the other members of his gang crouching along the side of a brick wall.

Cautiously, Al peered around the side of the building. The coast seemed clear. *No! That idiot policeman is coming back!* Releasing a string of profanities in his mind, Al pounded his fist against the side of the wall, ignoring the pain.

Tony whispered a curse. "He still there?" he asked incredulously. "Don't this . . ." He spit trying to come up with the most appropriately scathing designation, which he finally found. "Have nothing better to do?"

Al angrily swiped his hand at him, motioning for him to be quiet. This was the fourth time they had tried to get to the warehouse to get the rest of their stash, but this same policeman was always there! The gang leader pushed Tony and Junior away from the alley and grabbed their shoulders to talk to them.

"We gonna hafta go for it anyways," Al said in a low voice. "This guy ain't gonna go away befo' we can get what we want. The next time he crosses back over to the other buildings away from dis one, we makin' a run for our stuff. Got it?"

The other two gang members nodded with tight lips and

tense expressions. Al released Junior's shoulder and tightened his grip on Tony's. "Tony and I gonna run in. Junior, you cover us."

"Want me to just kill the cop?" asked Junior, whose hulking frame and massive biceps and legs did not reflect his name at all.

Al shoved a pistol into his hand and said, "Only as a last resort . . . only if one of us gonna get caught. I don' think most of the police . . . 'cept this stupid cop, be trackin' us down for what we done so far. We kill a cop, though, and we gonna be dead. They ain't gonna mess 'round wit' dat. It may come to dat, but not yet."

Junior nodded tersely and slipped down the alley, around the other side of the building. Al and Tony scrambled back over to where they could see the cop. He paused and was looking around with an intent gaze, as if he had heard something. Al held his breath.

The policeman tapped the gun by his side, then with a grunting sigh turned and began patrolling back over toward the other warehouses on his beat. The moment he was out of sight, Al pushed Tony, and the two of them bolted toward the back entrance, which was covered by boxes. Suddenly, Tony grabbed Al's shirt and yanked the big man down. Al fell hard with a thud and rolled against the side of the building as Tony dove by his side. Holding his heavy breathing, he heard the scuffing feet of someone running. He closed his eyes, willing himself to melt into the shadow. The policeman had not continued on his rounds but had circled back to the building.

Al heard the policeman go back and forth as though he wasn't sure which way to go. Then the sound of static as the policeman raised the radio to his lips. "This is Purdo requesting backup. Over."

He waited and a voice on the other end crackled, "I read you, Purdo. What's the problem?"

Al's mind raced, as he tried to figure out what to do.

Purdo raised the radio to his lips again. "Someone's here. I can almost smell their dirty bodies. Just get someone over here right now." The static of the radio sounded again, and Purdo began walking directly towards Al and Tony. Al tensed. He needed to do something—now!

Suddenly, a gunshot rang out in the still night. Junior. Purdo scrambled for cover and grabbed his gun and radio almost simultaneously. "They are here!" Purdo almost screamed. "I'm being shot at! I need backup *now*!"

Al didn't need any more encouragement to scram. Keeping his head low, Tony was already heading back toward the alley. Al followed him, crawling as fast and cautiously as he could. Suddenly, Purdo's gun rang out and brick shards rained down on Al from the spot where the bullet hit the wall right above him. Al didn't stop.

"I see you!" Purdo shouted. "Stop now in the name of the law! Dispatch, I'm requesting backup. Requesting backup now!"

A gun fired from the opposite direction at Purdo. Junior again.

"Cease and desist!" Purdo managed almost incoherently. He was securing his position behind the crates he had stacked up so that he would be able to defend himself.

Al and Tony made it to the alley and took off in a dead sprint. They heard one more gunshot, not sure who it was.

They rounded the corner of the alley and were met by Junior, who was carrying his still smoking gun. "Go! Go!" Al yelled.

It hadn't worked. They needed to find some way to get the rest of their drugs!

Greg leaned back in the bench at the little diner, pushing his empty plate away. He took a sip of his soda and observed the activity around him. Chris was sitting to his right, waving his hands demonstratively and arguing with Jack about something. Meanwhile, Zack was leaning over to pour some salt into Chris's drink while he was distracted.

Greg's eyes wandered to the three other tables that had been filled since Brother Joseph had brought in the kids from the skate park. Three girls were sitting at a table, gossiping about some kid from their school who was in juvenile detention now. At another table behind them, a couple sat close enough to breathe for each other, and two guys sat on the opposite side, one finishing his food and the other talking. Across from them, at the table behind Greg's, Brother Joseph, two guys, and a girl sat deep in conversation.

Greg was puzzled by Brother Joseph. Looking at the way he was talking with the three teenagers at his table, you would think he was genuinely interested in their lives. But if Greg knew anything about Christians, he knew that they were all just out to "win souls," as they said, and didn't really care about the people they were proselytizing. Greg shook his head in disgust. Brother Joseph must be a really good actor.

Suddenly, Chris spewed pop all over the table, making Greg jump. Jack shielded his face from the saliva. Zack burst out laughing. Apparently Chris hadn't noticed the large quantities of salt Zack had been dumping in his drink.

Jack grabbed a napkin and jumped out of his seat, yelling about how gross that was and wiping the sticky substance off his face. Chris jumped up, snatching some ice, and ran to Zack's side. Zack tried to slide under the table, but Chris grabbed his shirt and dropped the ice down it, then held it there so it would be extra cold. "Augh! Brother Joseph, help!" Zack cried, squirming.

Brother Joseph looked up and smiled. "You're on your own, Zack. But if you start throwing ice or pop or anything, take it outside. We don't want the restaurant personnel kicking us out. Besides, I don't want my nice-looking clothes getting messed up." The street preacher winked and Greg smiled at his sarcasm. The kid across from Brother Joseph laughed and punched him on the arm. "Nice-looking, bro? I'd hate to see your bad-looking clothes!"

Brother Joseph laughed and wagged his finger in the kid's face. "Hey, watch what you say about my clothes. I'm paying for your meal, remember?"

Zack had picked up a handful of ice, and Chris was making a hasty retreat to the front door. A short Mexican man with a handlebar moustache, apparently the manager, stopped him, and began waving his arms. "You pay, no?"

Chris groaned. "Oh man, sorry dude, I forgot!" He dug into his pocket for his wallet and grabbed a ten. "This should be enough to cover it, right?"

The manager waved it away. "You no pay me, you pay her!" He motioned toward the heavyset waitress who kept glancing over with an annoyed look at one of the tables where the conversation kept getting louder and louder.

Brother Joseph took the hint and looked at his watch. "Okay, gang," he said standing up. "It's one o' clock, I think it's time to load up. Pay for your meals, and if you don't have money let me know and I'll get it."

"Uh, Brother Joseph?" one of the kids over at the loud table raised his hand. "I think I left my wallet at home."

His friend elbowed him in the side. "Get out of here, I saw you with your wallet at the arcade, remember?"

The first kid lowered his head sheepishly and dug out his wallet.

Brother Joseph chuckled. "Does anybody here need a ride home?"

The kids all looked around and shook their heads.

Then Chris noticed Greg. "Hey, Greg, do you need a ride back to your hotel or whatever?"

Greg was about to say no, but then remembered he wasn't exactly sure where his hotel was. "Um . . . yeah, I guess I do."

Brother Joseph waved him over. "All right then, I just have to take the van back to the church where I left my car, then I'll drive you on over."

Greg slid out of the seat after leaving a ten dollar bill on the table. "Okay, thanks."

Two of the girls ran up. "Oh, hey, uh, Brother Joseph, could you, like, give us a ride back to the church, 'cause our houses are like totally closer to the church than here."

"Sure thing, come on. Okay, everybody clear out. See you tomorrow, or Friday maybe. Are you all coming to the youth service Friday?"

A couple of the kids said yes, and a couple shrugged. "Come on! Jordan," he said, addressing a specific teenager, "are you gonna be there?"

Jordan shifted his feet uncomfortably. "I don't know, it de- pends . . . maybe . . . well, yeah, I guess I can come. I'll be there."

"All right, good deal. If the rest of you can make it, I'll be glad to see you there. Okay, everybody with me, let's go."

The teenagers paid and began filing out of the restaurant, some walking together and some splitting off into the night, calling out goodbyes. The two girls, Greg, and another kid who just remembered that his house was closer to the church too, piled into the van and they took off.

It had started raining again when they were in the diner, so Greg was glad he was in the van. The church was fairly close, and they arrived in a few minutes. The three teens waved goodbye and ducked into the rain, running across the wet grass, trying to make it home before they got completely drenched.

Brother Joseph shut off the van and fingered his keys, lingering. He looked over to the skater. "Ready?"

Greg nodded. The two of them dashed over to a small silver Saturn and jumped inside. Brother Joseph started the car and turned on the windshield wipers. The car was relatively clean, though some papers and books were strewn across the back seat. A small air freshener hung from the mirror. Music from a Christian radio station was playing softly in the speakers. Greg leaned back in the soft padded seat.

Brother Joseph wiped the water off his glasses with his shirt. Suddenly, somebody knocked at the window. Both Greg and Brother Joseph jumped, and Greg heard the minister's sharp intake of breath. Then Brother Joseph let it out with a sigh and rolled down the window, a smile playing at the corners of his mouth.

A seventeen- or eighteen-year-old girl stood there, leaning over to face Brother Joseph, water running down her long black hair. "Did I scare you?" she asked, flashing a bright white smile that contrasted sharply with the dark night. Her bluish-green eyes twinkled with amusement, and her tanned face suggested she was of Hispanic descent. Even when she was soaking wet, Greg could see she was attractive.

"Ismeralda, what are you doing here so late?" Brother Joseph asked, shaking his head and ignoring her question.

She shrugged. "I was finishing some stuff up for the next

youth group lesson and didn't realize how late it was."

"Good grief, you should have gone home hours ago."

"I don't see you at home."

"I—" Brother Joseph threw his hands up in mock frustration. "Go home! You're soaking the inside of my car!"

She laughed and then seemed to notice Greg. "Hey, what's up?" She greeted him with a little wave.

"Hey," Greg responded.

"Where did you come from and why are you hanging around this old guy?" she asked, winking at him.

Brother Joseph rolled his eyes and made a gesture to roll up the window. Ismeralda quickly put her hand in the way.

Greg kept back a smile. He liked this girl. Her spunk reminded him of Renae.

"For your information," Brother Joseph interjected, "I'm giving him a ride back to his hotel. He's from Colorado."

"I'm Greg."

"I'm Ismeralda." She reached across Brother Joseph's seat to give Greg a fist bump. Brother Joseph leaned back in his chair and acted irritated.

Waving her off after she pulled her hand from the car, he said, "Now will you get out of here so Greg and I can get to our respective beds and go to sleep?"

"Who needs sleep?" Ismeralda retorted but grinned and stepped back. "Hope to see you again, Greg," she said.

"Yeah, for sure," Greg agreed, really meaning it. He wanted to see her again too.

"You gonna be at the youth rally Friday?"

"Probably not if he knows you're gonna be there," Brother Joseph shot back before Greg had a chance to answer.

"You kidding? I'm the only reason anybody even comes!" Ismeralda said, ringing some of the water out of her hair.

"We'll see," Greg told her. "I think I'll be around."

"Cool," Ismeralda said. "Well, since I know the old guy here needs some sleep, I'm gonna take off. See you guys later!"

"You better be well-rested on Friday!" Brother Joseph called after her.

She waved her hand and ducked into her car.

Brother Joseph chuckled and rolled up his window.

"She from your church?" Greg asked as Brother Joseph pulled the gear shift into drive and backed out of his parking space.

Brother Joseph nodded. "Yeah, she helps me out with a lot of stuff. She's a good kid. Comes from a rough background, but God has used her in some remarkable ways." He came to the edge of the parking lot. "Which hotel are you staying at?" he asked, waiting to see where to go. Greg told him and Brother Joseph turned out onto the street.

"So, what are you doing in Chicago?" Brother Joseph asked Greg.

Greg thought about telling him of Stefan's treachery about the alleged contest in Chicago and how he had rigged the contest back in Colorado but decided against it. This guy was a Christian, after all, and Greg wasn't sure he could trust him yet. "I won a skateboarding contest back in Colorado and this trip to Chicago was the prize."

"Oh, I see. Are you with parents or friends?"

"Uh, no, neither." Greg cringed, fully expecting Brother Joseph to lay into him about the dangers of coming to Chicago alone, without any friends or chaperones, but Brother Joseph simply nodded silently, as if that were completely normal.

"Tell me about Colorado. What do you do there?" He gave a quick grin. "I mean, besides skateboard."

Greg eyed him warily. What was motivating this question?

But the street preacher just sat there, waiting for an answer. Greg slowly started talking, and as Brother Joseph asked questions and laughed with him, Greg began to relax. Brother Joseph wasn't trying to convert him or win him over to Christianity. He was genuinely asking about Greg's life. But Greg knew he had to keep his guard up. This was a tactic Christians often used—put on a front of friendliness, get the heathens comfortable around you, and then begin dishing out the Bible studies before being polluted by the heathens' worldliness.

Greg told Brother Joseph about his life in Colorado, his school there, the small skate park, and a little about his mom. Greg even told Brother Joseph that his dad had left them when Greg was little. Brother Joseph seemed genuinely interested in it all, even down to the kind of music Greg listened to. Greg was starting to feel comfortable around this congenial street preacher.

Once Brother Joseph's questions about Greg's life had been exhausted, Greg asked, "So what about you? What do you do here?"

Brother Joseph looked up into his mirror as he changed lanes. "Well, as you know, I do the services for teenagers on Friday nights. I work at a small Christian publishing company. Oh, and I'm the youth pastor for the Pentecostal church my car was parked at."

A groan escaped Greg's lips involuntarily. "You mean you're Pentecostal too?"

Brother Joseph looked at him and said, "What do you mean 'too'?"

Greg looked down at his skateboard and rubbed his fingers across it. "Sorry, that just kind of slipped out. But, well, yeah, my mom's a Pentecostal."

Joseph nodded. "I take it you don't think much of her church then."

Greg shrugged and paused. "Well, to be honest, I think most Christians are . . . well, no offense . . . but I think most of 'em are hypocrites."

Brother Joseph studied him. "What do you mean?"

Greg shot him a glance, trying to read his face. The question had been asked sincerely and honestly, without an edge to it as Greg would've expected. "Well," Greg continued, fiddling with the wheels on his skateboard, "it's just that . . ." he took a deep breath then plunged in. "I don't understand how anyone could follow a God who is so cruel and unjust and . . . and . . . evil!"

There. He'd just insulted this guy's religion. Greg put his hand on the door handle, bracing himself for the tirade and for Brother Joseph to yell at him to get out of the car. He waited a moment and then looked over at Brother Joseph. The youth minister was glancing at his phone's GPS into which he had inputted the address of Greg's hotel.

"Greg, I think I made a mistake. Do you remember some of the places around your hotel?"

The innocuous question caught Greg off guard, but he listed a couple fast-food chain restaurants he'd noticed. Brother Joseph smiled sheepishly. "I entered the north address instead of the south address. I was wondering how you had come that far! But don't worry—we'll get on the right track."

Greg didn't say anything as Brother Joseph turned the car around. He felt strangely at ease with this man—more so than any other adult he knew. The only people he felt comfortable with at home were Renae and Doug, who were kids his own age. Never adults. But Brother Joseph was different somehow.

Once they were going the other direction, Brother Joseph

surprised him again by asking, "So why do you think God is cruel, unjust, and evil?" Greg had thought maybe that the preacher hadn't heard him because he hadn't reacted. But he obviously had and now wanted to pick up the conversation again like they were debating favorite sports teams.

"Oh . . . well." Greg grappled with what to say. "No offense, but if the God of the Bible is real, then it just seems like all He cares about are rules and trying to get people to be His slaves! He allows evil and suffering and horrible things, and punishes people when they do wrong, even sending them to burn forever in hell if they don't live exactly the way He wants! Sorry, but that just seems cruel, unjust, and evil to me."

Brother Joseph actually nodded. "I can see how it looks like that to you. But from knowing Him personally, I have a little bit of a different perspective. Do you mind if I share with you how I see it?"

"Uh . . . sure . . . go ahead," Greg conceded cautiously. Brother Joseph hadn't screamed and yelled and cried like his mom would have, so maybe it wouldn't be so bad to hear this. Not that he would agree, of course, but it might be good debate practice.

"You know, Greg," Brother Joseph said as he made a turn, "a lot of people think of God only in terms of a ruler, a king, or a judge, or a boss or something like that. But that's not the primary way Jesus taught us to think of God. He told us to think of God as our father."

Greg rolled his eyes. "No offense, Brother Joseph, but my experience with fathers is that most of the time they are selfish jerks who leave as soon as they realize they can't help their family . . . or don't want to."

Brother Joseph's eyes softened noticeably as he looked at Greg. "If that's your experience, Greg, then this is more important for you to realize than you know. God isn't like that . . . He is a *good* father. The best father. With love so great that no other father could compare no matter how hard they tried! If I were to explain what it means to me personally that God is my Father, I would say that God loves us and wants a relationship with us, and therefore, will love us, guide us, help us, encourage us, teach us, and correct us when necessary because He really does have our best interests in mind."

"That sounds good, Brother Joseph," Greg retorted. "But God hasn't done that for me! He hasn't been around any more than my real dad has. My real dad became an alcoholic and left when he lost his job and couldn't provide any more. He couldn't and hasn't helped us . . . and I don't see that God has done much to help us either."

Brother Joseph shook his head firmly, and the strength of the mild-mannered street preacher's voice when he answered surprised Greg. "You're wrong, Greg. God does love you and He has been watching out for you. He has and is going to great lengths to show you His love . . . you just don't see it."

A sharp comeback sprang to Greg's lips but died as he looked into the preacher's solemn brown eyes. Something in them stopped him from saying what he was going to say. "How do you know?" he asked hesitantly, after a moment.

"I know because He's done it for me," Brother Joseph responded. "My own dad passed away when I was young, and I could tell you countless stories of how God has provided and cared and protected me since then. But more important than all that, He wanted to build a relationship with me . . . so deep that now I come to Him with anything. The amazing part about it is that I didn't seek it out. God sought me out because He actually wanted to spend time with me, in spite of all I've done to hurt Him. That's what amazes me more than anything. And that's what He's doing for you right now, Greg. He's seeking you out."

The conviction in Brother Joseph's voice left no doubt in Greg's mind that the man believed every word he was saying. What were the experiences Brother Joseph hinted about that had so thoroughly convinced him of God's existence . . . and love? Part of Greg wanted to ask, but another part shrunk back. He wasn't sure he was ready to accept the existence of a God who had let so many bad things happen in his life. So, instead, Greg said, "Well, I haven't seen any evidence that God actually loves me. I'd have to see it to believe it."

"You will, Greg," Brother Joseph said softly. "But maybe not in the way you expect."

Greg was caught off guard by the preacher's gentle response and shifted uncomfortably in his seat. The youth pastor stopped talking for a minute to concentrate on a street sign, taking a sudden turn. It was easier to argue with his mom because his barbs made her defensive, and once they started volleying, he could usually get the upper hand. But Brother Joseph's approach had somehow disarmed him.

Greg looked out the window at the rain pounding the street. The street lamps cast a yellow glow over the otherwise dark storefronts. A few neon signs flashed, advertising how late the stores were open. He didn't want to offend the preacher by telling him what he really thought, but there was no way God really loved him, considering all the bad things that had happened in his life.

In the intervening quiet, Greg could hear the song that was playing. The words from one of the songs caught his attention and seemed to match what Brother Joseph was saying. "I love you more than all My creation!" Greg couldn't help rolling his eyes. It was obviously supposed to be God speaking here. "I call you, and seek you, and want you, because I love you more!"

"Yeah, right," Greg muttered.

Oops. He hadn't meant to say that out loud. He shot a glance over to the man in the driver's seat to see if he was offended. But Brother Joseph just looked over at him, inviting conversation. Greg looked down, embarrassed at his slip of the tongue.

Brother Joseph just waited. Finally, he said, "You know, you don't have to be worried about offending me with what you think. I'm not going to psychoanalyze you or rake you over the coals. I just like talking about what I consider to be the most important subject in the universe. But I'm used to people disagreeing with me." Greg could hear amusement underlying the last sentence. The minister continued. "So if you want to bring anything up, I'd love to hear your thoughts."

Greg shrugged his shoulders and flicked his skateboard wheel sending it spinning. "I'm sorry. I, well, I guess I don't believe all that Christian jargon about God being so loving and loving everybody on the planet and all that."

Brother Joseph nodded for him to go on.

"Well, it's just that, with all the evil in the world . . . you know, all the disease and hunger and terrorists and stuff . . . with all that, how can you say that God is loving and good and powerful? If He was really loving, He wouldn't want all that stuff to happen, and if He really was all-powerful, He could stop all the evil. The way I see it, you can't have it both ways."

The street preacher drummed his fingers on the steering wheel, then turned to Greg with a smile. "You know," he said, "the presence of evil in the world doesn't disprove the existence of God. It just proves the existence of evil."

Greg's eyebrows wrinkled in confusion.

Brother Joseph continued. "Just because you see something bad happening around you, doesn't mean that good isn't present.

For example, you can't say that evil proves there isn't a God any more than you can say that because a person hates someone that means they can't love anyone. Evil may just prove the existence of a devil, not disprove the existence of God."

Brother Joseph's train of thought made sense to Greg. "But still," he argued. "God is supposed to be all-powerful, right? Shouldn't He be able to stop bad things from happening?" *Like my sister dying or my dad leaving,* he added to himself.

The preacher gave a little shake of his head. "That question assumes there is no free will. By no means do I believe God is not all-powerful. But I do believe He gives us a choice. He created a perfect world, with perfect order, and then humans messed it up with sin, the rebellion against that perfect order. Just because there's crime in a city doesn't mean there is no police department. In fact, the very existence of crime proves there has to be a police department or a law system to enforce and set up the rules, or there would be no laws to break."

"That might be true about the terrorists and people who do wrong. But that doesn't explain how there's diseases and car crashes and natural disasters and stuff like that."

They turned onto another street. "Excellent point, Greg. That's something that theologians and philosophers have pondered for years. I've heard a lot of people ask that question before. How could a loving God allow evil in their lives?" He paused a moment while Greg sat there, waiting. Brother Joseph finally said, "I could tell you what I think about it, but I think it would be better if you got ahold of it yourself. So instead, I'm going to give you some scriptures that have encouraged me in my thoughts about this, and if you want, later you can look it up, all right?"

Greg shrugged and nodded.

"I'll write them down as soon as I pull up to the front door of your hotel."

The skater jerked his head up in surprise. He hadn't known they were here already. But yeah, there was the awning and the sliding glass door where Terrance had dropped him off only that afternoon.

Brother Joseph pulled up to the sliding glass door and found a scrap of paper and a pen in a little compartment underneath the cup holder. Greg opened the door but waited while Brother Joseph scribbled something down. He finished and handed it to Greg. Greg looked down at it. Romans 8:18-28. He took it and stuffed it in his pocket. "Okay, thanks," he said as he snatched his skateboard and emerged from the car into the bright lights outside the hotel.

"Oh, and Greg?"

Greg turned around and looked at Brother Joseph.

"This may not mean much right now, but I want you to know that I'll be praying for you."

Greg looked down and shuffled his feet. "Uh, yeah, okay . . . thanks." Then he lowered his voice and said, "But I'm not sure what good it'll do."

Brother Joseph chuckled softly. "It may do more good than you think. Talk to you later, huh, Greg?"

Greg grunted and waved, then turned and headed into the hotel.

o———o

Brother Joseph watched to make sure Greg got through the doors all right and then began to drive away. He sighed and closed his eyes for a moment. "Oh, God, help Greg," he said out loud. There were so many like him, so many teenagers that didn't have a clue of how much the Almighty God loved them. If only they realized the Lord really did love them! Brother

Joseph had felt His pain for the lost and the longing He had for the teenagers on the streets of Chicago . . . and everywhere else for that matter. If there was one thing this street preacher knew, it was that God loved them. God loved the young man who had just climbed out of his car, and Brother Joseph knew God's eyes were on him. He just wished he could have said more to him. Every time he spoke to teenagers, he always felt inadequate to the task the Lord had given him to do.

But there was also something wrong with his story. Brother Joseph frowned. Why is a fourteen-year-old boy wandering around Chicago alone? Where are the people who sponsored this trip? When they had pulled up to the hotel, the preacher had felt a sense of evil. Something wasn't right, and he was going to be watching . . . and praying.

Oh man, I needed more speed! Greg tensed his body as he barely made it up onto the rail. He began grinding across it when his phone suddenly vibrated and he lost his balance and toppled off the rail.

Chris and Terry laughed. "Ooh, looks like Greg's losing his touch!" Terry said.

Greg cussed and got up, dusting himself off. He fished his phone out of his pocket. The display read that he had a new text message. He didn't recognize the number. "I wonder who this is." He opened it.

Greg, come back 2 the hotel. I'll meet u in the lobby. Don't let anyone see u. –Stefan.

Greg cursed then quickly looked up to make sure Chris and Terry hadn't seen. They were both over at the ramps arguing about who was better at grinding. Greg cursed again and slipped his phone back in his pocket. *How did Stefan get my number? I didn't give it to him!*

Greg pulled out his phone again to look at the time. It was 2:30. He'd been at the skate park for a couple hours. Today had been pretty awesome. Sleeping in was blissful, and as soon as he'd gotten up and ready, he'd maneuvered over to the skate park. It took him a little while to find it again, but he had finally managed. Almost all the kids were impressed by his skateboarding abilities, and knowing Chris opened the door to meet anyone else who came to the park. He had felt free to just skate, without any responsibilities or commitments to tie him down. Until now.

Greg kicked a rail. He didn't want to leave. *Why does Stefan need me now, anyway? Aren't I going to do the errand for him at night? The jerk.* Greg wanted to express his anger in a more visible way but didn't want Chris and Terry to get suspicious.

Instead of cussing a blue streak like he wanted to, he turned to Chris and Terry and waved. "Um, hey, I have to get back."

Chris whirled around. "What? Why?"

Oh brother, why'd he have to ask that? "Uh . . . 'cause . . . I've gotta do some stuff." *Oh, sure, great cop-out, Greg.* He winced inwardly. *They're really gonna believe that!*

Chris gave Greg a strange look but shrugged. "Okay. See ya later, Greg. Check this out, Terry!"

Greg began trudging away from the skate park, fuming at Stefan. *Why did he have to ruin everything just when I'm beginning to have a little fun?* He threw his skateboard down on the concrete and was about to jump on and start skating when his phone vibrated again. With great reluctance, Greg opened the text.

Delete this & prev txt msg. –Stefan

Greg cursed and put his phone away, then jumped on his skateboard and began skating toward the hotel. *Stefan is sure going to get a piece of my mind when I get there.*

Greg reached the hotel and entered angrily, ready to lay into Stefan. He turned around in a circle in the lobby, looking for his adversary. Amazingly enough, Stefan was in plain view. He was at the vending machine in the hallway, talking on a cell phone. Greg took a deep breath and took a seat on one of the lobby's couches to wait for him. Greg had to admit, Stefan played his part well. He looked every bit like a visiting businessman.

The desk clerk was nowhere to be seen, and that surprised Greg. Usually, if she heard someone come in, she'd be at the front desk ready to help. But the two mainframe computers at the long desk sat vacant.

Stefan entered the lobby near Greg, still talking on his phone, with a soda in his other hand. He paused, trying to get a point across. "No, so I was late, and the kid stops me and asks for directions! Yeah." Here Stefan looked pointedly at Greg and casually began walking again. "Anyways, I didn't know you wanted those papers, so I threw 'em away. Oh, sure, I can still get them out. They're just lying in the wastebasket at my office." Stefan walked out the sliding doors and headed to the parking lot around the side of the building.

Greg rolled his eyes. *What is Stefan doing? Does he want me to follow him? Wait . . . what did he say when he looked at me?* "And the kid stops me and asks for directions." *Maybe I should act like I'm asking him for directions.*

A brunette desk clerk appeared just as Greg stood up to walk out. "Um, sir? I'll—" She stopped and looked around. She blew a puff of air out of the corner of her mouth and dropped a folder on the counter. "People are so odd," Greg heard her mumble to herself as he left the building.

He walked briskly down the sidewalk, carrying his skateboard, and looked around. *Where did Stefan go?* He came around the side of the building and scanned the parking lot. Nobody was in it. Greg punched his skateboard with his fist in frustration. *How does Stefan do that? Okay, that's it. I'm finished. If*

Stefan is going to pull these . . . these disappearing acts just for fun, I'm done. I'm tired of Stefan's games.

Greg was ready to turn back to the hotel when he spotted him. Stefan was at the curb of the sidewalk in front of the hotel, as if he were waiting for a taxi. *How did he get there without me seeing him?* Grumbling under his breath, he began walking in Stefan's direction. Remembering Stefan's hints about the kid asking directions, he looked around and hesitated, as if he weren't sure which way to go. Then, looking as if he had finally decided to ask someone, Greg approached Stefan.

"Hey, dude, uh, could you tell me how to get to—." *Oops . . . I didn't think this far ahead. I should have thought of a place.* Greg said the first thing that popped in his head. "To . . . um, the Willis Tower?"

Stefan looked at him as if seeing him for the first time. "The Willis Tower, huh? Well . . . I am waiting for my ride, but . . . let's see. I believe you turn left on the street up that way . . . wait, wait, no. Um . . ." Stefan looked around as if trying to get his bearings. Greg had to hand it to him; he was good at acting. "C'mon, over here, to the street corner." He waved Greg over, and Greg followed him. Greg couldn't resist rolling his eyes. *Was all this really necessary?*

At the street corner, Stefan lowered his voice. "Very good. I'm impressed you caught on."

Greg couldn't hide his disdain. "Did we really have to go through all that?" he asked, matching Stefan's low tone. "Why couldn't you have just told me to meet you at the street corner? And by the way, how did you get my number?"

"I did it so we wouldn't attract suspicion. When you've been in my business for as long as I have, you learn that caution is vital. You can never be too careful or take too many risks." Greg rolled his eyes again and set his skateboard down on the curb. Stefan's doubletalk never made any sense.

"Now, we don't have much time," Stefan continued. "Tonight at seven fifty, you need to go to the garbage can in the alley behind the hotel. You'll find a box. Get the box and catch the eight o'clock bus to Yorkshire Street. Are you with me so far?"

Greg sighed and nodded, looking off to the side.

Suddenly Stefan's eyebrows narrowed and he grabbed Greg's shoulder so hard it hurt. "Ow!" Greg said without thinking.

"Listen to me!" Stefan was not happy. "This is extremely important! Don't just flip it off like it's no big deal! If you fail me, it won't affect me in any way. I can always give them the slip. But your life will become miserable. If not by the police, then by us! Do you understand?"

Greg gritted his teeth and glared so hard at Stefan his eyeballs burned. If he could slap him just once . . .

Stefan released his shoulder with a shove and assumed a normal stance again. "Now, once you get off the bus at Yorkshire, turn left and go down the first alley you come to. Somebody will meet you there and take the box from you. That's all you'll have to do tonight. Think you can handle it?" It wasn't a question; it was an insult.

Greg jerked his head back to get his hair out of his eyes. "I can do it," he said, an edge lacing his voice.

"See that you do," Stefan replied. "I will pay you after you finish the job this time. Speaking of which . . . Where's the envelope?"

Greg had stuck it in his pocket that morning. He got it out and slapped it into Stefan's hand.

"Thank you," Stefan said, that annoying smile lighting his face. "If you don't understand what to do tonight, you can call the number Terrance gave you."

Oh yeah, I forgot about that.

"Are we agreed, Greg?" Stefan held out his hand. Greg wasn't agreed but shook hands with Stefan anyway.

"Excellent. I'll contact you later." Greg turned, but Stefan stopped him. "Oh, one more thing. Don't go back to the skate park until your mission tonight is complete."

Greg spun around to face Stefan. "What? But dude . . . Why?"

Stefan smiled. "Well, we don't want you compromising our secrecy, now do we?"

Greg threw his hands up in the air. "I won't compromise the secrecy, I—"

But Stefan was already shaking his head. "I'm sorry, Greg, but no."

Greg looked at him with disgust. "Why did you have me come back at two-thirty anyway for an eight o'clock mission? That's like a six-hour gap!"

"I couldn't have you come back in the evening, when people are getting out of board meetings and finishing their sightseeing, could I? That wouldn't do at all."

"Well, what am I supposed to do in the meantime?"

"I don't care, figure something out. Watch TV, go swimming, go out to eat. I don't care." Stefan looked at his watch. "I have to go. Don't let me down, Greg."

And with that, Stefan turned and strode off.

o——o

Greg creeped around the side of the building, glancing around to make sure nobody was paying attention to him. Nobody was. The last five and a half hours had crawled by. Greg couldn't remember ever being so bored. He had spent most of the time watching TV. Around five, he'd gone to a nearby fast-food restaurant for some dinner. By the time it turned 7:45, Greg was so bored he was more than ready to run Stefan's errand for him.

He came to the alley and took off his cap, running his fingers through his hair. The alley was empty. He looked up the side of the building to see if anyone was watching him. It was dusk, and he could see lights coming through some of the windows, but all the curtains were closed. *I guess people who come to Chicago like their privacy,* thought Greg.

He went to the metal trash can quickly, before someone decided to look outside, and slowly removed the lid. Flies buzzed all around him and a pungent odor hit his nostrils. Greg turned away and coughed. *Gross. Why couldn't they have picked a different place to hide the stupid box?* Greg turned back and peeked in. There it was. Sitting on top of a trash bag was a cardboard box wrapped in duct tape. Greg grabbed it and let the trash can lid clatter back onto the trash can. He froze. Had anyone heard that? He looked up, but no, all the curtains were still closed. Greg bolted out of the alley into the parking lot and snatched his skateboard up from where he left it. He ran to the bus stop and got his phone out of his pocket. It was 7:56. The bus would be here in four minutes.

A couple other people were at the bus stop, but everybody ignored Greg. At last the bus pulled up and the people filed on, Greg being last. Several asked if the bus stopped at a certain place and once satisfied, climbed into the back. Greg paid and took an empty seat near the front so he wouldn't have to talk to anybody and could get out quickly. The bus driver closed the door and took off.

"So, where you headed?" the bus driver asked Greg.

So much for not talking to anyone. "Uh, Yorkshire Street," Greg told him.

The bus driver looked curiously at Greg. "You sure you want to go to Yorkshire Street?"

"Well, sure. Why not?"

The African American bus driver shook his head. "You're not from around here, are you, son?"

"Why do you say that?"

"'Cause, well, 'scuse me for sayin' so, but no white kid from 'round here would ever set foot in Yorkshire. Not if they could help it. 'Specially not at night."

"Why not?"

The bus driver turned his wide, white eyes over to Greg. "Trust me, son. You jus' don't want to."

"Yeah, well, I know what I'm doing."

The bus driver held up a hand. "Okay, whatever you say."

The rest of the trip was silent between Greg and the bus driver. They made a couple stops, and people got on and off. Finally, they reached Yorkshire Street. The bus pulled to a stop. The mood felt ominous.

"Well . . . here we are," the bus driver announced, grimly. "Yorkshire."

Greg hopped off, making sure he remembered the box and his skateboard. The bus driver paused before closing the door. "Good luck, son," he said.

Now why'd he have to say that? Greg groaned. The door closed and the bus drove away. Greg was alone on Yorkshire Street.

As he started walking, Greg saw why the bus driver was so cautious. The street had a dark feeling about it. Broken beer bottles and used cigarettes littered the cracked sidewalk. The stripped frame of what was once a nice BMW was pushed off to the side. The lights were all dim, as if the light bulbs needed to be changed. Greg noticed most of the storefronts were liquor stores and night clubs. *Oh great, this is appropriate.* Greg felt his skin starting to crawl. *Stop it!* he ordered himself. *Quit being such a wimp!*

Greg's steps were long and fast. He just wanted to deliver the package and get out of there. A black homeless guy with a scruffy beard and a ratty dress shirt that wasn't buttoned up lifted his hand from the front steps of a building. "Hey, kid," he called in a wheezy voice. "Got some change for an old man?" Greg quickened his steps. "Hey wait, come back! I jus' wanna lil' booze," he said, slurring his words.

Thanks a lot, Stefan. Thanks a lot.

He noticed people watching him from dark corners, and he tried to stop the bus driver's words from replaying over and over in his mind. *I'm gonna be okay,* he told himself. *I'm just going to deliver the package and get out of here. Not a big deal, right? Just deliver the package and get out.*

Greg looked around, suddenly unsure of himself. *Have I passed the alleyway? Where is it?* Then he spotted it. *Aha, here it is.* Dark and threatening, just like everything else on this street. Greg stared at the entrance for a moment. *Oh boy, I so do not want to go in there.* Mold covered the crumbling brick wall. A dry wind whipped through, stirring up dead leaves. Greg darted to the alleyway and began to quickly walk down it. His footsteps seemed to echo with each step. The only light came from the street's dim lampposts. The shadows were long and dark. Broken glass was everywhere. Greg glanced at the graffiti along the wall. The words and pictures were graphic and cruel and made him shiver. *Just where am I, anyway?*

He came down the alley and reached a pile of broken-down cardboard boxes . . . and a wall. *A wall? This is a dead end! But that can't be! Where's the person I'm supposed to meet?* Greg didn't see anyone around. A noise from behind him startled him. Greg spun around to see what it was. He didn't see anything. *Oh boy, this is not good.* He heard a siren in the distance, and the long, high-pitched wail sounded eerie. Greg gripped the box tighter. *That's it. I'm leaving. Stefan will just have to deliver the box himself.* Greg started walking rapidly toward the street. *I am so out of here!*

Suddenly, a man stepped out of the shadows, blocking his path. Greg jumped, then stumbled back and tried to still his beating heart. *It's not a big deal, he just wants some money for liquor or something, then he'll be on his way,* Greg tried to assure himself. The man was huge. Six foot something. His finely-toned muscles bulged against his shirt. The man glared at him, and something gleamed in his hand. Greg thought his heart couldn't beat any faster, but it proved him wrong. The man was holding a knife. "Where you think you goin', punk?" he asked in a deep, gruff voice.

"Why does that matter to you?" Greg retorted, trying to hide his fear. The man moved closer, and to Greg's horror, he saw others moving in behind him . . . all with weapons. "I don't think you understand, kid. You're on our turf. You've crossed over to the wrong side of the line, white boy."

Greg realized then that all the guys ganging up on him were black. What was it the bus driver had said? "No white kid from 'round here would ever set foot in Yorkshire. Not if they could help it." Greg gulped.

The street thugs formed a wall, blocking Greg's exit. There were about seven of them. There was no way he could get through. He was trapped!

7

Greg began to back slowly away from the big guy with the knife. The man continued to step closer, raising his knife threateningly. Greg took another step back, clutching his skateboard in one hand and the box in the other. *If worse comes to worse, I can battle them with my skateboard. Yeah, right.*

"Please," Greg pleaded, all the toughness completely sapped from his tone. "I don't want to cause any trouble . . ."

"I don't wanna cause any trouble," the big guy mimicked. "You shoulda thoughta that before you came over here. We don't like strangers on our turf."

"Whadda we gonna do to 'im, Al?"

The man who spoke was a skinny guy with several chains draped around his neck, baggy pants, a baseball cap, and a T-shirt that was too big for him.

Al eyed Greg, never lowering the knife. "That depends on how well 'e cooperates wit' us." He spied the box and gestured toward it. "What's in the box, kid?"

"I–I don't know," Greg stuttered, too scared to think of anything intelligent to say.

"You dunno?" Al repeated with a sneer. "Then why you carrying it around?"

"Uh . . . 'cause, well, I was supposed to meet somebody here in this alley and give them this box, but . . . uh, they're obviously not here, so I guess I'll just be heading on out . . ."

Al looked at him suspiciously. "You was s'posed to meet someone? Wait . . ." Al turned around and groaned. "Tony, tell me he ain't who I think he is."

Tony shook his head grimly. Al spun back around and pointed the knife at Greg. "Okay, kid, who the one who sent you?"

Greg gripped the box tighter and took a step back. "I . . . I'm not sure I should tell you."

With one smooth motion, Al had lunged forward and grabbed the front of Greg's shirt, pulling Greg's face close to his and pressing the knife against his throat. "That help you make your decision?"

Greg nodded carefully, trying not to get cut.

This time it was another one of the gang members that spoke. "Hey, Al."

Greg noticed him behind Al's looming form. He may have been one of the shortest in the gang—only five foot one or two from the looks of it. In contrast to the other gang members, he didn't wear a lot of jewelry but was just in shorts and a T-shirt. "Maybe we shouldn't do nothing to him, man, I mean—"

"Shut your mouth, Michael!" Al shouted. Much to Greg's dismay, Michael stepped back and shut his mouth. Al pressed the knife harder against Greg's throat. "Now, tell me who the one that sent you!"

"H–his name's Stefan!"

Al's eyes rolled back into his head. He dropped Greg in a heap on the ground and cursed. Al walked a couple steps over and kicked a trash can, then cursed again. His gang just watched him. Greg wasn't sure what to do. Was this good or bad?

Al looked back at him. "So you mean you . . . you the . . . aw man!" He turned and cursed. "Of all the . . ." Al faced his gang. "Why on earth would Adikema send us some wimpy, skinny little white kid? Boy, when I get ahold o' that guy . . ." Al looked up into the sky and let out a deep breath. Then he held out a hand to Greg. "Okay, kid, you on our side now. I don' like it, but that how it be." As he helped Greg up, he let out another cuss word and muttered something about what he was going to do to Stefan the next time he saw him.

Greg staggered to his feet, unsure of how to react. Al held out his hand. "You gonna give me the ****ing box now or what?"

"Oh!" Greg quickly passed the box on and backed away. In a swift turn of his hand, Al slit the tape holding the box together and peered inside. He took a cursory glance, mumbling something to himself that Greg couldn't hear.

"Uh . . . c–can I go now?" Greg asked, still intimidated by the big guy. "I mean—"

Al's eyes shot up and narrowed. "You stay," he ordered.

"But I've done my part, and—"

"I said, STAY!"

Greg flinched and nodded rapidly. "Uh, yeah . . . like I was saying, I think I'll stay."

Al rummaged through the box a little, then lifted his head and turned to Greg. "So where the next pick-up point at?"

Greg stared at him blankly. "The next what?"

"Y'know, the next place we get the junk? C'mon, kid!" Al leered at him. "Or didn't Stefan tell you where it gonna be?"

Greg's mind raced. Stefan hadn't said anything about a pick-up point or anything like that! He'd just told Greg somebody would take the box from him. What was Greg supposed to do? Lie? Admit he didn't know? From the look of things, Al and his gang were looking for an excuse to hurt someone, and Greg didn't want to be that someone.

But fortunately, Tony saved him. "Hey, Al, c'mere," he said, waving the leader over. With a grunt, Al swaggered over. Tony began speaking to him in low tones, gesturing toward Greg and back toward the alley they had just come from. Greg chewed his lower lip nervously and wiped his sweaty palms on his pants.

Tony finished, and Al looked back at Greg with a sneer and nodded. "Yeah, I like it. That makes sense. Okay kid, c'mon."

"Uh . . ." Greg's throat was dry and he cleared it before speaking. "Um . . . come on?"

"Yeah, you familiar with the phrase?" Al said in his deep bass voice. "Follow me. We gonna use you, boy. You in this with us now, so we gonna make the most of it."

Greg clutched his skateboard tighter to hide the shaking of his hands. The gang moved in around him, preventing any possible way of escape. Al led them through the streets. He crossed Yorkshire and ducked into another alley. They went mainly through alleys after that, avoiding places with a lot of traffic. The gang was surprisingly quiet. Apparently they all knew where they were going and that they were supposed to remain silent. Finally, they reached what appeared to be the industrial section of town. It was dark except for the street lamps. All the buildings were dark.

Al hunched down his tall, bulky frame to Greg's level and lowered his voice to a husky whisper. "See that warehouse over there?" he asked pointing. Greg nodded. "Since you one o' dem skaters, I want you to ride your skateboard around the building, like you just be out skatin'. Follow? Then come back and tell us if you see anything suspicious."

Greg nodded. *Maybe I can get away or find someone to help.* That thought was his only consolation.

Just as Greg started to venture out of the alley onto the street, Al grabbed his shoulder with his big, meaty hand. "Oh, and kid . . . you know you won't be able to find your way back to Yorkshire, don' you? I led you so many different ways, there ain't no way you could find your way back. Don't mess up, hear? And if you let anybody know 'bout this here, I gonna make your life miserable. We ain't the only ones involved in this thing. You a part of it now too. Got it?"

Again, Greg nodded, his eyes wide with fright. *There goes my only consolation.*

Al clapped Greg's shoulder, making it sting, then gave Greg a little push. "Go on, kid."

Greg looked both ways, then cautiously emerged onto the street and began skating around the building.

o———o

Al crossed his burly arms across his chest as he watched the kid skate off.

Michael looked at Al. "You really think Purdo's back there?" he asked a little nervously.

"Dunno. Guess we gonna find out," Al said. "Knowin' that guy, nuthin'd surprise me." He gave Tony a side glance. "You know the kid ain't comin' back, don't you?"

Tony smirked. "Yeah, you probably right. But at least then we'll be rid of him. And if Purdo does grab him . . . it'll be to our gain, right?"

"Yeah, a win-win situation," Al said, watching the teenager skate off.

o———o

Greg skirted the perimeter of the building, trying to look as if he was doing what Al told him to. In reality, Greg was ready to ditch the gang and get as far away from there as possible. It didn't matter that he didn't know where he was, Greg was scared. He didn't want to have to be with Al and his gang any longer than absolutely necessary.

As he rounded the corner scanning the buildings for an escape route, suddenly a figure stepped out of the shadows and blocked his path. Greg couldn't stop and plowed into the man. It was a policeman. He grabbed Greg's shoulders to steady himself and pulled back in shock, looking as surprised to see a white skater in this part of town as Greg was to see him.

"What are you doing here, kid? You lost?"

"I'm just skating," Greg said, taking a step back, and reaching down to grab his skateboard.

The policeman stepped closer and motioned to the light of a street lamp. "Come over here," he said with a jerk of his head.

Greg looked at him guardedly. *Should I ask him for help? Is the gang watching right now? What does this dude want from me, anyway? Does he somehow know about the box I gave to Al and his gang?*

The policeman directed Greg to the pool of light on the sidewalk outside the large warehouse. "Do you have any idea where you are?" He looked at Greg suspiciously. "In fact, why are you out here, in this part of town, so late? You know there are dangerous gangs around here, right?"

All the questions flustered Greg. "I told you, I'm skating," he repeated.

The policeman narrowed his eyes at Greg. "Why are you skateboarding in this section of town? Isn't this a little far from any skate parks?"

I wish I was at the skate park right now, Greg thought. "Why does it matter to you where I skate?" he asked testily.

The restraint showing on his face, the policeman announced in a booming voice, "Young man, I am an officer of the law. My duty is to uphold the law and protect you from harm. This is a dangerous part of town, and I would recommend you find somewhere else to play."

Play? If you only knew what I was really doing, dude. Greg hated it when people talked down to him, and this policeman was definitely talking down to him. Greg stared at him defiantly. The policeman stared back at him.

"Okay, kid, level with me," he said suddenly. "What are you really doing here?"

Greg took a step back. "What?"

"You're not here just to skateboard, are you?" the policeman accused.

"Why wouldn't I be?" Greg asked, losing what was left of his confidence.

The policeman waved his hand at the warehouse behind him. "I'm going to be honest with you. There's been a lot of drug activity around this area lately, and I'm here to bring it to a stop."

The policeman looked hard at Greg, studying the skater's face. Greg shifted uneasily. "And if you've been involved in any of it, it's going to be painful for you. Show me what's in your pockets, please," he requested in an authoritative tone.

Greg fumbled for his cell phone and wallet and handed them to the guy, hoping his face expressed the resentment he felt.

The policeman flipped through the wallet quickly, pausing as he noted all the money. "That's a lot of cash for someone your age to carry," he observed.

Greg scrambled for an excuse. "I did a couple jobs recently and just got paid," he explained haltingly.

The policeman grunted. "Interesting they didn't give you a check." He looked into Greg's eyes as he handed back the wallet and phone. "I suggest you deposit your cash as soon as possible. It's not wise to carry so much . . . particularly in this section of town. Got it?"

Greg averted his eyes and didn't answer, putting his things back in his pockets where they belonged. The way the officer kept looking into his eyes unnerved him.

"Put down the skateboard and put your hands behind your head," he ordered.

Greg stepped back in shock. "What?" he asked, not sure the policeman was serious.

The policeman gestured impatiently. "Come on, kid. If you cooperate, things will be much easier for you. Just put your hands behind your head."

Greg gawked at him incredulously. "Are you searching me for drugs?"

The policeman nodded seriously. "That's right. Which shouldn't bother you, if you have nothing to hide, right?" He looked into Greg's eyes pointedly.

Shocked, Greg slowly set down his skateboard on the concrete and raised his arms. With one deft movement, before Greg even had time to react, the policeman grabbed Greg's hands, which were now behind his head, and came behind the skater. Greg stood there, feeling helpless and then angry.

The policeman began a quick pat-down of the skater's body, feeling his arms, chest, and legs. He finished and straightened up, releasing Greg with a rough push, and turned to face him again. Greg felt his cheeks redden as he stumbled forward, off-balance.

"Slip off your shoes," the policeman ordered.

Reluctantly, Greg did as he was told. When they'd passed the cop's approval, he gestured for Greg to put his shoes back on. Greg did so clumsily.

The policeman sighed. "All right," he said. "You're clean. But don't stick around this part of town, all right? There are a lot of gangs running around here. They use some of the old abandoned warehouses as hideouts and places to hide their illegal drugs." When he said drugs, the policeman spit out the word like it left a bad taste in his mouth. "Like I said, it's dangerous."

"I'll be sure to remember that," Greg mumbled sarcastically.

The police officer stared at Greg another moment. "Get out of here, kid," he commanded with a stern tone.

"You don't have to tell me twice," Greg said and picked his skateboard up, moving away from the officer. He set his skateboard down, then with one foot on it, pushed off with the other and began to gain speed, heading toward another alley. He glanced back once and saw the police officer staring at him, as if he still suspected him. Greg shivered and moved faster.

o——o

Purdo stared after the kid. There was definitely something going on with him. He wished he could follow him to find out what he was up to, but he had agreed to wait for Cambiano here.

Moments later, Cambiano walked up. His Italian partner ran a hand through his shock of salt-and-pepper hair. The older policeman shook his head. "I didn't see anything at the other warehouse, but there's something going on around here. The gangs are close." He pulled a cigar out of his pocket and lit it. "See anything?"

Purdo frowned. "A young teenage Caucasian boy. He was clean."

Cambiano raised his eyebrows. "Is that a fact?" He motioned for Purdo to follow him back to the car. "Why don't you tell me more about him?"

○———○

Greg skated into the alley, and turned a corner . . . right into the midst of the gang. Hands grabbed him and pulled him into the alley. One of the gang members gave him a menacing glare, put a finger to his lips, and slid a finger across his throat. Greg got the message. They waited a few minutes until Al came back from the direction of the warehouse with a couple others. He slapped Greg on the back. Greg pitched forward, barely keeping his balance. "That was great, boy. You might just work out after all." Al grinned and shook his head. "Let's go," he said and motioned down the alley. The gang followed with Greg trapped in the middle.

Greg wasn't sure what he had done, but Al was apparently pleased. *I guess that's better than the alternative.* Al led them to a tiny side street and went down a dark stairwell. *Oh no, not in there!* Greg thought. *Please not in there.* Fear pounded in his heart as the gang shoved him down the dark stairs and into the little room.

An old splintered wooden table sat in the center of the room underneath a bare light bulb hanging from the ceiling. The light bulb cast off a dim glow, barely bright enough for Greg to make out the rest of the room. The floor had no carpet, it was just concrete. The walls looked as if they had been painted at one time, but now they were stained and the plaster was peeling in so many places. Torn magazine pages and dirty newspapers littered the filthy, dirt-encrusted floor. Several cardboard boxes were stacked up in a corner. A hallway at the back of the room led into darkness.

The gang crowded into the room, and Al grabbed a cardboard box and set it on the table along with the one Greg had brought them that night. Ignoring Greg's box, Al dumped some small packets from the other box on the table. Each of them was filled with white powder. The policeman had been right. It was drugs.

Greg recoiled in horror. The whole scene brought back memories of that night when his dad had rushed at him with the tire iron. The skater slammed his eyes shut and gasped for air. He could still see his dad's wild eyes and hear him breathing strangely through his nose like a bull. Greg had escaped with one bruise on his back. Another fear hit him. *What would these drugs do to the already violent gang members?*

He and Doug had made fun of the way the kids at the skate park acted when they smoked pot. Greg had never felt the need for the drugs that would've made him look as stupid as some of the other kids. Skateboarding had always been his release, his comfort. But now he was in a completely different situation than making fun of how many tacos Matt ate. Now he was standing in a dark, drab basement in the midst of a dangerous gang, about to watch as they divided up their spoils.

One of the gang members hopped from foot to foot. "It's about time we got back into that warehouse to get the stuff we hid. I've been—" He let his sentence hang in midair and rubbed his fingers together nervously. Nobody seemed to pay any attention to him.

Al began separating the bags of powder on the table. "Hey, Al," someone spoke up. "Ain't you gonna pass out the oil pipes?"

"Wait till I'm finished," said Al in a menacing voice, not looking up. The guy who had spoken stepped back and shut up. Finally, the piles had been separated, and Al reached into the box and grabbed out a handful of what looked like paper and began rolling them. A couple guys stepped up to help. When they had finished, Al snatched a lighter from his pocket, lit it, and inhaled deeply, then passed it on. All the guys began lighting up and inhaling. Tony noticed Greg shrinking back. "Hey, kid, you wanna try some?"

The other guys took up the call and began urging Greg to take a drag. Greg shook his head and held up his hands. "No, no, I'm fine."

Tony took a step toward him. "C'mon, kid. Try a little. Or are ya too chicken?"

Greg continued to back up. *You'd better believe I'm chicken,* he thought.

Tony swaggered closer. "Here kid. Take one." He shoved it in Greg's hands.

Greg dropped the oil pipe as if it were on fire.

Tony snarled. "Whattsa matter with you, boy? That costs us money. I think you oughta show you appreciate it!" Some of the guys began hooting in agreement.

Greg shook his head vehemently. "N–no, no really."

Tony grabbed his knife and popped it open. "I think I should give him a little persuasion, how 'bout it, gang?" The gang howled their approval.

Suddenly the short gang member, the one called Michael, stepped up. "No, leave him alone," he said in a surprisingly firm voice.

Tony whirled around to face him. "What'd you say?"

Michael didn't back away. "Come on, Tony, he's jus' a kid. Let him go."

Tony took a threatening step toward Michael. "I think if he wants to run with us, he gotta show he can handle it!"

"He ain't runnin' with us, dude! He's jus' Stefan's little errand boy. Let him go. This is stupid."

With a flash, Tony swung the knife at Michael, which swished through the air, narrowly missing him, and Michael put up his fists. Tony lunged at him, grabbing his head with his arm. Michael connected a solid punch with Tony's shoulder, and Tony was about to let him have it when Al clapped his huge hands together and yelled for them to cut it out. "You idiots! Don't fight in here! And Michael's right, Tony. Lay off the kid. He ain't gonna give us no money anyhow. We gotta finish up this business first. Now get up here."

Reluctantly, Tony backed off. "We'll finish this later," he said to Michael, walking up to the table where Al began dishing out the bags and demanding the correct amount of money. One by one, the gang gave him the money and collected a bag.

While the gang was distracted, Greg suddenly realized that nobody was watching him. He glanced up at the doorway that led to freedom. If he could just . . .

Heart pounding in his chest, he began inching backwards. When he reached the stairs, he tentatively moved to the first step. Nobody was watching him. Taking another step, he glanced toward the gang. They were all engrossed with their transactions.

Moving quicker now, but still trying not to make any noise, Greg moved up the rest of the steps. Taking one last look, he burst through the door and ran without looking back. He ran down the street till his sides hurt. He didn't even try skateboarding. Greg didn't know where he was or where he was going, but it didn't matter. He just had to get away.

Greg paused to catch his breath when he reached a street, trying to decide which way to turn. Tears began to well up in his eyes, but he quickly wiped them away with the back of his hand. He had to think. Before he could decide what to do, a noise behind him startled him.

When he spun around, he found himself facing Tony. Greg backed up but Tony grabbed the front of his shirt and shoved him against a wall. "You thought I wouldn't notice you leave, huh, white boy?"

Greg's ragged breathing was heavy. Tony leaned close. "This is what happens to kids like you who cross onto our turf." He slapped Greg hard on the face and then punched him in the stomach and released him. Greg doubled over, gasping for breath.

Tony knocked him down, and he felt a sharp ache as the gang member kicked him in the side. Greg squeezed his eyes shut. *Why had he ever agreed to come to Chicago?*

Suddenly a siren sounded close by. Tony leaped back against the wall. The sound grew louder and Tony leaned over Greg. "If you go to the police or tell anyone about us, boy, you gonna get much worse, understand?" Then without waiting for an answer, Tony jumped up and ran off.

Greg kept his eyes closed. The car came down the street and passed Greg. The skater wanted to jump up and get a policeman's attention, but he didn't move. Tony's warning echoed in his brain and then the stony face of the police officer flashed through his mind. Greg could still hear his loud authoritative voice saying, "There's been a lot of drug activity around this area lately, and I'm here to bring it to a stop . . . And if you've been involved in any of it, it's going to be painful for you." No. Greg couldn't go to the police. There was too much at stake.

The skater wasn't sure how long he lay there. He knew he needed to get up and get moving, but somehow he felt immobilized. He ran his tongue over his lips and tasted blood. Where's my skateboard? At some point it had been cast off to the side and was lying in the rubbish. Greg's ball cap lay on the curb in front of him. Another car passed by, but it didn't stop. Maybe the driver didn't see him. Or maybe he just looked the other way. Greg had never felt more alone in his entire life. He didn't know what to do or who he could turn to. Stefan? Yeah, right. He was the one who got him into this whole mess. Besides, Greg knew Stefan would probably just laugh, call Greg a wimp, and tell him to get a tougher skin.

Mom? No. He couldn't turn to his mom. She loved him, yeah, but she didn't understand him. She didn't want him going off to Chicago in the first place. And he had been so rude to her he couldn't imagine going to her for help now.

Renae? He did want to talk to Renae. But what could she do? She would just go to his mom!

Chris and the kids at the skate park? Not a chance. They liked him but wouldn't understand. They didn't know him very well and would probably desert him anyway. He really couldn't trust anybody.

Then one face stood out among all the others. He was a Christian, so Greg knew he wouldn't turn him away. His sincerity and genuine interest in the kids at Denny's came back to him. The car ride home. Yes, if there was anybody Greg could go to, it would be him. That's what he'd do. It was the only option left. He'd go to the missionary—Brother Joseph!

8

Greg finally made it back to the hotel. The cab driver had seemed to sense Greg's need for silence and didn't say anything the entire trip over.

When the skater looked at the digital clock in the taxi, he was surprised to find how early it was. The readout showed it was just a little after 10:00. The whole thing with the gang, the drugs, and the police officer had taken only two hours. There was a chance Brother Joseph would be at the skate park and Greg could catch him.

Greg got out of the cab and trudged up to his room where he changed out of his clothes and washed his face. It wasn't too bad. He had a cut on his lip, and a bruise would probably form on his cheek. He rested both palms on the bathroom counter and finally let himself break down. Tears streamed down his face. *Why are people so evil? Why do they do the things they do? Why does God, if He exists, let it happen?*

After emptying himself of tears, Greg looked up in despair again and moved slowly out of the bathroom. As he walked across the room to grab his skateboard, he noticed the scrap of paper with the scripture Brother Joseph had given him on the table in the room. Greg picked it up and looked at it again. Romans 8:18-28. This was apparently Brother Joseph's answer for the problem of evil in the world. Greg hesitated a moment, then walked over in between the two beds and opened the drawer in the nightstand. Inside the drawer lay a phone book and a Bible. Greg removed the Bible and sat on the edge of the bed.

He flipped through the pages looking for Romans. When he didn't find it, he turned back to the table of contents and looked up the page number. Then he clumsily fumbled through the pages until he finally found it. And as he read it, there was something oddly comforting about sitting on the edge of his bed with the book full of ancient writings.

(18) For I reckon that the sufferings of this present time are not worthy to be compared with the glory which shall be revealed in us.

(19) For the earnest expectation of the creature waiteth for the manifestation of the sons of God.

(20) For the creature was made subject to vanity, not willingly, but by reason of him who hath subjected the same in hope,

(21) Because the creature itself also shall be delivered from the bondage of corruption into the glorious liberty of the children of God.

(22) For we know that the whole creation groaneth and travaileth in pain together until now.

(23) And not only they, but ourselves also, which have the firstfruits of the Spirit, even we ourselves groan within ourselves, waiting for the adoption, to wit, the redemption of our body.

(24) For we are saved by hope: but hope that is seen is not hope: for what a man seeth, why doth he yet hope for?

(25) But if we hope for that we see not, then do we with patience wait for it.

(26) Likewise the Spirit also helpeth our infirmities: for we know not what we should pray for as we ought: but the Spirit itself maketh intercession for us with groanings which cannot be uttered.

(27) And he that searcheth the hearts knoweth what is the mind of the Spirit, because he maketh intercession for the saints according to the will of God.

(28) And we know that all things work together for good to them that love God, to them who are the called according to his purpose.

A lot of the words were kind of hard to read. Greg had to admit he didn't understand most of it. He wasn't exactly sure what Brother Joseph's point with the scripture was. Maybe he'd ask him tonight. But he could understand bits and pieces. He noticed the word hope showed up a lot. Weird how it could talk about suffering and groaning in pain and then talk so much about hope right after that. *What was there to be hopeful about with all this suffering? Is that why Brother Joseph believed in God? Because without God there was no hope?* He looked down again at the last verse Brother Joseph had given him. "All things work together for good . . ." *How could that be true?* How could his sister dying, his dad leaving, getting tricked into coming to Chicago to be a runner for a dangerous gang and a psychotic supplier and then getting beat up ever work for good?

Greg rewashed his face, removing the tear streaks and trying to get the redness out of his eyes so no one would know he had been crying. He cleaned up the best he could and left his room with his skateboard. Oddly, though he disagreed with the scriptures, just reading about hope had rejuvenated him in some strange way. If Brother Joseph really believed this, Greg would see if he could point out some good in Greg's situation. He was ready to find Brother Joseph.

Greg reached the skate park without difficulty and walked up with his skateboard under his arm. *Ah, the skate park! There was a sight for sore eyes!* It was like an oasis in the desert or a ray of light in a dark tunnel. If Brother Joseph wasn't here, maybe Greg could simply forget his problems by skateboarding. It had worked before.

As he approached, he spied ten or twelve kids in and around the park, skating and talking. The boy and girl who had been making out the other night were on the bench again, sitting really close to each other and holding hands. Greg spotted Chris at the top of a ramp. *Doesn't he ever have anything else to do?* Greg wondered. Greg had met most of the kids that were there by this time. But as far as he could see, Brother Joseph wasn't there.

He walked closer and one of the kids noticed him. "Hey, Greg! What's up, man?"

Greg waved and walked in.

Chris skated over to him. "Hey, what happened to you?" he asked, motioning toward Greg's lip.

He doesn't beat around the bush, does he? thought Greg. "Uh, nothing," he lied, "I just took a spill on my skateboard."

"And cut your lip?" Chris asked. "Man, that must've been some biff! But if anybody could do it, you could," he said, draping his arm around Greg's shoulder. "Hey, check this out. I was almost able to do that heel flip today. Watch."

Chris showed him but biffed. Greg watched but was distracted. He needed to talk to Brother Joseph.

Chris laughed at himself and got up. "Wait, no, I can do it."

"Yeah, right, I'm sure you can," said Greg, grinning. "Uh . . .

I'm going to skate a bit, call me over when you get it."

"Aw, forget it," Chris said picking up his board. "I practiced that all day today. I'll skate over to the ramps with you."

Greg shrugged and the two skated over to the ramps. They had only been skating for a couple of minutes when a commotion outside the skate park caught Greg's attention.

"Whoa, what's going on over there?" Greg asked Chris.

"Hey, it's Brother Joseph!" Chris said, pointing.

Brother Joseph! Greg ran over to the chain-link fence. The youth pastor was standing outside the skate park with his hands held out in front of him, as if to convey he was non-threatening. The boy who had been on the bench with his girlfriend was advancing toward the preacher, a scary look in his eyes. His spiky jet-black hair glistened in the light as though he had used way too much gel.

His girlfriend was still on the bench, a confused and worried look in her eyes. "Steve?" she called out after the boy, brushing some of her short black hair with red highlights from her eyes.

The boy kept advancing. "Get out of here," he demanded in a low, threatening voice. "We don't want you here."

"Just take it easy, Steve," Brother Joseph said. "I'm not here to cause any trouble."

Steve suddenly leaped at Brother Joseph and swiped at him with his hand. Brother Joseph stumbled backward, barely avoiding the slap. "Don't lie to me!" Steve screamed. "I know what you're doing here! You've come here to make us leave!"

By now, all the kids in the skate park had stopped skating and were staring at the spectacle. "What's Steve talking about?" one of the kids asked. "Why would Brother Joseph want us to leave the skate park?"

But somehow Greg suspected it was something more. The way Steve was acting wasn't normal. There was something wrong. Steve was breathing hard. He glared at Brother Joseph, as if trying to intimidate him.

Brother Joseph began to take a tentative step toward him. "Steve . . ."

But the moment he moved, Steve tensed and raised his fists. "Don't take another step toward me!"

Brother Joseph stopped moving toward him but didn't back off. He held up his hands again. "Okay, Steve, okay. Please, calm down."

Steve shook his head wildly. "You need to leave," he repeated, his voice sounding strained.

"I can't." Brother Joseph's answer was solid and firm. "Jesus Christ has given me a message of light for the lost souls."

At that, Steve leaped forward, looking like he would strangle Brother Joseph. Quickly, Brother Joseph stepped out of the way, dodging Steve's attack. The momentum of Steve's lunge at the street preacher catapulted him forward and he tripped, falling onto the concrete sidewalk.

The street missionary cautiously began to approach him, but Steve began to writhe on the ground like some kind of a snake. Brother Joseph stopped, but understanding had lightened his eyes and a new resolve seemed to steel itself within him. Greg stepped back, even though he was inside the chain-link fence. *What is going on here?*

As soon as he stopped writhing, Steve jumped to his feet again and looked at Brother Joseph, then let loose a loud, terrifying scream. His girlfriend stumbled off the bench and ran backwards, horrified, then stopped, watching from a distance.

"Get out!" Steve yelled, taking another step toward Brother Joseph.

Brother Joseph looked straight into Steve's eyes. "No," he said in a calm but firm voice. "I have work to do here."

Steve began to circle him, his lanky body convulsing a little, and then began moving faster as he circled. "I know the work you have here!" he said, but the voice that came out of Steve was no longer his own. It sounded completely unnatural, more like a guttural snarl than a sentence.

Brother Joseph circled with him. "Steve? Can you hear me? Steve! Listen to me!"

Steve stopped running, but he was breathing hard and he wouldn't look Brother Joseph in the eyes. His hands were moving around like they were trying to find something to do but couldn't.

Brother Joseph took a step toward him and tried again. "Steve, listen to me. Jesus loves you."

Steve whirled around, facing the street preacher with his hands held out in front of him. "No! Please!" he cried. "Stay away from me!" To Greg's shock, he saw tears forming in Steve's eyes and begin to run down his cheeks. "Help me! It hurts!" he cried.

"Steve," Brother Joseph repeated. "I want to help you. I want to help you! But you have to let me!"

"No," Steve cried. "No, no! I can't! I can't! It hurts, it hurts! You're making it hurt!"

"I know," Brother Joseph said, his voice quivering. "It may have to hurt for a minute. But the only way to get completely healed is to go through that hurt. Sometimes pain has to be the passageway for something greater. I know what's wrong with you, and I want to help you. But you have to let me! Please let me help you, Steve!"

Steve was crying harder now, and suddenly he clenched his gut with his hand and doubled over and began heaving. A rumbling noise built itself up in his throat and spilled out over his lips, transforming into a horrible, terrifying scream that seemed to wind itself around Steve's face, which suddenly began to contort into an awful image. Greg's eyes widened. Again, he took a step back.

Brother Joseph suddenly put his hands up in the air and shouted, "In the name of Jesus, stop!" Immediately, dead silence followed. Steve stopped moving. "Stop, in Jesus' name," Brother Joseph commanded again. "Demon, I know you're in there."

At that, Steve hissed and raised his hands in a claw-like motion.

Brother Joseph continued, "But you no longer have any authority over this boy."

Then Steve's face contorted again into an image that reminded Greg of an orangutan, and vile cuss words and descriptions of evil began spilling forth from his lips in a voice and words that didn't seem to belong to Steve.

Immediately, Brother Joseph took an advancing step forward and raised his hand, murmuring as he did so, "In Jesus' name." This time, it was Steve who stepped back. Brother Joseph took another step repeating, "In Jesus' name," and Steve backed up again. "I'm not afraid of you!" he called to the preacher.

"Maybe not," responded Brother Joseph softly. "But you're afraid of the One I serve, and He has given me authority over you." And with that he took another step.

Steve bounced back again. "Stay away!" he shrieked. "You can't have him! He's mine! He's mine!"

Brother Joseph ignored the demon and looked directly into Steve's eyes. "Steve, do you want to be set free?"

"Nooooooo!" the voice screamed out of Steve.

"Be quiet!" Brother Joseph interrupted it, firmly. "I'm talking to Steve!"

Abruptly, Steve's mouth closed, but his eyes maintained

their wild look. "Steve," Brother Joseph repeated with more emphasis. "Do you want to be set free?"

Slowly, Steve looked at him and began to nod. All of a sudden, his body began convulsing again and he screamed. "Help!" he cried. "He's hurting me!"

Brother Joseph bounded to his side and laid a hand on his forehead. Steve squirmed, trying to get out from his grasp and swung his hands wildly, but Brother Joseph remained firm. Deliberately, and with some difficulty, Brother Joseph looked up into heaven briefly then said quietly, "In Jesus' name, Satan, I rebuke you. You have no more dominion over this boy. In the name of Jesus, demon, come out of him."

With that, Steve fell backwards and Brother Joseph lurched forward to keep him from hitting his head. Steve thrashed wildly on the ground, swinging his arms and legs and gnashing his teeth. There was another horrible scream that seemed to come from outside of Steve's body as he collapsed in a heap. It was finished.

Steve rolled over and lay on his back, tears streaming down his face. Brother Joseph leaned over him, breathing heavily as sweat dripped off his own forehead. "Steve?" Brother Joseph asked softly.

And then Steve was in Brother Joseph's arms, sobbing into his shoulder. Brother Joseph looked up into heaven and cried with him, thanking God for what had taken place. "Lord, you are great. God, I love you. It's okay, Steve, it's okay. It'll be all right now," he reassured him. "It's over. They don't have authority over you anymore." The two stayed that way for several long minutes while Brother Joseph gently rocked Steve and looked up to the sky, his eyes glistening and tears streaming down his face as he prayed for the boy. Nobody else moved or said anything.

Finally, Steve's girlfriend approached a little closer, still scared, and neared the bench she had been sitting at. "S–steve ?" she called timidly with a tremor in her voice. "A–are you okay?"

Brother Joseph wiped his eyes and waved her over. "Come here, Monica," he invited her, clearing his throat. "Let's you, me, and Steve go somewhere private where we can talk. I want to tell you both about the One who gave me the power to do that."

Brother Joseph stood to his feet and helped a shaking Steve to stand too. Steve stood with his head down, tears still flowing.

"B–but what just happened?" Monica felt anxious, still not coming closer but staying by the bench, eyeing her boyfriend warily. "Why was Steve acting like that?"

"He had a demon," said Brother Joseph simply and quietly. "And the demon in Steve recognized the Holy Spirit in me. Satan was struggling over control for his life. But now God wants to have it. Satan's control over you has been loosed, Steve, but Jesus told us that when a demon is cast out, he goes and finds seven other spirits more wicked than himself and comes back. If the house is swept clean and nothing is in there, he'll take control again. You have to stop that from happening. And the only way to do that is to fill your spirit with something else. Steve." Brother Joseph put a hand on the kid's shoulder and looked at him intently.

Steve wiped his eyes and looked up into the preacher's. "Yeah?"

"If you don't want the devil to have control over your life anymore, you have to give it to someone else. Completely. And I can tell you how to do that if you want."

Steve ran a hand over his nose and found himself nodding. "Yeah, preacher," he said in his normal voice, though it was broken and weak. "Talk to me. Talk to me."

Brother Joseph gently put an arm around Steve's shoulders

and motioned for Monica. "Then let's go over to the pavilion," he invited. "We can talk there."

The three of them walked off into the darkness toward a pavilion near the park. Greg watched them leave. The kids began to talk quietly amongst themselves.

Chris came up behind Greg, his eyes wide. "I've never seen anything like that!" he said. "What was that?"

Greg's eyes didn't leave the retreating figures. "I don't know," he admitted. *This has been a crazy night,* he thought.

Greg turned back to Chris. "I uh . . ." His voice caught and he cleared his throat. "Why do you think Steve was acting like that?"

Chris shook his head wildly. "I don't know, but I've never seen anything like that! I'm going to go ask those kids over there what they think!" Chris rushed off to compare ideas with the other skaters.

Greg stayed at his spot by the chain-link fence. He didn't know what had just happened with Steve and Brother Joseph, but it reinforced his desire to talk with Brother Joseph. Now he was certain Brother Joseph could be trusted. If he really didn't care about the kids, he wouldn't have stayed when Steve was acting so wild. And he wouldn't have been so caring and kind to Steve when the ordeal was over. In that moment, Greg made up his mind to tell Brother Joseph everything that had happened. In that moment, Greg decided to trust him.

Greg jumped up as soon as he saw Steve and Monica leaving the pavilion together. Brother Joseph had grabbed his Bible and was heading toward the parking lot. It was now or never.

Brother Joseph had his keys in his hand and was getting ready to walk through the parking lot when Greg approached him from the skate park, looked around, then shoved his hands in his pockets. Pausing, Brother Joseph jingled his keys, then put them back in his pocket. "Hi, Greg," he greeted him gently.

"Hey," Greg responded.

"What a night, huh?" Brother Joseph said, rubbing his eyes beneath his glasses. Suddenly the street preacher took a closer look at the skater. "What happened to your eye?"

Greg fumbled for an answer. "I . . . uh . . . well, that's kind of . . . I just got a little banged up . . . how did it go with Steve and his girlfriend?"

Brother Joseph raised his eyebrows at the change in subject but answered, "It went okay. I prayed with them. I think God will move in his life and use him if Steve will let Him." Brother Joseph's forehead wrinkled and he sighed slightly. "I wanted to go talk to his parents, but they've got some family issues and Steve didn't want me going over there. I'll probably be calling him tomorrow to make sure everything's still going okay. The devil's gonna want him back. He'll be a valuable asset to the kingdom of God."

"Oh . . . um, good." Greg stood there silently for a moment. He wasn't sure what all that meant, but he was impressed, he had to admit. *If Brother Joseph is a fake, he's an excellent actor.*

Brother Joseph seemed to realize Greg had more on his mind than the night's unfolding drama. His eyes focused on the skater, and he forced his thoughts to leave Steve and Monica and concentrate on this new problem. "What's on your mind, Greg?" he asked kindly.

"Uh . . . listen . . ." Greg struggled with his decision. Should he tell the Pentecostal preacher . . . the Christian . . . his problem?

Brother Joseph's gaze remained fixed on him. "Yes?"

Greg looked into his compassionate brown eyes behind his wire-rimmed glasses and took the plunge. "I need to talk to you," he said, swallowing hard.

"Okay," said Brother Joseph, giving Greg his full attention, waiting. "What about?"

Greg looked around at the bright lights of the skate park where kids were still lingering. "Uh . . . not here. Could we go somewhere else? Somewhere private?"

Brother Joseph answered, "Sure, why don't we go over to the pavilion where I took Steve and Monica?"

Greg nodded with his head down and scuffed the dirt with his toe.

"Well, let's go," said Brother Joseph.

The two walked over to the pavilion, which was barely lit by the lights from the skate park. They sat down at a picnic table, and Greg folded his hands on the table and stared at them. Brother Joseph waited patiently, gazing intently at him. Finally, Greg began his story, awkwardly at first, stumbling over words. As he began to release the story, though, he became more fluent and the words began bubbling out. Greg told the whole story of the skating contest, Stefan's deceit and treachery, his mom, coming to Chicago, the drugs, the gang—everything. Brother Joseph listened attentively, interrupting only to ask a clarifying question or two.

Greg finished by saying, "And that's what's happened. That's how I got this cut on my lip and how my eye got messed up. And . . . I . . . I don't know what to do. I think I've gotten in over my head."

Brother Joseph nodded silently and thought for a minute. "Have you talked to your mom about this, Greg?"

Greg shook his head vehemently. "No! No way! I could never

do that. My mom wouldn't understand, and . . . and I don't know what it would do to her. She would be so disappointed. And with my dad gone and . . . my little sister gone . . ." Greg choked back a sob and wiped his eyes. "I . . . I just couldn't, Brother Joseph."

Brother Joseph put his hand on Greg's shoulder. "Okay, Greg, okay. Um . . . oh boy." He let out a deep sigh. "Would you mind if we prayed right now?"

Greg shrugged and angrily wiped away another tear that was trying to form. "It wouldn't do any good," he mumbled. "God doesn't care about me anyway."

"That's not true, Greg," Brother Joseph said gently. "God does care. More than you know. He hates the hurt you have. He understands what you're going through and the pain you have. Greg, He knows you. And, believe it or not, He really does love you. Even if it doesn't seem like it in all the turmoil and uproar, God still cares."

Greg bit his lip, desperately trying to keep from crying. *What's wrong with me? Why are Brother Joseph's words affecting me like this?*

"Do you mind if I pray for you? You won't have to do anything. Just let me talk with God about you for a minute."

Greg shrugged again. Brother Joseph placed a hand on Greg's shoulder. Greg stared down at the picnic table as Brother Joseph began to pray. "Oh, God." There was a catch in his voice as he began. He stopped and he took a deep breath then began again. "Lord, I love You. Thank You for the ministry and burden You've given me for the youth at this skate park. And thank You for this child, Father, whom I know You love deeply. He's the one I want to lift up to You right now. Lord, You already know what he's going through. You know how he's hurting and what he's going to do next. Lord, reveal to us Your will in this situation. God, we want Your will to be done. Reach into his heart, because that's the main thing You're concerned about. Touch Greg. Surround him with Your angels and place Your protection upon him until this whole situation is settled."

The intimacy with which Brother Joseph prayed struck Greg. You'd have thought Brother Joseph was really communicating with God. It was as if he were talking to someone he knew. Greg could tell the prayer was from his heart. "Touch his mom, Lord," continued the street preacher, "who I'm sure loves him more than anything. I ask You to be with her and give her peace and comfort during this time. God, help her to lean on You. I bind the forces of darkness. The devil cannot have Your child. And Stefan has no authority over Greg in Jesus' name!"

Brother Joseph paused, and Greg thought he was done. But then Brother Joseph continued, "And Lord? Please show Greg that You love him. Make it real to him, Jesus, by Your own hand in an undeniable way. So that he knows that You love him."

Greg's head shot up to see if Brother Joseph were joking. But Brother Joseph still had his head bowed and eyes closed, with complete sincerity. *Is he serious?* Greg wondered. *He's asking God Himself to show me His love? Give me a break. If God really is who they say He is, He wouldn't stop everything to show someone as unimportant as me His love!*

Meanwhile, Brother Joseph was finishing his prayer. "In Your wonderful name, Jesus. Amen."

Greg looked up at him. Brother Joseph thought a moment then took a deep breath. "Well, tell you what, Greg. I'm meeting with a computer executive tomorrow in his office near this part of town to have a Bible study. I'll give you directions to the building. We should be done sometime around eleven o'clock. Come at eleven, and we'll see what we can figure out. Okay?"

Greg nodded. "Sure," he agreed trying to regain his composure.

"I'll be thinking and praying about your situation," Brother Joseph promised, looking Greg in the eye. "Tomorrow we'll talk about what we're going to do. I still have to work through some things tonight."

Greg nodded again. He felt an enormous relief just telling someone. Usually he didn't have this feeling, but tonight he did. He was glad to have someone to depend on.

"I guess I'm going to go back to my hotel now," he said.

"Do you want a ride?" Brother Joseph asked. "Or maybe even come to my house?"

"No thanks," Greg told him. "I don't want to just in case . . . well, in case Stefan's watching or something."

Brother Joseph dipped his head in acknowledgment. "All right then, tomorrow I'll see you at eleven. Please be careful, Greg. Do you have a cell phone with you? I can give you my number, and if you want to give me yours, we can connect that way." After exchanging numbers, Brother Joseph said, "I'll meet you tomorrow. God be with you, Greg."

Greg nodded and Brother Joseph walked back to his car. Greg watched him for a moment as he climbed in. Then the skater sucked in a shaky breath and took off into the darkness to return to his hotel.

Even though he felt like a huge burden had been lifted from his chest, he also felt a certain apprehension, a fear of what was going to happen next. He remembered Tony's warning, but he really didn't care. They couldn't do anything to him. He wasn't going to be going near the gang again, anyway.

But as he skateboarded down the street, he found himself glancing over his shoulder and jumping whenever somebody passed by. He skirted shady characters and drunks as much as possible, hoping to get to the hotel safely. A fear gripped him like he hadn't felt before. Thoughts of Al, Stefan, Tony, Steve, and Terrance ran rampant through his mind. It didn't help. He was getting edgier and edgier as he got farther and farther from the skate park and closer to the hotel. The demon-possessed kid's face was imprinted in his mind, and he couldn't seem to forget it. That wild look and evil voice sent shivers down Greg's spine every time he remembered it. And that scream! That horrible, taunting, evil scream! He skated into the street to avoid the opening of an alley and tried to stay in the light.

At last Greg arrived at his hotel. He was ready to go up to his room and get out of the night. As he came up to the front of the hotel, he saw movement over in the dark shadows on the side of the building. His heart was thudding in his chest, and he quickened his steps. Greg could vaguely make out the shadowy form of a man around the corner of the wall of the hotel. The man stepped out onto the sidewalk in front of the hotel, and Greg froze.

"Ah, Greg! I was wondering when you'd get here."

It was Stefan. But that didn't stop the pounding of his heart—in light of everything that had happened, it increased it. The voice was dripping with evil, or did it just suddenly seem that way to Greg? But there was no mistaking the coldness and the hardness in Stefan's face. Even with his fake smile plastered on, a sense of foreboding was still lingering in his features. And the fact that his eyes were constantly covered by sunglasses— even now in the dark of night—didn't help any.

"Come over here, out of the light, Greg, so no one sees us. Let's have a talk."

9

The red eyes of Gazez blazed like embers of hatred and malice as he gazed at the skater, yet a strange smile darkened his ghoulish face. He relished the destruction of human souls, and here was a young mortal being racked with fear and anguish. The skater was trembling slightly, perhaps not enough for anyone else to notice, but the tremor of the boy's hands did not escape the notice of Gazez, as an experienced, battle-hardened demon.

Of course the defeat at the skate park was regrettable. It was unfortunate and a devastating loss to the kingdom. Several demons would be severely punished in flames of fire tonight even though there was little that could have been done. The Name was too powerful, and no devil could stand against the Enemy's presence. However, Gazez did not need to concern himself with the effects of that battle in the least. He had a different project he was working on. The destruction of this soul. And even that awful defeat of the kingdom of darkness could be used to accomplish the evil of Satan. The night had obviously affected the kid, and that could be capitalized on right now.

Stefan crooked his finger at the skater. "Come here," he said indicating that Greg should come over into the shadows.

Greg stayed where he was. "Why . . . uh . . . why can't you come over here?" he asked, his mouth suddenly dry.

A surprised smile touched Stefan's face. "Why would I?" he said with a little chuckle. "We don't want anyone to see us, right?"

Greg shrugged but didn't move. Stefan waited a moment, then with a sigh he walked out into the light, glancing over one shoulder, then the other, to make sure no one was around. "At least it's nighttime," he muttered under his breath. "Why must you make things so difficult?" he asked Greg, facing him.

Greg didn't say anything, just stared at him with a guarded expression.

Stefan held out his hand. "Well?"

Greg looked at him. "Well what?"

Stefan rolled his eyes, impatiently. "Come on, Greg, what's wrong with you? You did deliver the box, right?"

"You mean the drugs, don't you?" Greg asked with a bite to his tone.

"Yes, the drugs," Stefan agreed, with a small smile, unfazed. "How did it go?" He looked at the cut on Greg's eye and snickered. "I see they gave you a warm welcome."

"Actually that was their goodbye," Greg shot back. "You didn't tell me it was going to be a gang I was giving the box to."

Stefan shrugged. "What's the difference? They would've done the same thing to you whether I told you who they were or not."

Greg bit his tongue, resisting the urge to lash out. He didn't want to make Stefan angry even though the man was making him mad.

Stefan looked pointedly and wiggled the fingers of his outstretched hand. "So . . . where's the money?"

Greg's hands started to get clammy. "What money?" he asked.

Stefan narrowed his eyes at him and said fiercely, "The money for the drugs, of course. Don't play games with me."

"I . . . I already gave you the money! You had me get it on the first night!"

"Do you think Al and his gang are the only ones I do business with?" Stefan shot back. "That was from a different deal. Now where's the money Al gave you?"

Greg's face went white and he shook his head.

"Don't play games with me!"

"I . . . I'm not! They, they never gave me any money!"

Stefan seethed and grabbed Greg's shirt threateningly.

"You never told me I was supposed to get money!" Greg protested defensively. "You just told me to drop off the box! I didn't know!"

Stefan raised his arm as if he were going to hit him. Greg cringed expectantly. Suddenly, Stefan's eyes were drawn to something behind Greg. His mouth opened and his arm froze in midair. "What the . . ."

Greg looked behind him to see what Stefan was looking at. He couldn't see anything that might have caught the evil drug lord's attention.

Abruptly, Stefan let go of Greg's shirt and took a step back. Greg looked at him, confused, his eyes asking for information. Stefan cleared his throat and nervously stuck a hand in his suit pocket, trying to appear casual. "Well . . ." he continued, then stopped.

Greg was shocked. What had rattled Stefan so much? He had never seen Stefan look uncomfortable before, as he was looking now. And strangely, as Greg watched Stefan, his fear left him. A certain peace came over him.

"Well," said Stefan again, struggling to regain his composure. "You are most certainly not getting your money until you get the other money from that gang!" Stefan shuffled his feet and looked over his shoulder. It was obvious that he had suddenly grown uneasy for some reason. Greg was bewildered at the sudden change that had come over his "employer" but didn't care to spend time dwelling on it.

"What do you want me to do?" Greg asked him, stifling a yawn and feeling his eyes growing heavy—noting with surprise that he was no longer scared of Stefan since he was now yawning in front of the man!

"I'll contact you tomorrow," Stefan told him, his eyes still searching the area surrounding them. "Sometime before ten o'clock in the morning. You're going back to get that money. Do you understand?"

Greg didn't say anything. He was supposed to meet with Brother Joseph at 11. Will this conflict?

"Do you understand?" Stefan asked again, sharply this time, looking at Greg.

"Why at ten?" Greg asked him.

"Do I have to have a reason for everything?" Stefan shouted at him.

Greg stared at him. Stefan seemed to realize he had just lost his temper and took a deep breath, forcing a smile. "Uh . . . listen, I . . . we need to get the money as soon as possible, all right? This is important, because the gang might not pay the rest now that they have the drugs in their possession. I should've gotten someone more suited for this work, but it's too late for that now. You're to be ready before ten, got it?"

Stefan's attitude changes were giving Greg a headache. The events over the last couple hours were beginning to take their toll on him.

"I'm tired and I wanna go to bed," Greg told him irritably, starting to walk past. "I'll talk to you tomorrow."

"Wait." Stefan grabbed his shoulder. Greg tensed and turned to look at him. Stefan opened his mouth to say something then closed it again. He stared at Greg for a long moment. "Uh, never mind. It's nothing," he said, licking his lips. "I'll contact you tomorrow sometime before ten," he said brusquely, a glare punctuating his sentence. He released Greg's shoulder, and Greg quickly turned and walked into the hotel. The skater didn't even look back. If he had, he would've seen Stefan's glare following him all the way in.

Gaddiel sheathed his sword, breathing heavily. He had caught Gazez off guard. But he knew the demon wouldn't let up without a fight. The demon was strong, and Greg was weak. He knew if it hadn't been for Brother Joseph's prayers, he would have lost this battle, and Greg may have been harmed.

Greg's eyes flickered open the next morning sometime around nine o'clock. He yawned and started to get up when a searing pain had him flopping right back down on his pillow. The cuts and bruises from his beating the night before added discomfort to his already sore limbs. With a groan, he sank farther back into the comfort of the pillow.

His first thought was remembering Steve's tormented face before Brother Joseph cast the demon out of him. Remarkably, Greg had not had any nightmares about the incident. Peaceful sleep had ruled the entire night. The last thought Greg had before drifting off to sleep was wondering what had caused Stefan to be so uncomfortable around him. His mind returned to Brother Joseph's prayer the night before. "Touch Greg. Surround him with your angels, and place your protection upon him until this whole thing is settled." Could that be the reason he hadn't had any bad dreams? The encounter with Stefan flashed into his mind. *Maybe the prayer was even the reason for Stefan's sudden nervousness last night . . . Nah.*

Greg brushed the thought aside and forced himself to sit up, ignoring his aching ribs. He glanced at the clock then stiffly rose, grabbed some fresh clothes from his suitcase, and headed for the bathroom.

After his shower, while trying to fix his hair, Greg's cell phone rang. Even after being awake for a while, Greg moved sluggishly to answer the phone. "Hello?" he said, groggily.

"Hey, Greg, how are you doing this morning?"

It was Brother Joseph on his way to the Bible study, calling to give Greg directions. Greg fumbled to find the pad of paper and a pen hotels always seem to supply, and wrote them down.

"Okay, I just got to the building," Brother Joseph informed him. "I've got to go. See you at eleven, Greg."

"Okay, later."

The teenager had scarcely hung up when his phone rang again. Greg answered without looking at the caller ID, thinking maybe Brother Joseph had forgotten something.

"Gregory?" the voice on the other end said.

"Mom?" Greg asked with a little bit of surprise. He hadn't been thinking about his mom. *I should've known she'd be calling.*

"How are you doing?" she asked.

"Okay," Greg responded. He felt a sudden urge to tell his mom what had been going on. The concern in her voice reminded him that she cared. But then, just as quickly, he felt a sudden panicked urge to hide it from her. She couldn't find out, no matter what. He had to keep this whole thing a secret.

"I thought you were going to call me yesterday," his mom said.

"Oh yeah, I forgot. I was really busy with the contest and stuff."

"So how's the contest been going?"

"Uh, great. Yeah, great! I'm having a blast!"

"Good, so you've competed already?"

"Um . . . no. I mean, yes!" Greg squeezed his eyes shut. Oh brother. He hadn't planned on what he was going to say. He wasn't ready to talk to his mom! "I, uh," Greg cleared his throat. "I went the other day."

There was a short pause on the other end. "Gregory? Are you sure you're doing okay, honey? You don't sound—"

"No, no, no, I'm fine, I'm fine. And don't call me Gregory. I'm just a little tired. I only got up a few minutes ago."

"Oh, I see," his mom said in a voice Greg could tell meant she didn't believe him. "Have you been staying up late?"

Great. How do I get out of this one? "Well . . . sort of. I've been hanging out with some kids I met at the contest, skating with them at the skate park."

"So you've made some friends?"

Greg couldn't tell whether she thought that was good or bad. "Yeah. They're really cool. I've been . . . well, I went out to eat the other night with them, and it was fun."

"Oh. Good. So the people at the contest have been treating you well?"

"Uh-huh." *If only you knew, Mom.*

"Well, tell me about it! How do you think you did? Did you do well?"

"I did okay." That's it, Greg praised himself. Give her short, generic answers so she won't get a lot of information.

"I read in the packet of information that the best contestants will compete in the finals. Is that happening today?"

"Uh . . ." Great, what did the packet say? "No. I think that's tomorrow. Today more kids will go, then they'll announce the finalists tonight."

"Oh. Um . . . do you think you're a finalist?"

Suddenly the phone beeped in his ear. Greg held it out and saw Call Waiting on the display. It wasn't Brother Joseph's number. In fact . . . Oh no.

"Gregory?" his mom's voice came from the phone. "Are you still there?"

"Huh? Oh yeah . . . I um . . . what did you ask?"

"I asked if you thought you were a finalist."

"Oh, right. I don't know. I guess I'll find out tonight." The phone beeped demandingly again. As much as Greg didn't want to talk to Stefan, if he didn't . . . well, he knew that Stefan wasn't above physical violence. Or getting someone else to be physically violent, like Al and his gang. "Hey, Mom, an official from the contest is trying to call in. I've got to go."

"An official? Are they calling to announce the finalists?"

"Uh . . . no, probably not. He's probably just calling to let me know when I need to be back at the skate park."

"Oh, well make sure you call me after you find out about the finalists, okay?"

"Uh, yeah, sure." There went the phone again. "Hey, I've got to go."

"All right. I love you, Gregory. Make sure you call if you need anything."

"Okay, I will. Talk to you later. Goodbye."

Greg ended the call and quickly switched over. "Hello?"

"How come it took you so long to answer?" Stefan's irritated voice came over the phone.

Greg rolled his eyes. *I guess he's not one for hellos.* "I was on the phone with my mom."

"Well, I don't have long. Next time, think of a way to end the conversation quicker."

Greg gritted his teeth against a cuss word that was dancing on his tongue, waiting for a chance to come out.

"I set it up on my end of things," Stefan continued. "You're to meet Al and his gang in the same alley on Yorkshire at eleven forty-five. My sources tell me the gang should be there around that time. You don't need to stay long, got it? All you need to do is get the money and move out. If you had gotten it right the first time, this wouldn't even be necessary."

"Hey, it wasn't my fault the first time!" Greg yelled into the phone. "All you told me to do was deliver the box to Al!"

"All right, all right, calm down, kid. Just don't let us down this time. Everyone's nerves are on edge. I need you to come through for us, okay?"

"Okay," Greg said grudgingly, running his fingers through his hair.

"I'll talk to you sometime tonight. And get you your money," he added as an afterthought, "if you do everything right. There's a lot riding on you, Gregory."

Since when did Stefan start calling me Gregory? "Just call me Greg," Greg instructed him, some irritation coming out in his voice.

Stefan laughed. "Very well. I'll see you tonight." With that, the line went dead.

Slowly, Greg hung up the phone and ran his fingers through his hair. *Hopefully Brother Joseph has come up with a plan.*

Greg reached the building and carried his skateboard up the steps. A little self-conscious, he began to tuck in his shirt and adjust his backwards cap. The building was tall and impressive looking. The sun reflected off the windows while their spotless glass glared down at Greg. The bushes in front were all neatly trimmed. Even the railing leading up the concrete steps to the doors was clean. An immaculate white sign out front announced that this was the computer software company where Brother Joseph had told Greg he was having his Bible study.

Greg reached the sliding doors, leaned his skateboard against the side of the building, and began to walk in, wondering what he was supposed to do now. Brother Joseph hadn't given Greg any instructions about what to do when he arrived, just to wait for him.

Greg approached the reception desk, where a secretary was busily typing away at a computer. Suddenly, he wasn't sure of what he was supposed to say. Should he tell her he was looking for Brother Joseph? No, that wouldn't make any sense. This was a large company, and the secretary probably didn't even know all of the employees' names, let alone everyone who met with the employees. Greg didn't remember Brother Joseph saying the name of the person he was meeting with. Maybe I'll just wait here.

The secretary paused her typing and looked up. "Yes, can I help you?"

"Uh, no, I'm just waiting for someone."

The secretary moved her hand over to the intercom. "Would you like me to page this person?"

"No, it's okay. I'll just wait."

The secretary tapped her long red fingernail on her lips. "There's no loitering, you know," she said, running her eyes over Greg's skating attire.

Greg rolled his eyes. "I'm just waiting for someone! Why would I want to loiter here anyway?"

The secretary started to say something, but then the phone rang. With one last warning glance at Greg, she answered, her voice immediately transformed as she cheerily thanked the person on the other end for calling and asking how she could be of help.

Greg looked around and sat down in a soft easy chair over against the wall by a glass coffee table. The secretary finished her phone call and went back to work, now ignoring Greg. Five minutes passed. Greg sighed and rested his chin in his hand, slumping down further into the chair.

Ten minutes later the elevator finally dinged. Greg got up from the couch, feeling irritated at Brother Joseph for taking so long. Brother Joseph and a man in a suit got off the elevator. Brother Joseph's eyes immediately searched the room, caught sight of Greg, and shot him an apologetic glance, mouthing the word, "Sorry."

The man was still very caught up in the conversation with Brother Joseph, but as they walked into the lobby, he spotted Greg and shot the secretary a questioning glance. "What is he doing in here?" he asked.

Brother Joseph immediately stepped up before the secretary could answer. "This is the next appointment I told you about. His name is Greg."

"He's the one you're meeting with?" the man said in a tone that suggested he was really asking, "Why in the world are you making time for a teenage skater?"

Brother Joseph nodded as if it were the most ordinary thing

in the world and turned to Greg. "I'm sorry it's taken so long, Greg," he apologized.

The man shook his head and shrugged. "I'm sure a small delay in his skateboarding plans won't make a difference," he said with a wave of his hand. Greg felt his cheeks grow hot. "This is actually a perfect example of what I'm talking about. You're so caught up in the fruitless process of trying to deal with each individual kid . . ." He shot a glance at Greg, which Greg felt no scruples about returning with a glare. ". . . when we could be implementing programs that impact the culture at large by instilling good values into them." The man turned back to Brother Joseph as if Greg had ceased to exist.

Brother Joseph nodded patiently. "I understand your perspective, but that's my whole point. Good values alone won't help to eradicate evil."

Greg shifted impatiently. Here these people were philosophizing about evil, when he was caught in the throes of it and needed help right now . . . in just a few minutes, in fact!

"I don't follow you," the man said. "Surely the only way to counteract evil is by educating people to do what's right."

"The only true way to counteract evil is by the blood of Jesus Christ," Brother Joseph said in quiet but firm disagreement. "That is the only true antidote for sin."

The man waved his hand dismissively and looked away as if suddenly bored with the topic. "Yes, yes, you keep bringing that up. Look, I'm fine with talking about Jesus and God as we implement these programs. Jesus taught good principles about morality, and if we emphasize that God's example is one of love, it can certainly be used as a teaching point for those who have that sort of background. What frustrates me is that you seem to want to isolate a huge segment of the population by getting hung up on things like baptism and things that don't really have any real, practical effect on these young people's lives."

Brother Joseph shook his head and his voice lowered slightly as he said with heavy conviction, "On the contrary, baptism has everything to do with their lives."

The man rolled his eyes. "Oh come on! I'm talking about kids selling drugs and vandalizing buildings and raping young girls and growing up as menaces to society! I want to teach them about basic morality, while you want to tell them they need to get dunked in water to join a church or something! What's more important?"

Brother Joseph chuckled slightly but held firm. "I think there's a misunderstanding about what the root issue is."

"I agree," the executive said.

The street preacher ignored the comment. "The Bible is very clear what baptism is all about, and it's not just about getting dunked under water to join a church. It's about being buried with Jesus Christ and rising again to walk in new life. See, the problem with these kids isn't education. The problem is that they need a heart change. They need new life. I know many kids that have a basic understanding of morality but choose to do what's wrong and evil anyway. Why?"

He paused, but the man didn't say anything. Brother Joseph continued, "It's because the problem is with their hearts, not their heads. They need a change of life. Their sins don't merely need to be pointed out but washed away. And the only way remission of sins is possible is through Jesus Christ, and His death, burial, and resurrection. What you see as mere jargon and ritual is in actuality a new birth—the beginning of a brand new life of following God."

Greg shifted uncomfortably as he listened to the exchange. He actually would have rather sided with the other guy's opinion, even though he hated the way that the guy was just philosophizing rather than doing something about the problem of evil like Brother Joseph seemed to be doing. Greg's philosophy of life had always been to just be a good person and help other people, inasmuch as it served him. But here Brother Joseph was saying that wasn't enough and he needed to believe in Jesus to be good? Maybe Brother Joseph really was one of these closed-minded Christians. If he hadn't been the only one who had shown an interest in actually doing something to help Greg, Greg would have rejected his ideas outright. But maybe he could put up with the man's strange ideas in exchange for help out of this mess he was in.

Greg glanced out the window and suddenly caught sight of a slender form coming gracefully up the steps toward the computer software company. Is that . . . what's her name? Ismeralda? Sure enough, when she brushed some of her long black hair out of her face, she saw Greg looking at her and waved. Greg waved back but was confused. *What is she doing here? Does this mean I won't get to talk to Brother Joseph alone?*

"Still," the executive was saying after a brief silence, "it seems like by always talking about the blood of Jesus and Christian ritual and tradition, you are isolating a lot of people that could be helped by just being taught good values. People will agree on the characteristics you talk about God having, like love and mercy without needing to go through any Christian rituals."

"Good values don't mean anything without the blood of Jesus," Brother Joseph asserted.

At that moment, Ismeralda entered the doors of the company and called out cheerfully, "Hi, Brother Joseph!"

The secretary shot Ismeralda a warning glance, then looked at the executive, exasperated at all the young people intruding on their place of business.

Brother Joseph saw her and smiled briefly, giving her a little wave.

Ismeralda saw the man standing next to Brother Joseph and put her fingertips over her mouth. "Oops, I'm sorry. I didn't mean to interrupt."

"Hang on, Ismeralda," Brother Joseph said. "We'll be done in a second."

The executive ignored Ismeralda and said, "Joseph, all I'm saying is that I am not as interested in the individual cases because I want to influence society as a whole. I don't understand why you're so involved with these young people when you could be influencing laws and legislation and providing programs so that these juvenile delinquents can become more accountable to society."

"The kind of change you're talking about can only start by transformation in the lives of individuals, which is only possible by the blood of Jesus."

Greg tapped his foot impatiently, then looked up to see that Ismeralda had crossed over to stand beside him. "I should have known he'd still be talking," she whispered to him. "Once you get Brother Joseph going, he doesn't stop!" She winked.

Greg rolled his eyes and grinned. "Yeah, they've been at it since I got here," he responded in a low voice. Despite not having Brother Joseph all to himself, he liked this girl. Maybe it'd be okay if she stayed.

Brother Joseph seemed to be finishing up. "So in each individual's life, it is in reaction to the incredible grace that Jesus has shown to us by dying on the cross, and in gratitude to His great love, we think of ourselves as being dead to sin but alive to Him. Believing in His attributes like love and mercy is great, and that's where it starts, but it's not where it ends. Reacting to His love is the most important thing you will ever do in your life, and that's what brings about real change."

The executive looked at his watch. "Well, I really should be going. I enjoyed our discussion."

"As did I," said Brother Joseph warmly, grasping his hand. "Hopefully we can talk again sometime."

The man nodded. "I don't agree with all of your ideas, but there's something different about you, and I appreciate you, Joseph. We'll talk again soon."

The executive headed back up to the elevator, and Brother Joseph turned to Ismeralda and Greg. "Sorry. That took longer than I thought," he said with a smile. Looking at Greg, he explained, "Ismeralda is coming along with me to pass out flyers for the service tonight after this."

"Oh, okay," Greg said, looking at the clock. 11:20. "Um, Brother Joseph, can I talk to you over here for a second?"

Brother Joseph also looked at the clock, then took a glance at the clearly frustrated secretary and motioned for Greg to go outside. "Why don't we talk out here? Ismeralda, would you mind dividing the flyers into two separate stacks? I didn't have a chance to do that this morning."

Ismeralda nodded cheerfully. "Where are they?"

"They're in the backseat of my car. Here are the keys," he said, tossing them to her. "Come over here, Greg."

The two walked a short distance off, in front of the computer company on the sidewalk. The traffic roared by and Greg noticed the sky was beginning to cloud up again.

"So what's going on?" asked Brother Joseph, facing Greg. "Has something else happened?"

Greg nodded and solemnly told him about meeting up with Stefan last night, and how the money mix-up occurred. Brother Joseph looked thoughtful when Greg got to the part about Stefan's sudden nervousness and asked him to describe how Stefan was acting before allowing Greg to go on with the story.

"Anyways, I'm supposed to meet the gang at eleven forty-five, which is in like . . . twenty minutes."

"Well, then we'd better get going," Brother Joseph answered.

Greg raised his eyebrows and took a step back in surprise. "We?" he asked.

"Of course," Brother Joseph said, beginning to walk back toward the car, waving for Greg to follow. "I'm not letting you go alone this time, and you might not make it in time on your skateboard. Besides, it will give us a chance to talk about what to do."

Greg followed behind, shaking his head. Brother Joseph never ceased to amaze him.

Before they got to the car, Brother Joseph fell in step with Greg and lowered his voice. "I was going to drop Ismeralda off to pass off flyers before we talked, but now since you have to meet the gang so soon . . . Do you mind if Ismeralda overhears what we're talking about? I can promise you beyond a shadow of a doubt that she's trustworthy, but I completely understand if you don't feel comfortable talking about it around her. If not, I can pick her up later after I take you."

Greg thought for a moment then shook his head. "No, it's okay," he assured the preacher. "If you trust her, I trust her."

Brother Joseph nodded and opened the passenger side door for Greg before going around to the driver's side. Greg's statement surprised even himself; he hadn't really thought about what he was saying. But it was true. He did trust Brother Joseph, he realized—in a way he hadn't trusted many people before. And he had only known the man for a couple days! What made him feel so comfortable around the street preacher? Was it his sincerity? Or the way he connected with teenagers? No, Greg decided. That was part of it. But the peace enshrouding the preacher was rooted deeper than that.

Greg got in the small silver Saturn, and Brother Joseph turned in his seat to ask Ismeralda, "Are you ready to go?"

Ismeralda looked up from the flyers and flashed a grin. "I'm ready for whatever you can throw at me."

Brother Joseph chuckled and started the car. He pulled out of his parking place in front of the building and out into the busy street. Like someone who had lived in Chicago for a while, he skillfully navigated through the heavy traffic and headed in the direction of Yorkshire.

Then Brother Joseph turned to Greg. "I've been thinking about what to do," he told the skater. "And maybe the three of us can come up with a solution. Do you mind if I fill in Ismeralda on what's happened?"

Greg shook his head, and Brother Joseph gave Ismeralda a summary of Greg's adventure, telling her only what she needed to know and leaving out any details he thought were irrelevant or that might embarrass Greg. Ismeralda listened quietly through the whole thing. When he finished, there was a silence in the car, as if nobody felt like they could lift the weight of the situation with a suggestion.

Finally, Ismeralda spoke up. "Aren't you already working to stop the gangs from selling drugs?"

Brother Joseph sighed and nodded affirmatively. "Any true preacher of the gospel is always working to stop the control of Satan on people. But, to answer your question more directly, yes, I am more involved in stopping the drug trade than others. The problem is that so many people are selling drugs that it's hard to make any difference. Even if a couple people who sell drugs get arrested, it won't make a big impact.

"But if this is as big as you say, Greg, I'm thinking that Stefan is the leader of a large drug ring. He's probably got lots of influence in the drug industry and hundreds of contacts and people working for him. Drugs make good money, so it's not hard to get people interested in helping out. If we can somehow stop Stefan, it might bring a major drug ring to an end. He seems to be the link between those selling drugs and the smugglers. It looks like he's a supplier for the gangs. So . . ." Brother Joseph drummed his fingers on the steering wheel. "What we need from here is information. We need proof against Stefan. Names, dates, places, stuff like that. Find out how big this is, so we can stop it."

Greg nodded. "I can probably do that."

"And since you're involved with the whole thing, you'll be able to get a lot more information than I ever could. And then when we have some solid evidence, we can go to the police with what we know, and—"

Greg bolted upright in his seat. "What? No! No police!"

Brother Joseph gave Greg a quizzical look. "But . . . don't you—"

"You said it yourself! I'm involved with the gangs and the drugs and Stefan and everything. If we go to the police I'll get in trouble, and Stefan will just find some way to pin it on me! I know it! We can't go to the police!"

"But . . . how else can we stop the gangs? What were you thinking of doing if we don't go to the police?"

"I . . . I don't know. But I can't go to the police. I already almost got caught by one policeman, and . . . I . . . I just couldn't."

"But then," spoke up Ismeralda softly from the backseat, "why did you come to Brother Joseph to help you?"

Greg looked down at his familiar skateboard, suddenly feeling uncomfortable. "I . . . all I wanted was to get out of this whole thing. I didn't want to go to the police."

"So you don't care if it gets stopped or not? You just want to get yourself out?" Ismeralda asked a little sharply.

"Ismeralda," Brother Joseph said in a low, warning voice.

"Well, yeah, I guess," Greg agreed.

"Then why didn't you just ride it out, instead of coming to Brother Joseph? It sounded like Stefan only needed you for a couple days. If you don't really care about all the people getting hurt by drugs . . ." Ismeralda's voice was growing angrier.

Greg turned in his seat to face her. "What are you saying?" he demanded.

Ismeralda threw her hands up in the air. "I'm saying you shouldn't be so selfish, thinking only of yourself and not of the people we're trying to help! The people whose lives are being ruined by the drugs you—"

"Ismeralda, that's enough," Brother Joseph reprimanded her sharply. Ismeralda fell silent.

Greg gritted his teeth and turned away from her to face out the windshield. An awkward silence prevailed for a few minutes. "I can't go to the police," Greg muttered resolutely.

"Okay, Greg. It's okay," Brother Joseph assured him, trying to break up the tension. "You don't have to go to the police yet, okay? Just think about it, will you?" Greg didn't say anything and Brother Joseph sighed. "Just get some information about the whole operation, and we'll take it from there, crossing each bridge as we come to it, all right?"

Greg nodded, still upset with Ismeralda. *Who does she think she is, anyway? Telling me I'm selfish!*

Silence reigned in the car for several minutes. Finally, Brother Joseph came to the street leading to Yorkshire.

Greg put his hand on the door handle. "You can just let me off here," he suggested.

Brother Joseph grew somber and shook his head grimly. "This is a bad part of town, Greg."

Greg smiled wryly and pointed to the bruise on his cheek. "I know. I've been here before, remember?"

Brother Joseph bit his lip. "I'd feel a whole lot better if I could drop you off at the actual alley, so I could be close by if something went wrong."

It was Greg's turn to shake his head. "No, that would just make it worse. They'd know something was up. It'll be better if you drop me off right here."

Reluctantly, Brother Joseph pulled up to the curb and gnawed at his lip for a moment. Then he turned to Greg and confirmed, "You've got your cell phone, right?"

Greg nodded.

"Put me on speed dial, so you can have your hand ready on the button if you need help."

Greg agreed to the plan and took a few minutes to do just that. He wasn't exactly looking forward to the meeting with the gang himself.

Greg didn't have any more excuses for staying in the car, so he put his hand on the door handle.

"We'll be waiting right here in case anything happens," Brother Joseph reminded him.

Greg didn't answer but got out with his skateboard.

"God be with you, Greg," Brother Joseph said softly. "And be careful."

Greg gave him a brief smile and closed the car door. Inside, his heart was pounding. If there was anything he did not want to do, it was face Al and his gang again. But it was too late. He was walking down toward Yorkshire to the alley where the gang would inevitably be waiting for him again. But this time, he was doing it knowing he was trying to betray them. That made Greg's fear even worse.

Greg put down his skateboard and apprehensively began to skate toward his meeting place with the gang. He had asked Brother Joseph to drop him off before he got to Yorkshire, just to be safe. He wanted to make absolutely sure the gang didn't see Brother Joseph. Now, he turned on Yorkshire. This is it. He was out of Brother Joseph's view. He was on his own from here.

Greg skated down the sidewalk to the alley. The street was as forbidding as he remembered it. But this time, nobody was on it. At last he reached the alley and turned the corner. Al, Michael, and two other gang members were in plain view now, obviously waiting for him. All except Michael were smoking.

The moment Al saw Greg, he jumped up and pointed. "There he is," he announced to his gang. The gang leader threw down his cigarette, crushed the light out with his heel, and started toward Greg, his nostrils flaring. "You! Kid! Get over here!"

As he said this, the other guys began following him. And they didn't look happy. In fact, they looked rather angry.

Greg grasped for his cell phone in his jeans pocket and put his hand on the button, ready to press it if anything happened, and held up his other hand.

"Look," he told them in a shaky voice. "I'm just here for the money, that's all. I didn't know I was supposed to get it last night. St–Stefan never told me to. Honest. There's no reason to get angry about it or anything."

Al had reached him by this time and grabbed him by the shirt. "That's not what we're angry about, punk. Get in here," he said, jerking Greg forward.

The other gang members parted as Al forced Greg into the alley and up against the wall.

With a swift flick of his wrist, Al had his knife out. "You didn't deliver all the goods, kid, and we ain't paying you no money till we gets it all."

10

Stefan threw a roll of packing tape against the wall and yelled in frustration. Then he whirled toward Terrance, who was leaning against the wall, his face expressionless. "Why can't you idiots ever get anything right?" Stefan was furious. Terrance didn't respond, and Stefan began pacing. "Nothing's been going right lately!" he cried, throwing his hands up in the air. He turned on Terrance again. "How big was the mix-up?" he demanded.

Terrance slowly uncrossed his arms and stood upright. "Nearly half of what they were supposed to receive never arrived."

Stefan clenched his fists into tight balls, causing his knuckles to go white. "Why did you—" He seethed through his teeth, apparently too angry to think of how to finish.

"Maybe they won't notice," another man suggested from the corner, his face partially hidden by the shadow of boxes, looking as if he were ready to duck in case Stefan's wrath was directed toward him.

Stefan delivered a swift kick to a cardboard box, sending it skidding across the room, and punched the wall. "Of course they'll notice!" he shouted. "These are drug addicts! Drugs are their life! They paid for a certain amount and they'll be expecting to get a certain amount. They weigh every speck of powder, and they will be furious when they don't get exactly what they wanted. There's no way they won't notice; don't be a fool!"

The man shrunk back and began loading up the boxes again. Stefan started pacing the length of the small room again. "They're gonna kill Greg," he muttered.

○———○

Al pressed Greg hard against the wall, slamming him into it. "What was you trying to pull, huh?"

"What are you talking about?! I did what I was supposed to do!"

Al leaned in so close Greg could smell the lingering smoke on his breath. "Don't give me that. You know what we do to—"

Greg was starting to get angry. "Why are you treating me like this?" he yelled. "I'm your only link to Stefan and you should—"

Al let out a roar and swung back his fist. Greg didn't see it till it connected with his eye. Al effortlessly lifted Greg a couple more inches off the ground and gripped the collar of Greg's shirt tighter, nearly choking the skater. "Yeah, tough guy?" Al hissed through his teeth, breathing hard. "You wanna finish that thought? Or should I just waste you now, since you ain't fol-lowin' your end of the deal anyway?"

Greg's face was pale as he grimaced. "Wh–what are you talking about?"

"We trusting you to deliver the stuff, and come to find out you didn't give us all we asked for!"

"Wh–what, but, I . . . I . . ."

"And the people we doin' business wit' ain't gonna be happy

'bout it neither!" Al continued angrily without waiting for Greg to respond. "You costin' us valuable money!"

"I . . . I didn't know anything about it," Greg said in a barely audible voice that was choked with fear.

Al snorted in disgust and threw Greg to the ground. The gang leader walked a couple steps away and clenched and un-clenched his fist. Greg couldn't remember ever being so scared in his life. The black man's anger was flaring dangerously close to rage.

Suddenly Al turned and grabbed Greg by the shirt collar, forcing him up against the wall again. "Now listen to me," he said in a low voice. "I don't think you had nuthin' to do with this. And I need to keep Adikema as a contact. So I gonna let you go—"

"What!" one of the gang members shouted in shock. "You gonna let him go?"

"Shut up, Junior!" Al yelled.

Junior, who was maybe only half an inch shorter than Al, threw his hands up in the air. "We should kill this kid for—"

Al swore and pointed a finger at Junior. "I'm the leader, and I said he didn't have nuthin' to do with it, so shut up!"

Junior's fists clenched.

Al pointed at the other gang members. "If he does anything stupid, you know what to do."

Junior cursed and dropped his fists. "I ain't gonna do nothing stupid," he said. "I think it's just stupid that we ain't gonna use him as an example."

"Well, we ain't, so quit mouthin' off. But listen, punk." Al looked at Greg again. "You are gonna go back to Adikema and get the right drugs and then you gonna meet us again. But don't meet us here. Meet us at the warehouse we was at before. It's at this address." Al reached into his pocket, pulled out a creased, folded piece of paper, and pressed it into Greg's palm.

"What if Purdo is there?" Michael piped up.

"If he is, we'll take care o' him." Al grunted. He looked Greg in the eye. "You ain't gonna let us down. Are ya, kid?"

Greg shook his head.

Al nodded in satisfaction. "Better not." He let go of Greg and shoved him down the alley away from the gang. Greg stumbled and grabbed his skateboard, which he'd dropped when Al grabbed him. Suddenly, the thought of returning to Stefan without the money horrified him. "Wait, what about the money?" he asked, turning around. The moment the question was out of his mouth he regretted it.

Al, Junior, and the rest of the gang were already angry, and there was no telling what they would do to him for a careless inquiry like that. But Al just snorted a laugh and motioned for Greg to leave. "We ain't givin' you nuthin', kid. Come back with the right goods. Then we'll talk money. Now scram!" Al took a threatening step toward him.

Greg needed no further encouragement. He nodded rapidly and took off running. The gang's guffaws reached his ears as he took off toward the corner where Brother Joseph's car was parked. Apparently they enjoyed making younger kids run for their lives.

Greg didn't stop running until he got to Brother Joseph's car. Brother Joseph jumped when he saw Greg coming and quickly reached over and opened the door for him. Greg practically leaped in and slumped down in the seat. "Greg, are you all right?" Brother Joseph asked the moment Greg was in the car.

"Start driving!" the skater ordered, out of breath. Brother Joseph started the engine and sped away from the dreaded Yorkshire Street. "What happened?" he asked, wide-eyed. "Are you all right?"

Greg pressed his fingers against his temples, covering his black eye so Brother Joseph couldn't see it. He felt like crying, but he couldn't do that in front of Ismeralda.

"Did they hurt you?" Ismeralda asked with genuine concern in her voice. "Do you need something out of the first-aid kit?"

Greg gritted his teeth and shook his head.

Brother Joseph eyed him. "I think he's fine," he finally said. They drove in silence for a couple of minutes.

"So what happened?" Brother Joseph asked softly.

Greg lifted his head a little and mumbled, "They didn't get the right amount of drugs or something. And they won't give me the money until they get them. I don't know what . . . what to . . ." Greg was beginning to choke up, so he let his voice trail off.

"Oh, Greg." Brother Joseph reached over and placed a hand on his shoulder for a moment before taking it away. "I'm going to pull off up here near the skate park. That's where we're going to start passing out the flyers."

Greg's black eye was beginning to throb now. He could hardly open it at all. *Another thing to show for God's so-called protection,* he thought bitterly. *God doesn't care. He's never cared. I don't know why I went to Brother Joseph.*

Brother Joseph pulled off on a side street and turned the key. With a final purr the engine died. The three of them sat there for a minute. Nobody said anything, and that was fine with Greg. All he really wanted to do was sulk. There was a click, click, click as they waited.

"Greg," Brother Joseph started.

Before he could say anything, Greg cut him off. "I don't want to talk about it right now."

Brother Joseph's eyes were full of concern. "But don't you think we should—"

"No, I mean it!" Greg interrupted. "I don't even want to think about it." He hung his head down lower and closed his eyes.

Nobody said anything for several minutes. Finally Brother Joseph said, "Hey, Greg, why don't you come with us to pass out flyers?"

Greg shook his head, looking down at his board. "I don't know . . ."

"Come on," Brother Joseph persisted, "it'll be fun. You might need something to take your mind off . . . well, you know."

Greg thought a moment. *I don't really have anything else to do, except go to the skate park again. But I'm not sure I want to pass out flyers.*

Brother Joseph cuffed him lightly on the shoulder. "Come on, don't leave me alone with Ismeralda! You've seen how feisty she can be." At this, the youth pastor turned and grinned at Ismeralda, who then smiled too. Greg bit back a smile of his own. Finally, Brother Joseph won out.

"All right," Greg agreed. "I guess I can."

Brother Joseph smiled, but suddenly the smile faded and he looked over at Greg as if he wanted to say something. Instead, with a sigh he changed his mind and got out of the car. But before he got out, Greg detected something else in his expression. It was something he couldn't quite place. *Hurt? That doesn't make sense. Why would Brother Joseph feel hurt for me? Nobody has before.*

Ismeralda had divided the flyers into three stacks while Greg was gone and now grabbed them as she too got out of the car. Greg stayed slumped down in his seat for a moment. He really didn't want to get out and act like everything was all right. But he didn't exactly feel like talking about it either. What he felt like doing was going to the hotel room and numbing his mind with TV. But the thought of going there alone made his stomach turn. Greg put his hand on his head. All these back-and-forth thoughts were making his head hurt.

At last he got up and opened his car door, just as Ismeralda was turning around. She let out a little gasp. "Greg! Your eye! You said they didn't hurt you!" she said in an accusing tone.

Greg shrugged his shoulders and shook his head. "You sound just like my mom," he grumbled.

Ismeralda reached back in the car and grabbed a water bottle filled with ice. "Don't be ridiculous," she scolded him. "You need some ice on that."

Greg waved her off. "Give me a break. I'm fine."

Ismeralda ignored him and held out the water bottle.

Greg shook his head. "I'm okay," he said. "I don't need any ice!"

Ismeralda put her hands on her hips and let out an exasperated sigh. "I may sound like your mom, but you sound just like my little brother." She waited a moment to give her next statement more weight, looking straight at him with her piercing green eyes. "He's three," she added.

Greg scowled at her. Ismeralda tossed her hair over her shoulder and returned his stare with her head cocked. Greg half-turned, and Ismeralda beckoned with her hand. "Come on, then, I'll put it on your eye for you, if you're too dense to do it yourself. I think there's a rag or something in here." She climbed back in the car and Greg looked to Brother Joseph for help. He could tell Brother Joseph was fighting back a smile. The street missionary lifted his hands as if to say, *What do you want me to do?*

Ismeralda reappeared and Greg grudgingly allowed her to put the frozen water bottle wrapped in a rag on his eye. She gingerly pressed against it, and Greg yelped with pain. "Hey, what kind of a nurse are you?" he demanded.

Ismeralda smiled sweetly. "A nurse who takes care of patients that need a little common sense pounded into them," she replied with a toss of her head. "Now keep that on your eye; you don't want it to get swollen."

Greg looked at her with his one good eye. "You want me to hold this water bottle against my eye the entire time we're going to be passing out flyers?"

"Maybe I can find something to wrap around your head to make it stay," she mused, rummaging through the first-aid kit.

"You've gotta be kidding. Who do I look like, Jack Sparrow?"

Ismeralda found some bandage and began winding it around Greg's head. "This is ridiculous," Greg muttered.

"It'll go away faster if I do this," Ismeralda said.

"Yeah, but in the meantime, I'll scare everyone away from your church service. 'Arr, hello there, matey, would ye like to go to a Bible study?'"

Brother Joseph laughed and Ismeralda suppressed a grin, trying to keep a stern face. "Arr, do ye want me to run ye through with me sword?" she said, imitating him.

Now it was Greg trying to keep back a smile. "Yes, please!" He groaned. "Put me out of my misery!"

Ismeralda finished her bandaging and stepped back to admire her handiwork. "There. Perfect," she said.

"This is crazy!" He turned to Brother Joseph for support. "I don't really have to wear this, do I?"

Brother Joseph grinned and waved for the two of them to follow. "Come on, let's get going. We're burning daylight."

Greg moaned. "You have to be joking! I hope none of the kids from the skate park see me."

Ismeralda smiled and followed Brother Joseph, who now had the flyers.

They spent the rest of the afternoon hanging up flyers and inviting kids to come to the service that night. Brother Joseph allowed Greg to skateboard as they hung them on light poles and walls. Greg was able to sneak the ice pack off his eye pretty quickly, to the chagrin of Ismeralda and amusement of Brother Joseph. As the afternoon progressed, Greg found himself growing more and more comfortable around Brother Joseph and Ismeralda. It was the first time in a long time he'd felt like he was truly accepted. He didn't feel like he had to put on a show for them, with the exception of trying to impress Ismeralda a little. The more time he spent with them, the less he found himself showing off, and the more he relaxed a little and just tried to be himself.

He was surprised how much fun he had just passing out flyers. Good-natured teasing and ribbing flew between the three of them the entire afternoon. Later when they were almost done, Brother Joseph took the two young people to a coffee shop and bought them drinks. By the time Brother Joseph drove Greg back to his hotel, Greg had almost forgotten about his problems with the gangs and the drugs. Almost.

Brother Joseph pulled up in front of the hotel, and Greg was getting out of the car when Brother Joseph stopped him. "Wait, Greg. I let it go earlier because I figured that you needed some time. But shouldn't we talk about what you're going to do next?"

Greg was silent and scuffed the toe of his shoe against the asphalt.

Brother Joseph continued in his soft voice. "I mean, wasn't that the main reason we came out today? I know you said you didn't want to go to the police but maybe we could work out something."

Brother Joseph's voice faded in Greg's mind as the skater squeezed his eyes shut. *No! Stop!* his mind screamed. He did not want to think about this. He wanted it to be over with and his mind to be numbed to everything but some sitcom or reality TV show. *Can't I just leave it up to someone else to deal with?* But Greg knew he couldn't. His head hurt thinking about it. He felt as if he couldn't trust anyone and yet he really wanted to. He wanted someone else to deal with it. But all the people one might normally go to for help—parents, relatives, friends, the police, and especially God were all out of the question for him. It seemed that Brother Joseph was the only person he could go to with this.

"Greg?" He snapped out of his reverie. Brother Joseph had apparently asked him a question.

Greg sighed. "Listen, I don't really want to talk about this."

Brother Joseph looked shocked. Ismeralda looked for all the world like she wanted to spout off at him but was using all her self-restraint not to.

"But . . . we have to!" Brother Joseph said. "How else are you going to deal with this? You can't be tugged between these two warring factions for the rest of your life."

Greg shook his head a little incredulously. "What the heck? 'Warring factions?' I'm sure Stefan's people and Al's gang will get things sorted out," said Greg. "I won't be between these warring factions the rest of my life." He was having second thoughts about trying to get out of it by going to Brother Joseph. *This whole thing will blow over once I get out of Chicago, won't it?* But even as the thought ran through his mind, his throbbing black eye told him that was a stupid idea.

Brother Joseph was shaking his head. "Those weren't the two warring factions I was talking about."

Greg was already turning towards the hotel, but Brother

Joseph's words made him pause. *What was that supposed to mean?* "Listen, I'm really tired. Can we deal with this later?"

Brother Joseph looked really uncomfortable with that idea, but he sighed. "Well, I can't force you to talk. Sure, Greg, whatever you want. I'll keep checking into some things though . . . and praying."

Greg nodded. "Thanks for the drink," he said as he closed the door.

Brother Joseph rolled down his window. "Hang on a second," he said as he motioned for Greg to come over. "You may not want to think or talk about it right now, but do you have anything that I could check into for you? Were you able to get any more information? About Stefan's operation, or the name of the gang, or where the drugs came from, or anything else?"

"Well . . ." Greg thought of the piece of paper in his pocket with the warehouse address on it. Greg's hand dangled uncertainly over his pocket. He had to decide now whether or not to trust Brother Joseph. *Well, where else can I turn?* With sudden resolve, he plunged his hand in his pocket and offered the paper to Brother Joseph. "Here," he said. "This is the address they told me to meet them at when Stefan gives me the drugs. I guess it's the same warehouse they took me to the first night. I don't know how much good it'll do," he offered with a shrug.

Brother Joseph took the address, wrote it down on the palm of his hand, and handed it back to Greg. "Thanks, I'm sure this will help."

Greg ran his fingers underneath his hat and through his hair and shifted his skateboard to his other hand.

Brother Joseph heaved a big sigh as if he were reluctant to leave and looked at Greg. "Are you sure you'll be okay till tonight? You could come home with me or . . ."

Greg smiled and shook his head. "I'll be fine, dude, don't worry about me."

Brother Joseph forced a smile and nodded. "All right. See you tonight then?" Greg nodded. "Seven-thirty?"

"You got it." Brother Joseph held out a fist and Greg punched it lightly. "All right then, Lord willing I'll see you tonight."

"If you can stay out of trouble until then," Ismeralda spoke up with a smile, trying to lighten the mood.

Greg smiled. "Don't count on it."

Brother Joseph still had a somber expression on his face. "Be extremely careful, Greg," he said.

The skater bobbed his head again and began backing toward the hotel. "Right," he said.

"See you later," Ismeralda called.

Greg waved. "Yeah, bye!" He turned and walked into the lobby, sipping his Frappuccino and noting that Brother Joseph made sure he got into the building safely before driving off.

As Greg pushed the button for the elevator, he suddenly noticed a shadow out of the corner of his eye. Nervously, he lifted the drink to his lips and tried to act nonchalant. The elevator seemed to be taking an eternity. He tapped his foot impatiently and casually turned his head to see if he could see anything. Nothing was there, but that didn't mean there hadn't been.

The ding of the elevator made him jump just a little. Quickly, he got on and pushed his floor, jabbing the close-door button a couple times to speed things up. As the elevator started to rise, he took a deep breath and tried to think about something else. He decided to let the afternoon replay itself in his mind. To his surprise, he'd actually had a lot of fun as they passed out flyers for the night service. What a strange concept. *Hanging out with Apostolics can be fun?*

He got to his room on the third floor and opened the door, draining the last of his drink out of his cup, and glanced around as the door clicked shut to make sure no surprises were waiting for him. Stefan had a tendency to show up at the worst times for the pure intention of scaring Greg to death. And Greg really wanted to avoid Stefan right now. Besides, if he showed up unexpectedly at this moment, Greg was sure he would scream.

Greg tossed the cup to the side and kicked off his shoes as he flopped down on the now-made bed, letting his hat flop off and his eyes close. He was tired! He had been staying up late every night and had been going through a lot anyway. He thought of turning on the TV, but the remote was all the way on the other side of the bed in the drawer.

The silence started to feel oppressive, so he sat up and quickly reached over to get the remote and flip it on before laying back down. That's better . . . background noise. His black eye still hurt and he was exhausted. *Maybe I'll take a little nap before the service tonight.*

As Greg waited for sleep to overcome him, his thoughts drifted to the service. Why was he going to this thing anyway? It was an Apostolic/Pentecostal/Christian service, after all! One of the prevailing reasons he had wanted to come to Chicago was so he wouldn't have to put up with the Apostolic Bible-thumping, weird Pentecostal worship, and Christian standards. Yet here he was in Chicago going to a youth meeting held by an Apostolic Jesus freak! His mom would pass out.

So what was he doing this for? *I guess it's for Brother Joseph, since he's helping me out,* Greg mused. *Maybe Ismeralda. Yeah, she's pretty hot. I wouldn't mind hanging out with her some more.* But even as he thought about it, he knew that wasn't the whole reason. It wasn't that he was going out of obligation or reluctantly. He wanted to go. It was almost as if he felt a pull from some outside force drawing him to the meeting, and he didn't understand it.

But at the same time, his stomach flopped when he thought about it. He got that fluttering feeling he always got right before doing certain flip tricks or getting on a roller coaster. And it wasn't because of Ismeralda. It was because of God. While he wanted to go to the meeting to hang out with the people he had met and to feel safe, one thing didn't make him feel safe. It was the fact that Brother Joseph fully expected the presence of God to be at the meeting. And Greg certainly didn't want to be around Him. What a strange thought. Being around God. It seems so normal to Brother Joseph. *But after what God did to my family . . . there's no way I want to come into contact with this cold, distant Deity.*

Something Brother Joseph had told him the other night replayed in Greg's mind. "God does care . . . Greg, He knows you. And, believe it or not, He really does love you. Even if it doesn't seem like it in all the turmoil and uproar, God still cares." Even as the thought entered his mind, Greg scoffed. *There's no way God loves me. Even if God was real and really did love other people, there is no way God could love me—a rebellious, lustful, sinful teenaged skater.* Greg opened his eyes to look up at the ceiling and glared hard at the white bumps. The fact that God couldn't love him was certainly evidenced by all the bad things that had happened in Greg's life.

But, even if God even exists, just for the sake of argument, does that mean He loves other people too? Brother Joseph sure thought so. But then why was Samantha killed? She was innocent and never did anything wrong to anyone. So was her death just a way to punish me? The loving, kind God Brother Joseph served apparently didn't have the Martin family's number.

Suddenly the phone in his hotel room rang, making Greg

start. God might not have Greg's number, but somebody else did. Greg reached a hand over and set it on the phone, looking at the digital clock next to it. Did he really want to answer the phone right now? Who could it be? His mom, Brother Joseph, and Stefan usually called his cell phone. Why don't these stupid hotel phones have caller ID? Maybe it was the hotel staff. Greg tentatively picked it up and answered, "Yeah?"

"Out front," a voice on the other end responded, then just as quickly he heard the dial tone.

Greg hung up the phone. *Out front? What was that all about?* The thought crossed his mind that it was a prank call. But the voice sounded familiar. Could it be a trick? Quickly Greg crossed over to the window in his room to look into the alley behind the hotel in case someone was waiting out there. But, no, it was empty.

Greg stood in the middle of his room for a minute, his heart pounding, trying to decide what to do. Should he leave the hotel? Why did that voice sound so familiar? There was a hint of an African accent to it, so it might be someone in Al's gang. But they all had heavier accents. Who else could . . .? Wait . . . Suddenly, an image of a tall bald African American entered his mind. An African American who wore a nice, clean suit and spoke in short sentences, hardly saying anything at all.

Curiosity got the best of him. Greg slipped his shoes back on and walked out into the hallway, letting the door close behind him. He rode the elevator down to the lobby and when the doors opened, sure enough, through the front doors of the hotel the skater could see a limousine. Greg walked out to see Terrance standing beside the back door. Stefan's right-hand man opened it and waited for Greg to get in.

"What's going on?" Greg asked suspiciously without getting into the car.

Terrance just jerked his head to the limousine. "You'll find out. Get in."

Greg walked cautiously over. "Where are we going?"

Terrance didn't answer but impatiently motioned for Greg to get in. Intrigue won out. That and Terrance's impatient hand gesture to his side where Greg imagined a gun. No sooner had he stepped in than the door slammed shut behind him. Terrance walked around to the driver's side and got in. There was a soft purr as the limousine started and began to roll smoothly over the street.

Greg looked around for the intercom button and finally found it near the cup holder. He pressed it. "Hey, are you taking me to Stefan?" He let go and waited for an answer. There was nothing. He pressed it again. "Could you let him know that the gang didn't get all the drugs they wanted? And they're not giving Stefan any money until they get what they want." Again, Greg clicked off. Still no answer came. Greg pressed it one more time. "So don't be expecting me to be bringing any money, and you guys better not threaten me or I'm not helping any-more." No answer. Greg rolled his eyes. He should have known. This was Terrance after all. "Where are we going anyway?" After Greg let go, there was a short pause.

Finally there was a click and Terrance's voice came over the other end, all of his words very clearly enunciated with a hint of irritation. "You will have to wait and see. Quit talking."

Greg slumped back down in the seat with a snort. Right. His eyes flickered to the TV. The case that held the video games was empty. *Figures,* Greg thought. But he really didn't feel like playing video games right now. His mind was on other things like how to make a quick escape if Terrance planned on kidnapping him or something.

Fifteen minutes later, the limousine pulled up to a huge wrought-iron gate and high voltage security fence with warning signs posted at intervals. Terrance rolled down his window and punched in a code on a small keypad by the gate. Greg watched, fascinated, despite his uneasiness.

They had driven into the industrial area of Chicago, close to the skyscrapers and important buildings. But this place was way back in the slum, in a dank alley. It had a dark feel about it. Hardly any people were around and since the sky was overcast again, it lent to the eerie vibe of the place. It was an old warehouse that stood tall against the gray sky but was hidden by other tall buildings that gave it an atmosphere of seclusion.

The old wrought iron gates swung open slowly, and as Terrance drove the limousine in, Greg noted the address. This would be good to give Brother Joseph. A big concrete opening was on the side of the building that Terrance went through before going down into an underground parking garage that Greg hadn't noticed at first. The place was bigger than it appeared to be. The lights inside were dim, the way parking garages usually are, but it seemed to have even less light than usual in this place. Terrance parked and when he opened the door for Greg, a blast of cold air hit the teenager. It felt damp too. *It's like a cave or something.*

Terrance began walking away, without a word passing between them. Greg assumed he was supposed to follow him. They reached some elevator doors with a keyhole instead of a button. Terrance fetched a key chain from his belt loop with about twenty keys on it and inserted one into the keyhole. They waited a few minutes until a green light flashed and they entered the elevator. The elevator doors closed, and Greg felt as if he had just been trapped with no hope of escape. He was stuck here. A claustrophobic feeling threatened to creep up his back. Terrance leaned casually against the rail in the elevator, oblivious to Greg's feelings. Greg shuffled his feet nervously. It appeared to be a very confined space without much room to move around. The elevator ride seemed to last a long time, with nobody talking, just waiting.

At last, a ding signaled they had reached their destination. They walked out into a large warehouse room. Crates and boxes were stacked up high, and forklifts were bringing in more from a loading dock near the back. Seven or eight people were stacking boxes and busily working. Terrance walked quickly through an aisle on one side of the boxes, never looking anybody in the eye or acknowledging their presence. For the most part, the workers ignored them too. If Greg didn't know better, he never would have guessed that this was the heart of an enormous drug ring.

Terrance led Greg to a back room and rapped on the door a couple times. Stefan's voice came through annoyingly pleasant, "Yes, who is it?"

Terrance crossed his arms and waited irritably.

Greg could hear Stefan chuckle. "I guess it's my driver. Come in, Terrance."

Terrance opened the door and stepped back, allowing Greg to go in before him. Greg walked in, trying to appear confident.

Stefan was sitting behind a big desk with his feet up. When Greg walked in, he stood and pointed to a folding chair on the other side of the desk. "Have a seat, Gregory," he invited, waiting until Greg sat down to sit down himself.

"Uh, just Greg, okay?" Greg reminded him.

Stefan ignored him and clasped his hands on the desk in

front of him. "We're in a sticky situation here," Stefan began with no preamble. "I am not saying that it's entirely your fault. But if we give the gang the right drugs, chances are they'll take advantage of you and refuse to give you the money. Another problem is one you weren't aware of. Somebody mixed up the boxes and gave them the wrong drugs, so Al didn't receive something else he was supposed to."

Stefan paused and looked at Greg. Greg didn't say anything. Stefan set this meeting up; let him carry the conversation.

Stefan continued, "The reason we arranged this little trip to Chicago for you was because our last meeting place, where Al would receive drugs and then sell them to the other gangs, was busted by the police. Somebody slipped, a couple gang members were arrested, and now the police are watching the location twenty-four/seven. So we obviously had to find a different place. Your purpose here was only to deliver that one box of drugs with the next address in it, get the money, then apart from some other small odd jobs we might think up, we'd fly you back to Colorado and begin shipping the drugs for Al to the next address. Simple. Except for the fact that they didn't get the address. I've called you here to give you the shipment personally so no other mistakes will be made. We have to make up for lost time and can't afford to have any more goof-ups, understand?"

Stefan leaned back in his chair and motioned out a glassless window that looked out over the warehouse. Somebody approached the window and gave Stefan a box, much like the one Greg had delivered before, but bigger. Stefan took the box and set it on the desk in front of him. "We now not only have to deliver the misplaced drugs, but also the time has come for the next shipment. And this envelope . . ." Stefan opened a drawer and withdrew an envelope ". . . contains the correct address. You are to deliver this personally this time. I wanted to give this to you myself so that there wouldn't be another mix-up. That's why I brought you here."

Greg just sat there, not saying anything while he listened to Stefan's long monologue.

Stefan held the box out, looking intently at Greg. "Don't mess up this time, do you understand? We simply cannot afford any more mistakes."

Greg sensed that that was the end of the conversation so he rose, took the box and envelope, and started to turn.

"Oh, and Gregory," Stefan caught Greg's wrist just as Greg was starting to walk out, pulling him back, and leaned close. "If you even think about betraying us, to the police or anyone else, there will be incredible consequences. You know that, don't you? By bringing you here, I have given you a vote of confidence. However, if you betray that confidence it will be you who suffers, not us. I have proof of you doing some terribly illegal things, like selling drugs to gangs." He leaned closer. "Stuff you wouldn't want the police to know about. But against me, you have no proof. I can escape any situation you throw at me, but you won't be able to. You are expendable, and we would have no trouble getting rid of you if the situation calls for it . . . without drawing attention to ourselves. Remember that, all right?" Stefan released his wrist, satisfied he had gotten his point across. "Terrance, you're dismissed. Drive him back to his hotel. Talk to you later, mm, Greg?"

Greg was shaking when he walked out. He couldn't wait to get to his hotel so he could get ready for the church meeting tonight. He no longer had any apprehension about Brother Joseph's service. Now he needed some security.

11

Azgad surveyed his troops with a look of uneasy approval. The demons were finally falling into formation after a bit of stern punishment. The lazy devils weren't happy with these new assignments. Ever since Brother Joseph had started holding youth services at the skate park, the normal routine of easy temptation and debauchery had been interrupted. Now they actually had to do battle and be ready to try to quench the fire that the street preacher was trying to start in the hearts of their charges.

By the uneasiness and fear starting to creep up the back of his neck, Azgad could tell the missionary was close. He glanced at the demons in their various posts around the park and saw a squabble had started up between two of them. Swiftly, he made eye contact and snarled in warning. Sulkily, the demons fell back into place. As much as they hated this, they must be ready. Great potential for disaster lurked here.

"Preparation of troops will not destroy the Lord's purpose, Azgad."

The voice amplified through the air without warning like a sudden trumpet blast. Startled, the demon slipped and stumbled backward. He recovered quickly and flapped his bat-like wings to rise up to meet the intruder.

Gaddiel stood there, in full glory, his white raiment shining out bright light in the gathering dark of the city park. His massive wings vacillated ever so slightly, with little effort, just enough to keep him in the air. Intuitively, Azgad shielded his eyes for a moment but then remembered his image and rested his scaly claws on his paunch, assuming a posture of indifference.

"Must you always wear those annoyingly bright clothes, Gaddiel?" he asked airily, eyeing the angel critically.

"The darkness hates the light, doesn't it?" Gaddiel responded with a smile.

"With good reason," Azgad sneered. "What are you here bothering me for?"

"I have only come to tell you that the presence of the Lord will be manifested in this park tonight. His hosts are entering, His servants coming. The children of the Most High will be here. The Spirit of the Lord is pursuing these children tonight. Just thought I would give you fair warning in case you and your minions want to leave."

Azgad made a noise that sounded like cross between a snarl and a chuckle. "You forget, Gaddiel, that these children are not the Enemy's yet. This is our territory that you are entering. The despicable humans' very nature is working against you here. My troops really have to do very little to keep your heavenly host at bay."

"The blood of the Lamb will take care of that, Azgad. The Lord is coming, and His power is greater than your troops."

Azgad's narrowed his eyes and said in a low tone, "If your street missionary would just keep out of the way, there would be no problems here. This isn't the place to do battle, Gaddiel."

"The Lord will work wherever there is an open heart, General of Darkness."

Azgad turned his head in disgust. "Shouldn't you be watching your charge, Angel?"

Gaddiel lifted a little higher in the air. "Indeed! I have delivered my message." He nodded to the demon. "Worthy is the Lamb, Azgad!"

With a growl, Azgad lost his composure and leaped at the angel, but Gaddiel was already flying up through the air, off to Greg's side.

Angrily, the demon whirled and yowled for his second in command. The minion was instantly at his side. Azgad pointed his clenched fist at him. "Make sure our troops are ready. We must not let the skaters' hearts soften!"

o——o

Brother Joseph had told Greg that the youth meeting was going to be in the open field behind the skate park. As Greg got closer, he saw that where once had just been green grass and a couple trees, a stage had been set up and several rows of chairs were arranged in front of it.

The skate park was deserted, but a crowd of kids were over by the stage. On the stage were a couple microphones and a keyboard with two loudspeakers on either side. Greg saw Brother Joseph talking with a couple teenagers as he brought out some more chairs from a little trailer hitched up to a truck. Greg didn't see Ismeralda yet.

The kids were milling about. Greg spotted Chris near the front of the crowd. Jack and Terry and a couple other kids he recognized were there too. Steve and Monica were there with some adults who appeared to be their parents. Brother Joseph apparently saw them too, because he set up the chairs he had brought out, excused himself, and made his way over to greet them. Steve hugged him, and Brother Joseph began talking with his parents.

Greg's eyes drifted and he caught sight of Ismeralda talking to a tall guy by the trailer with the equipment. She was looking at a sheet of paper and apparently trying to follow the guy, who was talking and pointing to something on the paper every once in a while.

Suddenly Greg felt out of place. He wasn't sure what to do. Everyone he knew was talking to someone, and he felt awkward standing on the edge of the park. Just then Chris caught sight of him and waved him over.

Grateful for someone to talk to, Greg walked over to Chris and the group of kids he was with. "Hey man, what's going on?" he said, pounding fists with him.

"Not much, dude. Hey, sorry I couldn't make it to the skate park today. My old lady had me doing chores and stuff around the house," Chris apologized.

"Don't worry about it, man," Greg waved it off. "I wasn't there either." He looked around at the crowd of kids by the stage. "So what happens at these things anyway?"

Chris looked around at the other kids for help then shrugged. "Well, first they play a couple songs, if they have music, and it looks like they do tonight."

"Yeah, then Brother Joseph has some 'icebreakers,'" Terry said, making quotation marks with his fingers.

"Icebreakers?" Greg asked, raising his eyebrows.

"You'll see," Chris promised. "Then they sing a couple more songs, and after that Brother Joseph gets up to preach."

Greg stifled a moan. It sounded just like one of the boring Pentecostal services his mom went to. And if it was anything like that, well . . . *I'm just here for Ismeralda and Brother Joseph,* Greg told himself. For them, he would sit through this. A voice in his mind reminded him: *No, that's not why you're here. You're here because you're scared.* He pushed it away.

"What then?" he forced himself to ask.

"Well, then if the kids want to go up and pray, they do."

Greg gnawed at his lip. "So . . . why do you come to these things?" The group stared at him.

"What do you mean?" Chris asked.

"Uh, never mind," Greg responded.

"Hey," one of the skaters piped up. "It looks like Brother Joseph is getting ready to start."

Gaddiel hovered above the group of skaters, scaring off any demons that ventured to come near him by simply brandishing his sword. Occasionally a brash little devil would dart at the angel in attack, and the angel would block him off with a swift blow. These small annoyances were not a cause of worry, however. The small devils were simply taunting him at the beginning, as they were inclined to do. The real battle would begin shortly.

A thundering noise above Gaddiel's head caused him to jerk his head upwards. His fellow angel, Zimri, zoomed toward the field, heading for the stage. He nodded at Gaddiel as he passed by, and instantly Gaddiel shot up above the field and the demons began to close in tighter.

Gaddiel kept his eye on Greg as the skater turned his head and saw Brother Joseph on stage, testing a mic. David, the keyboard player, was adjusting things on a soundboard in the back, behind the stage. Finally Brother Joseph gave him a thumbs-up and turned back to the crowd.

Zimri moved into place on the stage, and Gaddiel took up a

position near the first row where Ismeralda was standing. As soon as Gaddiel had moved away from the group of skaters, Azgad made a swift swooping motion with his talons, and a line of demons filed into place, forming a wall between the skaters and the stage. Zimri placed his powerful hand on Brother Joseph's shoulder as he began the event. Gaddiel glanced to the chairs, where a circle of demons had already formed a tight circle around the group of skaters.

Tension was building.

Greg's group sidestepped into the row of chairs they were standing nearest.

The tall guy Ismeralda had been talking to moved into place behind the keyboard, and Brother Joseph held up his hand to quiet the crowd. "Okay, let's get started," he said into the microphone.

The tall guy started playing a catchy, upbeat, contemporary song on the piano, and Brother Joseph started clapping. He waved at the crowd to join him, and soon all the kids were clapping in time to the music. Brother Joseph and the piano player started singing a Christian praise song.

Azgad surveyed the crowd. The Spirit of the Lord was going to try to influence the hearts of these mortals, and he knew his troops must do all in their power to stop Him.

Several of his lieutenants were stationed at key points, and he saw one in particular that was shifting uncomfortably but not doing anything. Growling, he flew over to him and hissed, saying, "Why aren't you doing anything?"

The demon sulkily glanced up at his commander, then looked towards the keyboard player and sneered. "Surely, they will not be influenced by the poor quality of this music. Brother Joseph isn't even singing on key. If they just focus on the music—"

Swiftly, Azgad whopped him on the head. "You idiot! The quality of the music doesn't matter if the Spirit of the Lord is moving! You must keep them distracted! If you leave them alone, their thoughts may turn towards Him. Drop thoughts in their head of lust, family problems, impressing their friends, the beat of the song, whatever! Use the poor quality of the music if you must, but keep dropping thoughts into their heads to keep them from thinking of Him! It is better for them to be light-hearted at this point and not think of anything serious rather than criticizing the songs. Their whole focus needs to be on having fun, and we must use that desire and the peer pressure created to distract their friends! Discomfort can be used by the Enemy. Make them comfortable and lethargic!"

Greg felt a little awkward, and he could tell he wasn't alone in his feeling from the sheepish grins some of the other kids were giving each other. Some of them started dancing or joking, drawing laughs. Greg joined in making a couple wisecracks and gestures, getting the guys in his group to laugh. If Brother Joseph noticed, he didn't let on but continued to sing right along with the song.

Greg noticed Ismeralda standing in the front row on the opposite side, her long eyelashes covering her pretty eyes and her slender lips moving. Her forehead crinkled with sincerity at whatever she was saying. If nothing else, it would seem she wasn't there to impress anyone. The question rose in Greg's mind again. *Why had she come? Why would an attractive girl like Ismeralda forgo all of her plans on a Friday night to hang out at a church service? What was her motivation?*

They sang a few songs and the kids were starting to get restless. A couple of them were cutting up and getting rude, interrupting the songs with yells and whistles. Brother Joseph finally signaled the keyboard player with his eyes and as the last song ended, Brother Joseph brought up a stand that looked like a music stand. It could hardly be called a pulpit—it was discreet and understated. But it served the preacher's purposes.

Azgad smiled. The preacher knew he was losing control and was trying to regain the teenagers' interest. He looked over to where the angels were mobilized and battling against the demons who were fully engaged in distracting the young people. His smile faded a bit as he saw Gaddiel bat away a demon from Greg. This was a precarious situation, and they needed to maximize the icebreaker the preacher was using as an opportunity to distract them more.

As Azgad began to move in to give the order, a smaller demon swooped up to him and saluted. "Gazez has arrived, sir."

Azgad whirled around with a start. "Gazez is here?" he demanded in shock.

The small demon saluted again.

Azgad snarled. "He didn't think we could handle this on our own, did he? Well, we'll just see about that."

"All right," Brother Joseph announced, his eyes sparkling

mischievously. "It's that time again." A couple people groaned and a couple laughed. Greg had no idea what he was talking about.

"What's going on?" Greg asked.

"Icebreakers," Chris whispered back. "You'll see."

Brother Joseph casually walked a couple steps to the side on the stage with the microphone in his hand. "I don't think church was intended to be dull or uninteresting," he said. "Ecclesiastes says to enjoy life in your youth, but remember your Creator. So let's have a little fun." Brother Joseph paced the stage, looking out into the audience. "I'm going to need some help. Can I have a couple volunteers?" To Greg's surprise, a couple people actually raised their hands. There was no way he was going to volunteer! "David," Brother Joseph motioned to the keyboard player. "Bring out the meal." David disappeared behind stage and emerged with the Happy Meal, then disappeared again to get something else.

As David went behind the stage, Brother Joseph's eye suddenly caught a man standing at the edge of the park, just under a tree, watching them. The man had slicked back hair and was wearing a suit, which was highly unusual for someone at a skate park, especially this late at night. He wasn't doing anything . . . just standing there, observing. The hair at the back of Brother Joseph's neck suddenly and inexplicably stood on end. He had never seen him before, but he sensed something suspicious and dangerous about the man. *If he has evil intent or intends to harm any of these kids . . .* Brother Joseph offered up a quick prayer to the Lord, asking for angels to protect the place.

Gaddiel received the order instantly but was engaged in combat. He shoved his sword hard into the demon to hold him off and looked to Zimri, who caught his eye and nodded upwards. Palti had already shot like a streak of light across the sky.

Brother Joseph grinned. "Now how many of you think you can eat a regular fast-food hamburger meal? I need three people who think they can eat one. We're going to have a little contest to see who can eat one of these meals the fastest." Several people jumped up, and Brother Joseph picked two guys and a girl to come up to the front.

"But to throw in a little twist, and help you eat this faster, we're going to do something else." David came out from behind the stage with a blender. The three volunteers began groaning, and one of the guys started to run away. Brother Joseph caught his shoulder. "Ah, ah, you volunteered," he said with a laugh. "David, go ahead and blend everything up." A cheeseburger, French fries and a Coke came out of the bag and were thrown into the blender, which was then turned on.

Expressions of disgust rippled throughout the crowd of teenagers. The girl was looking a little green. Brother Joseph finally turned off the blender and poured the concoction into three paper coffee cups. "Now when you can't stand it anymore, you can quit. You can quit before we start if you want. But whoever lasts the longest or can drink the most will win." All three said they would try. Brother Joseph gave each of them a cup, then crouching down to eye-level with them, said, "On your marks . . . get set . . . go!"

David began heading off the stage just as the contestants began, but Brother Joseph caught his shoulder. "I want you to watch that man over there under the tree," Brother Joseph instructed under his breath.

Casually, David let his eyes wander over to the tree till he noticed the man with the suit coat. "What do you think he's going to do?" David whispered back.

Brother Joseph shook his head. "Just keep an eye on him, and on all of the kids. Make sure none of them wanders over there."

The boy who had tried to run away was already spewing out the green concoction back into the cup. Brother Joseph grabbed his cup and called out, "Oh, one less contestant! Let's see if Ashley and Pete can pull it off!"

Ashley lasted a couple more seconds before groaning and handing the cup back to Brother Joseph. Brother Joseph laughed at the look on her face.

"Your consolation prize is a glass of water," he said and motioned for Ismeralda, who brought out three cups of water. "And, ladies and gentlemen, Pete is the winner!" said Brother Joseph.

David went behind stage and brought out another box. Brother Joseph glanced back over to the tree. The man was still there but had shrunk further back into the shadows.

"And your prize," Brother Joseph announced, "is a brand-new skateboard! Let's hear it one more time for Pete!"

Everybody began applauding and laughing as the three contestants gulped the water, swished it around in their mouths, and spit it back onto the grass.

Gazez let out a guttural roar. Stefan tensed and readied himself. Gazez wanted nothing more than to intervene.

His attention was arrested by a small devil motioning towards him. Clenching his fangs so tightly together they almost snapped off his tongue, Gazez swiveled his head in its direction. "What in heaven's name do you want, you imp?" he said.

"Into the trees," the imp said and disappeared.

Gazez was enraged but turned into the trees for a moment. Azgad was there waiting for him. Gazez unleashed his pent-up curses on him and swiped at his skull. Azgad dodged his blow and batted his wings to fly up higher.

"I came to undo your incompetence!" Gazez said.

"You're here to mess everything up," Azgad accused him. "We have this under control! If you go manifesting yourself with all your dark arts, they will be in tune to the supernatural without distractions, and their attention will be considerably more focused on the preacher! As of now, they are completely in the flesh! Don't mess that up!"

"Stefan is here to destroy Greg," Gazez said. "And I am here to make sure that happens. This could completely undo everything we've been working for in our operation!"

"Don't let that fool get any closer!" Azgad ordered.

Palti suddenly appeared on the edge of the skate park with a host of heavenly beings. Huge, burly angels were ready to protect the skaters and Christians at all costs. There was no way Stefan could get any closer. Gazez bellowed out curses in rage and turned to smash in Azgad's face, but the other devil had already disappeared.

Brother Joseph paused a moment after the icebreakers to allow the laughter to die down and after a few moments, he gestured to David and motioned for silence.

"Okay, we're going to sing a couple more songs and get back into the attitude of worship. Let's be free. Don't let anything hold you back as you worship, okay?"

David began playing another contemporary worship song to which everybody was clapping and stomping their feet. Brother Joseph looked back over to the trees where the man had been standing but didn't see him. Hopefully he'd left.

Gaddiel wiped his face with the back of his hand. It was hard to keep the skaters' attention focused on the Lord when everything in their minds and everything that the demons were doing was distracting them from that focus. A snarl behind him alerted him to the presence of another demon. Gaddiel slightly turned his head and saw bared fangs as the demon leaped at him. Hand readied on his sword, the angel waited until the demon was almost to him, then with one fluid motion, whipped out his sword and sliced the demon in half. It was time for stronger measures. His eyes searched for Zimri, who was touching Brother Joseph's shoulder. Gaddiel permitted himself a short sigh of relief. Three demons suddenly leaped at him and once again, the angel immersed himself in the battle.

By the second song, the crowd was getting restless. As the song finished, Brother Joseph waved his hands for quiet and said, "Now I have one more special treat for you, before the message. Some of you have met Ismeralda."

Ismeralda waved her hand, and a few teenagers whistled and cheered.

"She's a teenager in our youth group who's helping me out. But for those of you who haven't met her, please welcome Ismeralda to the stage." Scattered applause broke out. "She's going to be singing a song for us. But remember, it's not about her. This is about God. She is not doing this for her own glory or to entertain you—she's doing this for God. So please if you feel compelled during the song to praise God, you can do it silently or out loud. But let's give the Lord the glory out of this, okay?" With that, Brother Joseph set the microphone in its holder on the stage and walked to the side.

The glory of the Lord radiated from Ismeralda. Instantly, every demon's gaze turned toward her. Several began hissing, yowling, and gnashing their teeth. Her sincerity and love for Him poured out of every pore in her body. Azgad's eyes bulged, and he impulsively threw a clenched-fist gesture in her direction. A troop of demons howled and rushed at the young godly girl, only to be repelled and some disintegrated as soon as they reached the glory surrounding her. Two burly angels suddenly descended from the sky and stood by the young girl.

Cursing, Azgad swiped down his talon and called off his troops. Infuriated, the demons turned their attention on the group of young people in the crowd. Azgad glanced over at Gazez's enraged face and could almost read, "I told you so," on it. Azgad turned away, spitting.

Ismeralda came on stage and some of the boys in the crowd began whistling and catcalling, a couple of them making crude remarks. Ismeralda ignored them and stood there quietly as she waited for the music to start.

"Hey baby, what are you doing tonight after this?" someone called out amidst the laughter and prodding of his friends.

Ismeralda didn't say anything. Finally, the keyboard player found his music and started playing. The catcalls died down a little. The tall guy played the intro, and Ismeralda's eyes shut, her lips moving slightly. Then the intro ended and she tilted her face toward heaven.

As the demons flowed into the crowd of teenagers, Zimri's large wings lifted him off the stage and took him to a position over the skaters. He hovered there for a moment, then raised his fist into the air and brought it down.

Gaddiel and the other angels leaped into the fray. The angels' swords clashed with the demons' daggers. Red eyes stared into bright luminous ones. Fist slammed up against talon.

Slowly but surely, the angels found themselves in the center of the circle of skaters and began pushing the demons to the outskirts.

Azgad realized what they were doing and howled in rage. He flew on his leathery wings above the circle and was about to plunge down on Gaddiel when Zimri met him face to face, brandishing his sword. The two spirits began battling.

While Zimri distracted Azgad, Gaddiel led the rest of the angels in the charge to widen their inner circle, pushing the front of demons farther and farther away from the skaters. The presence of the Lord was too strong for the demons to resist, and they soon found themselves hissing and snarling on the edge of the park, facing a bright wall of angels surrounding the skaters.

Ismeralda opened her mouth and from the first note, Greg was transfixed. Her melodic voice carried over the cool night air and seemed to reach into his very soul. As she started to sing, the whistles and yelling subsided and the crowd began to quiet down. Every eye was focused on Ismeralda.

Everything grew still as Ismeralda's clear voice cut through the night, gripping the hearts of the teenagers. "I will give you my life . . ." For once, Greg wasn't poking and laughing with the other skaters. Everyone was sitting there, quietly listening. It was as if her voice had a hypnotic effect on all those present. This time, nobody dared interrupt the unwavering, beautiful voice singing.

A chill settled over Greg. He couldn't stop listening. An almost tangible presence descended on the group. Suddenly scared, Greg glanced around at the other kids. All were watching Ismeralda. Why are they all acting like this? What's wrong with them? But even as he wanted to break the tension with a wisecrack, he felt unable to do so. The skater glanced over to Brother Joseph. The street missionary's face and arms were lifted to heaven, his eyes were closed, and he was apparently oblivious to what was going on around him. Then again, maybe he was more aware of what was going on than anyone else. Ismeralda continued to sing until her song seemed to fade away.

She sung the last verse, her last note carrying over the breeze to the fading notes of the piano. Ismeralda walked off the stage. Nobody moved. The audience was so still that not a breath could be heard. Brother Joseph wiped his eyes and made his way to the center of the platform, took his place in front of the microphone, and looked out over the crowd of kids. Not a word was spoken. Every eye was fixated on him.

There was a long pause as Brother Joseph looked out over the teenagers. Somebody sniffled and blew their nose. Another person coughed.

"What you just felt," Brother Joseph finally said, his voice broken, "was the power of God. I can feel His presence so strongly here. And do you know why? It isn't because of me. It's not even because of Ismeralda. Do you know why God is visiting this park tonight? It's because of you. You. It's because God loves you and wants to have a relationship with you. As I talk to you guys tonight, please don't think it's about me or what I have to say. This is about God and what He wants to say to you. He loves you. I know He loves you. I have felt the pain He feels over each and every one of you when you stray from Him, and He longs to bring you back to Him. Hopefully, I can make a difference for someone tonight."

Brother Joseph paused and let out a small laugh as he wiped his glasses. "Well . . . not me; I'm just the tool that God has chosen to use. The rest will be up to God . . ." he paused and looked down at his feet, before looking back up into the faces of his audience, ". . . and to you."

Brother Joseph shifted the podium and shuffled through his notes, then looked back out over the youth. "Tonight I'm going to deal with a question I'm sure many of you have had. You've probably heard this question brought up by skeptics of the gospel. Maybe in a science class at school or even in your own home by a wayward brother or sister or an unbelieving mom or dad. I'm sure many of you have even asked it yourself." He paused for dramatic effect. "If God is so loving and merciful, how could He allow evil into the world? That's the question I'm going to try to answer tonight. Some of you might not like the answer I give. But the truth is always harder than a lie . . . but in the long run much better.

"First of all, I'm going to open with Romans six verse twenty-three. It says, 'For the wages of sin is death; but the gift of God is eternal life through Jesus Christ our Lord.' We like to blame God when things go wrong. But to tell you the truth, I'm going to come right out and say it: it's our fault. And I'll show you why in a minute. Who knows the story of Adam and Eve?"

As Brother Joseph went on to explain the story of Adam and Eve, asking questions to the audience and taking questions, everyone relaxed. No longer were they being disruptive. Now they were paying attention.

Greg listened intently to Brother Joseph's message. It wasn't that Brother Joseph was an incredibly eloquent speaker; in fact, he stumbled and stuttered several times. But it was because Greg knew who Brother Joseph was. It was because Greg knew the message was from Brother Joseph's heart, and he meant every word he said. Greg had seen him hanging out with the teenagers, and he knew this guy was cool. And as Greg listened to the message, it began to make sense. Death, pain, heartbreak—they all came because of sin.

"You see, the fact that there's evil in the world doesn't prove the absence of God, it just proves the existence of evil," Brother Joseph explained.

Greg had heard his mom tell him countless times that Romans 6:23 said, "The wages of sin is death," but it never became clear to him what that meant until now. He'd thought it was just one of those Christian clichés that was always thrown out.

Brother Joseph went on to talk about how God really did love them, but how our sin separates us from Him. "God doesn't want any to perish but all to come to repentance. But since He saw that there was nobody to stand in the gap and intercede for His people, He came down to earth Himself, manifest Himself as the Son of God, and died for us sinners. He bridged the gap Himself, if we'll only go to Him."

Brother Joseph stood there on the stage looking out over the teenagers. Nobody said a word. "Come on up," Brother Joseph said. "If you want God to move in your life, come up front and let Him. Just open up and let Him in your life. He wants to help you. I can promise you: Jesus Christ, the Lord God Almighty, loves you. He loves you, and more than anything He wants to have a relationship with you." The street missionary paused and looked up into the night sky. Tears glistened in his eyes, and as he spoke the last sentence, the passion he had been preaching with all night came forth so strong; there was no doubt that he believed what he was saying. "Please. I know He wants to touch you. You wouldn't believe the grief the Lord feels when you don't know Him. Connect with Him. Come up front and connect with Him tonight! God's waiting! All He needs is you!"

Kids began pouring out of their seats and going up to the front. There in the wet grass they kneeled down and began pouring out their hearts to God. Sobs and crying drifted over the rest of the teenagers in the crowd. The tall guy began playing softly on the keyboard, and Ismeralda moved into the crowd to pray for the girls that went up. Brother Joseph started praying for the teenagers, placing his hands on their heads.

Greg watched it all, perturbed. *What is going on? Why am I feeling this way? I can't take this.* Greg pushed past Chris and walked away from the stage. All the things Greg had been so sure about, all the arguments he'd had with his mom, Brother Joseph had blown out of the water with his scriptures and explanations—well, maybe not with his scriptures and explanations—with his love. Brother Joseph claimed that it was because of sin that the bad things happened; it was humanity's fault that there was so much evil in the world not God's. And the main punchline: God really did love everyone.

But Greg just couldn't bring himself to believe all the things the street preacher had said. *It wasn't my fault that Sam died, or that Dad left! God doesn't really care! I know He doesn't!* Greg's mind screamed angrily. *If He did, my sister would still be alive! He doesn't care! HE DOESN'T!* His eyelids closed in an effort to push back the tears. *What Brother Joseph said isn't true for me*, he told himself, with a lump rising in the pit of his stomach. *Maybe for him but not for me.* The tears spilled through his closed eyelids and ran down his face. He fell to the grass and began to punch it with his fist. *God doesn't love me. I know He doesn't.* An urge to go to the front suddenly overwhelmed him. Greg pushed it away. *God's not even real!* his mind screamed, trying to drown out the pull toward the altar with the kids praying.

Greg jumped to his feet and looked around wildly for his skateboard, ready to run back to his hotel.

"Greg," a soft voice behind him said.

Greg whirled around. Brother Joseph was standing there, looking straight into Greg's eyes. Greg averted them and started to turn back around. "I think I'm gonna go back to the hotel," he told the street preacher, wiping tears from his eyes with the back of his hand.

Brother Joseph moved closer. "Why are you running, Greg?" he asked softly, a touch of pleading in his voice. "God really does love you, and He wants to show you—"

Greg turned around so fast that Brother Joseph put up his hands and took a step back. "No He doesn't!" yelled the skater, clenching his fists by his sides. "You don't know anything! Do you know what it's like? God may love you, but He doesn't love me!" Greg knew he was almost incoherent, but he couldn't stop himself.

Greg could see tears mingling with the sweat on Brother Joseph's face. "That's not true, Greg. I know—"

"No you don't! If God loves me, why did my dad leave? Why did He kill my little sister, huh? Answer that, Bible man!"

"Greg—"

"No! I don't care what you say! God doesn't love me!" With that, Greg turned on his heel and began running furiously away.

"Greg! No! Wait! Come back!" Brother Joseph called. His hand reached out for the fleeing skater. Greg didn't turn around. Brother Joseph bit his lip and hung his head. Waves of sorrow washed over him as Greg disappeared into the darkness. His throat constricted and he gripped the back of a chair to keep from falling. "Oh, Father, what did I do wrong?" he whispered hoarsely. He looked around. *Should I go after him?* His eyes went back to the kids praying at the front. No, they needed him right now. *This is where I need to be. I'll have to follow up with Greg later.* As Brother Joseph began to trudge back up to the front, his eyes lighted on Greg's skateboard. Oh, good. This would be insurance that he would see Greg again. The missionary picked it up and carried it to the stage before going to pray with the other kids.

Stefan's eyes followed Greg as he ran from the skate park. He started after him but abruptly stopped, as if hitting a wall. Quickly, he stepped back behind a tree and adjusted his sunglasses to watch Greg as long as he could.

As soon as Greg disappeared, Stefan slowly, casually strolled to the edge of the skate park, glanced over to where the Christians were distracted by their service, and then began walking in the same direction Greg had gone.

Greg ran through the streets. The tears didn't stop blinding his eyes, but he kept running. He didn't know where he was going and he didn't care. Sobs racked his body. Why did Brother Joseph's words affect him like this? *I don't care if God loves me or not!* Another enormous sob came and he collapsed on the ground behind a building. *Why should God care? Nobody else does.*

Greg lay there for a long time. *If He really loves me . . . He would prove it, he thought. But I've got nothing to show for God's so-called great love.*

A dozen thoughts bombarded him as Greg struggled to fight off the demons of depression and hopelessness that were constantly whispering in his ears. If this is true, there's nothing to live for. If not even God, who's supposed to love everyone, loves you, what is there to live for? Nobody else is going to love you. Greg tried to brush off the suicidal panic that was overtaking him. But the thoughts continued to plague him.

Finally his tears seemed to run out. He wasn't even sure what to think anymore. All the absolutes and certainties Greg had built up in his life had collapsed, demolished in a pile of rubble.

After so much time had passed that both of Greg's feet had a chance to fall asleep, Greg slowly sat up on his haunches and wiped his runny nose on his sleeve, wincing at the pain from his feet.

"If You're out there . . . prove it to me," Greg muttered in a broken voice to the God he wasn't even sure existed. Nothing but the wind blowing through the alley answered his plea.

Slowly, to avoid any unnecessary pain from his feet, he rose and looked through blurry eyes to the dark sky above him. He closed them and breathed a deep wavering sigh. Again, he wiped his snot-encrusted nose with his hand, wishing he had a tissue.

Sluggishly, he started walking out of the alley. As he did, he noticed a light on in the building next to him. Hopefully nobody had heard him. Greg emerged out onto the street and self-consciously looked around for his skateboard. Then he remembered. He had left it at the park. Greg stood there uncertainly for a minute. Should he go back for it in the morning and leave it at the park tonight so he wouldn't have to face Brother Joseph? Or could he slip in without being noticed and get it tonight? Without his skateboard in his hand, he felt lost.

Turning to a direction on the sidewalk, he made his decision. He would go back. *Maybe they'll be gone by now.* As he trudged back down the street, wishing he had his skateboard to ride back on, he glanced at the sign of the building he had been sobbing next to. Saving Grace Church. Greg shook his head in disgust and painfully turned his head away from the sign. He had been crying in the shadow of a church.

o——o

Getting back to the park seemed to take a long time, probably because he had been running without thinking of where he was going before. With a groan, Greg saw that small groups of people still gathered in clusters around the stage. Apparently the service was over because the area in front of the stage was empty except for two people—one was on her knees crying, and the other had her arm around the first girl. As Greg drew closer, he saw that the girl comforting and praying for the other girl was Ismeralda. He tried to shield his face so she wouldn't recognize him if she turned. He didn't see Brother Joseph anywhere. David was still there, putting away the microphones into the little trailer and directing a couple kids who were helping to gather chairs. *Maybe I can get my skateboard without anyone seeing.*

Starting to walk toward where he thought he'd left it, he stopped. Now he couldn't remember where it was. *Did I put it by that tree? Yes . . . but, no, it's not there. But I distinctly remember leaving it there,* he thought with a frustrated grunt. *If somebody swiped it . . . Maybe it was in the row where Chris and the others had been sitting.*

As he walked toward the row, he saw Chris talking with a couple other kids in one of the clusters. Chris started to glance his way, and Greg tried to put his head down before the other skater recognized him but to no avail. Chris waved him over and started to yell his name. Greg acknowledged he had seen him and indicated he was coming over. Chris nodded and turned back to the conversation.

Reluctance slowed Greg's steps. He really didn't want to talk to anyone. All he wanted was to just go back to the hotel and sleep these weird emotions off. But whatever . . . maybe it's for the best. Peeking into the row where they had been sitting, Greg didn't see his skateboard. *Maybe Chris or one of the others knows where it is.*

As Greg approached the group, Chris stepped back, widening the circle, and put an arm around Greg's shoulder. "Hey, where'd you go, man? We didn't see you after the song ended."

"Yeah, well . . ." Trying to think of a good excuse, Greg rolled his tongue around in his mouth. Fumbling, but not finding one, he just muttered, "I decided to leave but couldn't find my skateboard, so I came back for it."

Chris stared at him and laughed. "I can't understand anything you say when you're mumbling like that. Hey, do you want to come grab pancakes? We're going again tonight."

"Uh . . . well, all I wanted was my skateboard."

"Dude, you're mumbling again. If you don't have any money, I'll pay."

Greg shrugged Chris's arm off his shoulder. "Yeah, well, it's not that . . . it's just . . ."

Chris looked at him. "What?"

"I uh..." Greg took a deep breath. "I just came back for my skateboard. Do you know where it is?"

Chris shrugged and looked around, shaking his head. "I don't know, dude. I haven't seen it."

"I have." The voice startled Greg, and as he looked over his shoulder, he saw Brother Joseph making his way through the chairs with Greg's skateboard. Greg's heart sank, and he looked down at his shoes. He didn't want to talk to him right now. *Why is everyone being so difficult?* The missionary walked up gave the skateboard to Greg.

Thanks," Greg mumbled, taking it from him. *I guess I should apologize,* he thought. Even though he didn't want to, he started, "Listen, dude, I'm sorry I was so . . ."

Brother Joseph put an arm around Greg's shoulders reassuringly and gave him a side hug, cutting him off. "Don't worry about it. Will you come with us to the restaurant?"

Greg looked down at his feet. "I . . . I don't know . . ."

"Please? I want you to be there."

Greg fumbled for an excuse but couldn't think of one. He felt himself nodding slowly. "Yeah, okay. I guess."

"All right!" Chris slapped Greg a high-five. "Let's go! Your van?" he said, looking at Brother Joseph.

Brother Joseph chuckled. "Yes, my van."

Chris bolted toward the van and called over his shoulder. "Last one there has to ride in the death seat!"

"The death seat?" Terry asked.

"Yeah, where Zack threw up last time," one of the kids said. "I'm outta here!"

Brother Joseph smiled, watching them run for the van. Greg started to walk over, but Brother Joseph caught his shoulder. "Greg, listen to me. I do care about you. And I'm never going to try to hurt you intentionally, okay? I need to know that you're okay."

Greg nodded silently, looking anywhere but the missionary's eyes.

"Hey, Greg, please." The tone in his voice caused Greg to look up, and Brother Joseph's brown eyes locked with his. "I need to hear you say it. I don't want there to be any rift between us, all right?"

The sincerity in Brother Joseph's eyes once again took Greg aback. There was a pause as the defiant teenager and the compassionate street missionary looked at each other. At last, Greg nodded. "Yeah, sure."

Brother Joseph held out a hand, keeping his other hand on Greg's shoulder. "We're friends?" he asked, looking for confirmation. "Now you've gotta say yes, or I'll be a miserable man."

Greg began to choke up again, but he quickly swallowed it back. *What was with all of these emotions tonight?* He wasn't sure how to handle Brother Joseph yet, but he forced a smile for the street missionary's sake. "Yeah. Friends," he said.

"Thanks," Brother Joseph said softly. "I love you, Greg. I hope you know that. But even more importantly, God loves you. You'll remember that, won't you?"

Greg nodded, once again surprised by Brother Joseph's straightforwardness. How many preachers would just come right out and tell a teenager they loved them? The strange thing about it was that it didn't make Greg uncomfortable at all, as it would under normal circumstances. This time, it was something he needed to hear. "Thanks," he whispered.

Brother Joseph smiled and clapped him on the shoulder. "Now, you better hurry if you don't want to ride in the death seat," he said, lowering his voice to make it sound spooky.

This time Greg didn't force the smile. It came on its own. "Okay," he said.

Brother Joseph watched with a smile as Greg ran to the van where the other kids were already screaming about something.

Little did he know the trust he'd just established with the teenager would be broken quicker than he thought. Much, much quicker.

12

Purdo burst into the office. For some reason, his entrance always seemed to be loud and chaotic, Cambiano had noticed. "What is it, Cambiano?" he demanded. "We have a new lead?"

Cambiano motioned for the chair in front of his desk. "Go ahead and have a seat, Officer Purdo."

Purdo glanced around as if he should be combing a house or interrogating a prisoner but finally settled into the chair. "Well?" he asked impatiently. "What do you have?"

"A contact." Cambiano slid his notebook across the desk. "I just received this address from the man we've been working with who's in contact with the gangs."

Purdo snatched it up and hungrily read it, then threw it down in disgust. "That's the warehouse we already knew about!"

"But now we have the runner."

Purdo leaped to his feet. "What?"

"We know who's been going in between the dealers and the gangs."

Purdo was excited. "Then we've got him!"

"Providing we play our cards right," Cambiano cautioned. "But, yes, it looks like our nets are closing in on our target . . . a man who is now going by the name Stefan Adikema."

○———○

"Ah, I wasn't expecting to find you here. I thought you'd be at the skate park. Again."

The voice broke through Greg's thoughts, interrupting his reverie of the night before. As it turned out, Brother Joseph had been too swamped with other conversations to actually talk to Greg, whose disappointment at this turn of events surprised him a little. But the night had turned out well. Greg had finally loosened up enough to enjoy the time at the restaurant. He even got to sit at Ismeralda's table for a while, which he enjoyed. But the fact that he enjoyed being with the group didn't change the thoughts that he continued to wrestle with. When he'd arrived back at the hotel, these musings had haunted him until he fell asleep. And now, this morning they hadn't quit either. In fact, the thoughts were so intense that this encounter with his adversary seemed trivial in comparison.

Greg didn't have to turn around to know that the voice belonged to Stefan. Only Stefan could sound that cocky, uncaring, cold, and cynical while at the same time maintaining his composure and confidence.

He slowly turned his head, hoping his eyes weren't still red-rimmed from crying. "What do you want?" he asked, spinning one of the wheels on his skateboard.

He was sitting in the alley behind the hotel, listlessly spinning his skateboard wheels because he didn't think anyone would bother him there. Of course, he hadn't counted on Stefan. Truthfully, he had thought of going to the skate park, but he didn't feel like it, which was definitely unusual. *Maybe I'm coming down with something,* he thought, putting a hand to his forehead.

Stefan raised an eyebrow. "Is everything okay?" he asked.

"As if you care," Greg muttered.

Stefan stared a moment longer, wondering whether to pursue that line of thought or not. At last, he decided not to, cleared his throat, and said, "I was wondering if you'd gone to give the stuff to the gang yet."

Greg wasn't focused. Trying to concentrate on the question, he muffled the thoughts of Brother Joseph and God in his mind and sighed. "No, I haven't."

Stefan's eyebrows narrowed. "I see."

Silence lingered between them like an oppressing fog for a few minutes. Greg averted his eyes from Stefan's sunglasses. The silence grew thick and unbearable.

"I'll go do it right now," Greg finally mumbled.

"Fine," Stefan responded, though his mind seemed somewhere else as he studied Greg.

Greg was tired of this. He rose to his feet, grabbed his skateboard, and started walking out of the alley.

Stefan's gaze followed him. Right before Greg exited the alley, in a low hoarse voice Stefan called, "I don't know what's going on with you, Gregory. But if you compromise this mission . . ." He let his sentence hang in the air for a few seconds.

The hair on the back of Greg's neck stood up involuntarily and Greg froze. What is it with Stefan? Suddenly angry, Greg spun around and faced the drug dealer. "What is your problem?" he asked, not caring if his voice was loud enough for others to hear. "Listen, I'm doing everything you've asked! I'm giving the drugs to the gangs, all right? And if you want me to keep helping you, why don't you shut up and quit acting so creepy!"

Stefan leveled his gaze on Greg and lifted a finger, pointing it right at the skater's face. "Just stay away from the missionary," he commanded in the same low creepy voice.

Goose bumps ran up Greg's arm. *Stefan knows?*

"Don't think we haven't been watching you!" Stefan said, his voice rising. "And if you don't cooperate with us, you will have no end of problems! I'm going to give you till tonight to accomplish your mission, but then if you haven't done it, you will suffer severe consequences. Do you understand me, Greg? I am running out of patience with you. Get . . . it . . . right!"

With one final withering glare at Greg, Stefan lowered his finger and turned and left the alley. Greg's heart was pounding in his chest. It wasn't Stefan's threat, it was the fact that Stefan knew what he'd been doing . . . that he was watching him. And that voice! That wasn't a natural voice! A terrifying blend of human and inhuman tones were mixed into that tone. Scary.

Heart thudding but trying to act unconcerned, Greg walked quickly from the alley to the hotel. He slipped quietly up to his hotel room and snatched his cell phone from his pocket. *I have to call Brother Joseph! No . . . wait. What if Stefan has the room bugged or something? Go into the bathroom. Yeah . . . like that movie. But . . . who's to say he doesn't have bugs in the bathroom? Turn on the shower.* Greg walked into the bathroom and turned on the shower, then quickly dialed Brother Joseph's number. The phone rang a couple times. *Come on, Brother Joseph! Come on!*

Brother Joseph sat in a meeting, waiting for his turn to speak. This was an important meeting for his company, and he hoped he could present his case well. But the street missionary's thoughts kept drifting to the skaters and teenagers that he was trying to help. Especially Greg. The turmoil going on inside the teenager was so apparent. Brother Joseph longed to help him, but Greg wouldn't let him. *Jesus, give me the opportunity to lead him to Your love,* he prayed silently. Another thought struck him. *And I need to call Officer Purdo.*

The speaker was saying something, emphasizing his point by shaking his pointer at the audience. *What is the point, anyway? Stay focused,* Joseph chastised himself. *You have to get your mind on the meeting.*

The speaker finished his presentation and everybody began to clap. Joseph was up next. He began gathering his charts. Just then his phone vibrated in his pocket. *Oh no, great timing,* he thought to himself. Quickly, he slipped the phone out of his pocket and looked at the caller ID. Greg. Joseph looked up at the ceiling. *Lord, are you testing me?* The president of the company was calling his name. Joseph gathered his charts and stood up, mumbling a quick apology to the Lord and starting to walk to the front.

Then the gentle voice of the Lord prompted him, "Answer it." Joseph tried to brush it aside. If it wasn't the Lord, he was in a heap of trouble with his bosses. The gentle voice prompted him again. "Answer it." Joseph paused, undecided. He'd ignored God before. But he'd also been wrong about the voice of the Lord before. The phone vibrated one more time, and he decided.

"Joseph?" the president asked.

"I'm sorry, sir, but I'm receiving a phone call that I need to answer. Would someone else present before me?"

The president didn't look too happy but slowly nodded. "We'll have Carlos give his presentation next instead. Go answer your phone call. Carlos?"

"Thank you, sir." Brother Joseph dipped his head toward the president and slipped out into the hall, answering the phone. "Hello?"

o———o

Greg closed his eyes and started to disconnect the call. Surely Brother Joseph would've answered by now. Just when he was about to press "end," he heard, "Hello?"

Greg quickly put the phone back up to his ear. "Brother Joseph?" he asked, relieved.

"Hi Greg, what's up?"

Greg lowered his voice as an extra precaution. "I need your help. I think . . . I think Stefan knows that I've been telling you about the drug operation."

"What? How?"

"Today Stefan came to see if I delivered the drugs to the gang yet, and he told me to stay away from you and gave me until tonight to finish the mission. And he was talking in this really creepy voice and . . ."

Suddenly the thing about the voice sounded foolish to him, and he chided himself for telling Brother Joseph about it. But Brother Joseph didn't seem to notice because he thought for a moment then said, "Okay, this is what I want you to do. You still have the drugs Stefan wants you to deliver to the gang?"

Greg nodded, then remembered Brother Joseph couldn't see him. "Yeah," he said.

"Okay, hang on. Let me think." There was a pause and Greg imagined Brother Joseph pressing his fingertips against his temples in concentration. "Why are they having you deliver these drugs now? Surely the drugs can't be all they're delivering."

"What do you mean?" Greg asked.

"I mean, I don't think they'd go to all the trouble of having a contest in another state, pay for your airfare over, and risk another link in their system and possibly a breach of security just to have you deliver a couple boxes of drugs. It wouldn't be worth it."

"Oh!" Greg quickly recounted Stefan's conversation with him in his office.

"So the address for the next drug deliveries is still in the box?"

"Right."

"I can't let you take the drugs to the gang. Who knows how many more lives could be ruined because of that stuff?" Brother Joseph murmured, half to himself. The preacher went silent again then finally took a deep breath. "Okay, Greg. I've got a plan."

o———o

Greg crept stealthily out of the hotel. He was wearing a hoodie with the box bulging underneath. Under his breath he repeated the address of the warehouse to himself. He hurried down the street to the bus stop. Thankfully, it was a different bus driver than before. The skater took the same seat as last time, and this time the bus driver was a gruff character who didn't ask any questions. Greg got off the bus without any incidents.

The clouds were dark again, and the wind whipped at Greg. He looked up into the sky and ran a finger through his curly brown locks sticking out of his backwards cap. Adjusting the box, he moved into an alley and dropped his skateboard onto the sidewalk. With ease, he began navigating through the alley around boxes and dumpsters to get to the warehouse.

He neared the end of an alley, and just before he moved out into the open, he heard footsteps walking toward him. Greg deftly leaped off the skateboard, leaving the wheels spinning, and stepped back into the shadows against the wall.

A shadow fell across the opening of the alley and paused. A nightstick was being twirled in the shadow's right hand. A familiar hat rested on the shadow's head. Greg caught his breath. It was a policeman.

There was silence for a few moments, then the policeman emerged into the opening where Greg could see him and stopped again, looking around suspiciously. Greg pressed harder against the wall, hoping he faded into the blackness and that he wasn't able to be seen from the street. The policeman turned his head in Greg's direction, and the light from a nearby street lamp illuminated his shadowy face. Greg nearly gasped in surprise. It was the same policeman he had run into before, the one who had searched him for drugs. What did Al called him? Officer Perez, or Purdy or something? *Of all the policemen to run into, it has to be one who would recognize me!*

But the policeman's scowl-hardened face turned away from Greg, and he continued on his patrol, passing by the alley. Greg waited a couple minutes before cautiously stepping out of the shadows and peering around the corner into the alley Purdy had been in. Or whatever his name was. It was empty.

Just then, Brother Joseph's plan came to his mind. Quickly, looking both directions again, he stepped back into the shadows and removed the box from his hoodie, lowering it carefully into an old metal garbage can. After a few minutes, he dusted off his hands and moved forward.

Greg slipped into the alley, carrying his skateboard, heading the opposite direction the officer had and turning as soon as he had a chance. It wasn't until he was so far away he was confident the officer wouldn't surprise him that he risked riding the skateboard again. Not that he would normally care so much about what a policeman would think, but he was involved in an illegal drug operation and didn't want to waste time messing with the cops.

A couple streets later, Greg reached into his pocket to pull out the address, checking it with the one on the street sign above him. *Yep. This is it.* With a deep breath, Greg hopped on his skateboard and maneuvered around the building into the back. He paused. Around the corner, he could hear a bottle break and the gang jeering, laughing, and making racial jokes and sexual innuendos.

Greg flipped his hair back from his eyes with a snap of his head and rounded the corner on his skateboard—right into Tony. With horror, Greg watched as Tony stumbled backwards and fell into a wall. A couple other guys in the gang laughed at him. One called out a rude name at Tony, but the rest stared at Greg, unflinchingly. Tony was quick on his feet, trying to right himself, only to knock his head on a brick ledge. The guys in the gang started laughing again until they saw how angry their second-in-command was. Greg backed up, stuttering and apologizing. Tony jumped up with fire in his eyes. "That's it, kid! You goin' down now!" A few cheered.

Greg leveled his fists, ready to fight if necessary, though he wasn't sure how he would do against the experienced black gang member. Tony's eyes were wild, and he took a couple monstrous steps toward Greg, ready to lay into him, when Al stepped in between them and gave Tony a hard look.

With a curse, Tony stepped back a step and said through clenched teeth, "Let me at 'im, Al. I've had enough o' dis—" At this point Tony began to describe Greg, using a lot of four-letter words in his description. "He ain't—"

"Shut up, Tony," Al said. "We ain't bein' paid to like 'im." Turning to Greg, he said in a low voice, "You got the stuff, kid?"

Greg's mind went blank and he forgot everything he and

Brother Joseph had talked about. Al's eyes narrowed as Greg stood there silently. "What the—" Al started. "Kid, you better have—"

Tony jumped up, spittle flying from his mouth. "See?" he said. "He ain't got it, Al! Let me rip into 'im! Let's work this one over good and send him back to Adikema with—" A string of curse words punctuated his taunt—and Al's meaty fist clubbing him in the jaw.

"I SAID, SHUT UP!" the gang leader screamed. "Who the leader o' this gang, huh, Tony? Is it you? Step back, ya hear? I gonna call the shots around here! I tol' ya to back off!"

Tony rubbed the tender spot on his jaw where Al had hit him, his eyes glaring daggers into Al. He looked like he was ready to punch Al back but didn't. With another curse, Tony threw his knife down at Al's feet. "Fine, Al! You handle your business with this little—" Tony spit at Greg as he called him an unrepeatable name. "I'm outta this thing!" he shouted pointing a finger at Al. "I warned you 'bout this kid, and I still think he be trouble! If you gonna keep actin' so soft and light den I'm out! Call me when you decide to start leadin' dis gang again." Angrily, Tony stalked off, clenching his fists and pushing a gang member as he walked off.

Al stared after him, then grunted. "He'll be back," he muttered. Then with his nostrils flaring, he turned to Greg. "And you. I'm gettin' fed up wichyer games! Where's the crack?"

"I don't have it," Greg admitted, hand on his skateboard ready to make a quick exit if he had to. "But that's why I'm here! I've got a message."

"From Adikema?" Al asked suspiciously.

"Uh…" A little white lie won't hurt. "Yeah. He wants you to meet him here at this address." Greg pulled out the slip of paper he had removed from the box of drugs. "Tonight at any time after six. This is where the new drop-off point is."

"We gonna start gettin' the drugs there?" Junior spoke up to clarify.

Greg nodded. "Yep, that's it." Trying to hide the shaking of his hand, he held the address out to Al.

Al snatched it up roughly and studied it before crumpling it up and putting it in his pocket. "A'right. Good. Guess we won't be seein' you no more, kid," he said looking at Greg.

"And good riddance," Greg heard one of the gang members mumble as they got up to leave.

"See ya 'round, punk," said Al, who was smirking.

Hopefully not, Greg thought as he began to leave.

o——o

Al stared at the kid as he left. Michael watched the gang leader as Al shook his head. And at the moment, Michael was puzzled; Al wouldn't usually let a white kid go that easily. These gang members liked to hurt people and wouldn't hesitate to kill that kid if he got in their way. But something about the kid touched Michael. *I hope Stefan doesn't view him as a liability now.*

o——o

Greg's feet pounded against the pavement, and he pumped his fist in jubilation. *Yes! They believed it!* The skater slapped his skateboard against the sidewalk as he brushed some hair out of his eyes. *Wait until Doug hears about this! Of course, Doug probably wouldn't believe him. Nobody will believe it! Greg Martin, skater kid from Colorado, involved in a drug-busting operation.* A grin tugged at the corners of his mouth as he skated down the street, this time trying to stay close to traffic. The thought of the box of drugs flitted through his mind. *Should I go get it?* At first, he opted not

219

to. Then he imagined the officer or one of the gang members finding the drugs, and he moved faster on the skateboard.

He reached the abandoned alley, where he had hidden the box and looked hurriedly. *Where is it?* Greg started to panic. *I know I hid it here!* Then his hand brushed against something in the rubbish. It was still there. Carefully he removed it and started off in the direction of the bus stop. He felt exuberant. Things were going to be okay now. Revenge was in store for Stefan, kids at the skate park liked him, Ismeralda was cute and he could probably get her phone number, not to mention the fame he'd get for helping end this drug operation. Lives could be saved from what he was doing, and TV and radio stations would probably jump all over it. Teenage Skater Infiltrates Drug Trade From Inside! the headlines would say. Girls would swoon. Sweet.

Greg got to the right bus stop and checked again the address for Brother Joseph's trailer park. Good, it wasn't that far. He would get there quickly.

Ismeralda jogged lightly up the steps of Brother Joseph's trailer home. They were going to be going out to talk to skaters, but Brother Joseph had to do something concerning Greg and the drug dealer. For some reason, he had wanted her there.

She knocked once, then opened the door like usual. "Hi, Brother Joseph, it's—" she stopped as she noticed Brother Joseph talking with a policeman in the middle of the living room. "Oh," she put her hand to her mouth. "I'm sorry. I didn't realize you were . . ." She paused. *What are they doing?* ". . . that you were in a meeting."

"That's all right, Ismeralda," Brother Joseph said, waving

her into the room. "It's why I wanted you here. Ismeralda, this is Officer Purdo."

"Nice to meet you," she said politely, offering her hand. The policeman nodded briskly and shook her hand formally, looking incredibly bored with the business and anxious to get back to whatever he and Brother Joseph had been talking about.

"Ismeralda has been helping me minister to some of the teenagers around Chicago," Brother Joseph explained to Officer Purdo.

Officer Purdo nodded. "Oh," he said in a different tone of voice. "Then is she—"

Brother Joseph shook his head quickly, cutting him off. "No, she's not. He's still coming."

"I see," Officer Purdo said, facing Brother Joseph again and seeming to forget about Ismeralda. "So were you able to get any more information other than what you've told me?"

"No, but I assume the one in contact with the gangs will have new information for us. I can contact you when—"

"No need," Officer Purdo said, waving his hand. "I think it would be best if I met this kid myself."

"Brother Joseph?" Ismeralda asked, uncertainly. "What's going on here?"

Brother Joseph started to answer when suddenly the door burst open.

Greg hopped off his skateboard when he got to Brother Joseph's trailer park and ran lightly up to the trailer number Brother Joseph had told him. *Wait till Brother Joseph finds out how well I did!* Greg bounded up the steps and opened the door.

"Brother Joseph!" Greg burst through the door. The room

froze and Greg stopped cold, looking from one face to the other. He still had the box tucked under his arm. Brother Joseph, Ismeralda and a police officer? Not only a police officer but . . . what is going on?

Recognition briefly flashed across Officer Purdo's face before he regained his composure. "Greg," Brother Joseph said with surprise. "I didn't think you'd be here this early. Officer Purdo, this is Greg—"

"So you're the runner," the police officer spoke up, giving Greg a condescending smile. "I should have known. Great work, Brother Joseph!" His nostrils flared like a bloodhound upon reaching its quarry. "I had my suspicions about this kid and now you've brought him right to us!"

Greg took a step back. "What . . . what's going on here?" he demanded.

The police officer put his hand on his gun and fumbled with his handcuffs eagerly. "Brother Joseph here is your downfall, kid. We've been working with him for quite some time. He gave us the information to bring the little drug ring you and your friends have been running to a screeching halt!"

He dropped the handcuffs on the table and clapped his hands to punctuate his sentence. Leaning in towards Greg with a sneer he said in a low voice, "Did you really think you could get away with this? You thought when I searched you that would be the last time you'd see me. But thanks to Brother Joseph here—"

Brother Joseph rose up out of his chair, "Now hang on—" he began.

But by this time, Greg was steaming at the ears. A thousand thoughts were rushing through his mind as he tried to process what was happening. All of Stefan and Tony's warnings about what would happen to him if he betrayed them to the police suddenly came to the forefront of his mind. "Are you saying you're going to arrest me?" he demanded. "You can't arrest me!"

Officer Purdo stepped forward menacingly. "Oh yeah, tough guy? You think you can do whatever you want with no consequences? Then you and your buddies are in for a big surprise."

Brother Joseph grabbed the policeman's shoulder who was lunging towards Greg, and said sharply, "Officer Purdo!"

"They're not my buddies!" Greg spat. "You think I get along with any of them, and they treat me like I'm part of their team?"

"Well, maybe you can all work that out in prison together," Purdo quipped snidely, shaking Brother Joseph's hand off.

The thought of being in prison with Stefan and Al terrified Greg. *That's not how it works with minors, is it? But even if they let me go but didn't catch Stefan, wouldn't Stefan hunt me down? He'd know I was the one who had tipped the police off! And he would find me!*

He had already said the police couldn't pin anything on him and he was slippery enough Greg could almost believe it. Why would Brother Joseph hand Greg over to the police like this? Suddenly, all of Greg's fear was turned into anger towards Brother Joseph. The realization hit him like a brick wall . . . Brother Joseph was working with the police and had just used him to get information and now . . . now he was going to hand him over to them.

Greg turned to the youth pastor. "You're turning me in?" he asked in disbelief. "But you promised you wouldn't take me to them!"

Brother Joseph looked stricken at how Greg was reacting. "Greg, how else are we supposed to stop these guys?"

"That's all you care about, huh?" Greg's cheeks were heating up. He felt slightly lightheaded. "To you I'm just one of those sinners who needs to be stopped, aren't I?"

Brother Joseph stepped back half a step like he'd been slapped. "How could you . . . you know I—" his voice trailed off, and for the first time since Greg had met him, the preacher seemed at a loss for words.

"I think we've wasted enough time," Purdo said, snatching up his notebook and a pen. "It's time to move in for the kill. Maybe we'll go easier on you if you tell me everything you know."

Greg looked from Brother Joseph to Ismeralda, disbelievingly. Ismeralda just stood there as if she'd been struck dumb. She opened her mouth as if to say something, but nothing came out. Purdo was asking him a question, but he couldn't understand what he was saying. Only one word hammered through Greg's mind. Betrayed . . . Betrayed . . . Betrayed . . . Betrayed.

"You used me!" he interrupted Purdo, his voice rising, staring in shock at Brother Joseph.

"Greg—" Ismeralda started, putting a hand out toward him.

Taking a step back, Greg ignored her and glared at Brother Joseph. "How could you? All that stuff about loving me and wanting to be there for me and—you lied! All you wanted was information! You used me, Brother Joseph! You used me!" Greg realized his sentences and words were running into each other but he didn't care. *The one person I thought I could trust.* Well, he didn't have to take this. Purdo would NOT get him today! Greg turned and slammed the door open angrily, smacking it against the side of the house and bolted.

"Greg, please!" Ismeralda cried.

Greg didn't listen and bounded off the steps, running as fast as he could, his vision being blurred by tears, which he angrily wiped away.

"Greg, no! You don't understand!" he heard Brother Joseph call. "Wait!"

It didn't matter what Brother Joseph said now. The betrayal sunk deeper with each step Greg took. *I should have known!* he thought angrily, trying to brush away tears. *All Christians are alike! I should have known!*

Brother Joseph sunk onto an easy chair with his face buried in his hands. Ismeralda rushed over to his side to comfort him. Brother Joseph's moans were muffled from behind his hands. "Oh, God, please reach out to Greg. Oh God, I'm sorry. I'm so sorry. Please touch him. Let him know I really do care! Oh Jesus! Jesus!" Brother Joseph began sobbing.

Officer Purdo shifted his feet uncomfortably, not sure what to do in this dramatic display of religious fervor.

Ismeralda put her hand on Brother Joseph's shoulder. "It's okay, Brother Joseph," she said softly. "It's not your fault."

Brother Joseph lifted his head up. "No, Ismeralda," he said in a husky voice. "It is. I never should've gotten involved with the police. I should've thought of the kids and how it would look to them! I . . ." He buried his face in his hands.

Officer Purdo adjusted his notepad and pencil and decided to step in. "Now, listen here, sir. Catching these drug abusers is, I believe, much more important than hurting some kid's feelings. You've gotta consider the cost/benefit analysis. You might lose a couple kids in your ministry or whatever it is, but it's worth it. After all—"

Brother Joseph jumped to his feet with such swiftness that Ismeralda nearly fell backwards. His eyes were blazing with an anger that she had never seen before. Even Officer Purdo was slightly taken back by Brother Joseph's sudden moves. "No, officer," Brother Joseph said firmly. "Losing one kid's confidence isn't worth all the drug busts in the world to me. I will never, ever place a mission or operation above a person's soul, do you understand? I brought Greg here to give you some more information and ID the people involved, but you shouldn't have intimidated him the way you did! And if that's what you're going to do in this investigation, you can count me out! The only reason I'm helping you at all, is to save kids' souls, not lose them. It is not worth it, Mr. Purdo. You are doing this to put people in prison, but I'm doing this to set people free. I care more about Greg than I do about the police catching a couple crooks. And that's what you can expect from me in any further dealings we have. Understood?"

Officer Purdo took a step back and raised his hands. He cleared his throat and forced a chuckle to lighten up this conversation. "Uh . . . listen . . . sir, I'm sure if you just think about it—"

"Officer Purdo." Brother Joseph cut him off with a wave of his hand and sat down in a chair with a weary sigh. "I think it would be best if you left now."

Ismeralda put her hand on his shoulder. "I'll go after Greg," she told him. "Maybe I can explain to him what really happened. After all, you didn't really promise you wouldn't go to the police. You told Greg he didn't have to go to the police yet! He's taking things out of context."

Brother Joseph stared at her and started to say something, then stopped himself. Looking at her another moment, he nodded. "Okay, Ismeralda. I don't know if he'll listen but . . ." As his voice trailed off, he stared off into the distance with an empty look in his eyes. Then he turned and nodded at the girl, forcing the corners of his mouth to turn up a little. "I . . . I think that would be great."

Ismeralda nodded and went to the door, slipping out swiftly and letting the door close behind her.

Brother Joseph rested his forehead against his hand.

Officer Purdo's eyes narrowed. "Joseph, I hope this doesn't mean you aren't going to help us anymore. We're counting on your support in this endeavor, and without your assistance—"

"I'll contact you at the police station from now on," Brother Joseph interrupted. "But please do not come to my home any longer."

"Well, all right." Purdo reluctantly accepted that answer as his promise to continue helping and turned to the door. "Thank you, sir. I'll be in touch." The police officer tipped his hat and turned on his heel. With his shoulders straight, the officer strode out the door.

o———o

Greg fled the trailer park, angrily spitting at a little girl who was staring at him with wide eyes. *Why did I ever listen to that creep?* he screamed in his head.

"Greg!" He heard Ismeralda running behind him. "Wait!"

He slowed his pace a little but didn't stop.

Ismeralda's black hair blew behind her as she ran to catch up to him. She grabbed his shoulder and stopped, trying to catch her breath. "Greg, please stop!"

Greg shook her hand off his shoulder. "Get away from me," he ordered, tossing his hair out of his eyes. "I don't want anything to do with you."

"Greg," she pleaded. "It wasn't what it looked like! You don't understand what—"

"What Brother Joseph was doing?" Greg whirled on her and she took a step back. "I know what he was doing! He was trying to stop the drug trade! And he used me as his little pawn to get the information he wanted! That's all he ever cared about from me. All of the things he said: 'No matter what, I'll be there for you,' 'You can always come to me if you want to talk,' 'I'm praying for you,' 'I'll never turn you away,' 'I love you, Greg!'" Greg spat out the last one. "Ha!" Pouring out some filthy cuss words aimed at Brother Joseph, he shook his head, turning away slightly. "All you all ever wanted was to get information from me for the police."

"Greg, that's not how it is," Ismeralda said quietly.

He flung his hands up and stared at her, eyes flashing. "Oh yeah? Then how is it, Ismeralda? Why was the policeman there? Huh? He said he wouldn't go to the police! He lied! How do you explain that? Does your Christian God love like that?"

"I . . ." Ismeralda faltered.

"Yeah, that's what I thought," Greg said bitterly.

Ismeralda stood speechless for a second, fighting for words. Finally she said, "Listen Greg, I don't know why things turned out the way they did. Brother Joseph was involved with the police long before you came on the scene. But we do care about you and—"

"Yeah, right!" Greg interrupted her. "Shut up! Just shut up, okay? I'm not going to let you stall me until the police catch me! Just leave me alone!"

The skater turned to leave and Ismeralda grabbed his sleeve. "Greg, please let me—" A cold glare from Greg cut off her sentence. Angrily, he shook off her hand and took off running.

Greg didn't look back to see what Ismeralda was doing. He didn't care. Nothing mattered anymore except for saving his own skin. Greg weighed his options carefully. He hated Stefan, Brother Joseph had betrayed him, the police sure weren't an option, and that left the gang. Al's gang. If there was any way he was going to get out of this thing, siding with the gang was the only way to go. *I could bribe them with the box of drugs to protect me and make up some story about Stefan to get them to turn on him.* Clenching his fist tighter around the box of drugs, he ran a little faster. Brother Joseph's words ran briefly through his mind. "Who knows how many more lives could be ruined because of that stuff?" Greg pushed them away. *It isn't about them. It's about me. And I'm going to do whatever it takes to come out of this on top.*

13

Old Elmer McArthur paused reverently at the end of the aisle in the sanctuary of the Pentecostals of Chicago church to look at the light streaming in from a window onto the old wooden altar. Dust swirled lazily in the stream of light. Elmer's eyes wandered over the piano, the glass-enclosed drum set, the microphones set up for the singers, the offering plates, the baptismal, the pews. He closed his eyes and allowed himself a moment of reflection. He could remember the times of intercessory prayer at that altar. He could remember Edna, bless her soul, bringing in huge Crockpots full of food to the potlucks in the basement while he talked to the elders. Times of repentance, revival, and restoration. Times of fellowship, food, and fun. All the memories contained in these walls . . .

Elmer shook his head to bring himself back to the task at hand. He turned and began slowly up the steps into the loft of the church, wincing occasionally at his aching joints and pausing once to set down his toolbox and give himself a minute's rest. This stuff didn't come to him as easily as it did when he was younger.

He reached the top of the loft, walked past the wooden door that was always propped open, and wiped his brow with a handkerchief. *Boy, it's sweltering up here! No wonder the choir complains during practices!* he thought. The air conditioning didn't circulate properly in the old building, so during the summer the balcony was a point of constant complaint from the choir and the people who worked the sound booth. There was one window, but it had been painted shut a long time ago. Often a sweating choir director or dehydrated sound booth worker had proclaimed they were going to fix it to let some air in, but it was such a small project and nobody ever had time, so it remained undone. That was about to change today.

During his prayer time that day, Elmer's mind kept going back to this window in the balcony and the grievances of the people who worked here. Fixing the window so it would open would be easy enough to do, but people kept putting it off. Elmer had brushed it aside at first too, thinking of the gardening he wanted to get done. But the thought kept returning, so Elmer promised the Lord the choir would have no more need for complaint. The old plumber might not know much about air conditioning, but he could sure fix a window! He would take care of that window today!

Elmer approached the window to look at his foe. This won't be so hard with a couple of minutes and the right kind of tools. He knelt to open his tool box. A few seconds later he was chipping away at the paint with sawdust, splinters, and dust flying. He jiggled the rusted latch. Now for the outside. He went back downstairs and took out an old ladder from the storage closet. He walked around to the alley adjacent to the building and adjusted the ladder. *Why did they make these buildings so close together?* There was hardly any room for the ladder between the fire escape on the building next to the church and the church wall where the window was. But if the years had taught Elmer anything, it was patience and determination. Stuffing the tools in the pockets of his overalls, he started up the ladder.

Within minutes he had finished and was putting away the ladder. He took a rag upstairs to clean up his mess and test his handiwork. Proudly, he observed the window sliding open and shut with ease. With that, old Elmer McArthur loaded his toolbox into his truck, locked up the church, and went home to finish his gardening. The whole scene went unobserved. By human eyes, at least. The old man had done what the Lord had told him to do. It was just a little thing, something to ease the discomfort of the sound workers and choir members so they wouldn't be so hot. Unimportant, some would say, a little thing that didn't really matter much in the grand scheme of things. But with the Lord, even the little things are important.

Al paced the sidewalk, stifling curses. He couldn't afford to let anyone find them again. The last couple weeks had been pure torture, ever since the PD had found their last drop-off point. *And Stefan's sure keeping a tight lid on the drugs,* he mused, his eyebrows knit together. It didn't make sense, at least not recently. Hiding the drugs from the gang is not a smart move on Stefan's part. Adikema has to know that. *So why is he doing it?* All it could mean was that he was staying a step ahead of them, and Al didn't like to think about that prospect. If the drugs weren't delivered on time that night, the gang would go after Adikema.

The gang leader reached the corner of the brick building he was next to and peered around it. He could barely make out Junior's shadowy form. Good. Junior sensed Al behind him and turned. With a slight furrow of his brow, he shook his head. Al nodded grimly and returned to pacing. So, Tony ain't back yet. *That ain't a good sign neither,* he thought, letting his eyes drift up to the cloudy sky. The clouds had grown darker, mirroring Al's mood. If Tony wasn't back, that either meant he was really mad or he had found something or he'd been caught. *Tony ain't the type to stay this mad over a little spat like we had earlier. Get mad over it? Yes. Stay mad over it? No.*

Suddenly Al heard a scrambling, and he whirled around to see what it was. A loose rock skid across the pavement as Michael raced up to the gang leader. His short body was sweating with exertion.

"The white kid is back," Michael told Al in a whisper. "Greg."

Shock registered on Al's face before he quickly dropped the curtain of his normal facial expression, hiding his thoughts. This was completely unexpected. Surely Stefan wouldn't send the white kid to deliver the drugs again. Not to the new drop-off point. There was too much risk in that. Then again, he might figure the pipsqueak already knew about it and couldn't do any more harm than he did before.

"What do you want me to do?" Michael asked nervously. He seemed more nervous than the situation warranted. The short gang member was glancing to both sides for the third time since he'd approached Al. *What was making him so agitated?*

Al looked at him and waved him back to his position. "Just stay where you at," he ordered in his low, baritone voice. "We'll see what he wants before we do anything."

Michael ran back to his hiding place and crouched down again, and Al ducked into one of the alleys leading to the warehouse. Undoubtedly that's where the kid was heading. Al signaled a couple guys from the gang to back him up and entered a space on the side of the warehouse unseen by the street. Leaning against a wall, Al folded his arms across his chest. The other guys followed his cue and took up bored stances. *Whatever this kid wants, he ain't gonna catch us by surprise.*

Greg came up to the alley cautiously, not wanting to be jumped again. Some of his earlier arrogance was gone, and as he flicked a lock of brown hair out of his eyes he caught himself checking the area for Al and his gang. He didn't have the box of drugs with him. This was the one sticky point of Greg's plan. On the way over, Greg decided he would need the drugs as leverage. If Greg had the drugs, Al could knock the skater out with one blow and take them. That wouldn't do any good. Instead, Greg had stashed them and was preparing to deal with the gang. Worry twisted his gut. He ignored it. This was what he had to do.

Forcing himself to walk upright, he rounded the side of the warehouse, entering an alley. Al and his gang were leaning casually against the side of the building. Only he didn't see Tony or Michael. The fact that Tony was gone was a good thing. The fact that Michael was gone may not be. He and Al had been the only ones to stick up for him.

A couple gang members were trying to light cigarettes and didn't look up from shielding the flame from the wind as he walked up. Al acknowledged him by dipping his eyes as he puffed on his own cigarette. The gang leader didn't seem surprised to see him, which puzzled Greg. Al pinched the cigarette between his thumb and forefinger and stared at Greg, daring him to speak first. Greg hesitated.

"Well? What do you want?" Al asked, eyeing the skater.

Suddenly, Greg wasn't sure if his plan was such a good one. But he was already here so he couldn't back out now. Swallowing hard, Greg said the words he'd hastily rehearsed on the way over. "I'm, uh, I'm coming to join you guys. Uh, your side, I mean." So much for rehearsing.

A look on Al's face showed he didn't understand what Greg meant. An amused smirk appeared. "You want to join the gang?"

"No," Greg sputtered, trying to get across what he'd come to do. "I just want to be on your side . . . not Stefan's."

The gang leader studied him, tapping his knife in his hand for good measure. "What do you mean you want to be on our side, not Stefan's?"

"I mean Stefan's been double-crossing you."

The knife froze in Al's hand, and it was obvious he had the rest of the gang's attention now too. He was definitely committed now.

One of the gang members leaped to his feet, his teeth clenched and eyes glaring. "This better be a joke, man," he said.

Al cut him off with a wave of his hand. "Quiet, Sonny. How?" he demanded, directing his question at Greg.

"With the drugs," Greg explained. "Why do you think you haven't been receiving the right amount of drugs or any drugs over the last couple weeks?" Al's eyes narrowed, and Greg pressed on. "Stefan's been charging you way more than the other gangs, and is secretly dealing you far less than you should be getting."

"He said he was cutting us a deal," Junior said doubtfully, looking over at Al.

"And you believed him?" Greg asked. "Stefan's been using you to get money from other gangs on the market and has been selling to your rival gangs constantly. By the word you're spreading and the meager money you get off the drugs you sell, he's hauling in money and he's been straight up playing you. In fact, he may even be working with the police."

"What?" a loud chorus of voices from the gang questioned.

Greg looked to Al to see if he was biting. Al looked suspicious.

"You think Stefan was planning on delivering all the drugs tonight?" Greg asked. "He was supposed to give you the drugs this morning too, but he didn't. Now he wants to lure you guys into a trap."

"You saying he's working with Purdo?" Al asked, staring hard at Greg.

"I don't know who he's working with," Greg said. "But Purdo's probably in on it."

"You got proof?"

"No. But I have the drugs." Glancing at a couple of the other gang members, Greg could tell he definitely had their attention.

"Where they at?" Al demanded.

"I'll take you right to them. But you have to agree to protect me from Stefan. If he finds out I double-crossed him, he'll kill me. But I'm on your side now."

"He lyin'." The distinct accent caused Greg to turn around.

Tony was standing in the alley, blocking his path.

Al raised his eyebrows. "Tony, you're back?"

Tony didn't take his eyes off Greg. "Yeah, I am. And I woulda been back sooner . . .'cept I been followin' this kid all day."

Greg's heart started beating faster, and he felt his palms going sweaty. *Did Tony see me at Brother Joseph's house with Officer Purdo?* The consequences were too terrible to think about. Hoping his voice came out normal and without squeaking, Greg challenged, "Yeah, so what?"

Al's eyes shifted between the two of them, trying to weigh the situation.

"What you got on this punk, Tony?" he asked, a smirk tugging at the corners of his mouth as if he thought the whole thing was amusing.

Tony was still looking at Greg. "Once I left, I hid in the alley, and as soon as he started walking away I followed him. I saw him go into an alley and come out with a box." Tony's eyes bore into Greg's accusingly. "It don't take a genius to figure out what was in it. Dat kid had the drugs da whole time." Al's tugging smirk disappeared and he stared hard at Greg. "I watched him get on a bus, so I slipped in the back and followed him," Tony continued. "He walked into a trailer park and went into a house. I waited a couple minutes, knowing he was up to something."

"What happened?" Al demanded.

"I didn't see what went on inside, but I sure saw who came out after this little punk. Guess who it was." Tony's voice was mocking.

"Who was it, Tony?" Al's tone carried a quiet, deadly ring.

Pausing for effect, Tony stared straight at Greg. "Try Officer Purdo."

There was silence for a moment as what Tony said began to sink in with the gang members. Suddenly Al turned to Greg, any trace of warmth or humanity gone from his face. With cold eyes he stared at the boy and said in a low voice, "You betrayed us?" The gang members jumped to their feet and grabbed their knives. An evil glint glistened in Tony's eye as he took a step toward Greg. Greg knew he had only one chance.

Keeping his eye on Al and the others, Greg took one step back, then without looking, grabbed his beloved skateboard and shoved it into Tony's stomach as hard as he could. Greg released his skateboard and leaped over Tony who gasped and tried to keep his balance but fell backwards. Greg bolted into the street. "After him!" Al yelled. The guys in the gang began whooping and hollering and tore after Greg, leaving Tony lying in the street. Greg didn't look back but ran as fast as he possibly could toward the street, the gang right on his heels. *Maybe if I can make it to the street where people are around . . .*

Without looking, Greg jumped into the street and dodged a car, which slammed on its brakes. Horns were blaring as cars screeched to a halt and zoomed around Greg, leaving skid marks. When Greg reached the median he risked a look back. The gang didn't stop at the street, but they were having trouble getting around all the cars. One of the cars hit a gang member. A siren sounded in the distance. A man stepped out of his car, cursing at the gang. Three gang members lunged toward him with their weapons and the man leaped back in the car.

Greg ran into an alley, adrenaline racing, hoping he could lose them in the city maze. For the first time in his life, Greg wondered if he were going to die. In desperation, a thought crossed his mind. *A loving God . . . .* Gulping air, Greg made a rash decision. *God, I don't know if You're out there. But if You are and You love me, help me!*

Al scowled and folded his arms, a thousand cuss words playing on his lips. *How did the kid manage to get away? No matter. He won't get far.* The gang had split up and was searching for him. Al had to reluctantly admit that the kid was smart. The skidding cars in the street had stalled them—not much, but enough for the kid to get away. Al spat on the ground and grabbed his cell phone. Stefan was going to hear about this.

Stefan slowly hung up the phone, an amused smile playing across his face. This was turning out better than he could've hoped. "Robert!" Stefan snapped his fingers at the young man moving boxes. "Get Rush and Terrance for me."

Robert dropped the box he was carrying and headed to the door. "Yes, sir."

Stefan slowly shook his head. Greg was making things interesting for all of them. Robert appeared in the doorway followed by Terrance and Rush. Stefan waved his hand at Robert in dismissal. "Leave us," he said.

Terrance and Rush stepped into the office, and Stefan motioned for them to shut the door. Terrance leaned against the wall, his face expressionless.

"What's going on?" Rush asked, shifting his weight.

The smile remained on Stefan's face as he tapped a pen against his chin. "Things just got more interesting," he explained. "Apparently Greg betrayed us and has now betrayed the gang as well. And they aren't happy about it."

Rush's mouth opened in shock, and he frowned at Stefan's apparent amusement.

"And that's a good thing?" he asked disdainfully.

"The game, Mr. Stein." Stefan waved his hands in the air and leaned back in his chair. "It's all about the game. What fun is the chase unless the object you're pursuing is running? What good is a fight unless the opposition is strong enough to give you a challenge? The stronger the opponent, the sweeter the victory."

"But this is a drug ring. Don't we want to keep it . . . you know . . . easy? Low-key? In the dark? We don't want resistance from cops and stuff. Right?" Rush ventured.

Stefan laughed. "So much more is going on here than a simple drug ring, Rush. Terrance, get the car. I want you two to find out where the kid is. I'll be out in a moment."

Terrance immediately slipped out the door, his facial expression remaining the same the entire time.

Rush lingered a moment longer. "You're coming with us?" he asked.

"Of course," Stefan answered. A cocky grin lighted his face. "I wouldn't miss this for anything." He laughed. "The chase is on!"

o——o

Greg paused to catch his breath and doubled over, resting his hands on his knees. *Maybe I've escaped them.* Tears welled up in his eyes. *Why is this happening to me? What did I ever do to deserve this?* Despite his desperate prayer to God, Greg still had his doubts about Him. If there really was a God and that God loved him, why would He allow this to happen?

Suddenly Greg heard a shout come from down the street. "There he is!"

He turned, his curly locks falling partially in his eyes, and saw three black guys from Al's gang at the end of the sidewalk, running toward him. Tony was leading them. Greg gulped one last breath of air and took off.

"Get back here!" a voice shouted, followed by the sound of a garbage can clattering to the ground. The skater didn't turn around but kept running. It felt weird being without his skateboard. Greg wondered if he would ever get it back. It sure didn't look like it. Greg turned a corner and his legs pumped harder. He was already feeling the strain on his muscles. A stomach cramp had begun to form. *I can't make it,* Greg told himself. *They're going to catch me!*

Suddenly the neon open sign of a bar caught his eye. *My mom would kill me,* Greg thought. *She's never even . . .* With irritation, Greg cleared his mind of the thought and bolted for the door. Funny the things you think of when you're about to die.

The door slammed open, and a couple guys looked up with a glare from their poker game. The rest didn't notice but continued on with their conversations in the smoke-filled bar.

One drunk staggered toward Greg with a crooked smile. "Say, ain't you a little young to be in here?" He started laughing, but doubled over in a coughing spell that ended up with him retching all over the floor. A guy near him cursed and shoved the drunk away.

Greg ignored them and ran through the tables trying to get to a back door. Out of the corner of his eye, he saw a short, thin Asian man in a white smock, cleaning a table. He reached the counter and paused, sweating. *Why is it so hot in here?* He absolutely couldn't run anymore. The door opened again and the three guys from Al's gang walked into the bar. Greg dropped to the ground and rolled under the counter, hoping nobody noticed him. A door in the back of the bar swung open and Greg saw the feet of a burly bartender approach the counter. Some muffled voices grew louder and something crashed to the ground. Greg winced.

The bartender who had just come to the counter scowled. "What's goin' on over there?" he said.

The combined smells of alcohol, urine, vomit, cigarette smoke, and sweat was about to make Greg puke.

A voice cut through his thoughts, stopping his labored breathing. "We lookin' for a white kid," he heard one of the gang members say. *It was Sonny,* he thought.

"That so?" the bartender said, as he set something down on the counter. "What makes you think he's in here?"

"We saw him come in," another gang member, maybe Junior, piped up.

"Is that so?" The bartender leaned back against the wall.

"Yeah," the other one, which sounded like Tony, said. "And

we gonna tear your bar apart unless you give him to us."

"Is that so?" the bartender said again with more emphasis.

"Yeah, that's so," Tony said. "Where is he?" Another crash echoed in the background. What's going on out there? Suddenly, Greg noticed a crack in the wooden counter. He peered out and choked when he saw the gang members' legs and realized how close they were to him. He held his breath and tried to keep still, his body shaking with adrenaline and tension. "Well?" Tony broke in again. "You gonna give him to us?"

The bartender stood up straight and stared at the gang members. "No," he said firmly.

Tony cursed. "Fine, then we gonna take this place apart," he said in a sneering voice.

The bartender leaned on the counter, placing both hands on the spot right over Greg. "Is that so?" he bellowed.

Before they could react, the bartender leaped over the bar and plowed into them. Greg stared at the scene through the crack in the counter in shock, his eyes wide and burning. A table was knocked over and a glass bottle shattered. Junior tried to pull out his knife but was knocked down by a strong uppercut to his chin. Tony and Sonny were swinging wildly, but the bartender was all over the place. The dazed Junior scrambled to his feet with a curse and tried to hit the bartender, but the back of the bartender's meaty hand swung back and hit him in the throat. With a thud, Junior toppled to the beer-stained floor.

The bartender targeted Sonny and sucker-punched him in the stomach. Tony lunged at the bartender from behind, only to meet with the bartender's right foot flying up for a kick. As Sonny swung at the bartender's face, Tony lunged for his feet, but the bartender ducked Sonny's swing and tackled Tony to the ground. With his strong fists, the bartender pummeled Tony, then with a deft jump, grabbed Sonny by the back of his neck and flung him across the bar. The poker game players jumped out of the way, and the gang member smashed into their table. Tony was struggling to his feet. The bartender whirled around and grabbed his throat, smashing him up against the bar. There was silence for a minute as the patrons of the bar looked on in stunned silence. Tony slid to the floor, limp, and fell over in a clump. The short, thin Asian man in the white apron looked on in shock, staring at the bartender.

The bartender walked back around the side of the counter and knelt down, staring right into Greg's face. Greg jolted in shock. The bartender put his finger to his lips and in a coarse voice whispered. "Get out of here, kid. You ain't got much time."

The skater was frozen in fear.

The bartender scowled at him. "I just risked my life helpin' you, you better make good use of it."

Shaking, Greg crawled out from under the bar and moved toward the back door. The bartender pushed him through the kitchen to the back door and opened it, giving Greg a nudge to go through. The door led to the back of the building where there were some garbage cans, boxes, and broken bottles. A street was at the end of the alley. Greg began walking that direction. Why the bartender helped him and how he knew he was under the counter was a mystery to Greg.

At the end of the alley, Greg paused and turned back. The bartender was leaning against the doorway. Speaking hesitantly, Greg said, "I . . . I just wanted to say . . . thanks."

The bartender's eyes twinkled. "Is that so?" he asked.

Greg smiled and waved, then began running back toward the street.

The bartender watched Greg until he made it around the corner. Then with a smile, the bartender closed the back door and disappeared.

14

Greg leaned against the side of a building. He knew he had to rest or he wouldn't make it much longer. A couple times he'd heard the gang members shouting in the distance, and each time his heart pounded a little faster. It was a miracle they hadn't caught him yet—though he didn't mean the spiritual kind. Greg wasn't convinced God had anything to do with it. *If He does exist, why did He let all this happen? If God wants me to love Him like Brother Joseph said, He sure isn't doing a very good job of drawing me.*

Suddenly there was a clatter in some garbage cans to his left. Greg jumped and tensed, ready to run. Slowly, one of the garbage cans moved to the side and Michael's face appeared. Startled, both Michael and Greg jumped back when they saw each other.

Then Michael whispered, "Greg, please don't run! I ain't trying to catch you for the gang!"

Greg eyed Michael and raised his fists. He could probably take him on. This gang member was short, and he might be able to overpower him in a fight.

Michael held up his hands to Greg the way one would to a scared, hurt animal. "Shh!" he whispered. "I'm here to help you!"

Greg didn't lower his fists. He was breathing hard.

"I'm going to take you to Brother Joseph," Michael whispered, taking a step closer.

Greg took a step back. *Brother Joseph? How did Michael know Brother Joseph? More than likely, this is a trap. But by Al? No, Al doesn't know about Brother Joseph. Stefan? Then again, Michael has been the nicest to me . . . No. This has gotta be a trick.*

Michael threw up his hands in frustration. "Please," he said, beckoning again. "They could find us any minute."

"Why should I trust you?" Greg finally managed to get out, breathing heavily.

"Because he's telling the truth." Ismeralda appeared behind Michael. "Greg, please, for your own sake! Michael told us what happened! You have to come with us to save yourself from the gang."

Greg's mouth dropped open, then he felt anger bubbling up inside him. "Ismeralda? What are you doing here? How do you know him?" he asked, jabbing a finger in Michael's direction.

"He knew my brother. We don't have time to talk about that, though! The gang will find you! If Michael hadn't decided to help us, you may have already been dead!"

"You don't think I can take care of myself? I'm still alive, aren't I?"

Michael spat into the dust. "Kid, if you're still here, it ain't because of no skill on your part. There's no way you could escape this gang for this long unless God Himself was helping you."

"Well, I guess I have, 'cause God sure hasn't taken a real good interest in me lately."

A shout from a couple streets down heard over the din of Chicago traffic interrupted them. All three heads jerked in that direction. Ismeralda looked for a minute, listening, then turned back to Greg, saying, "Please, Greg! There's more at stake here than you know! Come with us, Greg. I promise we're not going to hurt you."

"Yeah, I've heard that promise before," Greg said bitterly.

Suddenly Ismeralda grabbed his shoulders and screamed, "Listen to me!"

Dumbfounded by her aggression, Greg snapped his head back to look at her. Tears were streaming from her beautiful green eyes and her long black hair was tousled, strands of it hanging in her face, some blowing in the wind. He could feel a slight tremor in her hands as they loosened on his shoulders. He stayed silent, letting her continue.

"Listen to me," she repeated more softly, her voice trembling a little this time. "You don't understand how dangerous this is. Chicago is dangerous all by itself, but when you get mixed up with drugs and gangs—" A strangled sob tried to wrench itself from her throat, but she choked it back and took a moment to get ahold of herself, finally dropping her hands from Greg's shoulders and wiping tears from her eyes.

Greg gave her a few minutes and didn't turn away or say anything this time.

"My brother was killed because of his involvement in one of these gangs," she said in a broken voice.

Michael looked down at his feet and turned his head away.

Greg remained silent and Ismeralda continued. "Our home life wasn't great. The times my dad was home he was drunk, and my mom wasn't much better. But my siblings and I looked out for each other. My brother was the oldest and I was the second oldest. Because we each had such a heavy responsibility, we became very close. But as he got older, he began to get mixed up in drugs, just like my dad, and that led to his involvement in the gangs."

She stopped for a moment and wiped her nose with her

sleeve before continuing. "I kept telling him not to go out, but he wouldn't listen to me. Kept saying it was just a little bit longer, for the good of the family. One night, we got word he was killed in a gang fight. Over drugs." She paused and looked at Greg. "That's why I got so upset that day in the car. It's a very personal subject for me." She sighed. "Anyways, Ray's death caused me to do a lot of soul-searching. I didn't know where I was going. That's when Jesus found me, and my life has never been the same since. I started going to the church Brother Joseph attends, and thankfully, I've been able to bring a lot of my younger siblings to God.

"But my heart is to stop the drug trafficking in Chicago and get as many people out of the gangs as I can! About a year ago, Michael came to me out of the blue. He and Ray had been great friends, and he had known him in the gangs. Ray's death affected him a lot, and he wanted to find me and say how sorry he was, knowing how close I'd been to him."

Michael scuffed his shoe in the dirt and looked nervously down the alley.

Ismeralda continued, ignoring his uneasiness for the moment. "I've been talking to him a lot lately about quitting the gangs. There's no peace in it. Only bloodshed." Greg noticed the bitter emphasis she placed on the last word. "When I heard about what you were going through, I knew I had to help. Brother Joseph wasn't sure it was such a good idea to get me involved, but when we found out by accident that Michael's gang was the one you were involved with, we realized it could only be God who set that up."

"So you're doing this for your brother?" Greg asked flatly.

"I'm doing this for you, Greg. And so is Michael. I care about you. And I don't want to see you get hurt, because I know how much God loves you."

"How do you know we can trust him?" Greg asked in a low tone, gesturing to Michael.

"Greg, Michael came to us," Ismeralda said.

Michael finally spoke up again. "I've seen too many people get killed recently, kid. A lot of blood's been spilt. I just wan' get you out of here. I don't wanna see another killin'."

"Then why haven't you quit the gang?" Greg snapped.

After a moment's hesitation, Michael mumbled, "I ain't got nowhere else to go. They the only family I got."

"Greg, come with us," Ismeralda said. "We have to—" Suddenly she was cut off by someone turning down the alley they were on. It was one of the members of Al's gang. Michael quickly ducked into the shadows so the gang member couldn't see him. Ismeralda looked torn, not knowing what to do.

The gang member stared at Greg. He looked startled at finding Greg at first but then began yelling, "Guys! Hey, guys, I found him!"

"Greg, we have to go!"

Greg bolted down the alley where Ismeralda and Michael were, not so much to follow them but because it was the only way to turn. Ismeralda and Michael began running, leading him to some place they had apparently decided on earlier. The other gang member had stopped and was still screaming for the others to hurry up. With a curse, he ran down the alley a little ways trying to find somebody to help him.

Greg's side was hurting like crazy as he panted alongside Ismeralda and Michael. He couldn't take much more of this. Vomit rose in his throat and he fought it back. This was not the time to throw up. He had to keep going.

Michael turned a corner and Ismeralda followed him. Greg lagged behind, not completely sure he still wanted to follow.

Michael whispered, "Brother Joseph!"

Brother Joseph rushed up to them. "Did you find him?" He caught sight of Greg and lifted his face to heaven, briefly closing his eyes. "Oh, thank God! Greg, are you okay?"

Greg stopped when he saw him and took a step back. *I do not want to be with this traitor. How have our paths managed to cross again? I mean, this is Chicago, for crying out loud!*

Brother Joseph didn't wait for Greg's answer but beckoned hurriedly for them to come with him. "We have to hurry! They could be here any second!"

Ismeralda nodded and turned. "You're right; we have to get out of here." She looked pointedly at Greg then took a few strides in the other direction. Michael skittishly ran down to the next turn and looked around.

Brother Joseph beckoned toward Greg again, who hadn't moved. "Come on, Greg, we have to go!"

Greg stared at him in disbelief. *Is this guy for real? After betraying me, he still expects me to blindly follow him?*

Brother Joseph stood there, still waiting for Greg to move. "Greg?" he asked, searching the skater's face.

Suddenly, they heard shouts and whoops. Both of their heads spun in that direction. The gang had found them. They were on their way.

Brother Joseph took a step toward Greg. "That's it; we can't waste time any longer! We have to go now!"

"I'm not going anywhere with you!" Greg shouted, taking a step back.

"Would you rather go with them?" Brother Joseph asked, jerking his thumb toward the direction Al and his gang were coming from.

Greg glanced furtively in the direction Brother Joseph pointed to. The gang was shouting directions to each other about which way to go. Suddenly, he caught a glimpse of Al's face at the far end of the street as the gang leader turned a corner. Al's eyes were brimming with hate, and his fists were already curled into balls. Greg looked back to Brother Joseph and their eyes locked.

"Greg, you have to trust me," Brother Joseph pleaded softly.

"Hurry!" Ismeralda yelled, pushing Michael ahead.

Greg took one last glance at the gang then ran after the three trying to help him.

Al had caught sight of them by now and was yelling at his gang to hurry up. Curses flew at the four of them as they ran away from the gang, going up and down alleys.

They came to an intersection and Michael halted.

"Which way?" Ismeralda asked.

"I dunno this section of the city that well."

"It doesn't matter!" Brother Joseph said, breathing heavily. "We have to get away!"

Michael took a chance and ran down one street. Greg, Ismeralda, and Brother Joseph were hard on his heels. The gang was gaining on them but hadn't seen where they turned. The four took another turn then skidded to a halt. It was a dead end.

They looked at each other for a second in disbelief. Then they heard shouts ordering some of the gang members to split up and go down a different street. Half of them turned to the street Brother Joseph, Michael, Ismeralda, and Greg were on. It was too late to turn back. The gang had reached them. They were trapped!

Brother Joseph put a protective hand on Ismeralda's shoulder. "Michael, if worse comes to worst, will you be able to fight?" he asked in a soft, low voice.

Michael nodded and Greg noticed a trace of fear in the gang member's eyes. For the first time, he realized what a chance Michael was taking by helping them. "Yeah," he agreed. "Yeah, I can do that."

Brother Joseph leveled his gaze at Michael and waited until he caught the gang member's eye. "Just enough so Greg and Ismeralda can escape. Once they've gotten away, don't worry about me. Do you understand?"

Ismeralda opened her mouth in shock. "No! Brother Joseph!"

Brother Joseph put his hand over her mouth and stared at Michael. "It's very important, Michael. You might not get away if you continue to fight for my life. Don't worry about me. This is our last chance."

Michael swallowed hard and nodded. "Okay. Whatever you want me to do," he said.

Brother Joseph took his hand off Ismeralda's mouth and grabbed her and Greg's shoulders. "I need you both to listen to me," he said gravely. "There's a good chance we won't get out of this alive. But if we do—"

A sound further down the alley interrupted him, and Brother Joseph's head shot up. "It's them. Grab a board or whatever you can get your hands on to fight with," Brother Joseph commanded in a low voice.

Greg nodded and picked up a rotting piece of wood. Ismeralda grabbed a brick and held it at the ready. Michael tensed, holding his knife in his hand.

Greg glanced over at Brother Joseph and saw that he had no weapon. His eyes were closed and he was mouthing words. Praying. Greg turned back to face the oncoming gang. Shouts were heard as they closed in. They knew he was trapped.

The gang rounded the corner, and Brother Joseph opened his eyes, bracing himself.

Al stepped forward with a sneer. "All right, kid, the game is up." Michael quickly stepped into a shadow so Al couldn't see his face. The gang leader looked around and scowled at the rest.

"I don't know who you all are, or why you tryin' to help this—" he called Greg something unrepeatable. "But all we want is the kid, and we gonna take you all out, if the rest of you don't get outta here right now."

He waited a second. Nobody moved. Al's scowl hardened. "You bunch of . . ." a list of cuss words followed. "Who are you? You, old man, step into the light."

Slowly, Brother Joseph stepped forward. Al's mouth dropped open and a startled, stifled murmur ran through the gang. Al's face visibly paled.

"Hello, Al. Good to see you again, though I'd prefer to see you without the knife in your hand."

Al fumbled for a response. "Brotha Joseph . . . I . . . I . . ."

Greg turned to Brother Joseph. "Wait . . . you mean you know him?"

Brother Joseph dipped his head. "Our paths have crossed a few times," he admitted softly.

"Crossed?" Al said. "Man, you helped me when I was wandering down the street blitzed with no place to go. You took me back to some mission thing or somethin' and gave me clothes and food and stuff. I was all messed up from some gang fight and you helped me out. And then later we was at a bar, hangin' out and when you saw us you didn't ignore us like most preachers woulda done. You recognized me and came over an' talked to us. 'Member, guys?"

Al turned and addressed the gang. "This is the preacher dude that talked to us about God and stuff." The gang leader turned back to Brother Joseph. "Man, I never forgot that. But why you helping him?" Al asked, gesturing to Greg.

"Greg's a friend of mine."

Al shook his head grimly. "Preacher, you picked the wrong person to be friends with tonight. This . . ." He started to say a cuss word then stopped himself. "This kid double-crossed us and we ain't gonna let him get away with that."

"Yeah, well according to some people, I picked the wrong person to be friends with the night I picked you up off the street," reminded the street preacher softly. "I'm not going to leave."

"Preacher, I don't wanna hurt you," Al said in a low voice. "Get outta here before somethin' bad happens."

"To get to him, you're going to have to go through me first," Brother Joseph answered. "Greg, get behind me."

Al shook his head and pointed his knife toward them. "That was the wrong thing to say," he muttered.

The gang members started forward. Brother Joseph and Michael tensed, and Ismeralda moved back another step with a whimper. Greg closed his eyes, bracing himself.

"No!"

Greg opened his eyes.

"No!" Al suddenly shouted again, waving his arm. "Get back and put your weapons away! I ain't gonna hurt Brotha Joe." The gang members paused for a second, as if unsure of what they'd just heard. "Man, I said get back!" Al shouted again. Shocked, his gang backed off, falling into place.

Brother Joseph looked surprised. "Al . . . I thought—"

Al shook his head violently, cutting him off before he could say anything else. "I may be a lot o' things, and I know I ain't perfect, but I don't forget when someone helps me, Preacher. One o' the things you taught me 'bout was forgiveness. That stuck. We gonna forgive this kid, gang, and we gonna let Brotha Joseph go."

"How touching," a sarcastically amused voice came from behind them. Al spun around to face who was speaking, and Greg's heart dropped. Any hopes he'd had of escaping disappeared. The speaker continued. "But I'm afraid we won't be as forgiving as you were."

"Adikema!" Al gasped.

Stefan was standing there with a gun. Behind him were Terrance and Rush.

Greg hadn't seen Rush since they were at the airport. "Hey, that's—" Greg stopped himself.

"Remember Rush Stein, Greg?" Stefan asked playing on Greg's surprise, with a small smile turning up the corners of his mouth.

Greg closed his eyes again. He hadn't really realized till now how well arranged this whole thing had been. It had all been planned from the beginning.

The whole group was silent for a moment. Nobody in the gang said anything, all their eyes diverted to the ground. Brother Joseph, Ismeralda, and Michael quietly stared at Stefan. Rush and Terrance were grimly standing behind Stefan, blocking the exit.

"Well, I have to admit, this is a wild card," Stefan said, smugly striding forward. "I wasn't expecting this. But you can be very resourceful, can't you?"

Greg looked around, confused. *Is he talking about Brother Joseph or Al? Or is Stefan referring to me?*

Stefan turned to the gang leader. "Al, Al, Al," he shook his head in mock disappointment. "I never thought you'd let me down. So I assume you aren't going to attack them now?"

Al's face was pale and slowly he shook his head, eyeing the gun.

Stefan tsked and shook his head again. "Pity. And here I thought I was going to see some excitement. Well, it doesn't matter. I suppose you've done your job. You can leave now."

"Leave?" Al asked in a smaller voice than he'd used before.

"Yes," Stefan said coldly. "Your job is done. You may not want to keep helping me, but you're not getting in my way. You can either tell your gang to file out of here nice and quietly, or I can use my gun to persuade you, and right now it's aimed at you."

Al remained silent.

"Of course," Stefan continued, "there's always the option of pulverizing Brother Joseph and his friends anyway. Well? What's it going to be?"

Al shook his head slowly. "I ain't gonna hurt Brotha Joe," he said, drawing out his words slowly. "Guys, you heard what he said. Get back."

A smile toyed with Stefan's lips. "That's right. Get back. You've had your fun for the day, and now it's Stefan's turn."

Sorrowfully, his head down, Al turned and began walking away from Brother Joseph, down the alley. Silently, the gang followed, single-filed.

"You too," Stefan glared, looking at Michael, pointing his gun to the retreating gang members. "Go with them."

Surprised that Stefan knew who he was, Michael stepped back. "What?"

"Go with them," Stefan said, waving the gun slightly, acting suddenly impatient. "You are with the gang, aren't you?"

Fear lit his eyes and Michael nodded.

"Then please join your fellow gang members. You don't want to get hurt, do you?"

Michael looked scared, looking from Brother Joseph to the gang. "I . . . I only came to warn him," he said, waving a hand at Brother Joseph.

"Yes, and now that your little act of mercy is done, don't you think you should be following your friends out of here?"

Michael stood wavering for a couple seconds, avoiding

Brother Joseph's eyes. Brother Joseph looked at him with sorrow burning through his expression, begging Michael to do the right thing. There was a tense silence. Stefan cocked his gun.

Finally, Michael backed up. "Yeah, yeah, okay. I'm going."

Stefan nodded coldly, a smile gripping his face. "That's right. We wouldn't want anything bad to happen to you, would we?"

Michael shook his head and moved off to the side with the gang. Stefan eyed Brother Joseph, Ismeralda, and Greg. All three of them looked in shock after Michael.

He betrayed us, Ismeralda wanted to say but was too scared, a strand of loose hair falling into her face.

The gang filed out, quietly, leaving them alone with Stefan and his henchmen in the dark alley.

Stefan displayed his plastic, evil grin again. "Now you three. What will it be? Are we going to make this interesting?"

"What do you mean?" Brother Joseph asked.

"Well, the only one I really wanted was Greg. But now that you're here, I'd say you're an added bonus. You've been working against our little drug operation here, and I can't really afford to leave any loose ends lying around."

"Meaning you're planning to kill us?" said Brother Joseph.

Ismeralda let out a gasp.

Stefan stared at him for a moment then began chuckling. Rush joined in. Terrance was silent, resuming his bored look.

Hatred coursed through Greg's body as he glared intensely at Stefan. *Kill him!* his mind screamed at him. Greg had never felt so much hatred for another human being before. Stefan had ruined his life . . . and now might end it.

Stefan hadn't moved yet. He still had the gun but he wasn't firing. "You know, I'm kind of like a cat," he said, examining his fingernails for a moment before looking up at them with a smile. "I like to play with my food before I eat it." Stefan tossed Rush the gun. "Let's make this interesting."

At that moment, Brother Joseph pushed Ismeralda and Greg past Terrance and yelled, "Run! RUN!"

Terrance jumped into action and lunged at Greg but barely missed, tripping and falling to the ground. While Rush was fumbling with the gun, Brother Joseph plowed into him, knocking him down. Greg and Ismeralda began running down the alley. Rush lay flat on his back, and Brother Joseph jumped up and leaped over him, running after Greg and Ismeralda.

"You fools!" Stefan screamed, snatching the gun. "They're getting away!"

The gun went off and a bullet fired over Greg's head, narrowly missing Brother Joseph's ear just before they rounded a corner.

Rush scrambled to his feet, and Terrance looked to Stefan for instructions. Stefan was scowling in the direction the three had run. "Go after them," he said through his clenched teeth, brushing some dirt off his suit coat. "They're not going to escape me, no matter what."

15

Greg was breathing hard. His mind could scarcely grasp the danger they were in. All he knew was that he needed to focus on getting away.

Ismeralda glanced fearfully behind her. "Where's Brother Joseph?" she asked.

At that moment, Brother Joseph rounded the corner and urged them on. "Hurry! Don't wait!" he shouted. His legs pumped harder and he caught up with them, matching their pace. With a quick gesture, the street missionary pointed out another turn to make. Greg and Ismeralda immediately did what he said.

So far, Stefan, Rush, and Terrance hadn't caught up with them, but they were bigger and faster, and it wouldn't be long. Greg knew they'd have to do something to shake them.

The three of them ducked down another alley. Nobody said a word. Unlike last time, when the gang was shouting and yelling to each other and it was easy to tell where they were, this time no noises indicated where Stefan, Terrance, and Rush were. It was a silent, deadly, game.

"Greg, do you have your cell phone?" Brother Joseph asked quietly.

Greg felt his pockets as they were running. A look of horror appearing on his face, he shook his head. "It must have fallen out in the bar."

Brother Joseph winced but kept running. They still needed to shake Stefan and his cronies. Suddenly, the street preacher's eyes lit up as he saw what he was looking for. "Down this way," he whispered, turning one more time. Greg and Ismeralda followed him out onto a busy street.

They slowed to a stop at the curb. Cars roared by. "Great," Greg said, spitting on the sidewalk. "What now?"

Brother Joseph ran out into traffic in between a lapse in the cars, reaching the median.

"What are you doing?" Ismeralda cried.

"Come on!" Greg called, following Brother Joseph.

Shaking her head, Ismeralda followed. All three of them made it across safely.

"We need to go this way," Brother Joseph told them when they caught up. He started running down a side street.

"Wait," said Greg, trying to stop him. "Do you know where you're going?"

"We have to get to a safe place where we can use a phone and call the police," Brother Joseph said firmly, ignoring Greg's question and starting to jog in the direction he had pointed. "This is too big to handle by ourselves. It's out of our hands. That man back there is a maniac, and he isn't going to stop until we're dead or worse."

"What could be worse than dead?" Greg asked.

Brother Joseph didn't answer.

"And where are we going to find a phone in this part of town?"

Brother Joseph shook his head. "You have to trust me, Greg."

"I did trust you, dude. You let me down."

"Then give me another chance!" Brother Joseph shouted. Taking a breath, he calmed down. "Look, I'm sorry, Greg. As I tried to tell you before, I never meant to hurt you. I really do have your best interests in mind. But right now, the most important thing is to get out of this mess. We have to get help."

Greg frowned. "What about that gas station over there?" he asked, pointing down the road.

Brother Joseph glanced over but shook his head again. "No, it's not safe enough. From what I've seen of Stefan, I doubt simply having witnesses around will deter him from doing something dangerous."

"You really think he'd shoot us in public?"

"I'm not going to take that chance."

"Then where are we going?" Greg asked.

"Somewhere safe," he answered.

Ismeralda suddenly looked around in surprise. "Wait, I know where we are!"

"This way."

Just as Brother Joseph turned a corner, Ismeralda screamed, "They're coming!"

Greg's head jerked back to look behind them. Sure enough, Stefan, Terrance, and Rush were standing on the sidewalk across the street. Stefan was staring straight at Greg. A shudder ran up and down Greg's spine, and he rounded the corner after Brother Joseph.

That's when he saw the safe place Brother Joseph was talking about. A church steeple rose imposingly in the sky. Pentecostals of Chicago, the sign said. He remembered the parking lot in which he had first met Ismeralda. *Great, just what I need*, thought Greg.

"In here," Brother Joseph ordered. "Where are my keys?" he muttered, standing on the top step.

"Hurry, Brother Joseph!" Ismeralda urged.

Brother Joseph fumbled with his keys, finally found the right one, and shoved it into the lock. The three of them stumbled into the sanctuary and closed the door behind them. Ismeralda quickly turned the lock.

"Now what?" Greg asked.

"To the pastor's office," Brother Joseph instructed.

o——o

They approached the church steps. "They went in here," Rush volunteered.

"I can see that, you idiot," Stefan said, irritated. They stood there for a moment, waiting. Stefan turned on Rush and Terrance and threw his arms up in the air. "Well, what are you waiting for? Go get them!"

Rush looked confused. "Aren't you coming?"

"I am NOT going in there!" Stefan screamed. "Go get them!"

Rush shrugged and he and Terrance bounded up the steps.

Stefan paced outside, quivering with rage. *Of all the places they could hide, it had to be a church! Outside forces are at work here . . . I can feel it.*

"It's locked," Rush said from the stairs.

Stefan spun around. "Well, then find another way in!"

Rush nodded quickly.

"You go that way," Stefan continued, pointing to Terrance. "And you go that way," he added, pointing at Rush and handing him the gun. "I'll stay here to make sure they don't escape."

Without a word, Terrance set off quickly to obey his orders. Rush did as well, going the other way.

Stefan turned away from the church. Deliberately trying to

calm himself, he closed his eyes and took a deep breath. The familiar surge of power coursed through him, and he slowly unclenched his fists. *This will turn out well. The Enemy has a plan, but so do I.* A small box on the side of the building attracted his attention. Withdrawing a knife, he turned to it quickly.

"Hello? Police? Yes, we're in trouble. Three men are chasing us. They're armed and extremely dangerous. We're at 1102 Colfax Lane at the Pentecostals of Chicago church." At that moment, the lights went out, plunging them into darkness. Brother Joseph paused. "Uh, hello? Hello?" He shook the phone then hung it up in disbelief. "The line went dead."

Greg threw his hands up in the air. "Well, why don't you have your cell phone?"

Brother Joseph sighed. "When I heard you were in trouble, I ran out the door so fast I didn't think about grabbing it."

Greg slumped down. "Great. Just great."

Shards of glass shattered across the basement floor. Terrance climbed through the window without reacting to a cut he received from the broken glass. The light was off and no one was in sight. After removing his sunglasses, Terrance's eyes adjusted quickly, and he skillfully surveyed the fellowship hall of the church. Several metal folding chairs were set up around a couple of tables, and he noticed only six doors. Striding over to them, he flung three doors open, one after another—a closet and two classrooms. Terrance paused. It was obvious nobody was down here. Determination written across his face, Terrance headed for the stairs.

○——○

Ismeralda jumped. "What was that?" she whispered. Brother Joseph and Greg looked at each other. "It sounded like a window breaking in the basement." Brother Joseph held up his hand. They listened for a moment. "But I don't hear anything else."

"They found a way in," Ismeralda said.

"We need to go somewhere else." Brother Joseph motioned for them to follow him.

The three of them quietly moved into the entrance hall. "Someone's probably waiting outside this door," Brother Joseph said in a low voice.

"How about the back door in the sanctuary?" Ismeralda whispered.

"I guess we'll have to try," Brother Joseph agreed. "But be careful."

Brother Joseph opened the door to the sanctuary. It was dark. Tiptoeing down the aisle, Greg thought he could hear his heart thudding in the quiet sanctuary. Suddenly, Brother Joseph stopped so abruptly that Greg ran into him. The youth leader held up his hand for silence. A scraping noise was coming from the back of the sanctuary behind the altar.

"Quick, move to the opposite aisle," Brother Joseph said. Greg and Ismeralda stumbled over the pews to the other aisle. Ismeralda looked to Brother Joseph, wondering what to do next. Brother Joseph nodded toward the staircase leading to the loft.

"Up there?" whispered Ismeralda.

Suddenly, there was a crash at the back of the sanctuary and the back door caved in. Brother Joseph shoved Ismeralda and Greg up the stairs.

○———○

Rush smiled, surveying his handiwork. One more quick shove with his foot . . . Rush kicked the cracked door one more time and the rest of it collapsed. He snorted. *This church's doors sure weren't very strong.* Cautiously he stepped into the sanctuary of the small church. The only light was from the green exit light in the back. A scuffle grabbed his attention. Rush stepped farther into the church. *What was that?*

At that moment, the door to the sanctuary opened and Rush tensed, ready to fly into the man and two kids. A head poked through the door, but it wasn't the preacher. Rush lowered his hands in disgust as Terrance caught his eyes with an expressionless look. Rush stepped over some cords leading to the microphones and stepped lightly off the platform. "What are you doing up here?" he asked.

Terrance shook his head.

"Nobody was downstairs?"

Another head shake.

"Well, they've got to be in here somewhere," Rush said, looking around. "There's no other way they could get out. Let's start taking apart the church."

Without a word, Terrance grabbed a pew and toppled it over. With a smile, Rush walked across the aisle and did the same.

○———○

Ismeralda's head lowered after looking over the rail, and she looked at Greg in horror. "They're tearing apart the church," she whispered.

Greg shook his head in disgust. *How can she be thinking about that now?*

"There's no other way out of here?" he asked Brother Joseph.

Brother Joseph lowered his head with a sigh.

"No," Ismeralda answered. "There aren't any doors or anything up here."

Greg resisted the urge to let a cuss word out and punch the rail. Why Brother Joseph led them up here was a mystery. They had run up the stairs and closed the wooden door, which thankfully didn't creak, and locked it, which effectively blocked them in. "So we're trapped," he muttered.

Brother Joseph didn't raise his head. Greg ground his teeth. After everything that had happened, he was trapped in a Pentecostal church. *Is this going to be the way I die?* Something in Greg snapped in rebellion. *Not a chance. This is not going to be the way I die!* Searching for any possible ray of hope, Greg looked around wildly. "What about the window?" he whispered.

Ismeralda leaned back on her haunches. "What window . . . oh, you mean that one?" she said, looking to the far left of the wall.

Greg nodded.

Ismeralda shook her head in disgust. "That window hasn't opened in years! It's an inside joke at our church. Forget it, it won't work." She looked around and peeked over the top at the men searching through the pews. "I . . . I don't think there is any way out of here!"

Brother Joseph had been sitting quietly, but now he got up and began moving quickly over to the window. "Well, where there's no way, the Lord always makes one."

Ismeralda looked over in shock. "Brother Joseph, what are you doing? They might see you!"

Brother Joseph flung back the window latch, pushed it, and the window slid open effortlessly.

Ismeralda's mouth dropped. The three stared at it for a moment. "I . . . I think . . . I just witnessed a miracle," Ismeralda said quietly.

"Well, instead of wondering at how much of a miracle it is, let's get out of here!" Greg returned with a fierce whisper.

A small grin lit Brother Joseph's face. Greg didn't waste any time following his own advice. Quietly he got up and began moving along the wall furthest away from the balcony. Ismeralda wasn't far behind. Brother Joseph was ready with a chair to help them climb out the window.

Greg got up on the chair and started squeezing himself out the window. "Try to climb onto the roof of the next building," Brother Joseph instructed quietly. "Thank God these buildings are so close together."

The building adjacent to the church was a taller, four-story building, but a fire escape attached to it in the little alley was close to the window, and it led up to the roof. If it had been even a couple of inches farther away, it might not have been an option for escaping.

Greg climbed out the window and managed to grasp the metal pole on the fire escape, swinging his legs over to it. He winced as he clanged against the metal fire escape and hoped he hadn't attracted attention as he clambered into a position on the stairs. Ismeralda was next. Brother Joseph bit his lip as he looked behind him in the darkened church. Why Stefan's two thugs hadn't yet thought to check the loft was nothing short of a miracle. But there was no telling how much time they had left.

Ismeralda, with ease that surprised both Brother Joseph and Greg, made it to the fire escape. Then Brother Joseph stepped up onto the chair and began squeezing himself out the window. Suddenly he froze.

"What is it?" Greg asked. "Hurry!"

○———○

"Did you hear that?" Rush asked, pausing by the baptismal tank where he'd been searching.

Terrance had already stopped and was holding up his hand for silence. With a scowl, he looked around the church and suddenly caught sight of the stairwell leading up to the loft. If the man spoke more, he might have cursed. *Why didn't we notice that before?*

Rush saw it at the same time and glanced over at Terrance. Without looking to see if Rush was following, Terrance strode over to it. Rush bounded after him. The two of them clambered up the steps, and Terrance grasped the doorknob.

"Locked?" Rush asked.

Terrance wasn't listening. Taking two steps backwards so he could see into the loft, he fixed his gaze on something. Rush saw it too—the legs of a man disappearing out the window.

"There they are!" Rush bellowed and fired his pistol. The bullet smacked into the frame of the window.

With a snarl, Terrance cut him off with his hand and looked pointedly toward the door. Rush got the message and moved toward it. Then with amazing agility, Terrance leaped over the side of the stairwell and grabbed the edge of the railing on the loft. Rush watched with his mouth open as the man pulled himself up over the rail and bounded over to the window.

"Hey, what about me?" Rush called after his partner.

Terrance paused only a second before reaching over and unlocking the door so Rush could get in.

"Come on," Rush said. "We got to get them!"

The three ran up the fire escape and made it onto the roof.

"Come on, let's go!" Brother Joseph said as soon as they had reached the top. "We have to keep moving!" Greg and Ismeralda didn't argue.

They bore left and ran across the roof past some smokestacks. They approached the edge of the roof and were looking out on the building right behind the one they were on.

"Ready?" asked Brother Joseph.

"Ready for what?" Greg asked.

"Jump!" Without waiting for a reply, the street preacher catapulted himself into the air and landed on the lower roof of the other building.

Ismeralda glanced fearfully behind her before she and Greg did the same. As soon as their feet touched, they were running again, following Brother Joseph to the ledge of the building. Brother Joseph stopped and looked across, breathing hard, as if trying to decide what to do next.

The next building was a skyscraper that towered above the surrounding buildings. It seemed to be joined to a shorter building, with a roof about level to the one they were on, and connecting to a fire escape leading up to its roof.

Greg looked behind him, expecting Terrance and Rush to appear at any moment.

Finally, Brother Joseph seemed to make up his mind and pointed to the building. "We're going to jump again," he said in a low voice. "Then as soon as we make it over, run to the fire escape and start heading up."

"Up?" Greg asked incredulously. "Why don't we go down?"

"It'll be safer to go up," Brother Joseph said. "I don't know what Stefan has planned for us at the bottom. Besides, any confrontation would be more likely to be seen from higher up."

"Are you kidding?" Greg protested. "The top of the building is so high up nobody would even see us!"

"They will when we climb the fire escape. We need to get someone's attention to get some help. Please, Greg, we don't have time for this. We have to go. You two jump across first and I'll follow."

Greg hesitated.

Brother Joseph gave him a gentle push. "Now!" he ordered in a firm voice.

Reluctantly, Greg took a few steps back, then ran and launched himself in the air. Wind whistled past him as he flew over the gap between the buildings. Then he was over and landed on the roof of the lower level of the skyscraper. He heard a thump as Ismeralda landed beside him. They looked back, and Brother Joseph signaled for them to move out of the way so he could come over.

Ismeralda stood and ran toward the fire escape, taking a couple steps up the stairs. "Come on, Greg," she urged, pausing to wait.

Shaking his head, Greg jogged over and followed Ismeralda up the fire escape. Brother Joseph leaped across the gap and followed close behind.

As they ran up the flights of metal stairs, Greg kept glancing back to see if Stefan's henchmen were following. He didn't see them anywhere. Down on the street below, a couple cars drove by with their headlights on. Greg wondered if they noticed the three people running up the fire escape to the top of the skyscraper. Nobody gave any indication that they did.

At last they reached the top of the building. A crow squawked and flew away when they came up. A gusty breeze blew across the roof, chilling Greg. Dark clouds had rolled across the already darkening night sky, and rain was beginning to fall as they came to a halt. Lightning branched across the horizon as they stood there, catching their breath. Nobody said anything. There couldn't hear any sound indicating their pursuers were following them. For a couple minutes they stood still, waiting tensely, wondering if they had gotten away. The three of them surveyed the buildings in the direction they had just come from, not seeing anybody anywhere.

Brother Joseph wiped his brow. "Well, I think we escaped them."

A voice came from behind him. "You may have escaped them, but not me."

Brother Joseph spun around, almost losing his balance. Stefan was standing on the opposite edge of the roof, near the other fire escape, with his arms crossed and his suit coat billowing in the wind.

A cry caught in Ismeralda's throat. Brother Joseph looked stunned. Greg couldn't breathe. Stefan had found them.

With a laugh, Stefan began walking confidently across the roof toward the trio, but he was only looking intensely at one of them. "Hello, Greg. I guess I've finally caught up with you."

16

Officer Purdo charged up the steps of the Pentecostals of Chicago church and kicked the door open.

"You could've used the handle," Cambiano muttered. Cambiano was cool and collected as he surveyed the church. He had seen his share of bloody, gory scenes and nothing ever moved him. He was as close to desensitized as one could get. Purdo, on the other hand—whose forehead was glistening with perspiration and whose eyes were gleaming with the thrill of investigation— was hungrily searching the church with his eyes.

"Yup, we're on to something." He rubbed his hands together in glee. "We're gonna get these guys, Cambiano."

Cambiano ignored him and eyed the stairs leading into the basement. "You check the sanctuary. I'm going to look around downstairs."

Purdo nodded and flipped a light switch. "Hmm . . . lights are off." Purdo switched on his flashlight and waved it like a search beam.

Cambiano rolled his eyes and moved downstairs. Purdo began picking his way through the damaged, scattered pews, doing a quick run-through with his eyes to check for clues. Then he noticed the loft. The policeman aimed his light at the window frame and immediately noticed the bullet hole.

"Cambiano!" he yelled and whirled around.

Cambiano was just coming up the stairs. "Nobody downstairs," he reported. "Just a smashed window." He stopped when he noticed Purdo's face. He walked into the sanctuary and looked up at the bullet hole Purdo was pointing to.

"There was a fight in here," Purdo said excitedly. "We've gotta—hey! Where are you going?"

Cambiano had already reached his conclusion. "Let's go, they've already left."

"You're right. Hurry so we can catch these guys! I can't wait to see 'em trembling behind bars. They've had their run of this city long enough."

They stepped outside and felt the first few rain drops of another thunderstorm.

Cambiano lifted his radio to his lips. "We're going to need backup. Over."

The person on the other end responded affirmatively.

Purdo was already waiting impatiently by the squad car. Cambiano was just about to join him when four figures caught his eye on a skyscraper to his left. "What the—" he began to say. Quickly, he raised his binoculars. A flash of lightning lit the scene just long enough for him to catch a glimpse of Brother Joseph.

Purdo jerked his head in the direction the older officer was looking. "Cambiano!" he roared. "We gotta get to that building! I want the leaders of that drug ring in jail tonight!" Immediately he leaped into the squad car and flipped on the siren.

Cambiano pushed the button back down on his walkie-talkie, praying they weren't too late.

Thunder rumbled above them, and lightning cracked like a whip behind Stefan as he began to stride across the roof. The rain was pelting them harder now, and Stefan seemed to take advantage of the weather around them to prey on Greg's fears. His slick, black hair had stayed amazingly perfect throughout the entire chase, and now he looked at them through his sunglasses with a smirk, drawing closer.

"So," he said above the wind and rain. "We come to a climax. Me or Brother Joseph, Greg. That's your choice."

"What?" Greg asked, not understanding Stefan's proposal.

Stefan chuckled at Greg's naivety. "You still don't understand, do you?"

Brother Joseph and Ismeralda tensed as the man took another step forward. He seemed to be drawing out the process to terrify them as much as possible.

Stefan continued, "Well, I suppose it doesn't matter. You don't have much longer anyway. You know too much already. And now I'm going to destroy you."

"Not today, you won't!" Before anybody knew what was happening, Brother Joseph had leaped at Stefan, knocking him off balance. Stefan stumbled back but recovered quickly enough to deliver a blow to Brother Joseph that knocked the street preacher back. Then, as Stefan righted himself, his sunglasses clattered to the roof.

Greg froze. It was as if one of the laws of nature had been defied. From the first time Greg had seen the man, he had always been wearing sunglasses. They had become like a permanent part of his face. Stefan froze too, as if in shock, his face slightly turned so they couldn't see it. He stretched out his hand as if about to reach down and grab the sunglasses but then seemed to change his mind. Slowly, Stefan's head turned to face the little group.

Ismeralda let out a gasp, and Greg could see why. He felt lightheaded, as if he needed to sit down. The iris of one of Stefan's eyes was a brilliant blue—the clearest, most beautiful blue you could ever hope to see. But the other eye . . . what a contrast! Stefan's other eye was badly deformed. Revoltingly deformed. A sordid blackish-bluish color surrounded his eye socket, and ghastly, cracked, brown lines ran from the eye. It looked a little like a black eye that had never healed. Veins bulged out all around it. But the worst part was that what was supposed to be the white of his eye wasn't white—it was black. There was no color at all in the iris either; it was only black up to his pupil. His pupil might have been the most repulsive thing about the entire eye. It was completely red—a black eye with a red dot right in the center.

Ismeralda had squeezed her eyes shut, and Greg heard Brother Joseph say a breathy prayer that came out like, "Oh, Jesus!"

Greg took a step backwards.

A small smile played on Stefan's lips. "So, now you know," he said, as if terribly amused by the whole thing. He began to walk slowly toward them. His steps were deliberate, and the sound of his footsteps echoed into the night sky. Nobody else moved. "You know, it's funny," Stefan said in a reflective voice, "you're the first outsiders who have ever seen my eye in this way. I suppose it's quite appropriate, though. You three were the ones who were to be my undoing. But not any longer. Now you're trapped."

"T–trapped?" Greg managed to find his voice. But it sounded distant as if it came from someone else's mouth. "What are you talking about? We . . . we outnumber you!"

The smile spread slowly across Stefan's face. "You think so, Greg? Human power isn't the only contributing factor here."

The evil ringleader took a step closer then stopped, lifting his hands up in the air, as if demonstrating something. But Greg didn't see anything. All he knew was that the creepy look on Stefan's face frightened him more than anything else ever had. A chill washed over him.

"I have many others on my side. Not necessarily humans, however. I have supernatural aid." He cocked his head and laughed, looking at each person on the roof with an air of confidence and delight. "We have a slight advantage," he continued. "They have been seeking you out to destroy you, Greg. Why do you think I chose you out of all the others to come to Chicago? I was guided. They chose you, Greg. Not me." Again, Stefan raised his arm and addressed the group. "So many people scoff at the idea of a supernatural dimension. They don't believe it's real because they can't see it." Swiftly, an evil glare darkened Stefan's face and he swung his fist down adamantly with a grunt. "Fools! But I know. I know because I've experienced it! Spiritual forces are at work here."

Just then a clear voice broke through the pattering of the rain. "If that's true, then we do outnumber you."

Stefan turned and glared at Brother Joseph coldly. "What are you talking about?"

Brother Joseph matched Stefan's stare evenly. "You might have the power of demons and devils on your side. But you are weak because we have a power stronger than any other power, natural or supernatural! You know why, Stefan?"

Stefan snarled and took a step toward Brother Joseph. Brother Joseph walked a few steps to the side but continued to face him.

"Because we have Jesus on our side. And His power is greater than any demon."

Stefan growled and leaped at Brother Joseph, drool flying

out of his mouth. "Don't you ever mention that name again!" he said, looking like he was ready to push Brother Joseph off the roof. "How dare you insult my power? You don't have the slightest inkling of the kind of power I hold!"

Brother Joseph sidestepped him and whirled to face him again. "Not as great as God's, Lucifer."

He and Stefan faced each other on the roof. The blackened sky provided an eerie backdrop. They circled, each eyeing the other, waiting for the other person to make a move.

"You never quit trying, do you?" Brother Joseph asked quietly. "Always trying to be greatest. Always thinking in your heart that you can ascend up to be like the Most High. But you're wrong. There is One who has power over you. And I know His name."

Stefan's body tensed, shaking with rage. Greg couldn't help but wonder what was making him so angry. But whatever distraction Brother Joseph could provide was worth it. They had to get away from this maniac.

Brother Joseph had moved into a position in which he was standing in front of Greg again.

"Step aside, preacher," Stefan demanded in a low tone. "Just stay out of this. None of this even has to concern you. My business is with the boy alone."

"I'm afraid I can't do that. Greg is my friend, and I'll stand by him no matter the cost." He stared at Stefan with resolve.

"Oh please," Stefan said, taking a step back and waving his arms. "Greg is my friend!" he mimicked. Swiftly, he stepped toward Brother Joseph.

Brother Joseph moved slightly to the side again.

Stefan turned in sync. "What if the cost is your life, missionary? Think of all the people you will no longer be able to help. All of the good things you will no longer be able to do.

Would you forfeit your life for one insignificant child?"

"You're asking me to forfeit my soul in exchange for my life. But what will a man give in exchange for his soul? If I gain the whole world, and lose my soul, I gain nothing."

Greg looked over to Ismeralda. Her face was white, but her lips were moving. His attention snapped back to Stefan when he heard a deep growling sound. It sounded inhuman but it was coming from Stefan's mouth. His eyes were focused on Brother Joseph.

"I'm warning you!" Stefan said then hissed, his rage mounting higher, shaking so hard it almost looked as if he were convulsing. Drool was coming from his mouth and his black eye was quivering. "You can't possibly imagine my power!"

"His name, Stefan. Let me tell you His name."

"No! Stop!"

"Jesus."

With that one word, everything seemed to stop. Nothing moved.

Then with animal-like fury, Stefan flew across the roof, throwing himself at Brother Joseph, his hands clawing the air in rage.

Brother Joseph's hands flew to his face in self-defense and Ismeralda screamed, "No! Brother Joseph!"

Brother Joseph stumbled backwards and Stefan pushed him closer to the edge of the roof. Lightning streaked across the sky, illuminating the scene. Brother Joseph tried to stand against Stefan and keep his footing, but Stefan shoved him one more time, and Brother Joseph began to fall backward.

An evil, idiotic, crazed cackling came from Stefan's lips. It was no longer the dry, humorless chuckle Greg had grown used to. It was a full-blown, demonic laugh.

Stefan pounced on Brother Joseph's chest and grabbed his

shoulders as Brother Joseph's head hung off the edge of the roof. Brother Joseph struggled to right himself and to sit up, but Stefan was pinning his legs to the roof. His face was beginning to turn red.

Greg's mouth dropped wide open and yelled, "What is happening?"

"You have no power, you have no power!" Stefan was screaming. "You don't know what you've gotten yourself into, preacher! The lives of hundreds of teenagers are what I fight for every day. You don't realize how great my influence is! When you began fighting for their souls, you entered my territory and began fighting against me! But Greg's soul is mine! You can't have him! He . . . is . . . mine!"

Suddenly Greg's mind cleared. *This is insane. Stefan can't do this. I can't let this happen. All that talk about spirits and stuff didn't make any sense . . . but now it's like I'm seeing it before my eyes. If anyone has ever seemed possessed, Stefan does right now.* Greg shook himself. *But he needs to be distracted before he does something to Brother Joseph.*

"What are you talking about?" Greg shouted across the rooftop. Stefan paused and turned his hideous black eye toward Greg. Greg swallowed at the sight of the eye but kept going. "I'm not yours! What are you saying about taking my soul and stuff? You're really creeping me out!" *That's an understatement.* "I'm my own person, I don't belong to you!"

At this, Stefan erupted into mirthless laughter. "You poor, pathetic little fool!" he cackled. "You don't realize what's at stake here! There are only two options, my little friend. There is no middle ground! My way or his way!"

"That's . . . that's not true . . ." Greg began, but was stopped by Brother Joseph.

Brother Joseph had turned his head and was looking at

Greg with a pleading look like Greg had never seen before. But it wasn't a "help me" kind of pleading. For some reason, Brother Joseph seemed more concerned about Greg. Even though he was hanging precariously from a roof about to die, he still looked more worried about Greg. The preacher's brown eyes told it all.

"Greg, he's right," Brother Joseph managed in a strained voice. "You don't realize what's at stake here. There comes a time when you have to kneel down and admit you don't have control!"

Stefan's lips curled and he bared his teeth in an animal-like snarl. He pressed down harder on Brother Joseph's chest.

The street missionary struggled for breath, then in a labored voice tried to finish what he was saying, quickening his words before the deranged drug dealer cut him off completely. "But it's not my way or his way. It's either Satan's way," Stefan grabbed his throat. Brother Joseph gasped for air and wheezed, "Or God's way! You have to choose, Greg. You have to choose . . ."

With a shriek, Stefan lifted up his hand and swiftly brought it down onto a pressure point on Brother Joseph's chest. A gasp and rattling cough came from the street preacher and his eyes fluttered shut. He went limp.

Stefan stood up and towered over him, looking down at the fallen man of God with crazed eyes. "I told you not to mess around with my business," he said, sneering at his victim. "Nobody messes with me." Then he turned to Greg and Ismeralda. "Now for you two. The pretty little girl and the skater kid. Where do I start?"

Ismeralda was staring in shock at Brother Joseph. "Did you kill him?" she asked in a voice barely above a whisper.

"Actually, I think he's still breathing," Stefan intoned carelessly. "But he's not the one I'm focused on right now. He's merely a casualty. The high price you pay if you get in my way." He glared at Ismeralda. "Which is what you now have to decide."

"What do you mean?" Ismeralda asked, looking at him warily but not backing down.

"Are you planning to get in the way? If so, I'm afraid I'll have to make sure you don't interfere."

"I'm not leaving," Ismeralda said, her voice quivering. "You can do whatever you want to me because I'm a child of God, and you can't hurt my soul. Like Brother Joseph said, God's power is greater than yours!"

Stefan's eyebrow above his good eye jumped up in surprise. Then he looked at her fiercely and took a few steps in her direction, raising his arm. "Why, you little—"

At that moment, the group on the roof heard a high-pitched siren coming closer. Being in Chicago, the distant sounds of police cars were normal and just part of the background noise. What made this siren different was that it kept drawing closer. Another siren joined the first one, and a third wailed incessantly as they grew closer. Stefan paused, his eye shifting back and forth, making him look like a cat about to strike. The siren wailed right up to the building. Stefan cursed under his breath then held up his hand, indicating that Greg and Ismeralda should stay where they were. Stefan walked to the other side of the roof and peered over. This time, he cursed out loud. Three police cars pulled to a stop beneath the building. An ambulance wasn't far behind.

"Stefan Adikema!" a voice through a bull-horn shouted. "Come down with your hands up." Still cursing, Stefan backed away from the edge of the roof, then turned and looked at Greg through fiery eyes. "This is your doing!" he yelled.

Greg took a step back as Stefan came running at him, and

tried to think of what to do. The leader of the drug ring screamed and swung his fist at Greg, knocking the boy off balance. Quickly Greg righted himself, but Stefan didn't stop. His fists were a blur as he pummeled into the skater. Blow by blow, Stefan knocked Greg farther and farther back on the roof. Greg held up his arms, trying to shield himself against the onslaught of Stefan's fists. But it wouldn't stop. The rain was coming down harder and harder, as if mimicking the intensity of Stefan's attack.

"There's no use trying to resist," Stefan raved in between swings. "You have no chance. You are mine and will never escape. God could never love you after the things you've done!"

Greg could barely keep up with what he was saying. *Where did that come from? How did God get into the conversation?*

Greg was almost to the very edge of the roof. Stefan's eyes were wild and he was grinning like a maniac. He pushed Greg backwards across the roof. "You . . . are . . . mine," he said quietly, crazily. "You're mine!"

"No," Greg said firmly. "No, I'm not! I'm not on your side. I don't care what happens! I'm not on your side!"

Stefan didn't seem to acknowledge him and the intensity of his attack doubled, pushing Greg to the very edge of the roof. The teenager was trying to stand firm, but Stefan wouldn't let up and was pushing him back farther and farther. Stefan's face lit up with a crazed smile. "You are on my side because you are not on God's side! Your life showed it." *This is it,* Greg thought, his mind racing wildly. *I'm going to die! Oh God!* He choked back a sob. *I'm sorry!*

Suddenly, above the wind and the rain, Ismeralda's clear voice rang out like a bell. "Jesus, please help us!"

Stefan paused for one second, and Ismeralda continued crying out to the Lord in a firm, clear voice. "Lord Jesus, stop this evil man! We need your help! In Jesus' name I rebuke the devil out of him!"

At that, Stefan turned with a sneer. "You think you're going to defeat me that way?" he asked.

Ismeralda had dropped to her knees and was ignoring Stefan as she prayed. "In Jesus' name, come out of him!"

Stefan laughed loudly and mockingly. "It's going to take more than prayer to save you, little girl. You won't stop me from claiming this soul!" With that, Stefan turned toward Greg with a crazy look in his eyes, his black eye almost throbbing with intensity. Reaching into his suit coat, Stefan snatched something and withdrew it. A flash of lightning caught the broadside of a knife that glinted as Stefan raised it above his head. "You will be a sacrifice!" Stefan called out, his voice shrieking above the wind. "This knife will now claim you . . . and your life!"

"No!" Greg yelled helplessly. He was going to die. There was nothing he could do! The police would never reach them in time. At that moment, Brother Joseph's words came back to him: "There comes a time when you have to kneel down and admit you're not in control."

He was right. He was right all along. Greg wasn't in control. And that was never more apparent than this moment. This whole trip, Greg thought he could beat Stefan, thought he could get help from Brother Joseph and get out of this alive. But he was never in control. And now, the only One who really could help him was the God Brother Joseph talked about. Tears flooding his eyes, Greg dropped to his knees. *God, I admit I'm not in control. If You exist, please help me now.*

Suddenly, as Greg fell to his knees at Stefan's feet, a strong gust of wind hit Greg, blowing his hat off. His hair blew the wind out of his eyes. He fell to his side and looked up in surprise. Stefan was still standing in his position of power, the arm with the knife outstretched, his bad eye looking upward, but the wind had knocked him over a few steps. Without warning, the wind came again and slammed into him with a force unlike anything Greg had ever seen.

Greg, Ismeralda, and Brother Joseph were already down on the roof, but since Stefan was still standing, the wind caught him off guard and caused him to stumble backwards. Then, as Stefan tried to regain his footing, he slipped, and almost in slow motion, his foot came off the edge of the roof, and arms careening, he fell backwards. His eyes bulged as his upper half began to fall. He screeched before the wind slammed into him again. He began falling. Down, down, down, Stefan's body cascaded over the side of the building and plummeted to the sidewalk below. There was a sickening thud as he landed against the concrete sidewalk. The wind was still blowing strongly and Greg stood frozen, staring at the edge of the roof where Stefan had just been standing.

A moment of silence continued as the wind died down again, and then suddenly, shouts came from below. Greg lowered himself down flat on his belly and looked over the side of the building. Stefan's head lolled to the side, and his deformed eye stared up at him lifelessly. No movement came from the drug ringleader.

The shouting increased as the police officers and paramedics swarmed around Stefan and immediately began tending to him. Some were running around the building to the fire escape. The scene was total chaos. The paramedics loaded Stefan into the back of the waiting ambulance after checking his vital signs and a few climbed in with him.

A police negotiator had reached the top of the fire escape now, with paramedics not far behind. Greg turned from the roof and looked up through the rain at the policeman and then over to Ismeralda. She was still on her knees, but when the police negotiator made it to the top of the fire escape, she opened her eyes and saw the man and said, "Thank God." Then as if a dam burst, she began crying.

The police negotiator surveyed the scene from the top of the fire escape and saw Brother Joseph lying there with his eyes closed, Greg lying on his stomach by the edge of the roof, and Ismeralda crying on her knees in another section. The negotiator realized that the danger had passed and asked, "Is everyone all right?" After a short pause, he continued, "Everyone just stay where you are and remain calm." He had a gun out and motioned the paramedics behind him to come up and look at Brother Joseph.

Carefully, they crawled over to him and one put his ear by his mouth. "He's still breathing," one reported. "We need to find a way to get him down."

Stifling a sob, Ismeralda held up her hand. "Wait a minute, please," she said in a soft voice. "Do you mind if I come over?"

The police negotiator looked at her intently for a moment then said gruffly, "Carefully!"

The paramedic rocked back on his heels as Ismeralda made her way over to him. Ismeralda hesitantly laid a warm hand on Brother Joseph's forehead. Then in a shaky voice she started to pray. The paramedics glanced at each other as if they'd seen this kind of thing before and it worried them.

Brother Joseph's eyes opened and he groaned. The paramedics quickly knelt beside him. The memory of what had just happened flooded Joseph's mind and he struggled to sit up. "Stefan?" he asked in a weak voice. "Is he . . . what happened? Where's Greg?"

Greg cleared his dry throat and shakily got up on his knees so Brother Joseph could see him through the pouring rain.

"Right here."

Brother Joseph settled back down. "Oh, thank God," he murmured. "What happened to—"

"He's gone, Brother Joseph," Ismeralda said through her tears. "God saved us."

o——o

Brother Joseph and Greg sat side by side, watching the commotion. The police officers were swarming all over the place, taking notes and making calls on their walkie-talkies. One of the police officers had taken Ismeralda home. Several others were out looking for Rush, Terrance, and Al's gang. The police had high hopes they would find them.

Officer Purdo was there too, wrapping up the case, beginning to write a complete report based on what he'd heard from Ismeralda, Brother Joseph, and Greg. Purdo had been on this operation a long time, and a few minutes after they had climbed off the roof, he had swaggered up like a king, took charge, and began asking questions.

Brother Joseph had been a little queasy and shaky, and the paramedics had assessed his condition and taken his vitals, which were now stable. And while Greg, Ismeralda, and Brother Joseph had been the center of attention earlier, it seemed that now nobody needed them. The paramedics didn't believe Brother Joseph was injured seriously enough to take him to the hospital right then, though they intended to take him in later, and of course the police wanted Greg to stick around. As the police and paramedics were still talking amongst themselves and figuring out whatever they needed to figure out, Brother Joseph and Greg had sunk down together on the back bumper of an ambulance.

They sat there in silence for a moment until Greg dropped his forehead in his hands and heaved a quivering sigh, as if finally releasing all the tension from the night.

Brother Joseph looked over at him. This was their first opportunity to talk. "Greg? Are you all right?"

Greg shook his head without taking it out of his hands. "No," he said in a weak voice.

"I know," Brother Joseph said in a quiet voice. He waited in silence.

"I didn't have control, Brother Joseph," Greg mumbled into his hands with a cracking voice. "I knew I didn't. That's why I knelt down."

Brother Joseph was slightly confused, but he listened intently without interrupting.

"Stefan was the only one standing. And that's why he couldn't stand up. I mean, the wind was too strong, and he lost his footing and, and . . ." Greg said.

Brother Joseph had only heard bits and pieces from the investigators and Ismeralda and Greg, and he still wasn't clear on exactly what had happened. "Greg—," he began, but Greg interrupted him.

"I know what you're thinking," Greg said, finally lifting his head a little, and staring out at the rain and the glare of the street light reflecting off the wet asphalt. "You want me to believe in God. And I know I wasn't in control, and I know God is the only One who could have helped us up there. But I still don't understand." Tears were beginning to run down Greg's cheeks. "Why did He let my little sister die? Why? If He's in control, why do these bad things still happen? Why does He save some people and let others die?" Greg couldn't help it now, he was crying and his head sank back into his hands.

"Oh, Greg." Brother Joseph put a hand on the skater's

shoulder, which was now shaking as Greg cried. "I know it hurts. And God knows it hurts." Greg drew in a deep breath and tried to stop his shoulders from shaking.

"You know, this is what I was talking about at the youth meeting."

"Yeah." Greg's voice came out as a squeak. He cleared his throat. "I remember." He took another deep breath. "You said that the world is full of death and suffering because of sin and God hates it, which is why He came and died on the cross or something like that."

Brother Joseph nodded.

"Well, you know I've been kind of skeptical about the whole God thing. But tonight, when I saw how Stefan was acting and then the wind knocking him off the roof . . . I guess I'm not sure anymore."

Brother Joseph didn't say anything.

"I know what you're thinking," Greg went on. "You want me to accept Jesus or become an Apostolic or whatever, and think that after seeing all that it should be easy for me. But—"

"You can tell me, Greg," Brother Joseph prodded him gently.

There was a pause. Finally, Greg spoke. "Well . . . it's just that . . . my sister . . ."

Silence hung heavily in the air until Greg broke it with an unsteady voice. "It was . . . a rainy night . . . and a drunk driver. My dad was driving, and he'd let Sam sit up in the front. The drunk lost control and crashed into the side of the car, right where Sam was. There was no chance. My dad wasn't hurt, except for a scar on his face. The drunk wasn't hurt at all."

"I'm . . . so sorry, Greg."

"Sam never hurt anybody," Greg said, his voice choking up. "She was innocent. There was no reason for her to die. How can

I believe in a loving God when He let something like that happen? I think that's one of the reasons my dad left . . . he couldn't handle the guilt. Why would God let that happen, Brother Joseph? Why?"

Brother Joseph was silent. Then quietly he said, "That's just it. I don't know, Greg. This world is full of horrible pain and suffering. I'm so sorry about your sister."

Greg opened his tear-filled eyes and glared down at the sidewalk at nothing in particular.

"I . . . I don't have all the answers," Brother Joseph went on. "But I do know . . . that God loved your sister. And He's in control. That's part of trusting in Him . . . even when we don't understand what happened. We still have to believe that God knows what He's doing."

"That sounds like a cop-out," mumbled Greg.

Brother Joseph sighed. "Yeah . . . it does," he admitted. "But one thing I know for sure, Greg: God was right there with you when your sister died, and He was grieving alongside of you."

Brother Joseph's expression softened and he looked at the tired teenager. "Greg, in no way am I trying to disregard the hurt that comes with your sister's death. But I want you to see that God still loves us. Even when bad things happen, He is still reaching out to us and desiring to have a relationship with us. But that doesn't mean He'll bend the rules for us. The Bible says it rains on the just and the unjust. But it's up to us to choose Him. You're on the threshold of making a huge decision that will change your life, and you're scared. Stefan was right. You do need to make a choice. But it's up to you to make that choice."

Greg didn't say anything, but he could feel emotions warring inside of him.

Brother Joseph continued, "Greg, God loves you. I can't stress that enough. But you need to believe it. And the only way you'll be able to believe it is if you find out for yourself. You've got to get in touch with God and know from His words that He loves you."

Tears spilled over onto Greg's cheeks. He did want to know that God loved him . . . if not God then somebody. Really, Greg was just desperate for love.

Greg glanced over and saw a soft, warm yellow light coming from the open door way of the Apostolic church where they had been hiding just an hour ago. At that moment, he stood to his feet and wiped at the tears. "You know what? You're right," he said. "And I'm going to do something about that." The skater turned and began running.

Brother Joseph jumped to his feet and held out his hand. "Wait, Greg! Where are you going?"

Greg didn't answer. If he was going to do this, he was going to have to do this alone . . . that's the only way he could know for sure if it were true.

The door to the old Pentecostal church swung open effort-lessly. Apparently Rush or Terrance had gone out this way. Greg stepped gingerly into the foyer, then with resolve pushed his way into the sanctuary. The glow from a street lamp bathed the sanctuary in golden light. The pews were all knocked over and the church was in disarray. Broken glass and sharp wooden splinters were scattered up on the platform from where the two henchmen had done damage. The door at the back of the sanctuary was still cracked and busted in, but Greg hardly noticed.

The skater walked slowly up the aisle until he reached the altar. He stood uncomfortably for a couple seconds, unsure of what to do. He'd never tried to have a conversation with God before . . . at least, not like this. Well . . . he'd just do it how he'd seen others do it. Slowly, he dropped to his knees. *Is this right? Should his heels be underneath him flat, or kind of propping him up? . . . There, that's more comfortable. Uh . . .* Greg placed his hands on the altar, the edge of the platform and looked around. What to do now, he wasn't exactly sure. He'd had it planned out up to this point, but now he was uncertain. *How had others at the Pentecostal church done it?* They always looked so confident and knew exactly what to do when it came to talking to God. Brother Joseph probably had no problem doing this. Maybe he should have waited. *No,* Greg decided. *I'm gonna do this on my own. I have to do it by myself if it's going to be real.*

The skater started to lift up his hands but put them down again. This was a lot harder than he thought. *I should close my eyes,* he thought, and closed them. Then, he awkwardly lifted up his hands. "I . . . hi, God, it's me." *What am I doing? Talking to God like I'm a first grader? This isn't going to work. If there is a God out there, He isn't interested in me.* Greg started to get up to leave, but then resolve hit him. No, he had determined to do this. He was never going to know for sure if he didn't. *And if nothing happens, I'll know for sure that God doesn't live . . . or at least doesn't care for a punk skater.*

Slightly, and still uncomfortable with it, Greg lifted his hands again. The Sunday school teachers and preachers always said to talk to God like you would a friend. Just be real. "Well, here goes," Greg said aloud.

"Uh . . . God? Lord? . . . Are you out there?" Greg paused in the silence. "Um . . . I want to know if You exist. I've heard lots of stuff, but I never know if it's true and . . . well, Brother Joseph sure believes in You, and You and him seem to get along." *Boy, this sounds stupid.* Again, he almost gave up. But something in him forced him to stay down.

"I guess, if . . . well, they say I should . . . you know, say I'm sorry and . . . if You're out there I want to say I'm sorry . . ." The impact of what he was saying hit him. He meant it. A tear slid down Greg's cheek. "I know if You're real, I've messed up a bunch and sinned a lot. But I don't know how to say I'm sorry." Another tear fell, and suddenly he wasn't thinking about what an awkward a position his hands were in. In fact, he barely noticed them. "What I'm trying to say is, You say You're loving, but I don't feel like I'm loved. You . . . You can't care . . ." His voice quavered and he choked back a sob. "Because You never notice me or listen . . ." Another sob came up and this time escaped. "And I don't know what to do, God! You probably hate me! All the sin I've done and You're all good and holy . . ."

Suddenly, tears started to flow. Pain hit his chest and he sobbed out in anguish as he realized what he'd become. Funny he had never seen things from this perspective before. An intense sorrow and regret seemed to flow through his entire body, and he felt an intense desire to go back and fix what he'd done. He wasn't sure what was coming over him, but whatever it was, he had advanced to all-out weeping. And Greg could sense something—no not something, Someone was there. At first he didn't notice, he was weeping so hard and didn't really know why. But then he began to be aware of a Presence.

He buried his face in the altar and covered his head with his hands, the sobs coming stronger and stronger. Knowing Jesus was the only thing that suddenly seemed important. It wasn't as if Greg thought he was going to get to do that, but His Presence filled the whole building and Greg began sobbing louder. He knew. God was real. He knew. And suddenly he wanted to hide his face from His glory. It was too majestic and brilliant. Greg covered his face with his arms but it was still there. God's Presence washed over him and Greg cried out inside, *Why? Oh, why have I ignored it for so long?*

Then he heard a voice. It spoke! It wasn't a literal, tangible, out-loud voice. It was more like he felt it. In his consciousness somewhere it spoke to him. It was a clear, distinct thought that seemed to come from nowhere. But Greg knew where it was from. And it hurt more than anything else. More than his dad leaving, more than his sister dying, more than his mom yelling, more than the other kids rejecting him. No other hurt so consumed him like this did.

"Greg, why have you been rejecting Me? Why have you been running away?"

"I'm sorry, God! I'm sorry!" Horrible anguish and indescribable pain filled his heart. He cried out louder, trying to erase the horrible feeling. Nothing could. *Was this what church people called repentance?* If that's what it was, it seized him and wouldn't let go. He never wanted to commit another sin again. All he cared about was getting right with God and never going back.

"Greg."

And then what he'd been wanting to hear for so long washed over him in warmth. Sobs convulsed his body.

"I love you, Greg."

"No, no you can't," he said as he wept, pouring out his soul.

Oddly, he wasn't even noticing anything else around him. All the things in the universe had been brought down and contained to one spot before him where he was being dealt with by God. He felt warmth and pain at the same time. Greg sobbed out loud, uncaring of who heard him now. He was being dealt with by God, something he had needed for so long. He needed God. And now he could admit that he loved Him too. But the washes of grace that were coming over him in waves were almost too much to bear. His arms flung out in desperation for some motion that would give some meaning to the emotions he wanted to express, but nothing could possibly give God the glory He deserved.

"Help me, O God, I'm sorry! You were right! Help me!" He found himself doing the things he'd seen others at the Pentecostal church doing. Actions he'd laughed at before suddenly made sense. He sobbed, flailed his arms, and struggled to give God glory, in an up-and-down motion with his arms.

Then he felt Brother Joseph beside him. The street preacher's hand went to his forehead, and another wave of God's presence came cascading over him. Crying out louder and louder, Greg wailed at the pain he had caused God, struggling to give Him some praise, any praise that would make it better and convey the depth of his feelings. Brother Joseph was prophesying loudly in tongues, but Greg didn't care. All that mattered in the universe was happening in that little church in front of that little wooden altar as the Creator of the Universe dealt with His child. Finally, Greg was bowing his will to God.

Holiness, majesty, and glory surrounded him. He could feel it pressing in on all sides and all he could do was murmur, "Thank You, thank You!" So inadequate! Was there any way to express the depth of love he suddenly felt and gratitude at God's acceptance and forgiveness? And then, his tongue was rolling and sounds were coming out he'd never heard before. Brother Joseph began shaking as warm tears fell down his face, and he lifted up his face to heaven and shouted out praise to God. Greg was—it was almost unbelievable—but Greg was speaking in tongues! The words he'd known before were inadequate for communicating with God, but these seemed to express the true depth of his feeling and heart. God's Spirit filled him, and with it an incomprehensible joy.

Brother Joseph raised Greg's hands a little higher, and Greg tilted back his head and raised his arms in acceptance of God's love. Praising and loving his Maker in another language. His hands were outstretched, and a love and peace and joy and warmth he'd never felt before filled him as his mouth articulated words he'd never heard before. The Spirit was giving him utterance. The Holy Spirit was praying through him. Greg had never experienced anything like this before. And he never wanted to leave. Lifting his hands a little higher, he continued to praise the Lord Jesus Christ. And then those three words came out of Greg's lips. They were to be the most altering, life-changing words of his life.

"I love you. Jesus, I love you!"

17

The way to describe what Greg was feeling was warmth. After his time spent on his face talking to God at the altar, the wave of God's presence had run its course, and Greg was ready to get up. Now warmth settled over Greg as he wiped his eyes and sat up, still lost in the glory of God's presence. With a half-turn, Greg hugged Brother Joseph fiercely. Brother Joseph returned the hug just as intensely, tears glistening in his big brown eyes behind his glasses. A few moments later they released each other, and Greg murmured another, "Thank you, Jesus," wiping his eyes again.

Brother Joseph smiled his soft, warm smile, tears still running down his face. "The angels of heaven are rejoicing, Greg. They know the love you just felt was from God and they revel in it."

Greg nodded, smiling through a fresh flood of tears. "I know," he whispered. "God loves me. I don't know why it took me so long to accept it."

"It's hard for all of us," the street missionary said and nodded, looking reflectively past Greg. "There's certainly no reason for Him to."

Then wrapping the skater in another hug, Brother Joseph said, "And I love you too, Greg."

"Yeah. Me too," Greg said hoarsely.

A sound at the back of the wrecked sanctuary got their attention, and they pulled apart. A shadow stepped into the light, revealing itself as Officer Purdo.

Strangely, Greg felt no animosity toward the police officer. All he could feel right now was the love that had washed over his senses and separated himself from anything else.

"Brother Joseph?" Officer Purdo's voice thundered across the quiet sanctuary.

Taking off his glasses and wiping his eyes again, Brother Joseph stood up. "Yes, sir?" he asked in a soft voice.

"I, uh, don't mean to interrupt this religious . . ." Words seemed to fail him and he groped for the right thing to say. ". . . this religious . . . well, whatever it is here, but . . . I'm going to have to ask you and the boy to come down to the station for questioning."

"Why?" asked Brother Joseph.

"Just because he's found forgiveness from God doesn't mean he's found forgiveness from the Chicago police department or the state of Illinois. Whatever else he's done, this young man was still involved in a drug ring and needs to be questioned and then dealt with accordingly." Officer Purdo beckoned with his hand, then adjusted his hat and turned to walk away, as if that had settled everything.

Greg and Brother Joseph looked at each other. "Greg—" Brother Joseph began.

Greg shook his head as he blew his nose again. "No, it's okay," he assured the street preacher. "I'll come." He hesitated, then looked at Brother Joseph with a smile, "God'll be with me, right?"

Brother Joseph grinned. "You're absolutely right, Greg," he agreed, putting his arm around him. "You're absolutely right."

○———○

They walked into the police station, greeted by the sound of ringing telephones, shuffling papers, and dispatchers answering calls. Several policemen walked by or looked up from their work but didn't say anything. Officer Purdo led Greg and Brother Joseph to a cubicle, where Cambiano sat behind a desk. Cambiano was rummaging through a file and motioned for Brother Joseph and Greg to sit in the metal folding chairs positioned in front of the desk. Officer Purdo leaned against the wall with a smug grin.

Cambiano stopped rummaging and glanced up. "Thank you, Rob," he said and inclined his head toward the door.

Purdo straightened up in shock. "But don't you—"

Cambiano cut him off. "No, I think that's it. You may go."

Purdo turned on his heel and marched off. Cambiano returned to his file.

Despite his resolve to do what was right, apprehension filled Greg and he fidgeted nervously in the chair. Officer Cambiano's silence didn't help. *Is he using intimidation tactics?*

Brother Joseph glanced over at Greg. As if comprehending Greg's discomfort, he said, "Officer Cambiano, would it be all right if Greg called his mom? She doesn't know anything about what's going on."

Cambiano looked up from his file with a world-weary look and responded, "Actually, I'd prefer the boy to remain here, but if you wouldn't mind contacting her, I'd be grateful. We'll need to speak to her ourselves anyway, momentarily. But you may preface our call with one of your own."

"All right . . . is that okay with you, Greg?"

Greg agreed, and as he scribbled down the number on a scrap of paper, Officer Cambiano slid a cell phone across the table. Greg handed both to the street missionary, and Brother Joseph exited the room.

The scratching of Cambiano's pen was the only sound in the room after Brother Joseph left. Greg shifted his weight in the seat, growing annoyed. *Does he enjoy making me squirm?* he wondered. He wanted to confront the policeman and get this over with, but he bit his lip and held back his feelings. Now wasn't the time to get on the police officer's bad side. After an uncomfortable silence, they heard the street missionary's footsteps approaching the cubicle.

Brother Joseph returned the cell phone to Greg.

"What did she say?" Greg asked, afraid to hear the answer.

Brother Joseph smiled. "When she heard me tell her that you had gotten right with God, she dropped the phone and I could hear her dancing around the kitchen, shouting and crying and speaking in tongues." Greg smiled at the picture that conveyed. "I'm sure she'll call back soon, and we can tell her the rest," Brother Joseph continued.

"Did you mention I was at the police station?"

Brother Joseph nodded solemnly. "I did. And she knows it had something to do with drugs, but I'm not sure she understands the full extent of what that means. We'll see how she takes all of this."

Cambiano cleared his throat, and they looked over to the desk again. "Well, I have been doing the paperwork for this case, and young man, I'll tell you, it doesn't look good. Willing or unwilling, as an active participant in this drug scandal, you will be facing some steep punishments. To what extent I am uncertain, but you will be dealt with."

Brother Joseph put his hand on Greg's shoulder in silent encouragement.

"Now that doesn't mean we won't be able to work out some sort of alleviation for the fact that you helped stop Adikema, you turned yourself in, yadda, yadda, but I'm warning you, there will still be some aftereffects. But most likely it will mainly be community service things. All right with you?"

Greg nodded numbly.

"Now, in order to file a complete report, I'm going to need to ask you some questions. And I can promise you, it will go much easier on you if you tell us everything you know." The policeman looked down his nose at Greg. "Understand?"

Now Greg saw what he was doing. Before it would've made him mad that the policeman was patronizing him, but now he only felt a twinge of resentment before he nodded his head in agreement.

Cambiano let out a sigh, visibly relieved that Greg had decided to cooperate. "This will only take thirty minutes to an hour, depending on what information emerges. Joseph, I'm afraid I'm going to have to ask you to step out," he said, nodding toward Brother Joseph's direction. "There's a waiting room by the front entrance, and I'm sure there's some coffee in there as well. And try to get in touch with the boy's mother again. Or one of our staff can handle that. I'm sure Bradley, who's one of our parole officers who's been assigned to this case"—he cleared his throat and continued—"will want to speak with her. He'll probably contact you to get her number shortly."

Brother Joseph nodded hesitantly. "Well, okay . . . Are you going to be okay, Greg?"

Greg nodded.

"All right," said Brother Joseph, "but I'll be right down the hall if you need anything."

After Brother Joseph stepped out, Cambiano nodded tersely and pulled a tape recorder out of a drawer. "Standard procedure," he explained. Then he began asking Greg questions.

An hour and a half later, Greg and Brother Joseph walked out between two hefty policemen. The interrogation lasted longer than Officer Cambiano had anticipated. And now Greg was worn out. His head was slumped between his shoulders, and his hand was resting lightly on his forehead as if he had a headache. Brother Joseph glanced at him with concern but didn't say anything.

They climbed into the police car and drove down the Chicago street. Even though it was late at night, the area was still heavy with traffic. The two policemen chatted jovially with each other as they drove, but Brother Joseph and Greg were silent.

The officers had decided to take Greg back to the hotel, where the two parole officers would stay—one in the room with him, and the other outside the hotel. Brother Joseph was going to see them to the hotel, then return in the morning to take Greg to the airport to connect with his flight. That had already been set up with Stefan. The police had contacted Greg's mom and had gone over the logistics of his parole with her. She would pick him up at the airport and take him home.

The police car pulled up to the hotel by a side door, sloshing through a puddle, and the four of them stepped out into the pouring rain. Greg pulled his key out of his wallet and flanked on either side by the two policemen, led the way up to his room. The policemen then set about securing the room and explaining the situation to the hotel staff. Greg entered the room and collapsed on the hotel bed, putting his arm over his eyes. Brother Joseph stood in the doorway.

"Greg, are you okay?" he asked.

"Yeah," came Greg's muffled voice. "Just tired."

Brother Joseph didn't move. "Something else is bothering you, though, isn't it?"

"What do you mean?" Greg asked, remaining still.

"You're not just irritated with Officer Cambiano or Purdo. Something else is wrong."

Greg let his arm flop down on the bed and opened his eyes. "I'm just trying to think of how this will change things."

"Change things?"

"At home, at the skate park." Greg stared at the ceiling. "I don't even want to think of how Doug and the rest will react after finding out I've become a Christian."

Brother Joseph paused, concern clearly showing on his face. "You . . . you're not starting to doubt your experience, are you?" he asked.

Greg paused, then moaned and covered his eyes again. "No. No, I'm not. But I'm not looking forward to telling Doug and the others."

Brother Joseph started to say something, then hesitated. "Well, it's not like you don't have an ally," he finally pointed out. "God will be with you. Again, Greg, you have to decide whether God is more important to you than your friends."

Greg nodded wearily.

Brother Joseph hesitated. "I'm sorry if it seems like I'm prying, but I can't help but notice—is anything else bothering you, Greg? You seem a little irked." Greg didn't say anything, and Brother Joseph took that as confirmation. Brother Joseph walked in the hotel room and sat down in a chair facing the bed before asking, "What's the matter?"

"I'm still not sure about some of the stuff in your religion. Like . . . well, standards and hair and . . ."

Brother Joseph took a deep breath then said, "Well, Greg. I

know what you're saying, but I think you're just making an excuse."

"I just don't feel like I could do all—"

"Then don't."

Greg spun his head to look at Brother Joseph in shock. Brother Joseph was staring at him with a very serious expression on his face.

"Greg, if that's what's potentially getting in between you and God, then you need to get rid of all those notions. I tried to explain before, standards were born out of our love for God. Not because we have to, but because we want to. I won't deny that some Apostolics and Pentecostals have deviated from that and it's become more like salvation out of works. But that's not how it's supposed to be! God doesn't want anything to get in the way of your relationship with Him which is why He purchased us with His own blood. Our sin was separating us from Him, so He gave His only begotten Son that whosoever believes in Him should not perish but have everlasting life. Because He loves you, Greg. But the question is now, are you willing to let those standards get in the way of your walk with God?"

Greg looked away and rubbed his eyes.

"You say that's what's holding you back, but really, it's just an excuse. If you fall in love with Jesus, whether or not you follow those particular standards is not the most important thing. You need to follow God and what He directs you to do."

Reluctantly, Greg nodded then shut his eyes, letting a yawn slip.

Taking his cue, the street preacher rose and moved toward the door. "I'll be here early tomorrow to take you to the airport. God's with you, Greg." The door shut softly, and Greg lay in darkness, waiting for his parole officer to come in. But now the darkness wasn't as oppressing. He knew what the preacher said was true. He had felt it. God was with Him. And Greg had to admit he knew God loved him too.

Early Sunday morning, Brother Joseph's silver Saturn could be seen weaving through the traffic in Chicago, taking Greg to the airport. Ismeralda was in the car too, since she wanted to come along and say goodbye. They laughed and talked on the way. A peace Greg didn't understand had settled over him. He didn't feel any anxiety or fear or apprehension or anything. It was a little strange to him.

They finally reached the airport, and to Greg's surprise, rather than pulling up to the place where he would check in his bags, Brother Joseph parked in the parking garage.

"What are you doing?" Greg asked.

Brother Joseph turned the key in the ignition and turned to look at Greg. "Did you think I was going to just drop you off at the curb?"

"I wouldn't have been offended if you did," Greg answered.

Brother Joseph smiled. "Well, I'm not. We'll walk you up to the security screening."

The three of them got out of the car and went through the process of getting Greg's bags checked and finding their way through the busy Chicago airport to the security lanes. At last, they reached them. At first nobody moved. Nobody seemed to want to give Greg's departure closure, least of all Greg. It seemed as if something needed to be said or done. This whole trip had been such a significant experience. It needed something.

Suddenly, Ismeralda surprised him by stepping forward and giving him a light hug. "Bye, Greg," she said. Caught off guard, he awkwardly returned it, then stepped back with a half-smile on his face. Brother Joseph stifled a laugh, and Ismeralda grinned as she brushed a few strands of hair out of her face.

"Well, I guess I need to get going," Greg said, although it was the last thing he wanted to do. *Amazing. I've only known these people a few days—less than a week. But I'm already closer to them than to most of my other friends.*

"Thanks for everything," he added, meaning every word. "You guys are pretty cool."

Ismeralda feigned indignation. "Pretty cool?" she asked, placing a hand on her hip. "Did you hear that, Brother Joseph?"

"Yeah," Brother Joseph responded. "Isn't that great? We've risen to the 'pretty cool' status! A week ago, he thought we were both self-righteous hypocrites."

"I did not!" Greg protested. He paused. "Just Ismeralda."

Ismeralda slugged him lightly, with a glint in her eyes, acknowledging his teasing.

"Well, I gotta go," Greg said again.

Brother Joseph stepped forward and grasped his hand with a firm grip. "Listen to me, Greg," he said, staring at him with his brown eyes. "I couldn't be more overjoyed by what's happened to you. But don't stop there. God has a purpose for your life. Keep seeking Him. He loves you, and now you need to return that love by submitting yourself to Him and doing whatever He wants. I'm talking complete and total submission. Give everything to Him."

Greg met his gaze and nodded seriously. "I understand," he said softly. "Don't worry. I will."

Brother Joseph wrapped him in a bear hug, which Greg returned. "God bless you, Greg," Brother Joseph said when he stepped back. "I'll see you in a week," he added, lifting his hand in a parting wave.

A wide smile lit Greg's face, and he nodded enthusiastically. "Okay," he agreed, stepping backwards into the customs line. "See ya! Bye, Ismeralda," he said, winking at her. She made a face at him then broke it with a smile. They both waved until Greg got up to the front, then after making sure he made it through, they turned and began walking back through the airport.

On the way out the sliding doors, Ismeralda turned to Brother Joseph, saying, "You'll be seeing him next week?"

"Oh, you mean I didn't tell you?" he asked, feigning surprise.

She glowered at him. "You know you didn't!"

Brother Joseph smiled. "Well, as it turns out, this morning Greg talked to his mom and they decided to ask me to go up to Colorado to do Greg's baptism."

"You're going all the way up to Colorado for that?" Ismeralda asked in surprise.

"A soul is worth any price," Brother Joseph reminded her. "Whatever we invest in God's kingdom He will return a hundredfold. Not always with physical blessings but with spiritual ones."

"You're right," she agreed, holding up her hands in concession. "I hope Greg comes back to Chicago some time, though."

"Oh?" Brother Joseph asked, turning to her with a knowing, mischievous smile.

She rolled her eyes. "Now, Brother Joseph. All I said was that I'd like to see him again someday."

"Sure," Brother Joseph said with a wink.

"Brother Joseph!"

He laughed and dodged a shove she directed toward him.

A Week Later . . .

"Where is he?" Mrs. Martin craned her neck, searching for the face she'd never seen before in the crowd of usual church-goers.

"Mom, he said he'd be here," Greg said, irritated. "And, if you knew Brother Joseph, he'll show up when he said he would." Even after his conversion, his mother still got on Greg's nerves. Maybe he needed to pray about that.

Renae squeezed his arm and he took a breath and smiled at her. She had been there with his mom to pick him up from the airport. As soon as he saw her, he began apologizing and even broke down and began crying, which was embarrassing. But she was crying too and the whole ride home was full of emotion and excitement. They had been talking about going to church to-gether and had even decided to get baptized together. Renae was in the same goofy robe as him, which made it way easier.

"I'm a little nervous to meet Brother Joseph," she said now, at Greg's side.

Greg turned to her in shock. "What? Why would you say that?"

"After everything you've said about him," she faltered, "I feel like . . . like I'm meeting a celebrity!"

"Don't worry," Greg assured her. "When you get to know him, you won't feel that way at all."

Renae smiled. "Kind of like getting to know God."

Greg looked at her in surprise at her insightful comment. He was glad he had someone his age to go through this journey with him.

"But what if there was a problem with the rental car or something," Mrs. Martin was saying. "I should've picked him up at the airport."

Greg shook his head, shaking his hair loose, despite his mom's desperate attempts to keep it in place. "Mom, I told you, wait a minute, here he comes."

Sure enough, through the door of the Pentecostal church, unassuming and quiet, walked the humble street missionary. Brother Joseph blended right in with the crowd, until Mrs. Martin ran up to him, weeping. Trying to stifle his embarrassment, Greg followed. His mom embraced Brother Joseph and grabbed his hand and thanked him profusely for his influence in her son's life. The corners of Brother Joseph's mouth turned up slightly, and he said something Greg couldn't hear, shaking her hand. Then his eyes wandered past her, lighting on Greg. His face lit up, and Greg had to smile. From what he gathered, Brother Joseph was more comfortable with youth than adults.

Brother Joseph approached Greg, who introduced him to Renae. He shook her hand warmly and she said hi shyly.

"Are you both ready?" he asked in his usual soft manner.

Greg heaved a sigh and paused. "You honestly think I could go through all the things I went through in Chicago and not be ready? Of course I am!"

The street missionary laughed. "Glad to hear it."

One of the elders in the church caught sight of the three of them talking and walked down the aisle toward them. "You must be Brother Joseph," he said warmly, shaking the preacher's hand. "I'm Brother Andrews. If you don't mind coming up to the platform, we'll begin Greg and Renae's baptisms soon. Everything is ready." He looked over. "Except for you, Greg. Aren't you going to get changed? Right this way, Brother Joseph."

Joseph meekly followed Brother Andrews up to the platform where the elder caught the pastor's attention and whispered something in his ear. As soon as he heard it, he beamed and beckoned Brother Joseph to the front, grabbing his arm and yanking him toward him as soon as he was in reach.

The pastor, a large, heavyset man, clapped Brother Joseph on the shoulder and boomed into the microphone, "We have a brother here from Chicago, Brother Joseph is it?" Brother Joseph nodded and the pastor turned back to the congregation. "He is going to baptize Sister Martin's son and his friend Renae!"

The congregation erupted into shouts and clapping and the pastor grinned a wide, ear-splitting grin. "Brother Joseph, just step over to the baptistery, and Greg, you step in right here."

Brother Joseph did as he was told and walked to the baptismal tank. The keyboard player began to play another worship song, and Greg stepped gingerly into the baptismal. Mrs. Martin was close behind him, clutching towels for him to use afterwards.

The pastor waved the microphone and shouted in a booming voice, "Praise the Lord, church! This young man is getting baptized!" A chorus of hallelujahs and praise the Lords sounded out, and people began waving their hands in the air and jumping up and down. Greg smiled nervously and stepped into the water at the prompting of an elder. He still wasn't quite comfortable in front of all these people in this Pentecostal atmosphere. Renae winked at him and he tried to relax.

Brother Joseph smiled at him. "Are you ready, Greg?" he asked softly.

A peace settled over the skater. "Yeah," he answered. Mrs. Martin was standing off to the side, crying and praying in tongues.

"All right," Brother Joseph said. The pastor seemed to be holding his breath as they waited for the big moment.

"Gregory Martin," Brother Joseph said simply, his voice

swelling with emotion. "Upon the confession of your faith in the God who loves you as a Father, I now baptize you in the name of Jesus Christ for the remission of your sins."

With that, Greg went down in the water. When he came up, the church erupted into praise. The sister at the keyboard pounded out another chorus and began singing, "I've been redeemed! By the blood of the Lamb!" And as soon as Greg came up, he felt the gentle presence of the Lord surround him. Spontaneously, he raised his hands and began speaking in tongues. He was forgiven. And more than that, the skater, Greg Martin, now knew God loved him, which was confirmed by the soft whisper in his ear. It wasn't Brother Joseph or his mom or Renae. Greg knew who it was.

"I love you."

EPILOGUE

Poneros swung his enormous fist, and it landed with a loud crack on the demon's head. Sharath swayed dizzily, and Poneros grasped his neck with his long talons, puncturing it in every place they touched. Slowly, in a deep, hideous, raspy voice that started as a whisper but crescendoed into a loud cry, he said, "Another . . . soul . . . has . . . been loooooooooooooooooooost!"

Poneros' rage echoed through the warehouse, and any demons that had the courage or stupidity to remain cowered in fear and hatred. Most of them had already fled, knowing what was to come. A dark, heavy smoke hung in the room oppressively, mirroring the intent of the forces of evil at work there. All of the angels in heaven were rejoicing, naturally, but the demons in hell were seething. And Sharath had been the unfortunate, pitiful wretch who had delivered the news.

Poneros released Sharath, who collapsed on the floor in shame and fear. Poneros then swung his huge leathery wings in a wide arc, flapping them in irritation, growing angrier by the moment. "This is unacceptable! A soul has been taken from our kingdom and placed under the control of another!" He let loose in another loud roar, almost beside himself with rage.

Gazez stood to the left, his massive, stately wings covering his scratch-infested, bruised, lumpy frame. His eyes were cold, dark, and calculating.

Poneros turned to him, spewing sulfur into his face. "You have failed, you miserable little idiotic devil!" In truth, Gazez was neither little nor idiotic, but as an experienced demon had handled the situation as well as could be done.

Gazez hissed, a burst of flame escaping from his gaping, snarling jaw. "Fool! You know I stood no chance against the Host of Heaven in that situation! I was outnumbered. And as soon as the Name was mentioned . . ."

No sooner had the words floated on his stale breath out of his mouth than the room full of hissing, snarling, muttering spirits quieted, and each spirit turned on him with a withering glare. Gazez snarled back at them and spread his wings, showing his talons. Many of them spat and returned to the mischief they had been about before. But the intensity in the room had just risen a notch. Any mention of the Name that bound them so effectively was enough to make the hair on the most battle-hardened devil's neck stand straight up. They all hated it.

Gazez returned to his former posture and rewrapped his gargantuan wings about his body. "I should have had backup," he said to Poneros.

Poneros growled and bared his fangs.

Gazez smiled at the anger he had caused and picked his fangs with one of his talons. "But, as it was, the pathetic man's usefulness was used up. I disposed of him, as we will with all of those unfortunate enough to fall in with us."

"Yesssss," Poneros rumbled. "But this battle has cost us. And we must do something about"—he spat the name—"Brother Joseph. Sharath!"

Sharath crawled to his side.

"Send a contingent against the street missionary. We must dispose of him."

"Understood, my Ba-al."

"And you, Gazez," Poneros bellowed. "Immediately set to work destroying another soul. Your work through Stefan was well done. Now try not to slip up with your next instrument of destruction."

Gazez's eyes flashed but he gave a curt nod and swooshed upwards, spreading his wings and flying into the night sky of Chicago.

Poneros followed him until he was at the top of the warehouse. Here, he stopped and with a cruel gaze looked out over the city. Lifting his head, he raised his voice in a monstrous roar that even shook some of his minions' hearts. "This war isn't over yet! Do you hear, Hosts of Heaven? We may have lost one soul, but this war isn't overrr!"

The skate park was empty tonight. Empty with the exception of two figures—one seeable by human eyes, the other only with spiritual eyes.

The angel hovered over the skater and observed as the skateboard landed on the concrete with a familiar sound. He saw the skater view the well-known territory as he rested his foot on the glistening black grip tape of his new skateboard with a calm familiarity.

As the skater began to take a lap around the skate park, the angel came to rest on the half-pipe, emanating light, his flaming sword whirling in an impressive show as he kept watch.

An old memory lit the boy's face as the rush of freedom he had always experienced on a skateboard came back to him. But it wasn't the same as before. The angel knew that this time the sense of freedom was coupled with the knowledge that the skater was completely free. Not just for a short skating run—but for all of eternity. The wheels whirred underneath the skateboard as it began to pick up speed and the skater geared up for a flip trick.

A sound growing increasingly louder caused the being on

the ramp to turn and look up into the night sky. Two streaks of light were heading closer and closer to the earth, quickly approaching where he stood. A smile began to broaden on the angel's weary face as the streaks of light grew closer. He turned to face them.

When they were close enough to clearly make out their distinctive features, they slowed their pace, finally landing in the skate park.

The angel on the ramp sheathed his sword and bowed his head. Zimri approached him, the majestic angel's face warmed with a soft smile. "You have done well, Gaddiel."

Gaddiel looked up with joy. "Another warrior has been brought into the kingdom."

"And we were all rejoicing," Chelal said as he joined them at the ramp.

"How did things go in Chicago?" Gaddiel asked.

Zimri looked grimly off into the distance as if viewing the skyline of Chicago. "There are still so many lost souls," he murmured softly. He looked at them again. "It's true that the war is not over. Many people still need to be turned from the power of Satan to God. But this battle has gone well." He motioned for Chelal to fill in Gaddiel.

"The Spirit is at work!" Chelal announced. "Ismeralda has been strengthened and the Spirit of the Lord is moving upon her as she continues to fight for His glory. Attacks are being made against Brother Joseph, but he is well-guarded and is continuing in prayer. Stefan is in the hospital, and they are not sure if he will live. The policemen and doctors believe he tried to commit suicide."

Gaddiel nodded knowingly.

"Terrance and Rush have been arrested, and Officer Purdo is having a heyday breaking up the rest of the drug ring. Officer

Cambiano is doing a very thorough job closing the case. The gang members have also been arrested, but Brother Joseph testified and their sentences will be lighter than they otherwise would have been. Even now, Brother Joseph is visiting a few of them in prison, and both Al and Michael's hearts have been softened." Chelal's gleaming eyes twinkled. "And I do believe I detected a tear in Al's eye."

Gaddiel lifted up his head and laughed. "Perhaps all of us angels in heaven will be rejoicing yet again tonight."

Chelal pumped his fist in exuberance. "We just might, my friend. We just might!"

Suddenly, Zimri silenced them and pointed with his sword. "Look," he instructed.

Another figure was approaching the skate park. A human one. Greg was skating toward a ramp when the other figure tackled him. They both toppled over, then sat up laughing and talking over each other.

"Dude!" Doug yelled, when they finally paused for a breath. "How was Chicago?"

Greg swallowed and hesitated, then smiled. "Dude, do I have a story to tell you!"

About the Author

MICHAEL SCHROEDER has been passionate about stories and writing since he was a child. Michael was born and raised in northern Colorado. Through helping with short, audio drama skits, acting, and personal writing projects, Michael grew in his love for all things having to do with a story.

He attended the Lamplighter Guild for Creative Disciplines in New York several years in a row and obtained creative training from masters within the world of Christian audio drama. In 2012, upon graduating from high school, Michael went to college at Verity Institute in Indianapolis, Indiana, and received his degree from Thomas Edison State University in 2013 with his BA in Communications.

Since then, he has returned to Colorado and has been involved in writing Sunday school curriculum at Abundant Life Tabernacle, teaching voice acting with Lost Marbles Theatrics and teaching Bible studies for people of all ages.

9 781581 696646